Available
from Mills & Boon® Intrigue

THE COLONEL'S WIDOW?

"You think I caused all this?"

"I think all of this is here because of your decision to fake your death. I think your arrogance has ruined many lives. Not only mine, but all these other people who care about you and are loyal to you."

He grimaced and shook his head. "I had to do it."

She was way too close to him. Close enough that she could smell his fresh, clean scent. She held her breath.

He ran his palm down her upper arm. "We need to talk. *I* need to talk and you need to listen."

He held on to her for a few seconds, his head bent enough that he could look into her eyes. He wanted her to look at him. To yield to him.

She wouldn't. She couldn't. Not now. She had no idea what she was going to do, now that Rook was back. Yesterday he was dead. Today he was alive.

Until she could process everything that had happened in the past few hours, never mind the past two weeks or two years, she couldn't afford to allow herself to relax. She had to maintain control.

Control was all she had left.

CAVANAUGH PRIDE

Julianne stared at Frank, dazed. "I just threw myself at you."

And he would have liked nothing more than to catch her. But he knew he wouldn't. Not if he wanted a clear conscience.

"Yes, you did."

"Oh." She felt naked and vulnerable. "You don't want me."

He laughed then and shook his head. God, was she ever off base.

"Lady, you are definitely not as good at reading people as you think you are." Because they were standing outside her hotel and not inside her room, he allowed himself a second more to drink in her presence and all that could have been. "I don't think the word 'want' even *begins* to describe what I'm feeling right now."

All the characters in this book have no existence outside the imagination of
the author, and have no relation whatsoever to anyone bearing the same name
or names. They are not even distantly inspired by any individual known or
unknown to the author, and all the incidents are pure invention.

First published in Great Britain 2010
Harlequin Mills & Boon Limited,
Eton House, 18-24 Paradise Road, Richmond, Surrey TW9 1SR

The Colonel's Widow? © Rickey R. Mallory 2009
Cavanaugh Pride © Marie Rydzynski-Ferrarella 2009

ISBN: 978 0 263 88207 0

46-0310

Harlequin Mills & Boon policy is to use papers that are natural, renewable
and recyclable products and made from wood grown in sustainable forests.
The logging and manufacturing processes conform to the legal environmental
regulations of the country of origin.

Printed and bound in Spain
by Litografia Rosés S.A., Barcelona

THE COLONEL'S WIDOW?

BY

MALLORY KANE

CAVANAUGH PRIDE

BY

MARIE FERRARELLA

™MILLS & BOON®

THE COLONEL'S WIDOW?

BY
MALLORY KANE

Mallory Kane credits her love of books to her mother, a librarian, who taught her that books are a precious resource and should be treated with loving respect. Her father and grandfather were steeped in the Southern tradition of oral history and could hold an audience spellbound for hours with their storytelling skills. Mallory aspires to be as good a storyteller as her father.

Mallory lives in Mississippi with her computer-genius husband, their two fascinating cats and, at current count, seven computers. She loves to hear from readers. You can write to her at mallory@mallorykane.com

For Daddy, a hero by any definition.

Chapter One

Moonlight sprinkled pale silver across Rook Castle's bare back, buttocks and thighs. His muscles tensed and rippled as he thrust once, twice, again and again, filling her with familiar, exquisite heat.

Irina's fingers slid through her husband's softly waving hair. She arched upward, pressing her breasts against his hot chest, demanding more.

He lifted himself, his biceps straining, glistening with sweat and moondust. He gave her more—gave her everything she craved. His deep, green stare mesmerized her.

"Rook," she whispered. "Why did you marry me?"

He went still. The moonlight no longer shimmered along his flanks and shoulders.

When would she learn to keep her mouth shut?

His arms quivered with effort as he held himself suspended above her. His arousal pulsed inside her.

"Rina—" he muttered, something between a warning and an endearment. Dipping his head, he sought her mouth.

She longed to kiss him, to surround herself with his powerful body, to feel him in her and around her as she had so many times before.

But her hands acted against her will and pushed at his chest. Resisting. She struggled to maintain eye contact. "Why?" she repeated.

"You know why," he whispered, his breath tickling her eyelashes.

"Tell me."

He kissed her eyelids, her cheek, the sweet spot below her earlobe. Then he moved, rocking her with a slow rhythm born of trust and familiarity. His chest rumbled with languid laughter when she gasped.

"Shh," he whispered. "Come with me."

She tasted sweat on his neck—salty, delicious. "Rook, please?"

With a frustrated sigh, he lifted his head. A jagged shadow defined his rigid jaw.

"I had to marry you," he said. "It was the only way I could protect you."

"But what about love?" Dear God, she was pathetic.

"Love? Rina, don't—" His voice rasped.

Then blood blossomed on his chest.

"No!" She reached for him, but her fingers slipped in the hot, sticky liquid.

"Rook!" she shrieked. "No! Help! Somebody help!"

He clutched at his chest.

She screamed.

His eyes met hers and he whispered something—she couldn't tell what.

She grabbed his arm, but he was too heavy. She couldn't hold on to him.

The last thing she saw was his beautiful face distorted by the bloodstained waters of the Mediterranean as he sank beneath its waves.

Irina Castle bolted upright, gasping for breath.

"No!" The word rasped past her constricted throat, pulling her out of the dream.

She wasn't on their yacht. She was at Castle Ranch, alone. She kicked the covers away and gulped in air. The taste of his sweat stung her tongue.

No. Not his sweat. Her tears.

Harsh moonlight glinted like a knife blade on every surface. She covered her face with her hands, trying to block it out.

She hated moonlight. Hated night. Darkness brought the fear, and moonlight brought the dream.

Every night she promised herself that next time she wouldn't ask him. Next time, she'd take all the dream would give and hold out for more. After all, her memories were all she had left.

But every night she asked.

Sliding out of bed, she reached to close the drapes and shut out the moon's light. But her skin burned and perspiration prickled the nape of her neck, so instead she flung open the French doors.

Cold air sent shivers crawling down her spine. She took another deep breath, hoping the sharp April chill would chase away the tattered remnants of her nightmare.

No such luck. Her body still quivered with unquenched desire. The empty place inside her still ached with grief.

In the distance, the Black Hills of Wyoming loomed in magnificent desolation. Rook had loved the mountains. He'd drawn strength and purpose from them. And like the Black Hills fed him, his strength, his dedication, his larger-than-life presence had fed her.

Then he'd been shot. His body was never recovered.

So for the past two years, she'd poured money into looking for him.

Two weeks ago, her accountant had issued an ultimatum—stop her unending search for Rook, or dissolve Black Hills Search and Rescue, the legacy he'd devoted his life to.

She stopped the search. How could she have known that her decision would set events in motion that would nearly destroy his two closest friends?

HE COULDN'T SLEEP. Hadn't been able to since he'd been released from the hospital. The idea that he'd been shot—*shot*—still spooked him. He was lucky to be alive.

So he sat up, looking out the window toward the ranch house. Toward Irina's bedroom. One of his favorite pastimes was watching her bedroom at night. She rarely closed the drapes.

He saw movement. Irina stepped out onto her patio with the red gown on—his favorite. She couldn't sleep, either. He watched her for a while, noticing that the pain from his gunshot wound wasn't so bad while he watched her.

Then he saw something—someone—inside the bedroom.

"Irina, don't tell me you've got a man in there," he whispered.

A cloud drifted by and the moonlight got brighter. He could see the man's face clearly. *Cunningham.* He'd know that hard face anywhere. What the hell was *he* doing in Irina's suite? At midnight?

He stood carefully, groaning with pain and dizziness, and got his shaving kit. Inside, hidden with the rest of his stash of goodies, was a LoJack.

It didn't matter what Cunningham was doing in

Irina's suite. What mattered was that he had a window of opportunity to keep up with his every move.

He sighed and clenched his teeth against the throbbing pain. He didn't want to go out there. He wanted to take another painkiller and go to bed. But he had a feeling this late-night meeting between Irina and Deke was no lovers' assignation.

From the way Irina was acting, she didn't know Cunningham was there.

Was this the night Cunningham would lead them to Rook Castle?

Pulling on a jacket, he stuck the LoJack in a pocket and took one more longing look at the bottle of painkillers on his bathroom sink. He needed one—bad. But he had to take care of business first.

Novus Ordo was willing to spend millions to find and capture his nemesis, Rook Castle.

He wanted at least one of those millions as a finder's fee.

BLACK HILLS SEARCH and Rescue specialist Deke Cunningham moved silently through the east wing of the sprawling ranch house. Behind him, beyond the enclosed courtyard, past the living room and kitchen, was the west wing, home of the offices of Black Hills Search and Rescue. The building to the south housed the staff quarters.

Hard to believe it had only been two weeks since Irina had called Matt Parker back from overseas.

A lot had happened, not the least of which was that he'd become a father.

Unbelievable. And thrilling. An involuntary grin stretched his mouth as he thought of Mindy and his newborn son.

On the heels of his grin came a wince. His tongue sought the cut on his lip that matched the one over his eye as he stopped in front of the door to Irina's suite.

Damn, he didn't want to be here. He wanted to be at the hospital with Mindy and their baby. He wanted to be planning their future together as a family.

But even more, he wanted to be in a different world. A world where his best friend hadn't had to die in order to save his wife. A world where a terrorist hadn't made it his mission to kill Rook Castle and everyone close to him.

But that world didn't exist. So he had to do his best to clean up this one—to make it safe for the people he loved. And one of those people was Irina Castle, Rook's widow.

He took a deep breath and glanced up and down the hall. There were four suites in the east wing. Irina's, of course. Next to hers was the one he'd lived in until he'd left on a mission to rescue his ex-wife, Mindy.

The suite directly across from his belonged to Rook's baby sister, Jennie. For the past two years, she'd been living in Texas with a family friend and attending graduate school. The fourth suite, opposite Irina's rooms, was empty.

Satisfied that there was no one around, Deke gripped the door handle. He'd waited until two o'clock in the morning for a reason. If he'd ever been on a stealth mission in his life, this was it.

The door was unlocked. "Dammit, Irina," he whispered. "You know the danger."

He eased open the door and peeked around it. Moonlight angled across the rumpled bed.

The rumpled, empty bed.

Instantly on alert, he drew his weapon as he slipped

inside and closed the door. A movement caught his eye. Curtains ruffling in the breeze. The French doors were open.

His unease ratcheted up a notch. Dan Taylor had assured him that there wasn't a chance in hell anyone could sneak past the Secret Service's perimeter onto the ranch. But Dan didn't know Novus Ordo.

Deke did.

He'd experienced firsthand what the internationally famous terrorist Novus was capable of. Twice. So it would take more than the word of a young hotshot with lots of civilian training and zero field experience to put him at ease.

Deke moved silently across the room, trying to position himself to see the entire patio without stepping out of the shadows. The French doors faced south, which meant she could be seen from the guesthouse, where the three specialists lived. If she was out there, they could see her—and him if he wasn't careful.

He knew from the gate guard that all three were there. And he had a very good reason for not wanting any of the three to know he was here.

He took another step, craning his neck to see the southwest corner. Finally, he saw a flash of red. There she was, in a red gown and robe, bathed in moonlight. She had her arms wrapped around herself, and her head was bowed.

He blew out his breath in relief and frustration. She was all right. But she was exposed. He sank back against the wall.

Now what?

He had to get her out of here and on the road. Every second increased the danger that he'd be spotted.

He thought about calling out to her, but if someone was watching, her reaction would alert them.

And once they were alerted, it wouldn't take them long to figure out that there was only one reason he'd be spiriting Irina away from Castle Ranch—the one place on earth she should be safe—in the middle of the night. And right now he couldn't risk anyone knowing where he was taking her. Not even his fellow BHSAR specialists.

Gritting his teeth, he waited, absently rubbing at the bandage on his right forearm. The surgeon had done a great job of stitching up his arm—thirty-two stitches— but the deep slash itched and hurt like a sonofabitch, courtesy of the weasel who'd called himself Frank James.

He'd like to have five minutes alone with James. Hell, three minutes would be plenty. But that was impossible. The dynamite he'd set off in a last-ditch effort to save Mindy and their unborn son had taken care of James and Novus Ordo's soldiers—permanently.

A rustle of silk pulled Deke's gaze to the French doors. Irina's shadow stretched across the bedroom floor. She was coming inside.

No matter what he did, his presence was going to scare her, so he stood still and waited until she stepped inside and closed the heavy drapes.

She headed toward the bed, reaching for the sash of the shimmery red robe. Then she stopped, her palm pressed against her midsection. She'd sensed him. Slowly, she turned her head.

"Irina," he said softly. "Stay quiet."

SHOCK PARALYZED Irina. She tried to suck in enough breath to scream, but her throat seized. She coughed and gasped.

"It's Deke," the voice said.

Deke. She shuddered as relief whooshed through her, followed by ringing alarm.

"Deke?" she said, her voice rising. "What's wrong?"

"Be quiet. Okay?"

She nodded.

"I'm serious. Promise?"

"Yes," she whispered. "Is it Mindy? Or the baby?"

He put two fingertips against her mouth. "They're fine. Listen. I've got to get you out of here."

Fear tore through her like lightning. It had happened. Danger had penetrated her home. She'd known it would one day.

"I'll get dressed," she whispered.

Deke shook his head and grabbed her hand. "No. No lights. No movement. I can't risk anyone knowing I was here."

Nothing Deke said made sense. "But—"

"Irina, we've got to go now."

IT DIDN'T TAKE Irina long to figure out where Deke was taking her. The route was familiar. They were headed to a hunting cabin Rook had acquired years ago. He'd managed to keep the title and tax papers in the name of the original owner and hadn't told anyone about it, except Deke and Matt, his oath brothers.

He'd called it their getaway house. A place the two of them could go where no one could find them if they didn't want to be found.

She hadn't been there since he'd died. Their last night there had been too painful to relive. Besides, why go alone?

Irina folded her arms beneath the wool throw Deke had tossed her way when he'd gotten into the SUV. She stared at the road, not bothering to hide her annoyance.

Several times, she'd tried to engage him in conversation, to no avail.

He acted as if he were too busy making sure they weren't being followed. Rook's best friend had always treated her with loving respect, but for whatever reason, tonight he wasn't answering any questions.

So she clamped her mouth shut and snuggled deeper under the throw. Her flimsy silk robe offered little protection against the late April chill. She shuddered. Nothing short of a direct and imminent threat would have made Deke ignore her comfort or dignity. Fortunately, she had clothes at the cabin.

Once they reached the hunting camp and Deke was satisfied that she was safe, she'd unload on him. She didn't get angry often—temper rarely helped any situation—but she didn't like being bullied. Not even by the man who'd appointed himself her protector after her husband's death, and not even if it was supposedly for her own good.

Deke spoke only once during the hour's drive, and then not even to her. He pulled out his cell phone and dialed a pre-programmed number. He listened for a few seconds.

"Dammit," he muttered. After another couple of seconds, he hung up and glanced at the tiny screen, as if to check the number he'd dialed. Then he shot her an awkward glance and turned his attention back to his driving.

Irina bit her tongue to stop herself from asking who he was trying to reach. He'd tell her when he felt like it.

The road ended a quarter mile from the camp, but Deke barely slowed down. He circled around and drove up behind the cabin, where he parked and shut off the engine of the large SUV.

Irina reached for the door handle.

"Wait," he snapped.

He retrieved his phone and pressed the redial button, hissing in frustration through clenched teeth.

After a few seconds, he sucked in a sharp breath. "Where have you been?" he growled.

Irina held her breath and listened, but she couldn't hear the person on the other end of the line.

"You could have waited. I was afraid you—" he stopped. "Yeah, okay. We're here. I'll bring her inside, then put the car in the barn." He paused, listening.

"Nope," he snapped. "No way. You're on your own this time. I'm going to take a look around. I'll be in later." He hung up and got out of the car.

Irina didn't bother to ask who'd been on the phone. Judging by the brevity of the conversation, she figured it was probably Brock, the oldest and most experienced of the Black Hills Search and Rescue specialists. Brock O'Neill's conversational style was terse at best.

As soon as she entered the rustic kitchen, she saw dim light coming from the front room. "Is that a fire? Or is the generator running?" she asked.

He didn't answer.

"Deke, stop acting like a secret agent and tell me what is going on! Who's here? Is it Brock?"

He set down his black duffel bag. "I'm not playing. Don't worry, you're safe. I'm going to hide the car. Irina—" He laid a hand on her arm, as if about to say something else.

She waited, apprehension crawling up her throat.

"Just remember that all this—was for you." He turned and went out the door, locking it behind him.

Irina stared at the door for a few seconds, as Deke's words replayed over and over in her head.

All this was for you.

"All of what?" she whispered. Shaking her head, she stepped through the dining room and into the front room. One lamp shone dimly, competing with the fireplace for the privilege of staving off the darkness. The only sound she heard was the crackling of the flames.

But she knew she wasn't alone.

Her breath hitched. Deke had promised her she was safe, she reminded herself. He'd promised her, ever since Rook's death, that he'd take care of her, and he had.

"Hello? Brock?" She spoke softly. "Is that you?"

No answer. Yet she felt a presence.

"Who's here?" she asked sharply.

Did she only imagine she heard breathing? She squinted, trying to see past the shadows. From the corner of her eye she recognized the old bookshelf to her right. It was on the wall opposite the fireplace. It was one of many places in the cabin where Rook had hidden loaded guns.

She'd never liked all the weapons. He'd turned their secret getaway into a secret arsenal. She'd complained a million times that she'd seen all the guns she ever wanted to see during her childhood in Russia. Still, she couldn't deny that right now she was glad to have a loaded weapon within reach. If she remembered correctly, this one was a Glock. She took a step toward the bookcase.

"Hello, Rina."

She whirled, startled. Nobody called her Rina—not anymore.

A lone figure stood to one side of the fireplace. All she could see was a silhouette.

"Who—?" Before she could gather breath to say

more, the person took a step forward. When the light hit his face, a giant fist grabbed her insides and wrung them tight—so tight she couldn't breathe.

"What's going on?" she gasped, gulping in air and casting about, as if an explanation lurked somewhere in the room.

"It's okay." A whisper. The figure held up a hand. "Irina…it's me."

A sharp ache burned through her chest. An ache of loss, of grief. Of denial.

"No," she breathed, shaking her head. Whoever was standing there, whatever was going on, she knew one thing for certain. His words were a lie. It wasn't him.

It couldn't be. He was dead.

She took a shuddering breath. "I—I don't understand—"

"I know you don't."

The sound of the man's voice sheared her breath and spasmed her throat. The words were tentative, the voice was hoarse and hesitant, but she knew it. Just like she knew the broad shoulders, the long powerful legs, the rugged profile outlined by the flickering firelight.

Knew them, yes. But believe what she heard and saw? No way.

It was impossible.

She clapped her hands over her mouth as her brain denied what her eyes saw. Was this another, more astounding dream? A dream she'd never—even in sleep—dared to contemplate?

Her hands slid down to cover her pounding heart. "Who are you?" she asked. "Where's Brock?"

He took another step forward.

She instinctively stepped backward, maintaining the distance between them. Her heartbeat thundered in her ears. Her throat closed up. Her whole body contracted, as if turning inward in an effort to protect her.

For an instant, her panicked brain considered running. Deke was in the barn. But she'd have to go past—

Her breath hitched.

His brows drew down and he took a step closer.

She stiffened, and he stopped.

She couldn't take her eyes off his face. His cheeks were leaner, his hair was all wrong—long and shaggy and damp, as if he'd just gotten out of a shower—and his eyes were haunted and sad. He was wearing dress pants without a belt, and a dress shirt that hung unbuttoned and untucked over the pants. And he was barefoot.

It was him.

Or a dream of him.

Darkness gathered at the edge of her vision, like a fade to black.

Like a dream. That had to be it. It was the only explanation that made sense.

She hadn't eaten dinner, and she'd drunk a glass of wine. Maybe she'd never woken up at all. She was still in bed, immersed in dreams. She pinched her arm, feeling silly.

Nothing changed.

The man standing in front of her lowered his gaze to the floor, then raised it again. When he did, a burning log collapsed, sending more light splashing across his face.

His face. The last time she'd seen those lean cheeks, that long straight nose, that wide sexy mouth, they had been horribly distorted by the dark Mediterranean waters.

"Go away," she cried. "Why are you doing this to me? You can't be here, Rook. You cannot. You are dead."

Chapter Two

God in Heaven, it was really her.

That was her low, sexy voice with the faint Russian accent that increased when she was upset.

Rook Castle wiped his palms down the legs of the dress pants that hung a bit too low on his haunches. His skin was still warm and damp from his shower, but the moisture on his palms came from pure nerves. He hadn't seen his wife in two years. Hadn't dared to hope he'd ever see her again.

She was so beautiful his eyes ached. More beautiful than he remembered. Although her delicate features were masked by fear, and her slender frame looked fragile, engulfed by the plaid wool blanket that wrapped around her shoulders.

Without makeup, her blue eyes surrounded by pale lashes were as wide and innocent as a girl's. And right now, they were filled with confusion and disbelief that etched another groove into his already battle-scarred heart.

"Irina," he breathed, and dared to move one step closer.

She held up a hand in warning. Her gaze tracked

him like a doe watching a hunter. He hated seeing her like that—the way she'd been when he'd rescued her father, dissident Soviet scientist Leonid Tankien.

But he'd come to know her well in the past six years. Irina Castle was no doe in headlights. In about five seconds that wild-eyed fear was going to change to fury, and woe to anyone who stepped into the path of her storm.

Woe to him.

"Irina." His throat was scratchy and sore, his voice hoarse from disuse. He'd talked more today than he had in two years. He cleared his throat. "I'm not—"

"What is going on?" She stiffened her back and tucked her chin. Her eyes narrowed and the spark he'd been waiting for flashed in them. She eased sideways. Again.

A weak thrill fluttered in his chest. If he could've remembered what muscles to use to smile, he would have.

She was doing exactly what he'd expected her to do. She was edging toward the closest weapon—a Glock .23, hidden in a shelf of dog-eared paperbacks opposite the fireplace.

He pushed back his open shirt and slid his weapon from the paddle holster in his waistband. He held it up. "Here," he said, flipping the Sig Sauer's handle out. "Take mine."

He bent down and slid it across the red oak floor toward her, then straightened and leaned against the mantel, doing his damnedest to appear nonchalant.

She picked up the gun, never taking her eyes off him. The blanket slipped off her shoulders, and Rook saw her perfectly shaped breasts beneath a thin covering of silk. He gritted his teeth as his body reacted to the familiar, lush curves and hollows he saw, and those he knew only from memory. Her beautiful body, which he'd yearned for every night during the past two years.

Was that the red silk gown and robe she'd bought for their yachting cruise in the Mediterranean? He'd never gotten to see it on her.

He'd died on that trip. As the thought formed in his head, the heat in his groin dissipated.

Clutching the Sig, Irina pointed it at him and straightened. One shoulder of the robe slid down her arm. She didn't notice.

Her delicate shoulder was made more vulnerable, more fragile looking by the little bump of bone that interrupted its curve. Her skin stretched across it, appearing translucent. He knew that bump, and the matching one on the other side. He knew how it felt, how it tasted. Like clean, white linen. Like her.

Rook winced inwardly and lifted his gaze to her face. Her gaze met his with faint horror, as if he were a stranger ogling her and she could read his thoughts.

Suddenly, a different kind of sparkle lit her eyes, and it twisted his heart painfully.

He knew better than anyone that Irina never cried. And he knew why. That he'd caused the tears that reflected the firelight gouged another chunk from his heart.

She took a deep breath, lifted her chin and, miraculously, the dampness in her eyes disappeared.

"So tell me. What is the big emergency?" she asked tonelessly.

"What?"

"Obviously, you never planned to—" she paused briefly "—to come back here. But something has happened. Something involving me. Something you couldn't handle any other way."

She wrapped her left hand around her right to support the weight of the gun. "You were never fond of theatrics, so I have to assume that it is urgent, or you wouldn't have sneaked me out here in the dead of night. So get to it."

Rook nodded. *That's my girl.*

She was doing everything she could to stay in control. It was one of the things he loved about her. That need to keep everything steady in an unsteady world. It was embedded into the core of steel that had drawn him to her the first time he'd seen her. But that steel core made her slow to trust.

And if anyone ever betrayed her…

If he could hate himself any more than he already did, he would. But his self-loathing was maxed out. There was no way he could explain to her why he'd done what he had.

Hell, *he'd* been second-guessing his decision for two years.

"Is it because of what happened to Matt and Deke? I'm sure Deke has briefed you—" Her voice cracked.

"Deke didn't know," he said quickly. "Not for sure. Not until yesterday morning. Don't blame him."

"No. I do not blame him. I blame you." The staccato words were coated with frost. "Spare me the explanations. Just get to the point."

"Why don't you sit down—"

"Get. To. The. Point!"

Rook pushed his hands through his hair and wiped his face. He still wasn't used to his naked cheeks and chin. The beard—his mask—had been a part of him for the past two years. He lifted his gaze to Irina's. Her eyes were as hard and opaque as turquoise.

"Novus Ordo is after you."

"*Da,*" she said, then, "Yes. That I know."

"When you stopped looking for me, and called Matt back to Wyoming, it alerted him. Deke was right about—"

"About Novus acting on the theory that I stopped because I had found you," she fired back at him in a rapid staccato. "Not because I ran out of money or gave up. How silly of me. I waste so much time and money looking for you when I could have—" her voice broke and she laughed sharply, the sound like breaking glass. "You should tell me something I do not know."

"Fine. But I'm going to sit down. You stand there if you want." Rook dropped into a worn leather chair that smelled like oil and pipe smoke. It had been his dad's.

He couldn't believe how shaky he was. How unsure. He didn't remember ever feeling this way before. Back when he'd made the decision to fake his death to stop Novus Ordo from targeting Irina, he'd felt like his life was spiraling out of control.

But *this* uncertainty was new—born of lies and deception, of stealth and secrecy and living in exile.

He'd been alone too long. In the past two years he'd barely spoken a word to another person. He'd spent all his time studying and searching for his enemy. The world's most dangerous terrorist, Novus Ordo.

He feared he might never feel human again, now that he'd lived inside himself for so long. He'd hoped to find a way to keep up with her, to make sure she was all right.

But by the time he was healed, he knew if he saw her he wouldn't be able to stay away from her.

And if he didn't stay away from her, she could die.

When he looked up, she hadn't moved, although the gun barrel had tilted downward. Her face was still expressionless, but her body was rigid—so tense he was afraid her bones might break.

"You said you know Novus Ordo is after you. Do you understand why?"

Irina's throat moved as she swallowed. "I understand that it has to do with you. That secret mission to save the senator's son, before you left the Air Force." She took a shaky breath. "When you rescued Deke." Then she shot him a look of pure suspicion. "Not that *you* ever told me anything about it."

"Do you know why Novus wants me?"

She shrugged and her arms dropped. The Sig slid from her fingers and hit the floor with a thud. "You saw him."

He nodded wearily. "Apparently I'm the only person in two hemispheres, other than his trusted inner circle, who's ever seen him without his mask."

"Why didn't you kill him then, when you had the chance?"

He shrugged without lifting his head. "We've been through this. I was out of ammo. I was sure I was a dead man."

Irina moaned audibly. "But now, you're not the only one who knows what he looks like. The CIA has the drawing. Why can't they figure out who he is? Find him? Kill him?"

"Believe me, Irina, if it were that simple—"

"No!" She shook her head, and the clip that had been holding her hair slipped free and clattered to the floor. Waves of shimmering gold fell over her shoulders.

He swallowed against the lump that suddenly rose in his throat.

"No," she repeated. "Believing you is something I will never do again."

Rook slammed his fist down on the arm of his leather chair. "Then what do you want from me?" he yelled.

Too late, he realized he'd done what he always did when backed into a corner. He'd turned a weak defense into a strong offense.

And this time he'd aimed it at his wife. *His wife.* The one person in the world who least deserved it. Who had never deserved what loving him had put her through.

She winced, then lifted her chin. "I want the truth. But, as I am sure you can understand, I'm a little shy right now."

Gun-shy, he almost said, but he bit his tongue. She'd always laughed when he'd correct her English. She wouldn't appreciate it now.

"Why don't you ask the questions, and I'll answer them."

"Truthfully?"

Rook growled and rubbed his aching jaw. The muscles there and in his neck throbbed with tension.

"Did you plan all this?" she snapped.

He looked up at her from beneath his brows. "All what?"

Irina let fly a string of Russian that Rook was sure would have shocked her father, were he still alive.

"Sorry," he muttered, feeling mean and cornered and exposed. "I planned to die. It was the only choice I had—"

He clenched his jaw and pressed his lips together. No. She didn't deserve excuses.

He propped his forearms on his knees and nodded, looking down at the floor.

"If you planned the whole thing, then who did you hire to shoot you?"

He bent his head and squeezed his temples between his palms. He was tired. He was frustrated. He ached with the need to pull her into his arms. Just long enough to remind himself that he was a human being. That he was alive.

He hadn't felt anything in so long, he'd begun to wonder if he ever would.

"Rook? Who shot you?"

Her voice sizzled with venom. She hated him for what he'd done to her. And she had every right.

His very presence here put her in danger—her and everyone else involved with Black Hills Search and Rescue. That thought sent a shard of fear through his chest.

No. He couldn't afford to feel anything—not until all this was over. If he let his emotions get in the way, the consequences would be too great to bear.

He'd already pushed Irina too far. Answering the question she'd asked would sever the last frayed thread that bound them together. And he wasn't sure he could survive if that thread broke.

He took a long breath. "Deke."

Irina gasped audibly. "What?"

He lifted his head and met her shocked gaze. "You heard me," he muttered.

"D-deke?" she stammered.

As she spoke, the door from the kitchen opened.

"Deke shot you?" Her voice was shrill with shock.

"Oh, crap," Deke said.

IRINA MET the wary gaze of her husband's best friend. She shook her head back and forth—back and forth, while her stomach churned with nausea.

"I don't understand…" she whispered. Her throat was too tight, her chest too constricted, to speak any louder.

"Don't blame him," Rook said, standing.

He might as well have been in a different room. She barely heard him. All she could do was stare at Deke, who had been there for her, who had grieved with her, who had kept Black Hills Search and Rescue going and had taken care of her during the dark time since her husband's death.

"Deke? You—?"

"Irina, he was only following—" Rook started.

"Shut up!" She swiped a hand through the air in his general direction without looking at him.

Deke's tanned faced turned a sickly green. He opened his mouth, closed it, ducked his head and rubbed the back of his neck. "Irina—"

"You shot him? You shot Rook? It was you?" Saying it didn't make it any more real. In fact, it confused her more. The memory of those awful seconds washed over her like a volcanic wind. For that instant she was back there, on the deck of their yacht, feeling the downdraft from the helicopter, gripping Rook's arm as she asked him why it was flying so close.

"But that's impossible. The shot—it came from a helicopter. He was—" She turned her head to look at Rook. "You were hit in the chest. All that blood…" She had to force air past her constricted throat.

"It was so awful. How could you not tell me, Deke?"

"It was…a matter of national security—" Deke started.

"He was following my orders. He didn't know I was still alive until he contacted a prearranged number three days ago."

Irina's head was spinning. Too much information. "But I saw the bullet hit you. It made a little puff." She gestured with her fingers. "F-fibers from your shirt, I think. Then blood—your blood—spattered on my blouse. You fell into the water." She pressed her palms to her temples. "Were you wearing a bulletproof vest? No, you couldn't have been. We'd just…" Her voice trailed off as more memories flashed across her vision.

They'd made love. She'd watched him dress afterward. All at once she realized that was the origin of her recurring dream.

They'd made love and then he'd been shot.

Killed.

"I watched you die," she whispered. Then suddenly the floor tilted and her vision turned dark. Strong arms enveloped her.

Rook's arms. But no. It couldn't be. Rook was dead.

She came awake as he laid her gently on the sofa. She didn't open her eyes, afraid the room would tilt again. Afraid her world would turn right-side up again and Rook would be gone.

The next thing she was aware of was Deke's voice.

"—can't believe you're here in the flesh. But I gotta say, I'd like to strangle you right now. You could have let me know you were alive."

"After all that planning, it was too risky to take a chance like that. What happened to your arm?"

Their words confirmed what Rook had said. The two men, who'd been best friends and oath brothers since childhood, really hadn't spoken in two years. She could tell from Deke's voice that he'd feared he'd killed his best friend.

At least Deke hadn't betrayed her—not like her husband had.

"This? It's just a scratch, courtesy of a costume cowboy called Frank James, who insisted he wasn't working for Novus."

"It's wrapped up like a mummy. Looks like a little more than a scratch."

"Don't worry about me. I'm fine. More than I can say for your *widow*. Think she's okay?"

"I think so. But look at her. She's so pale, so scared. Dear God, I never meant to hurt her."

"Well, you did."

"You think I don't know that? If there had been any other way—"

"You know what, man? Just stop. I had to watch her, knowing the whole time what I'd done—what I'd let you do. I've learned a lot in the past two years. And even more in the past few days. One thing I can tell you for sure, it may take me the rest of my natural life to make up to Mindy for everything I put her through in the past. But I'll do it. And I won't waste time whining that there was nothing else I could do." Deke's voice was low, but Irina heard the disgust and anger behind his words.

Cloth squeaked against leather as Rook stood up. "You got anything else to say, Cunningham? Because if you do, maybe we should go outside. I'd rather my wife not be any more upset than she already is."

"Now you're blaming me for upsetting her? You arrogant—"

Their argument was fast escalating into a fight. Irina sat up, a lot more quickly than she should have. Stars flared at the edge of her vision. She pushed her hair out of her face.

Both men turned toward her. She could see Deke's sheepish expression and Rook's worried gaze through the fading starbursts.

"Hey, Irina." Deke's voice softened into gentleness. "Are you okay?"

"Not even near," she muttered.

"Stay still. Rest. Maybe you can even sleep for a while," Rook said.

She laughed. "Sleep? I don't know what sleep is. Not for two years. My brain is speeding ninety miles an hour. There are so many questions that I don't know where to start."

His gaze faltered.

"Okay. Answer this one. Why did Deke bring me here?"

Deke answered her. "Because he doesn't want you out of our sight for even one second."

She shook her head and smiled sadly. "No. That doesn't explain it. Why now? I've been out of your sight for two years—" She stopped. "Or have I? Don't tell me you have watched me all this time." Her stomach churned. "I think I may be sick."

"I swear, this is the first time I've set foot in the U.S. I couldn't chance being spotted."

She turned to Deke. "So how did you find him?"

Deke's gaze slid past her to Rook. "I'll let you field that one. I'm going to go take a look around outside—"

"No!"

Deke and Rook jumped.

She swallowed. Her vehemence surprised even herself. "No. You stay right here, Deke. You're involved in this, too."

Deke looked down at the toe of his boot.

Rook rubbed a hand across his face. Despite her hurt and anger, Irina's heart squeezed at the soul-deep weariness etched there.

"I set up a message service," he said flatly. "The fees are paid automatically on a yearly basis by electronic withdrawal from a bank in the Caymans. I used the name Kenneth Raven."

She stared at him. "A bank—" How had she been married to him and not known him at all?

"So who called you on this message service? I thought Deke did not know you were alive. You said nobody knew."

"That's right. Nobody. Deke had the number, but he wasn't to call it unless it was a life-or-death situation."

"You arranged your assassination. You planned for a contingency in case you needed—or wanted—to return to life. You left your sister, your wife, all your friends and family, to think you were dead." Irina's stomach was still churning. Her head was spinning. "We had a funeral. We grieved for you. And the whole time you were laughing at us."

"Trust me, I wasn't laughing."

Was she seeing things, or were his eyes brighter than they'd been a few seconds ago? She'd never seen Rook Castle cry before. Still, even if those were tears, it didn't matter. It was too late for tears, too late for apologies.

It was too late.

An awful thought occurred to her. "What about Jennie? Is she all right?"

He nodded without looking at her. "I hired a bodyguard for Jennie, using the Cayman Islands account. She has no idea."

"So you have decided the best thing for everybody, haven't you?"

"I didn't have a choice."

She lifted her chin. "Just so I know, how long had you been planning all this?"

"Rina, it wasn't like that—"

"How…long?"

Out of the corner of her eye she saw Deke squeeze his eyes closed.

Rook looked away and shrugged. "Six months. Maybe eight."

A short, sharp laugh burst from her throat. "Eight *months*. You lived with me, you made love to me, and all the time you were planning to—? Dear God, who are you?"

She stood and caught the arm of the sofa to steady herself. Then she glared at the man she'd married in a fever six years ago. "I do not know you at all."

Rook spread his hands. "Trust me, it'll all make more sense once you've had some rest. It's a lot for you to take in right now—"

"A lot to take in? You think?" She heard her voice rising in pitch. "But, yes, of course. I am sure I'll feel much better once I take a *nap*."

Deke reached out a hand, as if to soothe her, but she jerked away. "No. Don't touch me."

She wrapped her arms around her middle and turned back to Rook. "Where have you been? Who have you been in touch with?"

"Nobody. Irina, you need to calm down."

"You have no right to tell me what I need to do. You gave that up when you let me think you were dead." She held up her hands, palms out. "I can't—I cannot take any more. I'm going to make tea."

"Stay there. I'll make it for you," Deke said.

"No," she snapped. She couldn't be alone with Rook. She didn't know what she would do—or say. "I think I'll let you two talk. It's pretty obvious you need to."

She glared at Deke. "Maybe you can get some real answers out of him."

She took a cautious step, making sure her legs weren't going to collapse, then headed to the kitchen, with Rook's voice following her.

"Use the light over the stove. Don't turn on the overheads."

"Fine. Fine. No problem," she muttered. "Like I have no sense to figure that out."

She twisted her hair up and anchored it with a rubber band from a kitchen drawer, then pulled the tea canister toward her, hoping there was at least one tea bag. She opened the lid.

"Jasmine," she whispered. Her favorite. She dug the little package out and opened it.

She put the kettle on the stove eye and held the tea bag to her nose. The scent hurtled her back in time.

She and Rook had come up here a couple of weeks before the fateful trip to the Mediterranean. Just the two of them.

She'd brought up the idea of having a baby—again. And again, like always, he'd sidetracked her with jasmine tea and hot, passionate lovemaking. He'd never talked about having children. At least now she understood why.

She had to blink away tears before she could pour the hot water into her mug. Then she turned out the light over the stove and stood at the kitchen window in the dark, waiting for the tea to steep. In the distance, thunder rolled lazily and a pale flash of lightning lit the sky.

Before Rook, she'd always been afraid of thunderstorms. They reminded her of the guns and bombs from her childhood in the former Soviet Union. Thunderstorms had frightened her. But ever since she'd married Rook, she'd learned to love them.

He liked to lie in bed with the windows open, summer or winter, spring shower or gale-force winds, and watch the lightning and listen to the sounds of rain and thunder.

For her, lying in his arms, safe and secure in the

knowledge that he would never let anything happen to her, was the ultimate definition of safety.

But he'd left her alone—alone with the storms and the memories and the unrelenting grief.

She swiped her fingers under her eyes and set the tea bag aside. Then she wrapped her hands around the warm mug and sipped, sighing as the hot liquid slid down her throat to soothe her insides.

She closed her eyes. She'd spent the past two years living in a nightmare. Every night, she'd prayed she would wake up and find Rook beside her, safe and sound. Every morning, she'd woken with her prayer unanswered.

Now he was here, but she still didn't feel like her prayers had been answered.

This felt like the nightmare. The months of sleepless nights, of the recurring dream of loving him and then losing him, had become her reality.

Thunder rumbled again, closer this time. Irina's eyes flew open. A lightning flash illuminated the dense woods on the east side of the cabin and a deafening clap of thunder made her nearly spill her tea.

Then something moved—a shadow darker than the trees.

She froze, holding her breath as the thunder continued to roar. She waited for the next flash of lightning. It didn't take long.

The flare spotlighted a creature slinking along the edge of the woods. No. Not a creature. Not some *thing*.

Someone. And he was carrying a gun.

Chapter Three

Irina's breath caught. There was someone outside the cabin, and he was carrying a weapon—maybe a rifle.

Setting down her mug, she moved swiftly toward the living room.

Rook and Deke were still arguing.

"—surprised he hasn't tried to get to Rina before now," Rook was saying.

"Son of a— That's what I'm trying to tell you. He has." Deke's voice rose. "You don't get it. The level of security I've got around her—she might as well be the First Lady. I told you I'd take care of her!"

"Of course I get it. That's not what I'm saying."

"It's only been two weeks since she called off the search. Fifteen days! And he's already managed to send a man after Matt and put a plan into place to kidnap Mindy. That's why I knew I had to call you. He was obviously watching Matt. He knew the instant Irina called him. Hell, he knew before she got in touch with Matt. I'm thinking Novus knew she was calling off the search as soon as we did."

"That's not possible," Rook snapped.

"It is if he's got a mole on the inside. Look how he

got to Mindy and used her to get to me. The SOB was watching her. He knew she was pregnant, something neither Irina nor I knew."

"You can't think that one of the BHSAR specialists is working for Novus."

Irina stepped into the room.

"Would you listen?" Deke snapped. "My helicopter was sabotaged on the ranch. Right there in front of the hangar."

"Sabotaged?"

"Rook! Deke!" Irina hissed. "There is someone outside. He's armed."

"What?" Both men jumped up. Deke grabbed a fireplace tool and shoveled ash over the flames. "Where?"

"At the edge of the woods outside the kitchen window."

"Did he see you?" Rook asked.

She shook her head. "Not when I saw him. The lights were off. Maybe while I was making the tea."

"I thought you said you weren't followed," Rook flung at Deke.

"I wasn't. You?"

"Absolutely not. Are they Secret Service?"

"I've got a team on alert, but they won't approach until I call them." Deke cursed. "See? This is what I've been trying to tell you—"

"Who'd you tell about the cabin?"

"Just Dan Taylor. Today."

"Then how in hell did they find us? LoJack?"

"No way. I swept the SUV before I picked up Irina."

"But not after? If what you said about a traitor in BHSAR is true, someone could have tapped your car while you were inside."

Deke cursed and crossed the room. He peered through the corner of the wooden blinds.

Rook shook his head. "No matter. Too late now. Are there still automatic weapons in the safe?" he asked as he walked over to the metal safe set into the far wall.

"Yeah, plenty. I can't see anything out there."

Rook dialed in the code and opened the heavy door. He reached in and pulled out two machine guns, along with several magazines of ammunition. "Wow," he breathed. "You've upgraded."

Deke walked back over to the fireplace. "HK 416s," Deke said. "Secret Service gave me those after you disappeared. Part of their commitment to protecting Irina. You should find some super-hot night-vision goggles in there, too. And several flash grenades."

"Nice." Rook examined one of the 416s briefly and efficiently. His ease with handling the big weapon sent chills down Irina's spine.

Deke pulled out his phone and dialed a number. He spoke a few words and hung up. "The Secret Service team will be here in less than twenty."

"Hand me a com unit. And don't we have some Tasers around here?"

Deke had already pulled a small wired box out of his pocket. "Pocket Tasers and handcuffs are stowed in the duffel bag I brought in."

Irina watched them in awe. They hadn't seen or talked to each other in two years, yet they worked completely in synch, anticipating each other's needs. Their calm efficiency was reassuring and yet profoundly frightening at the same time.

As he grabbed the com unit and inserted the earpiece, Rook nodded at Irina. "You're going to the basement."

"Wait. I can take the Sig. I can help—"

"Now!" He pointed a finger at her. "And don't open the door until you hear my signal. There's a Glock down there, with plenty of extra ammo. Remember the safe word?"

She nodded stiffly, nearly paralyzed with fear. Years ago, when Rook had bought the cabin, he'd extended the basement to the barn and turned it into a safe room, reinforced with steel.

Since the barn was downhill from the cabin, a short tunnel was all that was necessary to join the two buildings. A door at the far end of the basement joined the back wall of the barn.

He'd gone over a long list of precautions with her. His insistence on such extensive safety measures had spooked her at the time, but they'd never had to use any of them.

For her, Rook's very presence had always meant safety. But no more. The man standing in front of her with cold determination hardening his face was not the same man she'd married.

"Go!" he barked.

"Don't—" she choked out through her constricted throat "—don't get killed."

ROOK DECIDED to follow Irina down the stairs from the pantry to the basement. He wasn't going to take any chances. He'd see for himself that she was securely locked in the basement safe room.

He didn't touch her—he didn't have to, to know that she was shivering with fear and confusion. That and more radiated from her like a fever. He couldn't blame her, but he couldn't reassure her, either.

He wanted to tell her how sorry he was. Wanted to somehow explain. But even if he could form the words, they were meaningless. Mere words couldn't make up for what she'd been through.

Hell, nothing could.

He opened the basement door and stepped back to let her pass. She went through the reinforced metal door and pushed it almost closed, then paused, peering at him through the narrow opening.

Long ago, he'd promised her that she would never be afraid again. He'd promised himself that she'd never have cause to regret marrying him. He'd broken both promises.

"Why?" she whispered, as if she knew his thoughts. "Why did you let me believe you were dead? All this time—"

He clenched his jaw. "Not now, Rina."

She recoiled slightly, as if dodging a blow.

He'd hurt her again. More. It seemed that all he'd ever be able to do from now on was hurt her.

Reassuring words lodged in his throat. If he said them, they could turn into yet another lie. She needed time to heal, time to learn that she could trust him.

But right now time was a luxury they couldn't afford, because Novus had found them. So he said nothing.

She lowered her gaze and closed the door.

Rook stood there until he heard the massive lock click into place, then he mounted the stairs.

He tapped the ultralight communications transmitter in his ear.

"Deke?" he muttered.

"Front room. And whisper, dammit. You're busting my eardrums." Deke's words slid through his head as if they were his own thoughts.

"Irina's secure," he mouthed, barely making a sound. "I'm in the kitchen. Whatcha got?"

"I see two, slinking around behind the trees."

Deke's voice was clear and as smooth as silk. These were damn good units. A far cry from the staticky ones they'd used during their Air Force missions.

"I figure there are four of them," Deke continued. "And two of us. That makes it even odds."

Rook's mouth twitched. "You're giving those four guys a lot of credit."

"Yeah, well, they may have explosives. How do you want to handle this?"

"The two you don't see—where are they?"

"My guess—one at the front door and one at the back, waiting for us to come out. I'm betting Novus wants you alive, so they'll try tear gas first. Then escalate to stun grenades if they have to."

"What about these grenades we've got?"

"New toy, courtesy of Homeland Security. Works like a regular grenade. The flash blinds the enemy for thirty seconds or so. The goggles you've got hanging around your neck will protect you."

"What if they have the goggles, too?"

"These babies are brand-new technology. Prototypes. Theory is you can stare at the sun for hours with them on. I doubt Novus has them yet. *We* don't have them—officially. Whoa!"

"What?"

"They're on the move."

"Deke, go get Rina and get the hell out of here. Through the basement into the barn. The keys are in the rental car. I'll hold them off."

"The hell you will! Four against one's not the same as four against two. You'll be playing right into their hands. You get Irina, I'll hold off these—" Deke spilled a few choice curse words. "I've gotten away from Novus twice before. I can do it again."

"With that arm you may not be able to handle the 416. It's heavy."

"You don't worry about me. I can handle anything you can."

Rook heard something clatter against the kitchen window. "Something hit the window. Probably tear gas."

"Rook—go! Take Irina and get to safety. They're after you, not me."

"No way. We'll take them together and then I'll get Rina. As long as she stays in the safe room, she'll be fine."

"Unless one of our visitors decides to check out the barn."

"The steel door from the barn into the safe room is rated for twenty minutes against dynamite."

"Good to know. So how do we want to take these guys? Stay together or split up?"

"You take the front. I'll take the back and then we'll catch the middle two in a crossfire. No casualties unless absolutely necessary. I want them in custody, spilling their guts."

He heard a hissing noise outside the window. "There goes the tear gas. They wasted that one."

"I'm at the door. You?"

Rook flattened his back against the kitchen door, mentally measuring the distance out to the yard. The door opened onto a small stoop and then down five steps. "Yeah. See anything?"

"Nah. I say we go on three. If you spot one, try the flash grenade, but be ready with firepower. I'll be shooting down from the porch." The edge in Deke's voice cut like a razor blade through Rook's head. He knew the tone. Deke was prepared to die to protect him. Rook felt the same way.

But it wasn't going to happen. Not today—not ever. Deke had every reason to stay alive. He had Mindy and their newborn baby boy.

And Rook had— He gripped his machine pistol in both hands and shoved those thoughts away. "On my mark," he growled.

"One." He tensed his thighs and pushed to a standing position, then pulled the night-vision goggles over his eyes. It took him a second to adjust to the *Matrix*-like look of the world through the infrared lenses.

"Two." He turned the key in the back door and reached for the knob, ready to angle around. Ready for anything. A heady rush of adrenaline buzzed through him, making him super-aware. He heard the whisper-light hum of a mosquito, noticed the faint cold breeze on his neck.

He took a long, slow breath.

"Three!" He slung the door open and slid around it, his finger on the trigger of the HK 416. The 416 was a heavy piece of equipment and carried plenty of ammo, but right now its weight was comforting.

A second wave of adrenaline jacked up his heart rate and sharpened his already-honed senses.

Deke's labored breathing sounded like a windstorm above the sawing of his own breaths. His nose picked up the fresh, earthy smell of rain from the brief thunderstorm. His trigger finger tightened.

In one long stride, he crossed the stoop and put his back against a wooden pillar.

Poised to shoot, he swung out and swept the backyard with his gaze and his gun. It was empty—no shadowy figures, no sound other than rain dripping off eaves and tree branches.

Where were they? If they were his men, they'd be covering the main entrances to the cabin.

He didn't like that he couldn't see them. Had they circled around to the barn? Or was Deke wrong? Were there just two of them?

He shook his head. Deke was rarely wrong.

"Whatcha got?" he whispered into the com mic.

"Nothing." Deke's voice was laced with disgust.

"Still think there are four of them?"

"Yeah. But maybe not."

A noise to Rook's left had him swinging his weapon in that direction. Glass shattered.

"They breached the kitchen window with a tear-gas grenade. Ready to go? Flash grenade first?"

"On your mark," his friend replied.

"One…" Rook hopped lightly to the ground and planted his back against the north wall of the cabin, east of the porch. The grass, wet from the thunderstorm, muffled his footsteps.

"Two…" He cradled the HK 416 in his right arm and pulled out a flash grenade with his left, noticing his arm, dark and edged with acid green, through the goggles.

"Three!"

He rounded the corner of the cabin in time to see a human-shaped green monster slink away from the kitchen window back toward the woods.

He jerked the pin with his teeth and tossed it a couple of feet beyond the man.

"Flash!" he muttered into his com unit. "Look out."

Suddenly the yard lit up like the midway of a state fair. Even through the goggles the flare was painfully bright. Someone screeched in pain.

Then all hell broke loose.

The air around him filled with the deep rat-tat-tat of

machine-gun fire. The blinded enemy were strafing the yard randomly, hoping to score a hit.

And coming damn close.

Rook shrank against the wall, making himself as small as possible as a flurry of bullets zinged past him. If he could dodge them long enough, their attackers would soon be out of ammo.

If he could dodge them.

"Deke?"

"I'm okay. You?"

"Soon as they're done wasting ammo, let's take them. Tasers and cuffs. Then we'll see how many buddies they've got."

"Say the word."

Rook stayed flattened against the wall until he heard the spit of machine-gun fire slow down and then stop. The volley that seemed to go on forever had probably only lasted a few seconds.

He pulled the fully charged Taser from the scabbard he'd attached to his belt and checked its setting.

Medium. He turned it to high. To the danger zone, in fact. He wanted the bastards helpless and moaning with muscle cramps.

Then, with his finger on the trigger of the HK 416, he tensed.

"Go!" he spat through the com unit.

He rounded the northeast corner of the house just as Deke appeared on the southeast end of the long front porch.

The guy who'd thrown the tear gas was dressed head to toe in black. He lurched across the bare yard toward the woods, obviously still blinded by the high-powered flash. Rook hoped Deke had the other man in his sights.

He slung the 416 over his shoulder by its strap and

ran toward the stumbling terrorist. He took him down easily, zapped him with the Taser and then, ignoring his moans, cuffed him and jerked his ski cap over his eyes as a blindfold.

"Move, and I'll shock you again."

The man squealed in protest. His legs jerked involuntarily.

The unmistakable stacatto of machine-gun fire broke the silence.

"Deke?"

"Over here. I got two for one. Had to take one out. Got the other one trussed up like a turkey."

"Mine, too. That makes three."

"Hey." Deke's voice brightened. "Here comes the cavalry, right on time."

As his voice faded, Rook saw the headlights. He jerked his captive to his feet by the neck of his black sweater, but the man's legs buckled under him.

"Get moving. I'll drag you if I have to," Rook growled and proceeded to do just that. By the time he got to Deke his arm muscles were protesting.

Rook dumped the man onto the ground next to Deke's prisoner and shoved his goggles up onto his forehead. "Where's the casualty?"

Deke nodded toward the bushes that hugged the edge of the porch. At that moment, the headlights of a black SUV shone on them like spotlights, and four Secret Service agents jumped out, dressed in flak jackets with weapons at the ready. The driver stepped over next to Deke while the other two took charge of the prisoners.

"Good timing, Dan," Deke said, nodding at the driver.

Rook glanced beyond the SUV as a second vehicle pulled up and four more flak-jacketed men emerged.

"Rook, meet Special Agent Dan Taylor, with the

Secret Service. He just took over as Agent in Charge of Security around the ranch. He's been briefed about your situation. Dan, this is Colonel Rook Castle."

Taylor shook his hand. "Pleasure, Colonel."

"Glad to meet you," he said. "Deke, I'm going to get Rina."

Deke nodded as he continued talking with Taylor. "Dan, we think these guys are working for Novus Ordo. I'm afraid the one in the bushes over there didn't make it, but these two are healthy. We need all the intel they've got."

"Any means necessary?" the Secret Service agent asked.

"That's right," Deke responded. It looked to Rook like Deke had everything handled for the moment. So he turned on his heel and headed for the house to fetch Irina from the fortified basement.

As soon as Deke and Agent Taylor headed off with the prisoners, and he and Irina were finally alone, they could talk. The thought sent apprehension skittering down his spine.

He was halfway up the steps to the kitchen door when the blast shook the cabin. The force of the explosion knocked him down the steps and on his butt. Heated air gushed over him.

Black smoke billowed up over the west roof.

The barn.

"Rina!" he screamed, pushing himself to his feet. He ran toward the smoke and flames.

"Rook, wait!"

Deke's hand brushed his arm. He jerked away, pumping his legs faster.

Then Deke tackled him. He went down heavily, with Deke's arms locked around his legs.

Rook struggled, kicking. "Let go!"

Deke propelled himself up and over him, wrapping his arms around his shoulders in a bear hug. "Stop it, Rook!"

Rook heard a shout and the pounding of boots on the wet ground. He kicked again and tried to buck Deke off.

"You'll kill yourself. Taylor's men are checking it out."

Rook barely heard him. He bucked again.

"Get off me you son of a bitch! I've got to get to Rina!"

Chapter Four

Rook finally pushed Deke off of him, or Deke gave up and rolled away. He vaulted over Deke and up the porch steps, heading for the basement safe room. From the color and height of the smoke coming from the barn, he was sure nobody could get to the basement going that way. The fire was burning too hot.

He raced through the kitchen and down the basement stairs. With a giant leap off the bottom stair, he hurtled himself against the metal door, pounding with his right fist and groping for the intercom switch with his left.

He prayed that the wires hadn't been burned or shorted.

"Irina!" he shouted through the intercom's speaker. "Answer me!"

Nothing.

His scalp burned with fearful anticipation. Had the explosion compromised the steel mesh-reinforced walls of the safe room? Had she been hurt? Or worse, had the men gotten to her?

He took a deep breath and shouted the safe word. It was actually a phrase, made up one night as they lay in each other's arms after an hour of nonstop lovemaking. Loosely translated to English, the phrase meant "Come here often?"

"Irina, *Priyed'te s'uda chasto?*" he said carefully, enunciating the words the way he'd learned. He'd never been great with the language, although he could speak it. According to Irina, he always bungled the pronunciation. She'd laughed every time he spoke. He wished he could hear her laughter right now.

"*Priyed'te s'uda chasto,* Irina." He hit the door with his fist again, then spread his palm against the metal, ridiculously relieved to feel its chill against his skin. Rationally, he knew it was too thick to allow heat to penetrate, especially after only a few minutes, but he breathed easier anyway.

Please, he begged silently. *Answer me.*

"*Tol'ko—*" a choked voice crackled through the intercom. "*Tol'ko, kogda suda vhod'at.*"

Only when the ships come in.

Relief sent shivers across his scalp and the nape of his neck, where sweat prickled.

"Irina, thank God. Are you all right? Are you hurt? Can you unlatch the door?"

He heard her fumbling with the lock, then with a cold metallic snick, the latch sprung.

For an instant, he paused. She hadn't answered any of his questions. What if she wasn't alone? What if one of Novus's men was holding her?

But, no. She knew what to do. If she weren't safe, she'd have answered *Vse vrem'a,* "All the time," if she were compromised.

He swung the door open, expecting her to throw herself into his arms. But she didn't. She stood, a couple of feet back from the door, her arms wrapped around herself.

He examined her closely, looking for any sign of burns or injuries. She looked unhurt, but she was shivering.

"You're freezing. Dammit. I should have grabbed that blanket for you. Come here." He held out his arms.

She looked at his outspread hands, then met his gaze. Her eyes were wide and dilated with fright. "Is it safe?"

His embrace or the situation? "We've contained the attack."

Her gaze held his for an instant, then she pushed past him and went up the stairs.

He turned to follow her, but the straight, stiff line of her back in the silk dressing gown spoke volumes. In fact, she couldn't have been clearer if she'd shouted.

She didn't want his help, nor his comfort. He couldn't blame her. She'd managed for two years without it.

He was terrified that during that time she'd decided that being without him was easier than being with him.

He didn't take his eyes off her until she disappeared through the door at the top of the stairs and closed it, quietly but firmly.

He couldn't make it up to her for leaving her. All he could do was make sure that everything around her was safe. So he stepped through the metal door and looked around. She'd turned on the solar lights that were fed by panels on the roof of the cabin, so it was easy to see that this end of the basement was undamaged.

However, the smell of smoke and burned wood and rubber permeated the air, and forty feet away, at the other end of the room, he could see where the steel mesh that reinforced the basement walls was bare in several places. Whatever they'd use to blow up the barn, it had generated enough heat to incinerate the plywood.

The basement was slightly soundproofed by virtue of the reinforced walls and metal doors. Still, it must have been terrifying for her, down here alone, listening to the gunfire. He couldn't imagine what she'd gone through as the explosion ripped the roof off the barn and burned through the walls he'd assured her were impenetrable.

For all his training and experience, in the Air Force and afterward, it occurred to him that beneath it all he was a naive idiot, thinking that because he thought he'd made her safe, she actually was.

Worse, he'd expected her to blindly accept his decisions—expected her to trust her life to them.

When had he become so arrogant and self-delusional?

The door behind him opened.

"Rook?"

He heard Deke's voice in his ears and through the com unit at the same time.

"Yeah."

"I saw Irina." Deke's footsteps were light on the wooden stairs. For his size, he could move almost without a sound. He stepped up beside Rook. "She didn't seem to be hurt—"

"Not physically," Rook finished, wincing. "She's never going to trust me again." He started toward the other end of the room.

Deke muttered something as he walked beside him.

"What? You might as well say it out loud. It won't be anything I haven't already said to myself."

"Have you called yourself an arrogant prick? Because that's what I'm calling you."

"Actually, yeah."

"Good. With your vote, it's unanimous." Deke widened the distance between them as they came closer to the far wall.

The smell of burned wood and rubber grew stronger, as did the heat. The crackling of flames filled the silence.

"It took nearly losing Mindy to make me realize what's really important."

"I know what's important. Why do you think I did what I did?"

Deke snorted in disgust. "Yeah, you know what *you* think is important. Don't put Irina through what I put Mindy through." He moved to the south wall. "Damn, that was some explosion."

Rook stepped to his left, to the north side. "Yep. Took the whole roof off the front of the barn."

"Aw, man. Look at my car." Deke's SUV was in flames, and several other small fires were still burning.

The rental car Rook had parked near the safe-room door appeared untouched. He took a few steps closer and pulled a small, high-powered flashlight out of his pocket. The roof was still intact over this end of the building, and he saw very little damage.

A beam of light crossed his on the concrete floor. Deke was checking out the south side.

"The SUV's leaking gas," Deke said.

Rook trained his light beam on the same area where Deke's light was shining. "How close to the flames?"

"Close."

Then Rook saw it. A line of liquid trickling along the floor, from the smoldering SUV to the rental car. As he watched, the center of the line caught fire.

"The gas just caught," Deke said. "It's spreading in both directions." He flipped on his com unit. "Taylor?"

Rook flipped the switch on his own unit. He heard

static. These fancy new units didn't work that great underground.

For a second, he debated running to the vehicles and trying to stop the gasoline before it caught the rental car on fire, but even as he thought it, he saw the flames brighten.

Time had run out.

"Taylor!" Deke shouted. "Get your men away from the barn. It's about to blow!"

"Deke! Run!"

They both turned and ran.

IRINA HAD THE blanket wrapped around her shoulders, but no amount of external insulation was going to help the chill that sat like a block of ice inside her.

Deke had come in a few minutes ago. When he'd asked how she was doing, she'd merely shrugged. How did she answer that question? In the past week and a half, she'd abandoned her last shred of hope that Rook might still be alive, she'd almost lost two of her closest friends—Rook's oath brothers—to terrorists and she had come face-to-face with the man she'd finally, after two long years, accepted as dead.

Deke had studied her for a few seconds, a worried frown marring his rugged features, then asked her if Rook was still downstairs. Without waiting for an answer, he'd headed down there.

She hadn't moved. She still sat in the same position, waiting, not even sure why. What was she waiting for?

She supposed she should be doing something. Maybe making coffee? Or cooling bottles of water?

She'd neglected to buy the etiquette book that covered entertaining Secret Service agents who'd helped save their lives. Was she obligated to provide a full meal? Or just hors d'oeuvres? And was it impolite to exclude the attackers?

A near-hysterical chuckle escaped her lips. She didn't know how to receive a husband who'd pretended to be dead for two years. She couldn't possibly be expected to handle Secret Service and terrorists.

Leaning her elbows on the table, she pressed her face into her trembling hands. None of this seemed real. If she opened her eyes right now and found herself in her bed at Castle Ranch, still a widow, still essentially penniless, she wouldn't be surprised.

A coughing spell interrupted her wandering thoughts. Her throat burned, and the smell of smoke lingered in her nostrils. She stood, pulling the blanket more snugly around the flimsy red gown and negligee. She needed to wash her face and get dressed.

As she turned toward the sink, she felt something under her feet. Did the floor shake? A low rumble hit her ears, followed instantaneously by a deafening explosion.

The safe room!

"No!" she cried. *No!* She dropped the blanket and rushed toward the basement stairs.

"Rook!" His name tore from her raw throat.

Before she got to the door, it slammed open. She got a split-second glimpse of two looming figures.

Then a hard body collided with hers, propelling her backward. Rook's lean, muscled arms immediately grabbed her up.

His warm strength enveloped her. His hand cradled the back of her head and pressed her face into the hollow of his shoulder. Holding her. Protecting her.

She felt the soft cotton of his shirt beneath her palms. Then her fingertips encountered a thick, harsh ribbon of fabric. It was the nylon strap of the gun slung across his back. "Rook, are you okay? Please, please be okay."

His arms tightened around her and his voice hummed near her ear. "Shh. Shh. I'm here."

She doubled her fists in the material of his shirt, sobbing with relief. Right this second nothing mattered except that he was here. He was safe. He was alive.

"This is Cunningham." Deke's voice broke into her consciousness.

Rook stiffened.

"Yeah, we're fine. The two vehicles in the barn went up." Deke continued. "Everybody okay out there?"

Rook took his hand away from the back of her head and adjusted the com unit in his ear. He cocked his head as the arm embracing her slid to her shoulder.

"Good," he said, staring at a point beyond her left ear. His jaw flexed with tension. "Meet us in the front room to debrief."

Suddenly, as quickly as her fingers had noticed the difference in his soft shirt and the harsh gun strap, she sensed the difference in him. The hand touching her shoulder belonged to a soldier. A commander. Not a lover.

Her Rook, her sweet, safe love, was gone.

She pushed away. "I need to get dressed."

Deke stepped past them. "I'll sweep the rooms first."

She watched Deke's retreating back helplessly, wanting to yell at him not to go. *Stop leaving me alone with him.*

But it didn't matter. Rook might as well have been one of the nameless Secret Service agents swarming around the cabin. He was distant, detached, as he removed the com unit from his ear and put it in the box that sat on the counter. Then he swung the gun down from his shoulder and unloaded it and broke it down. He laid the parts on the table. From the small of his back, he retrieved a handgun and checked it, then slid it back into the waistband of his pants.

He did all this without looking at her or speaking to her. Then when it seemed he'd done everything he could think of to do to avoid talking to her or even looking her way, his gaze slid up to meet her eyes and he took a breath, as if about to speak.

But she had no idea what he'd been about to say, because at that instant Deke reappeared.

"Everything looks fine in here. You can go ahead, Irina." He stopped, his gaze moving from her to Rook. "Or—"

She spoke quickly. "I will dress and then make some coffee."

Rook shook his head. "No. No coffee. Join us in the front room. You need to know what we're going to do next."

"Fine," she said evenly. "I appreciate you including me—this time." Then she turned on her heel and left.

Wincing at the venom-laced words that lingered in the air, Rook watched her exit. She'd never been one to flaunt her beauty or her femininity. But her slender body was perfectly proportioned, beautifully formed. She walked like a princess, head held high, back straight, with no wasted movement. Yet to him, everything about her, even the slightest brush of her hair across her shoulders or the sweep of her eyelashes, was alluring, and profoundly sexy.

"Uh, Rook?"

He glanced sidelong at his friend. "What?"

"Taylor and his men are waiting in the front room for the debriefing."

When Rook walked in with Deke at his side, Dan Taylor was standing near the fireplace, dressed in his flak jacket and police windbreaker, speaking quietly to a fellow Secret Service agent and jotting notes on a spiral notepad. Two other agents were standing near the front door.

All of them straightened perceptibly as Rook and Deke entered. Taylor accepted a manila envelope from one of his men and stepped over.

"Colonel Castle. I have something here I'd like you to look at." He opened the envelope and pulled out several photos.

"That's Lieutenant Cunningham's guy who called himself Frank James. Along with a couple of the others found in the explosion of the old mine."

"Explosion?" Rook looked at Deke, who shrugged.

"I had to get Mindy to safety, and I didn't have a whole lot of options. I found some dynamite."

Dan continued. "Lieutenant Cunningham believes there were at least six men there, counting James, but the others were so badly burned we weren't able to recover enough for a definitive conclusion."

Rook took the photos and studied them.

As soon as he laid eyes on the first photo, his pulse hammered in his ears. That face—or one eerily similar—had haunted him across three continents. It was of a thin-faced man with dirty-blond hair. He was obviously dead, and although he'd been cleaned up for the photo, one side of his face was unrecognizable.

"This guy's a dead ringer for Novus Ordo, except for Novus's receding hairline."

"I *knew* it," Deke said. "The first time I laid eyes on him I knew I'd seen him before. He looks just like your sketch."

"He's got to be Novus's brother," Rook said, tapping the picture. "So that's how Ordo found out so much about all of us," Rook said. "His brother must have been here the whole time."

His temples throbbed. Was he finally close to identifying the terrorist—finally close to bringing down the man who was responsible for thousands of innocent deaths throughout the world? "Can we ID him? Fingerprints? Dental records? Publishing his photo?"

"We managed to get two prints off him. Dental records aren't as easy as you'd think. If you've got a tentative ID, you can use dental records to verify it. But it's like your CGI of Novus's face. With no place to start, it's almost impossible."

"Why not start here, in Crook County, with prints and dental records?" Rook asked. "Have you met FBI agent Adrian Schiff? Good. Contact him. Then, if nothing comes of the fingerprints or the DNA, maybe we can at least verify whether he's been living in this area."

Dan nodded. "I'll ask the local FBI to help with matching dental records. I like the idea of publishing the photo, too. It might flush out some of Ordo's followers.

Dan jotted some notes on his dog-eared pad. "I suspect you'd like to be there when your specialists see these photos?"

"And I want their reactions recorded. I want to study each one of their faces when they first see this." He handed the photos back to Dan.

"Now, sir. We need to get you and Mrs. Castle away from here. Two of my men have cleaned up the casualty and taken the prisoners in for interrogation. Two are securing the grounds and waiting for the local authorities."

Rook winced. "Do we have to involve the locals?"

"Yes, sir. That blast was visible for several miles. We're spinning it as an accident—gas line exploded, place was empty. We'll take care of the rental car."

It was a good plan. Simple. Two years ago, letting someone else take charge of anything wouldn't have been in Colonel Robert Kenneth Castle's playbook, but after spending all those months as an expatriate and fugitive, he found it disturbingly easy to acquiesce to the Secret Service agent.

"So how are you going to explain your presence?"

Deke spoke up. "I'm going to tell them I was on my way up here. They probably won't believe it was a coincidence, but there's not much they can do about it."

"After you're safely away, we'll have a talk with the sheriff."

"I want to know what you find out about the prisoners," Rook said. "And who set the explosive in the barn."

Taylor nodded. "My recommendation is that we first get you and Mrs. Castle to a safe location. We'll debrief there once we're done here."

"No. Take us back to the ranch."

"Sir, security at the ranch may have been compromised. Plus the specialists living on the grounds will know you're there."

Rook shook his head. "I have an obligation to my specialists—to everyone who works for me—to keep them safe. I trust you to take care of security at the ranch. At least, as Sun Tzu said, we'll be keeping our friends close and our enemies closer." He glanced at Deke.

"Yeah," Deke agreed, "but so will they."

IRINA BURIED her face in the white towel, breathing in its fresh, clean scent. She sent a silent blessing up for

Jocelyn Talltrees, a local woman who kept an eye on the cabin and cleaned it twice a month. She peered over the towel into the mirror. Eyes clouded with fear and worry stared back at her from a pale, drawn face.

She had dreamed of finding Rook alive. It was why she'd spent a fortune the past two years searching for any clue that might give her hope. If anyone had asked her, she'd have told them that finding him would make her the happiest person on the planet. That getting her husband back would make her life complete once again.

But as she'd already realized, this reality she found herself in was no dream come true. In fact, it was a nightmare.

The man who'd come back to her was a stranger. He reminded her of the man who'd saved her father from execution as a traitor to the former Soviet Union.

Her father was one of only eight people in the world who could approximate the level of genius of Albert Einstein. When the Soviet Union broke up, Leonid Tankien was branded a traitor because of his belief that scientific breakthroughs belonged to the whole world. In poor health, he'd been placed under house arrest in the care of his only daughter and sentenced to hang for treason.

The president of the United States sent a special extraction team in to rescue Tankien and his daughter. Rook was the commanding officer on that mission. Like a superhero, he'd swept in and rescued them and brought them to the United States.

The plane ride to Washington, D.C., was twenty-two hours long. Rook and Irina sat together while her father rested. By the time the plane landed at Dulles, Rook had transformed from terse military commander to gentle yet strong confidant, and Irina had fallen hopelessly in love.

Too bad for her.

She hung the towel over the rack and rolled down the sleeves of her white silk shirt. The black pants she'd fished out of the closet were a size too large now, but the cotton socks and hiking boots fit fine. She pulled her hair back from her face and refastened the rubber band with a wince.

For a brief moment she again buried her face in her hands and worked on controlling her breathing and swallowing the nausea that kept pushing at her throat.

Someone knocked on the bathroom door. When she opened it, she found herself staring up at Rook's handsome face.

He didn't even bother to try and raise a smile as his gaze raked her from head to toe. "We've got to go."

She nodded without speaking. Picking up a wool jacket, she glanced around for anything else she needed to take back to the ranch.

Rook took a step backward. "Now." He sent a brief glance around the room, then turned on his heel, leaving her to follow.

By the time Irina got to the front room, Rook and Special Agent Taylor were talking intensely in hushed tones, and Deke was pacing. He looked up as she came in.

"Hey, Irina. How're you doing?"

"Fine," she said shortly, and immediately regretted it. "I'm okay. How are you? And Rook?"

Deke shrugged. "He's afraid someone's going to get hurt. He's trying to work out a failsafe plan with Taylor."

Irina frowned. "Well, first, he is too late. He has already hurt a lot of people. And second, when will he learn there is no failsafe?"

"I'd think you'd know the answer to that question. You've been married to him for what? Six years now. He'll never learn that lesson. Your husband is the most idealistic SOB I've ever met. He actually believes that Good will win over Evil and that one man can make a difference."

Irina raised her brows. "And you don't?"

Deke ducked his head. "I'm still working on happy endings."

"Don't worry, Deke," she said, laying her hand on his arm. "You've got yours. Just make sure you don't forget what a precious gift you have in Mindy and— Oh, my gosh! You haven't named the baby yet, have you?"

A grin transformed Deke's features. "Oh, yes, we have. Deacon Robert Cunningham."

Irina stood on tiptoes and kissed his cheek. "Oh, Deke, I love it. I'm so happy for you."

He squeezed her shoulder. "Don't give up on Rook," he murmured. "He loves you more than life."

She stared at him as he straightened. His mouth quirked and he tilted his head, as if to say "But then, what do I know?"

"Irina." Rook's quelling voice hit her ears. His gaze snapped from her to Deke and back. "Ready to go?"

She lifted her chin a fraction. "Yes."

Out of the corner of her eye, she saw Deke turn and practically run for the door. She couldn't blame him. The ice between Rook and her was enough to freeze his nose off.

She stepped past Rook and let Special Agent Taylor escort her out the front door of the cabin and into a black SUV with heavily tinted windows.

As she waited uncomfortably for Rook to get in the seat beside her, Deke's earlier words echoed in her ears.

I'm still working on a happy ending.

She pressed her lips together in an effort to hold tears at bay.

At least you *are working on it,* she thought.

Chapter Five

Irina set the coffee carafe down and glanced at the clock over the door of Rook's basement office/conference room. Eight-thirty in the morning. At this point she wanted more than anything to go to her suite and take a long, relaxing bath, then climb into bed and sleep for about a week, long enough to forget this nightmare.

But the nightmare wasn't over. In fact, it was only beginning. During the two-hour ride back to Castle Ranch, Deke had filled Rook in on the details of what had happened in the past two weeks.

He spoke calmly and matter-of-factly, as if he were presenting the details of a budget request, or outlining the advantages of one helicopter over another. But his deadpan delivery didn't soften the impact. Irina was shocked to hear all the details of what Matt had gone through, and all that Deke had endured.

The realization that every bit of it had been put into motion by her decision to call off her search for Rook was daunting and sobering.

Matt and Deke had put their lives on the line. Innocent people had been hurt and traumatized, because of her decision. People had died. Bad people—traitors, kidnappers, torturers. But still human beings.

By the time the SUV veered from the main road onto a gravel drive that led to a garage underneath Castle Ranch, Irina had been queasy with horror over the consequences of her innocent act. As soon as the garage door had closed, Rook had stepped over to the wall and pressed a code into an electronic keypad. A hidden door had opened into the room she now was standing in—another safe room. This one was a sound-proofed office suite, complete with a kitchen area and a bathroom. Even a minuscule elevator that ran to the large suite of executive offices on the main floor.

It had always baffled her that Rook, the bravest man she'd ever known, found it necessary to have so many safe rooms and secret hideouts. But now it made sense. Without such precautions, he'd already be dead, several times over.

Rook sat at the head of the conference table, with Deke and Special Agent Taylor to his right.

Irina watched along with them as the other specialists came in.

Per Agent Taylor's instructions, the agents were brought down one at a time. Matt was brought in first.

His face was as pale as the straps on his arm sling. Purplish shadows ran under his eyes. When he saw Rook, he swayed, grabbing the back of a chair to steady himself. But he recovered and greeted Rook with a big grin before lowering himself gingerly into the seat to Rook's left. Irina caught the meaningful glance he sent toward Deke, and she saw the infinitesimal movement of Deke's shoulders.

Irina felt indignant on Matt's behalf. Rook shouldn't have made him come. He was obviously still too weak from surgery. From the looks of him, he probably shouldn't have been discharged yet. After all, he'd almost died up on that mountain top fighting for Aimee and her little boy's lives.

The next specialist to arrive was Aaron Gold. A red scrape above his right ear spoke to his brush with death. The sniper's bullet had missed his brain by a fraction of an inch.

Aaron's dark eyes behind his rimless glasses glittered and his face went ashen when his gaze lit on Rook, sitting at the head of the table.

"Colonel!" he gasped. "You're— Oh, my God!" He shook his head. "We all thought you were—"

"Dead," Rook responded. "I know."

Aaron nodded eagerly. Pink spots appeared in his cheeks. "This is unbelievable. I'm— What happened? Where have you been? Are you all right?"

Rook nodded. "I'm fine. Have a seat, Aaron. We've got a lot to talk about."

Aaron's eyes darted around the table as he sat. "Did you know about this?" he asked Deke.

Deke shook his head.

Aaron started to say something else, but at that moment the door opened again and Rafiq Jackson was standing there, leaning on crutches. His right pant leg was slit and his thigh was bandaged.

Irina turned her attention to Rook. He hadn't met Rafe, and she wanted to know what his first impression of the young man was. She'd never gotten to know Aaron very well. He was quiet and introverted. But she liked Rafe a lot. Maybe because he was the only member of the team that *she'd* hired. Or maybe because he was outgoing and funny and he seemed to have less to hide than either Aaron or Brock.

When she looked back at Rafe, he smiled. "Good morning, Irina," he said with a nod. Then his deep brown eyes slid to Deke and he nodded again. He planted the crutches in front of him and, looking down, swung forward a step.

"Rafe," Deke said. "Meet Rook Castle."

Rafe's smile froze on his face. He stared at Deke for a second before turning toward the head of the table. Then, much like Aaron, his eyes widened and his face drained of color. He swallowed, opened his mouth, closed it and then opened it again.

"Mr. Castle. I mean, Colonel Castle. I—I'm—"

Rook waited.

"This is a true honor, sir. I've always regretted that I never got to meet you. I've been— It's been a privilege to work here." He stood stiffly, his knuckles white on the crutch handles. "I must say, I'm stunned."

Rook nodded. "I'm seeing a lot of that today."

Rafe's gaze turned back to Irina and his brows raised slightly. "I'm certain of that, sir. Mrs. Castle, may I help you with the coffee?"

She shook her head. "No, thank you." She intercepted an irritated glance from Rook. He'd told her to forget the hostess duties and concentrate on the debriefing, but she'd needed something to do. Otherwise she was afraid she might give in to panic and start screaming.

Rafe took both crutches in one hand and lowered himself into a chair, wincing. Irina quelled the urge to go around the table and take his crutches before he dropped them. He had no business being out of the hospital yet, either.

Two down and one to go. She glanced up at the clock again. Eight-thirty in the morning. Where was

Brock? Usually he was the first one awake in the mornings, the first one to arrive at a meeting, and the last one to turn in at night. Had Rook left him until last for a reason?

The doorknob turned and Brock came in. He looked like he always did. Crisp and neat—military neat. His shoes were polished, his slacks were pressed and his shirt was dazzlingly white. His good eye slid from face to face, until he met Rook's gaze.

Brock went still, reminding Irina of a champion bird dog on point. His body was perfectly balanced, his senses razor sharp. He exuded focus and concentration. No matter what might be required, he was ready.

Rook's head went up a fraction and his lips curved slightly. "Brock," he said.

"Colonel Castle." Brock nodded once. Nothing else. No effusive greeting. No exclamation of joy that Rook was alive. Merely that simple acknowledgment.

Yet she saw his hand twitch at his side. An odd reaction from the ex-Navy Seal whose survival had depended more than once on his self-control. Rook had told her stories about him. She glanced at Rook, wondering if he'd noticed, but his face revealed nothing.

Brock sat next to Rafe and rested his clasped hands on the table. They were steady, motionless now.

Irina picked up the tray of coffee-filled mugs and set it in the middle of the table.

The men reached for the mugs—even Rook, and the small wrinkles between his brows smoothed out a bit as he took a long swig of the hot drink. His reluctant appreciation sent a little flare of triumph through her.

After taking the last mug herself, she sat in the empty chair to Special Agent Taylor's right. She wrapped her fingers around the warm mug and took a sip. It *was* good coffee, which made her wonder who kept the coffee down here fresh and the pot and mugs dust free.

She realized Rook was speaking. With an effort, she concentrated on what he was saying.

"I'm sure you all have a lot of questions," he said, looking from Matt to Aaron, from Rafe to Brock.

Rafe laughed quietly. Aaron and Matt nodded, and Brock didn't blink or move a muscle.

"Well, right now, we've just come from a confrontation with several individuals whom I'm sure were sent by Novus Ordo." He nodded toward the right side of the table, where Deke, Special Agent Taylor and Irina sat. "So I apologize, but there's no time for discussion about me and where I've been. Deke or I will fill you in on a need-to-know basis."

He leaned forward. "What we need to talk about right now is what happened this morning, and what precautions we need to take at this point. What I will say as a preface, is that I'm here because of everything that's happened during the past two weeks. I look around this table. It's impossible to miss that each one of you has been injured because of me. I regret that, and I regret that I can't give you each time off to heal."

He waved his hand. "Don't bother shaking your heads. I know, and I appreciate it. All of you have met Special Agent Dan Taylor, right? He'll tell us about the prisoners. This is our first debrief, so I'd appreciate it if you'd hold any questions until Dan is done. Dan?"

"Yes, sir. Colonel Castle and Lieutenant Cunningham faced three attackers at a facility owned by Colonel Castle. We don't know at this point if the three were the only ones. Explosives destroyed the barn and two vehicles on the property. No casualties were found in the rubble. The three could have set the explosives prior to attacking, or they could have had help. We have two of the men in custody. The third was a casualty on site. No evidence of other accomplices."

Taylor flipped a page in his small spiral-bound notebook. "We had to notify the sheriff over there, because of the visibility of the explosion. We'll brief you as needed about any contact you may have with that office. The Crook County medical examiner took charge of the body of the single casualty. The other two are in custody in the former Treasury Department building in Sundance. I have two men guarding them, but we haven't had a chance to question them yet."

"Do you have photos?" Rook asked.

"Yes, sir." Taylor nodded to the Secret Service agent standing at the exit door. The agent retrieved a small manila envelope from his inside jacket pocket and handed it over.

Rook glanced quickly at the three photos, then shuffled them and scrutinized them more closely.

"We found a vehicle hidden in brush a mile south of the cabin. It's a junker with expired tags. We're tracing the last owner, but odds are it was bought or stolen from a junkyard. I don't expect there to be any way to trace it."

Rook nodded. He handed the photos to Matt and gestured for him to pass them around.

No one said a word as the photos changed hands. Rook watched as Matt, Aaron, Rafe and Brock examined the pictures.

"If any of you recognize anyone," Rook said, "speak up."

Dan jotted a note on his pad, looked at it for a moment, then leaned over and whispered something behind his hand to Deke. Deke cut his eyes over at Dan and then nodded.

For the first time, Irina noticed how Dan was dressed. His slacks were perfectly tailored and she wouldn't risk a dollar betting against that white dress shirt being handmade. His expensive clothes didn't fit with the dog-eared dollar store notepad and cheap mechanical pencil he carried.

"While you're looking at pictures, I've got three more for you to see." He gestured to the guard again and was handed another manila envelope.

"I've e-mailed all of these to our computer expert in D.C. She'll run them against our known terrorist database for a facial recognition match. I've ordered DNA and fingerprints and Special Agent Schiff has requested top priority for the results."

Dan handed the envelope to Rook, who looked at each one carefully. He glanced at Deke and then returned the pages to the envelope and handed them to Matt, who was seated directly to his left.

Irina knew the photos were of the man who'd named himself Frank James and two of the terrorists who'd worked with him on Mindy's kidnapping. And she knew the specialists' reactions were being recorded. She watched carefully, wondering if she'd be able to spot any reaction.

Matt took a quick glance through them and handed them on to Aaron, who seemed to know he was being scrutinized as he studied the faces. He quickly passed them on to Rafe and shook his head at Dan.

"Nothing. I mean, there for a minute I thought I recognized that first guy, but no."

"I've never seen them, either." Rafe handed the envelope to Brock. "You're up," he said, smiling.

Brock glanced through the small stack of photos, shook his head and laid them down on the table. "Who are these guys?"

"They're the men who were after Deke in the mine."

He looked at Deke. "That first guy is the one who called himself Frank James?"

Deke nodded.

"That's interesting." Brock slid the folder across the table to Dan.

"Interesting?" Dan repeated.

"Jesse James was the more famous of the brothers, but a lot of scholars think Frank was the real brains."

"That's what he said," Deke remarked. "I goaded him about naming himself after the *brother* of an outlaw, and he said Frank was smarter."

Irina kept her attention on Rafe and Aaron. Rafe was following the conversation with his typical engaging fervor. Aaron was listening, but as was usual for him, he didn't show much emotion.

Dan tapped the edge of the folder on the tabletop. "Do you think that's significant?" he asked, directing his question to Rook.

"You mean, do I think that it's a clue to Novus Ordo's identity?" He nodded. "I wouldn't be surprised."

At the mention of the terrorist, both Aaron and Rafe tensed. But then, so did almost everyone else at the table. The notable exception was Brock. Still, he was the one that had introduced the conjecture.

"I want to see the prisoners in the flesh," Rook said. "How soon can you arrange that?"

"If you don't mind, sir, I'd appreciate it if we could keep them isolated for at least twenty-four hours."

Rook looked like he was going to object. Irina knew he didn't find it easy to acquiesce to someone else's authority. Especially someone like Agent Taylor, who was younger and much less experienced than he.

Deke cleared his throat quietly.

Rook's chin lifted and his eyes narrowed slightly. "Fine. Make sure you understand that I'm not only concerned about the safety of my family and my employees. This is also a matter of national security."

"Yes, sir," Taylor said. "The White House made it very clear that this team's mission was to keep you and your family safe and to gather every bit of information we can about Novus Ordo. Oddly enough, Ordo seems to have disappeared around the same time you did. The destruction of the chemical munitions plant in Mexico two years ago was his last known attack.

"Homeland Security has ramped up its surveillance of audio and electronic transmissions throughout the world, and we've upped scrutiny and troop availability in the Far East, especially the areas that join Afghanistan, Pakistan and China."

Irina doubted anyone in the room, except maybe Deke, noticed a difference in Rook's attitude, but she had. A nearly imperceptible relaxation of the tension across his forehead told her that he was impressed with Agent Taylor.

"So how long have you been on this assignment, Taylor?"

"A month, sir. However, most of the team has been here since right after you disappeared."

Rook blinked. He was surprised. Another thing he hadn't known.

"A month. So I can assume you're not totally up to speed on the situation?"

Taylor's mouth quirked almost imperceptibly. "More today than yesterday. As Lieutenant Cunningham told you, he briefed me after he'd spoken to you. I was originally assigned here when the agent in charge had to take bereavement leave. At that time I was told we were guarding your wife, because of your connection with Novus Ordo and the international involvement and implications in your...death. That's the extent of my knowledge."

"Fine," Rook said curtly, setting down his mug. For a few short seconds he stared at the surface of the coffee, or at his hand—Irina couldn't be sure. "It's probably as good a time as any to bring all of you up-to-date."

He raised his gaze and looked at each specialist. "Four years ago, I was asked by the president to go into Mahjidastan to rescue Travis Ronson." He sent an apologetic glance in Aaron's direction.

Aaron nodded once, gravely.

"We lost Norman Gold on that mission—Aaron's dad. He died a hero. Matt and Deke were with the mission. Brock was holding things together back here, Aaron hadn't joined Search and Rescue at that time. He was still in school."

Dan nodded eagerly. "I remember that incident. Ronson's oldest son."

"Oldest of five."

Rook nodded. "He was a Navy fighter pilot and was shot down. Ronson is a close friend of the former president's, and he couldn't stand to think that Fred might lose another son. So we went in after him."

"That was you who pulled off that rescue." The awe in Taylor's voice was palpable.

Rook nodded at Deke. "We had intel that Ronson was being held by the terrorist who had bombed a nuclear plant in India, killing thousands. Deke—Lieutenant Cunningham—flew a grid over the entire area, searching for signs of their camp. It's damn rocky up there, but Deke spotted a small campfire and some tents. Before he could get away, Novus shot his helicopter down and took him captive, too." Rook finished his coffee.

Irina reached for his cup, but he checked her with a sharp gesture.

"At that time, micro-GPS locators embedded under the skin were investigational. Deke had one of the first. Luckily it worked. We extracted Ronson and him without any further casualties to our side, but—"

The tension and expectancy in the room was palpable. Dan Taylor leaned forward. Rafe and Aaron were both staring at Rook, entranced.

"I came face-to-face with Novus Ordo."

"Without his mask," Taylor breathed.

Irina almost smiled. The special agent, who had to be four or five years younger than Rook's thirty-three, was obviously starstruck by him. She could understand why. Rook had a presence about him. He was larger than life. Heroic.

"I saw his face and he almost killed me. He managed to grab my dog tags. So I can identify him, and he knows who I am."

"So faking your own assassination was—"

"A well-meaning but foolish attempt to stop Ordo from targeting me and my family."

Irina wanted to believe that. She *wanted* to believe everything Rook said. But in all the time they'd been married, the one thing she'd never had was Rook's complete trust. He seemed to view everyone as a potential enemy—even her. And this moment was no exception. He didn't glance toward her as he spoke. He didn't look at anyone. He stared at his clasped hands.

Matt sat up gingerly. "It was a good plan, until Irina was forced to abandon her search. Her decision was innocent, but Ordo had obviously been watching her for the past two years. He was alerted. He couldn't afford to believe that she'd stopped merely because of financial problems, or because she'd gotten proof that he was dead. Ordo had to operate on the assumption that she'd found him."

Hearing those words in Matt's low voice sent a shard of guilt stabbing into Irina's breast. She could never tell anyone about the surprising feeling of relief she'd felt when she'd finally made the decision to stop putting money into the futile effort of proving her dead husband wasn't dead.

The truth was, after two years of hanging on to that tattered shred of hope, finally letting go had been a relief.

Chapter Six

She turned back toward the coffeepot as her face heated with shame. She felt Rook's eyes burning into her back.

"So, clever bastard that he is, Ordo managed to put a complex plan together in a matter of hours," Deke threw in. "I don't care if he did have two years to work on it, the plan he devised shows he's a genius. The deadliest mistake we can make is to underestimate him."

Irina poured water into the coffeemaker and turned it on.

"I left Mahjidastan within twenty minutes of hearing from Irina," Matt said, "yet Ordo still managed to have me followed and contact one of his agents in the U.S. to kidnap baby William. He knew about my best friend's widow and her son. And he knew I'd drop everything to save them."

When Irina turned around, it was obvious that Rook was listening intently, although his expression was stony. She could tell this was the first time he'd heard all the details of what had happened. She studied his face. It was impossible to tell if he was affected by the knowledge that she'd searched for him all that time.

He really had cut himself off totally—and he'd done it for her safety.

No, not her safety. *The nation's.*

Rook's jaw muscle ticced. "Novus has made it his mission to know everything about the brotherhood, so—"

"Excuse me, sir. Brotherhood?"

Rook's face lightened for an instant, then sobered again. "Matt, Deke, me, and Bill Vick. When we were around nine or ten years old, the four of us went on a mountain adventure and nearly died when a storm blew in. A brave man named Arlis Hanks lost his life rescuing us. Hanks was a combat rescue officer in the Air Force during Vietnam. Their motto is *That others may live.* We took an oath to live our lives by the same creed. I started Black Hills Search and Rescue to pay forward what Arlis Hanks did for us."

Dan scribbled something on his notepad. "Where's Bill Vick?"

Matt spoke up. "Bill Vick was my best friend. He died last year."

"And how does Novus know about this oath you took?"

Deke shrugged. "He doesn't. But he's figured out that each one of us would give our life to save the others."

"Why we do what we do doesn't mean anything to you," Rook stated. "Just be aware that Novus Ordo has killed who knows how many people to protect his identity. And he will again."

Rook paused, watching the effect of his words on those gathered in the room. Brock and Aaron knew about the mission to rescue Ronson. Brock's reaction was exactly what Rook had expected. No sign of surprise or interest. Aaron had joined Black Hills

Search and Rescue just weeks after the rescue, so he knew most of the story.

Rafe appeared spellbound, like a kid in the presence of his favorite superhero.

Rook turned his attention to the Secret Service agent. Agent Dan Taylor was an interesting man. Six feet tall and well-built, he seemed more mature than his years. And something Rook said had affected him. Quickly replaying his recent remarks, Rook decided that it must have been the mention of the brotherhood. He filed that piece of information away.

Taylor turned to Matt. "Lieutenant Parker, you said you were in Mahjidastan when Mrs. Castle called you?" he asked.

Matt nodded. "Following up on a rumor that an American had traveled there recently. If Novus had a tail on me, it was a damn good one. I never caught the guy. But obviously, he knew the instant I left. Apparently knew I was there and was keeping an eye on me, so he had me followed back here to Wyoming. Then he kidnapped Bill Vick's widow's seven-month-old son in an effort to capture me."

"But his plan didn't work." Deke tossed back the last of his coffee and set the mug down on the table with a thud. "Any more than his plan to take my wife hostage to force me to reveal where Rook was. And now he's after Irina."

Taylor assessed Deke and Matt.

Rook knew what he was thinking. "You're wondering why Novus didn't try something more direct, like stopping Matt before he got on that plane, or going after Deke instead of capturing his ex-wife."

Dan shrugged. "I'm guessing he knew they wouldn't talk, with nothing at stake but their own lives.

I've got to agree with Lieutenant Cunningham. Novus has to be extremely intelligent to plan and carry out all this on such short notice."

"Oh, he is." Rook nodded. "But as Deke said, it's likely he's had tentative plans in the works for months—probably since I disappeared. Still, not only did he underestimate Deke and Matt, he underestimated Aimee Vick and Mindy Cunningham, as well. Even so, he accomplished his ultimate goal. He managed to flush me out. Now that he knows I'm alive—"

"He'll do whatever he has to do to destroy the man who exposed his true face," Deke said, then paused, looking at Rook.

"What about the CGI?"

Rook's gaze met Matt Parker's. He sent him a nearly imperceptible nod.

Matt stood and stepped over to a fireproof safe.

Dan's gaze followed him. "You have a computer-generated image of Novus Ordo? Who did the drawing?"

"The CIA, using my descriptions."

"No hits?"

Rook shook his head. "Not even close."

Her husband's disgusted tone reminded Irina of how obsessed he'd been with finding the man whose face he'd seen. The lengthy phone calls with CIA, Homeland Security and other government officials, the numerous trips he made to Washington to look at photo arrays. The memories weren't fond ones.

They'd married a few months after Rook's rescue of her father, six years ago. The first two years she spent learning to trust and love him and his country.

Then, right when she was becoming comfortable in his love, he'd gone on that mission to save Travis Ronson and seen Novus Ordo's face. So the next two years were lonely, as he spent most of his time obsessed with identifying the terrorist. And of course, these past two years she'd spent alone.

Right now, standing here, watching her husband and the two men he trusted most in the world, assessing the nature and the source of the threat against their lives, it occurred to her that she'd have to dig awfully deep to unearth *any* fond memories.

She held up the fresh carafe of coffee and glanced around the table. In response to the nods, she refilled mugs.

Matt closed and locked the safe, handed a manila folder to Rook and returned to his seat.

Rook forced his hands not to shake as he slid the photo out of the folder, just enough to see the subject's eyes and nose.

Novus Ordo. Latin for "New Order."

A surge of anger washed over him, surprising him. He hadn't expected to react so strongly to the drawing. After all, the man's face was engraved into his brain. He didn't need a computer-generated image to remind him of what he looked like.

Nor did he need to look at the photo of Frank James to know that the two men were brothers—that they could be twins.

But he wanted to. "Hand me that photo of Frank James."

Dan picked up the folder and passed it to him. Rook held the two images side by side.

No question. If they could get a hit off James's prints or DNA, maybe they could finally identify Novus.

He handed the two pictures to Dan, who grabbed them eagerly.

"Pass them to Rafe when you're done," Rook said.

Then he turned to Jackson. "You haven't seen the drawing yet, have you?"

Rafe shook his head, his gaze following the manila folder. "No, sir, I have not," he said in his faintly British accent.

Dan stared at the two images. Irina looked over his shoulder. The resemblance between the drawing put together from Rook's description and the photograph of Frank James was amazing.

"This is Novus Ordo?" Dan sounded stunned.

No one bothered to answer him.

"He's American!" he exclaimed, then immediately corrected himself. "I mean, he's—Anglo. Caucasian?"

"Yeah," Deke said flatly. "We know."

"And he and James are dead ringers!"

Rook nodded. "Except that Novus is losing his hair."

"And in all this time, the CIA couldn't find him?"

"I'd have done it differently, but the CIA felt that starting with a narrow sample and gradually widening would eliminate even the slightest margin of error. So rather than publishing the sketch, they chose to start with criminal records."

"Mug shots," Dan offered.

Rook nodded. "I looked at every ugly, two-bit criminal in Wyoming and the surrounding states. And nothing. Which didn't surprise me. My guess is that when we do find out who Novus Ordo is, he'll turn out to be some formerly mild-mannered guy with no criminal record. The kind who's easily swayed by whatever latest fad religion or cause comes along."

"Like Ted Kaczynski?"

Rook nodded. "Probably never got a parking ticket. I wouldn't have started with criminals, but I guess they had to start somewhere."

"What was their next step?"

"Driver's license photos. But I'm guessing that once I disappeared, they suspended the search. I mean, what would be the point? As far as they were concerned, I was dead."

"So not even the CIA was aware of your plan?" Dan asked.

Rook felt an overwhelming urge to defend his decision. But he suppressed it. What was done was done. No matter whether he'd made the right decision or not, he had to live with it. He sent the young agent a quelling glare. "No."

Dan's face reddened and he nodded. "Have you contacted them since you returned?"

"Agent Taylor, I flew into Casper yesterday, using a counterfeit identity I set up prior to my disappearance. When I'd thanked the attendant as I walked off the plane, that was the first time I'd spoken to anyone in the U.S. in two years."

Dan looked surprised. "No one? No one at all?"

Exasperated, Rook shook his head. "Not my wife. Not Deke. No one. It would have been too dangerous."

He glanced briefly at Irina, but she appeared to be involved in stirring her coffee. She was tired. He could read her exhaustion in the slope of her back and neck. She'd changed from the sexy red silk gown to a white shirt and pants that were too big for her. Even so, they didn't hide the enticing curve of her back or her vulnerable nape.

Dan lowered his gaze to his notepad. After a second of awkward silence, he took a deep breath. "I believe that's all the questions I have at this time—for the specialists."

Rook dragged his attention away from his wife. The

look in Agent Taylor's eye and the inflection in his voice told him a lot. He wanted to talk about Rook's employees.

Rook nodded his understanding. "Brock, Aaron, Rafe. Thanks for your time and input. Agent Taylor and I have a few more things to discuss. You're dismissed."

Once the three of them had exited and the door was closed, Rook turned to Matt. "You don't have to stay for this. Deke or I can fill you in later."

Matt smiled. "Not a chance. I'm here. I want to hear everything."

"Great." He turned back to Dan. "You have more questions?"

"I understand from Deke—Lieutenant Cunningham—that there's strong reason to suspect one of your employees of feeding information to Novus."

"That's what he told me. Deke?"

Deke leaned back in his chair and raked his fingers through his hair. "Dan, you've heard the short version."

Dan nodded. "Your helicopter was sabotaged. I'd like to hear how. Who could have done it. And who couldn't have. I've viewed the security disks. I'm assuming that whoever did the tampering knew how to avoid being recorded."

Deke nodded. "That's right. As for the how: Someone drained all the oil *and* tampered with the oil gauge, so it had to be someone with a little technical knowledge," Deke said. "I followed my usual start-up routine. I'd checked all the fluid levels the night before. I did my walk-around—to make sure there were no leaks. Then I did a visual check of the mechanics. I started the engine and checked all the gauges. But when I tried to take off, the motor seized." Deke rubbed his eyes. "Draining the oil is a pretty simple matter, if you know where the drain plug is. But doing it in the short time frame they had to work within, without spilling a drop? That takes more patience, skill and attention to detail than most people have."

"So which one of your specialists has those traits?"

Deke shook his head. "All of them."

He leaned back in his chair and raked his fingers through his hair again. "I've worked with each of these three guys and found them competent and trustworthy. Until my bird was sabotaged, I'd have said I could trust each of them with my life, but obviously I was wrong there. I've gone over everything I know about them, and I can give you at least one reason to suspect each one."

"*At least* one? Which ones have more than one?"

While Dan was speaking, Rook stood and stepped over to where Irina was sitting, near the coffeepot. She'd been getting more and more pale, and he could tell by the way her skin stretched across her cheekbones how exhausted she was. He put a hand on her shoulder and leaned down. The scent of gardenias wafted past his nostrils from her hair.

"Why don't you go upstairs? There's no reason for you to sit through this."

She stiffened under his touch. "I'm fine," she hissed.

"It's obvious you're not."

"I thought you wanted me to hear everything." Her voice was still icy.

"I can brief you tomorrow—or Deke can, if you don't trust me."

"I'm. Fine."

Rather than make any more of a scene than they'd already made, Rook gave up and went back to his seat.

She wasn't about to give him a break. Not that he deserved one, but it still hurt.

He pushed his thoughts back behind the steel wall of his heart, where he kept things he didn't have time to deal with, or didn't want to.

Behind him, Deke was filling Dan in on the specialists, and Rook needed to be listening.

"The one person I've always known I can count on is Brock O'Neill. He's been around the longest. He's a former Navy Seal, got a disability discharge when he lost his eye on a mission."

"He lives on the ranch?"

"Sort of," Deke said.

Dan's brows went up. "Sort of? What does that mean?"

Deke shifted. "He's here during the week."

"And on weekends?"

Irina caught the look that passed between Deke and Rook. She'd seen it before. The two of them sometimes communicated in ways that she didn't understand.

Deke turned back to the Secret Service agent. "We don't know."

"You don't—?"

"His weekends are his own. He doesn't have to tell us where he goes."

"But you have an opinion, right?"

"Nope. Not me."

Irina's gaze shot involuntarily to Rook's. She knew as soon as her eyes met his that he was thinking the same thing she was: Deke wasn't telling everything he knew.

She knew that Brock disappeared most weekends. He'd always done it, and Rook had always allowed it, unless Brock was on an active mission. She'd never asked Rook where the ex-Navy Seal went on his own time, and Rook had never volunteered the information.

Dan intercepted her gaze and started to speak, then stopped and mentally regrouped. He jotted a note on his pad, then looked up. "What's his specialty? What was the last job he did for Black Hills Search and Rescue?"

"Brock took over my job as mission coordinator when I took over Rook's position," Deke said. "He's got expertise in explosives, as well as several other areas. But at heart, he's a tracker. He's half Sioux Indian, so I suppose tracking is in his blood. He can track over ground, in water and over rock. Best I've ever seen."

"How can you be sure you can trust him?"

"Because I know him. He wouldn't betray his country."

"You said he's Sioux. Maybe he doesn't recognize the United States of America as his country."

Anger flared in Deke's eyes. To his credit, he didn't say anything.

Irina understood. It was one thing to speak in generalities about someone feeding information to Novus Ordo. It was quite another to specifically target each trusted employee.

"Brock's last assignment was a missing-child case," she offered. "A mother and her two boys went on a picnic in a supposedly safe camping area. The younger, a six-year-old, disappeared."

"He had a child locator on." Deke took over the story. "But the locator was found at the bottom of a ravine, smeared with blood consistent with the boy's blood type. The child hasn't been found."

Dan shook his head. "Sad story. Has that affected his work?"

"No," Deke said.

"I think he's still looking for the child," Irina put in. "I think that is what he does on his time these days. I tried to tell him to let it go. But he is a stubborn man, and I'm afraid he may have developed feelings for the mother. In any case, that's about the time my accountant started warning me about finances, so that was the last pro bono case we took."

"And when was that?"

She thought for a second. "Two months ago."

Dan turned back to Deke. "What about the other two?"

Rook spoke up. "Aaron Gold is our computer and communications expert. He's young, only twenty-three. His dad was a good friend of mine. One of my mentors. Like I told you, he died on that mission under my command." He rubbed his face.

"Aaron followed in his dad's footsteps and got his degree in computer engineering while he was in the Air Force. I hired him for his computer knowledge, and because I felt responsible for him after his dad's death."

"Think he resents you for taking his dad away from him?"

Rook shook his head. "I'd have said no, but—"

"Aaron was pretty shook up when he heard about Rook's death. I think he thought of Rook as a father figure," Deke put in. "Oh, and he does live here on the ranch, in the guesthouse."

Dan glanced down at his notepad. "And Rafiq Jackson. What kind of name is that?" He looked up at Rook, who shook his head and gestured toward Deke.

"Irina hired him several months ago. He was born

in England." Deke sat back in his chair and crossed his arms. "He's our terrorism and language expert."

"So he's not an American citizen?" Dan asked.

Deke nodded tersely. "Yeah, he is. Naturalized. He's never had military service, but he studied math in the U.S. and worked for NSA until he got sick of government bureaucracy—his words."

"Rafiq—what kind of name is that? It sounds—"

"His mother is from Saudi Arabia. His father is British."

Dan nodded. "Anything else out of the ordinary about him? Other than his heritage, I mean?"

Irina responded. "He was unemployed for two years after he quit NSA. According to his CV, he took a trip around the world. I hired him for his language skills."

"You advertised for a language expert?"

"No. We didn't advertise."

"So, how did you know about him?"

Rook sat forward. He wanted to know the answer to that, too.

Irina spoke then. "We received his CV in the mail," she answered Dan. "We were not advertising, but when we saw his credentials, we called him in."

"We both liked what we saw," Deke said.

"I can show you his introductory letter," Irina continued. "His education and experience were impressive. And he said he had always wanted to work search and rescue."

Her voice quivered slightly at the end. Rook understood why. She was questioning her decision. Had she unknowingly hired a terrorist? She had good instincts about people, but sometimes her feelings got in the way of her better judgment.

He turned his gaze to Deke.

"I vetted him," Deke said. "All the way back to Hampstead Garden, England, to his birth records."

"So tell me, why does a search-and-rescue operation need a terrorism and language specialist?"

Deke sent the Secret Service agent an exasperated look. "Because this particular search-and-rescue operation is on Novus Ordo's short list."

Chapter Seven

"Black Hills Search and Rescue wasn't created to be a typical search-and-rescue service like so many who operate here in the mountain states. You might say our scope is pretty broad."

Rook clasped his hands on the table. "Dan, I know you've only been here a month, but you were assigned here by the president. I'm certain you know the answers to many if not all of these questions you're asking." He paused long enough for the silence to become uncomfortable.

Dan didn't take the bait. He sat still, staring at his pad, waiting for Rook to continue.

"Given our customers, it makes perfect sense to me that Deke and Irina would hire a language and terrorism expert."

"Yes, sir," Dan replied. "I'm not questioning the decision. I'm merely interested in finding out why Rafiq Jackson sent his CV *here*."

The question hung there in the air until Irina spoke.

"Are you saying this is the only place he sent it?"

Dan's head turned sharply in her direction.

Rook nodded to himself. Excellent question.

After an instant of silence, Dan nodded. "I'll check." He flipped a page. "Okay. Moving on, tell me about Fiona Hathaway."

Irina looked surprised. "Fiona? How did you get her name?"

"Same as all the other specialists. From your assistant, Pam Jamieson."

"Fiona is on a leave of absence—maternity leave. Has been for the past two months. She has nothing to do with this."

"Fiona had a baby?" Rook was surprised. She'd never seemed like the type to want children.

Irina nodded.

"She was a major in the Air Force," Deke supplied. "Commanded a medical reserve unit until she retired four years ago. She's also a cartography expert. Her unit was deployed to Afghanistan, and she returned with medals for bravery, although there were some rumors circulating that she may not have deserved them."

"Oh, yeah? Why not?"

"I didn't ask," Rook said. "Fiona informed me about the rumors and assured me they weren't true."

Dan jotted down a quick note, probably to request the information from the Air Force.

"Who's the father of her baby?"

"Never asked that, either."

Dan nodded and flipped backward several pages.

"So that's four specialists. They're the only people, other than you, who could have access to the kind of information we know has been given to Ordo?"

Rook, Deke and Matt all nodded.

"But Fiona has a really good alibi," Irina pointed out. "She was in the hospital in labor when the helicopter was sabotaged."

Dan looked at each of them in turn. "So who is your traitor? Brock O'Neill, Aaron Gold or Rafiq Jackson?"

No one spoke.

Rook rubbed his palm down his cheek to his chin. "It could be any one of the three."

"WHAT ARE YOU planning to do? Hide down here in the basement all day?"

Irina didn't answer Rook's question. She didn't even look at him. She didn't have to. Even with her back turned, she knew exactly what he was doing. He was leaning against the door frame with his arms crossed and his jaw set. He was angling for a fight. It was how he always argued. Closed off. Irritatingly rational. And with a subtle undertone of sarcasm that could sting like an angry hornet.

As frustrating as his superior attitude was, she felt a disturbing nostalgia. She'd even missed this.

She'd stayed behind when the meeting broke up, using the dirty coffeepot and cups as an excuse, although what she'd really wanted to do was avoid the awkwardness of going upstairs at Rook's side. She wished she could slip into her suite and lock the door and avoid the question of where he would sleep.

She ran the coffee carafe under the hot water tap one more time and set it on the drain board in the small kitchen, then started on the mugs. Maybe if she ignored him long enough, he'd give up and go away.

"Irina, we have a cleaning staff to do that."

That did it. She slammed the mugs down on the granite counter, getting satisfaction from the sound. "I let most of the house and grounds staff go six months ago, when the accountant began talking about my dwindling funds."

His face reflected surprise. And that gave her satisfaction, too. When had she become so mean-spirited? When had she changed from a grieving widow who would have done anything to have her husband back again? When had she become this bitter shrew?

It was a silly question. The answer was easy— horrifyingly easy.

This morning. That's when. Around 2:00 a.m., when she'd come face-to-face with her dead husband.

"Irina, I'm sorry. I didn't expect the insurance company to drag out the investigation of my death. I guess I should have." He rubbed his palm across his cheek. "I know all this has been hard on you."

"Hard on me?" she squeaked. "Hard—? Yes. You could say it's been hard."

She neatly and carefully folded the dish towel and laid it on the counter, using the mundane movements to gather her composure.

"Is everyone else gone?" She tried her best to keep her tone conversational.

"Yeah. Dan Taylor went—wherever he goes. Matt went to the guesthouse, where he's staying with Aimee and her son. And Deke went back to the hospital.

"Oh, Mindy. How is she? I didn't get a chance to ask Deke."

"No, you were too busy making coffee and washing dishes."

"Do not—"

"Sorry. He said they've gotten her blood sugar back to normal, but they're keeping her there for observation. At least that's what she thinks. Deke has made arrangements with the hospital director to keep her there in a protective custody situation until he's comfortable that she's no longer in danger."

"Tangled webs," she muttered on a sigh. Exhaustion shrouded her.

"What?" he snapped.

She shook her head. She felt so tired. Bone weary, as she'd heard Brock say many times. She'd only had about two hours of sleep last night before the dream woke her. Two hours in thirty-six.

"Never mind. I heard you. You said 'tangled webs.' Is that what you think I've done? You think I caused all this?"

"I think all of this is here because of your decision to fake your death. I think your arrogance has ruined many lives. Not only mine, but all these other people who care about you and are loyal to you."

He grimaced and shook his head. "I had to do it."

"No, you didn't. That is the arrogance. You decided you were the only person in the world who could stop Novus Ordo. And you had to do it alone." She flipped off the light switch.

The room plunged into darkness, startling her. She hadn't realized that Rook had turned off the conference room lights. The only relief from total darkness was the glow of a couple of night-lights.

Lifting her chin, she stepped toward the door, but Rook didn't step aside, as she'd expected him to. So she nearly collided with him.

"Excuse me," she said coldly.

"No."

She was way too close to him. Close enough that she could smell his fresh clean scent. She held her breath.

"Ex-cuse me," she repeated.

"No." He ran his palm down her upper arm. "We need to talk. *I* need to talk, and you need to listen."

His hand was as strong and warm as she remembered. She stiffened even more and took a small step backward.

"Don't do this," she said evenly. "I will listen to you. But not tonight—today, I mean. You've been gone for two years. *Dead* for two years. I am sure one more day can't make that much difference."

He held on to her for a few seconds, his head bent enough that he could look into her eyes. He wanted her to look at him. To yield to him.

She wouldn't. She couldn't. Not now. She had no idea what she was going to do, now that Rook was back. Yesterday he was dead. Today he was alive.

Until she could process everything that had happened in the past few hours, never mind the past two weeks or two years, she couldn't afford to allow herself to relax. She had to maintain control.

Control was all she had left.

"That's not true," he murmured.

For an instant she thought he'd read her mind. Then he continued.

"One day *can* make all the difference. The most dangerous man in the world wants me dead, and he'll do anything—*anything*—to make it happen. That includes killing you."

His hand tightened for an instant, maybe with emotion? She didn't dare believe that. But she had to believe what he said. Her life was in danger, and apparently her safety was in his hands—the same hands that had held her heart and then broken it.

"All right. I'll listen."

She heard his breath escape in a sigh. His hand slid from her arm to the small of her back. "Let me reset the access code and we can go up to our—to your suite."

Just what she didn't want to happen. She'd almost gotten rid of his scent. And now he was going to stamp it on everything again. The bathroom, the bed linens. Her.

They rode upstairs in the elevator that was disguised as a closet in the executive offices upstairs.

Rook paused at the elevator door as he took in the changes she'd made to his masculine office in the past two years. She watched him as his gaze lit on vases and fresh flowers and candles, the new, colorful cushions that brightened the dark wood and tan walls, and the airy curtains on the wide windows that he'd always wanted bare.

He took a deep breath and his nose wrinkled, and she knew he'd noticed the subtle smell of fresh flowers and scented candles.

"Nice," he said, that edge of sarcasm tingeing his voice.

She could have predicted his reaction. He'd indulged her liking for beautiful feminine things, but reluctantly, in typical male fashion. It was one of the things they'd bantered intimately about. One of the things she'd missed so much.

"Don't," she snapped.

"Don't what?"

"Don't tease me as if nothing has changed. I had to do something. Your—your ghost in this house haunted me."

"So you had me exorcised with aromatherapy?"

Hurt arrowed through her. "This is not a joke. Maybe it was easy for you to wipe me out of your mind. You didn't have to live here, surrounded by *my* clothes, *my* scent, *my* ghost in every room."

He looked at her, and for an instant the veneer of

command and confidence that he carried with him fell away, and raw anguish etched new lines in his face. But the instant passed, as if it had never been.

He turned to stare out the picture window and ran a finger across the large mahogany desk. "Do you want to talk in your suite?" he asked.

Her immediate reaction was to say no. All her bravado about wiping his presence out of the house was a shield she'd thrown up to protect her vulnerable emotions. He would see through her as soon as he stepped into their bedroom. She'd made changes to the open areas of the ranch house, but their bedroom was the same as it had always been.

She'd been trying to convince herself that it was time to let him go. That two years of sleeping with his ghost was long enough. And she'd almost succeeded.

"That's okay," he added. "We can talk here. Hopefully no one will interrupt us. And I don't want to make things awkward for you."

Too late for that.

He looked past her. "Are the rooms across the hall from the suite empty?"

Suddenly, and inexplicably, Irina wanted to cry. Was he trying to spare her, or himself?

"No," she said. "I mean, yes, they're empty, but you have no need to do that. It's probably best if we keep a low profile." She uttered a small laugh. "Awkward would be if everyone knew we were sleeping in separate rooms."

"Fine. I'll sleep on the sofa." He sent her a look. "The sofa's still there, right? I mean—have you changed the bedroom?"

"Of course not." Unable to look at him, she headed out the door and down the hall to the east wing. Rook's shoes echoed on the hardwood floors behind her.

He was her husband, and he was back from the dead. So why did she feel like she was on her way to the guillotine?

BY THE TIME IRINA had finished her shower and come out of her dressing room, Rook had fallen asleep on the sofa that sat opposite the king-size bed.

She studied him closely. Was he pretending, in order to avoid the questions he knew she was going to ask?

No. He really was asleep. A glow of sunlight creeping around the edges of the drapes illuminated his face. His strong, even features were soft and relaxed, something that never happened while he was awake. Still, even in sleep, the lines she'd noticed earlier were still there, scoring the corners of his mouth. Lines that hadn't been there two years before.

She wanted to trace them with her fingertips. Wipe them away. Why were they there? Pain? Fatigue? Worry?

All of the above?

She was surprised and a little hurt that he could sleep.

She hadn't slept for two years. Every time she closed her eyes, she dreamed that dream. He was with her, in her, loving her, and then he was gone, sinking into the dark waters of the Mediterranean.

Her feelings were in turmoil. A part of her felt comforted by his presence, but at the same time, her limbs were rigid with trepidation, as if she were alone in a room with a sinister stranger.

Not surprising. In a way, that's exactly what he was. A stranger.

She wrapped the terry-cloth robe more tightly around her and lay down on her side, still watching him sleep.

After a few moments, her vision blurred and her eyelids prickled. She touched the corner of her eye and was surprised to feel a warm wetness.

She was crying. She who never cried. Hadn't for years. She blinked rapidly. There was nothing to cry about now. Rook was back. He was alive.

Nothing in her life could **measure** up to the joy of discovering that the man **whom she**'d loved from the first moment she'd laid **eyes on him** was alive.

However, nothing **could measure** up to the enormity of his betrayal, either. **He'd** let her believe he was dead.

She pressed her lips together as a sob gathered in her throat. It was too much to bear. To lose him only to find out that he'd lied to her—lied to everyone. He'd left her alone.

And he'd done it deliberately.

She thought back on the days, the weeks, prior to his death. He said he'd been planning it for months. When had he changed? Was there a moment that she could pinpoint as different?

She didn't know. All she knew was that the strong, dependable protector who had rescued her father and her from the wrath of the former Soviet Union, and the sweet, attentive lover who'd wooed her during the following months, then asked her to marry him, had somehow slipped away without her noticing.

By the time her father died, a year later, Rook was well on his way to becoming the soldier who'd appeared before her in the cabin, his olive-green eyes cold and opaque as jade, his demeanor more like a newly extracted deep-op than a returning lover.

She tried to think about her first glimpse of him in the cabin, his body lit by firelight and obscured by shadow. It had been several moments before she saw his face. He'd had plenty of time to mask his feelings.

What had he thought when he'd seen her for the first time in two years? Had his gaze turned soft as emerald velvet like it had when they'd first become lovers? Or had it been distorted by the raw pain she'd glimpsed when she'd accused him of wiping her out of his mind?

He stirred, startling her. His brows twitched and lowered, his chest rose and fell rapidly. He tossed his head and arched his back, as if gulping for air.

Irina sat up quietly. Rook had never had nightmares. She could only remember being awakened by him one time. It was a few months after he'd returned from rescuing Travis Ronson.

He'd cried out in his sleep but had quieted immediately when she touched his forehead. The next morning he hadn't remembered anything about it.

She glided over the hardwood floor without making a sound and crouched beside the couch. This close, she could see sweat glistening on his forehead and neck.

Maybe he was sick. Hesitantly, she reached out a hand. Her fingertips brushed his forehead.

His eyes flew open, and in one motion he threw back the blanket and pointed a big gun directly at her forehead.

She scrambled away but lost her balance and ended up on her butt. Horrified, she scooted backward across the floor.

The next few seconds stretched out in slow motion. Rook's eyes went from glazed with sleep to sharp and clear as green bottle glass. His knuckles turned white around his gun. His finger tightened on the trigger.

A subsonic rhythmic roar filled her ears.

Finally, he lowered the weapon. He stared at her,

blinked, stared again and then looked down at his hands.

Once he broke eye contact, time returned to normal. But that was the only thing that did. Her heart still pounded like a jackhammer, stealing her breath. Her arms and legs were rigid with tension. And her brain was spinning too fast to settle on a single coherent thought.

Her husband's shocked face filled her vision.

"What are you doing?" he gasped.

She held up shaking hands, palms out. "H-hoping you are not going to shoot me."

He eyed the gun as if it were a rat or a spider. Then he set it down on the arm of the sofa and sat up, pushing his fingers through his hair. "Go back to bed."

"Rook—"

"Just go. I won't bother you anymore. I'll sleep across the hall."

"No."

His head jerked up.

"This cannot continue, Rook. You told me you needed me to listen. Well, I am here. I am listening. I deserve explanations, answers." It was a struggle to speak evenly. Her throat closed up.

He lowered his forearms to his knees and leaned forward, his head down. "Yes, you do."

Her scalp tingled with relief. She picked herself up off the floor and sat on the edge of a slipper chair across from the sofa.

For a few seconds, Rook sat there, his head in his hands. Then he rubbed his eyes and his chin and stood.

For the first time, she noticed that he was dressed in nothing but dark dress pants. The belt was undone and the too-big pants hung low on his hips.

He'd always been lean, with long straps of muscles that rippled under his golden skin. But he'd lost at least twenty pounds in the past two years, so his body, which had always been buff and muscular, was now wiry.

Her gaze came to rest on a vaguely circular scar on his upper right chest. "Oh," she whispered.

Rook knew what she was looking at. His hand twitched to cover the scar—the place where Deke's bullet had entered his chest.

He still remembered the hot rush of panic as the slug impacted him. The instant of horror and regret. In all his planning, he'd never once thought about how the bullet would feel. He'd given Deke specific instructions to aim for his right upper chest. But until the instant of impact, he hadn't seriously considered that the shot might be fatal.

The self-consciousness he suddenly felt about his body heightened his awareness of hers.

She had on a white terry-cloth robe belted at the waist. It gaped open at the top and the bottom, revealing the curves and cleavage of her delicately rounded breasts and a glimpse of her thighs. She was decently covered, but her perfect body made the robe seem X-rated.

She'd lost weight during the two years he'd been gone, which meant she wasn't quite as curvy as she had been. Her hips didn't swell out from her slender waist like they once had. Her breasts weren't as full and plump. But she was as beautiful and desirable as she'd ever been.

More so. After all, he'd been alone for two years.

And so had she.

He forced his gaze away from her beautiful breasts. When he met her eyes, the awareness he felt flared like a flame. But too soon, her gaze wavered, reminding him that he had no right. Not anymore.

"What do you want to know?" he asked flatly.

Chapter Eight

Irina stared at Rook as his question echoed in her ears. *What do you want to know?*

He looked back at her, his face carefully wiped clean of any emotion, his body still—unnaturally so, even for him. He'd always radiated a calm command that put people at ease.

This was different. He looked as though he were facing a firing squad.

She shook her head, resenting the fact that he was turning it back onto her. He'd said he wanted her to listen. Now he was demanding that she figure out what questions to ask.

"I want to know everything," she said, spreading her hands, palms out. "Where have you been? What have you been doing? How did you plan this for months and never once let anything slip?"

His gaze didn't waver, but his chin lifted a fraction and he swallowed. He wasn't as calm as she'd thought.

"How—how could you leave me?"

Then his gaze did waver.

"I thought I had everything planned," he said. "I didn't realize how hard it was going to be, to be shot. To swim. To survive."

Irina didn't speak.

"I attached a wetsuit, diving gear and two air tanks to the bottom of the boat before we set out. But when I hit the water after Deke shot me, it knocked me unconscious for a few seconds. I thought I was dead. When I realized I wasn't—" he shook his head "—I was disappointed."

"You *wanted* to die?" she burst out.

He shrugged. "I thought it was the only way I could keep you safe."

The words from her nightmare. She shook her head. "No. I don't believe you."

"I managed to wake up before I drowned. I found the air tanks and gear, but I couldn't get the wetsuit on. The Mediterranean is damned cold. I swam for probably two miles, floating with the currents as much as possible. By the time I got out of the water I was hypothermic and I'd lost a lot of blood." His voice sounded strained. He sat down on the couch.

"I'd stashed local currency with the diving gear, so I ditched the gear, found an isolated farmhouse and pretended I had amnesia. I gave the farmer a lot of money to keep quiet about helping me."

Irina hunched her shoulders and crossed her arms. Who was he? This man who'd planned such an intricate deception? And how pathetic was she that she'd never suspected a thing?

"Where were you all this time?" She had to fight to keep her tone even.

"For six months I was with the family. I set up a trust for them through the Cayman account. Then I made my way across Europe and Asia to Mahjidastan. I'd been there about three months when Deke called."

"You were there, in the same place as Matt, for three months?"

"Mahjidastan is a tiny province, but I was doing my best not to be noticed. I'm sure Matt was, too. I had no idea you were searching for me until I got that message from Deke."

"If you wanted that terrorist to think you were dead, why did you go there? Is that not where the U.S. thinks he is?"

"That's one of the reasons I did it—to find him. To try and stop him."

"Was it worth it?"

Rook blinked. She'd gotten to him with that question. He opened his mouth, then closed it again. Then he lay back down on the sofa and threw an arm over his eyes.

"I don't know, Irina," he muttered. "I really don't know.

ROOK GASPED and clutched at his chest. It was wet. He checked his hand. *No blood.* Sweat, but no blood. Relief stung his eyes.

It was a dream. *The* dream. He wasn't bleeding— or drowning. He sat up and put his bare feet on the floor, and froze. The floor wasn't grimy, cracked vinyl with sand in all the crevices. It was warm, smooth wood. Polished, new, expensive.

He lifted his head and took a deep breath. The scent of gardenias filled his senses, a far cry from the smell of dust and sweat and heat.

He wasn't in Mahjidastan. He rubbed his eyes and looked around. The pale pink night-light played tricks on his eyes, just as the after-effects of his dream played tricks on his brain.

Irina. He was in Irina's bedroom. They'd argued and he'd fallen asleep on the sofa. Squinting at the king-size bed, he made out her gently curved form. She was lying on her side, with her back to him. She was still asleep—so far.

He made his way carefully into the dressing room and slid the pocket doors closed before he turned on the light.

He turned on the hot water and ran his hands under the flow. He'd forgotten the feel of clean, fresh, hot water. The best he'd gotten in Mahjidastan was a trickle of lukewarm brownish liquid. He splashed his face again and again, until the water got too hot to bear. Then he turned it off and started on the cold water.

After dousing his face with a few double handfuls, he cupped his hands and rinsed his mouth with the cold, delicious liquid. Then he leaned his forearms on the edge of the ceramic sink and waited for the nausea and panic to pass. A couple of deep breaths slowed his racing pulse.

He'd hoped he was done with the dream, now that he was back home—back from the dead. It was always the same—the sharp blow to his upper chest, the spasm of fear and regret as his arms and legs collapsed.

Irina's anguished screams—her fingers grasping at his arm, his shirt, his hair. But inevitably she couldn't hold on and he tumbled overboard into the dark waters of the Mediterranean.

The last thing he saw was her face distorted by water and the sun's brilliant glare.

He grabbed a towel and swiped it over his neck and chest, and then his face. The soft Egyptian cotton soaked up the water but didn't wipe away the dream.

He peered in the mirror—and stared. He still wasn't used to seeing his bare face. He still expected unkempt, untrimmed hair and beard—a simple disguise in a barren East Asian mountain village. Although he'd long ago accepted the bearded face. This clean-shaven face and neatly trimmed hair seemed more like a mask. Was not recognizing one's own face the measure of a good disguise?

With a nearly silent groan, he arched his sore shoulders and neck. The day before had been a long one. And today would probably be longer.

He ran his damp fingers through his hair and straightened, arching his aching neck.

He took a deep breath, wiped a dribble of water from his cheek and hiked up his pants from where they'd ridden down over the waistband of his briefs.

Instinctively, he reached around to the small of his back to check his paddle holster. But it wasn't there. The holster and his Sig Sauer were lying on the sofa.

He winced. He should have been more careful. Her terror-filled eyes had pierced his heart. He wished he could explain why he felt he had to sleep with a weapon, even here, even in her room. But she wouldn't understand.

He didn't want her to understand. She'd always hated guns. Her childhood had been permeated with guns and bombs. She'd grown up in the collapsing former Soviet Union, with its chaos and civil wars.

When he'd rescued her and her father, when he'd fallen in love with her, he'd promised her she'd never have to live in fear again. And he'd broken that promise. That one and many others.

A quiet knock at the pocket doors startled him. He opened them. Irina was standing there, in a sleek nightgown the color of candlelight. It was sleeveless and long. The material was opaque and draped across her breasts and waist and hips like wavelets in a shallow pool.

Her blond hair shimmered brightly against her pale shoulders, and her blue eyes were dark with worry.

"Rook? Are you all right?"

"Yeah, sorry. I didn't mean to wake you." He tried not to look at her, but his eyes refused to obey his brain.

"You—called out my name."

"It was just a dream," he said, rubbing the back of his neck nervously. "It's over now." He pushed past her, and his bare arm brushed against her breast.

She uttered a tiny gasp.

He clenched his jaw, determined to walk on by her, back to the sofa. But try as he might, he couldn't take another step.

He turned toward her, willing her to do what he couldn't. All she had to do was take one step backward. One small step, and he'd know she was rejecting him.

But she didn't move, unless leaning forward was considered moving.

He lowered his head. She raised hers. Their lips touched for the first time in two years.

Both of them jerked away, startled by the electricity that sparked between them.

Her gaze flickered, and he was sure she would stop, but then her eyelids drifted shut and she raised her head a fraction more.

He kissed her, deeply, fully, drinking in the feel of her mouth beneath his. Those full lips soft and trembling, her small sweet tongue, her breath.

Time swirled around them, meaningless. It had been two years, but it could have been yesterday.

Irina couldn't breathe, but she didn't care. Rook was breathing for her. He was feeding her life and breath through his kisses. Without his mouth on hers, she knew she would die.

He lifted his hands and cradled her face, as he deepened the kiss even more. She had a vague impression that his hands were rougher, more callused than she remembered them. As soon as that thought hit her brain, it was gone, lost in sensation.

He slid his hands down to her shoulders, her back, her waist. She leaned into him, pressing her breasts against his bare chest. Her nipples were tight and distended, almost painfully sensitized. When they brushed against his skin, a deep, erotic thrill surged through her, weakening her knees and stealing her breath.

She was sure nothing could surpass the feeling of his mouth on hers, his chest against her breasts, the heat of his hands caressing her body. But he slid his hand further, from her waist to her rounded bottom, and pressed her to him, until the searing heat of his erection branded her skin.

He lifted his head and took a ragged breath. His eyes were soft, questioning. His erection pulsed against her, leaving no doubt what he wanted.

She nodded and pressed her lips against his collarbone.

"Rina…"

"Yes," she whispered.

He lifted her and laid her on the bed. With a conciseness of movement, he was in her. She gasped and arched her back as she felt the familiar, unbearably erotic sensation of being filled by him.

"Oh, Rook," she breathed. "I've missed you so much."

He stopped her words with his mouth as he pushed deeper.

Irina couldn't control herself, and it was obvious Rook was having the same problem. He thrust deeply, desperately, sending her to the apex of sensation within seconds. He stopped and pressed his face into the curve of her shoulder, breathing harshly.

She pushed her fingers through his hair.

The phone rang.

She jumped as the shrill noise cut through her erotic haze, and pushed at his chest.

He rolled away.

She crawled across around the bed and picked up the handset. "Yes?" she said coldly.

"Mrs. Castle, this is Dan Taylor. I apologize for bothering you, but I need to speak to Colonel Castle."

Irina held out the handset without looking at him. "It's for you."

Rook took the phone from her hand. "Castle," he said shortly.

Irina got up and folded her arms across her revealing nightgown. She felt naked and exposed.

Rook rubbed his temples as he listened. Then he shook his head and muttered a curse. "When?"

The tone of his voice told her something had happened.

"Where are you? Where is he? I'll be right there." He hung up and turned.

"I have to go," he said, his voice tense and carefully even. He started toward the door, adjusting his pants and picking up his shirt along the way.

"What's wrong?"

He turned back to send her a warning look. "I've got to get out of here. I'll wash up across the hall. You stay here. Lock the door and don't open it for anyone but me. Brock's been shot."

FIVE MINUTES LATER, Rook headed downstairs. A long, shaky breath escaped his lips. Dan's phone call had interrupted something that shouldn't have ever happened.

He'd known the instant he laid eyes on Irina that if

he touched her, he'd be lost. He'd told himself a hundred times that he had no right.

But, dear God, he'd missed her. He'd missed that mouth, that body. He'd missed the way she opened to him, welcomed him. He'd missed being her lover.

He knew by the look in her eyes as he'd closed the suite's door that she felt abandoned.

But Brock O'Neill, the man he trusted most after his oath brothers, had been injured, and no matter what his personal feelings, he had a responsibility.

He headed through the house and out the front door. Immediately, he saw Dan Taylor standing beside the open passenger door of an idling black SUV. Taylor spotted him and climbed in. The SUV pulled up beside Rook and he got into the backseat.

"What happened? Did you catch the shooter?"

"I don't have specifics. Captain O'Neill notified one of my men via push-to-talk."

"What was Brock doing on that ridge?"

"Lieutenant Parker suggested a few days ago that the specialists patrol the perimeter, just to be sure that the remote areas of the ranch weren't breached."

Taylor continued to fill Rook in as he drove to the ridge. "I called and dispatched Major Hathaway over there immediately, since she has medical expertise, and sent two agents to meet her. Then I called you."

"Fiona's here at the ranch?"

Dan nodded. "I assumed you knew. She came in earlier this afternoon, according to my gate guard." He paused for an instant. "Timely."

The single word held a wealth of meaning. Rook sent him a sidelong glance. "You've added her to your suspect list."

"Just making a comment."

As soon as he got out of the car, Rook saw Fiona and Brock. Brock was sitting in the open door of an SUV, and Fiona was taping his upper arm.

"Fee, Brock," he called as he sprinted over.

They looked up. Brock's usually impassive face held a sheepish expression.

"Rook!" Fiona gasped, as the roll of gauze dropped from her fingers. Her hands covered her mouth. "Oh, my God. Brock told me, but—" she shook her head "—I can't believe you're here. You're— Oh, my God."

"Don't faint on me, Fee," he said gently. "It's good to see you."

"Oh, my!" She threw her arms around him and hugged him, then pushed back to look at him again. "It is great to see you! I don't know what to say."

"Just hearing that you're glad to see me is enough."

He met Brock's gaze. "Didn't take you long to get into trouble."

Brock's sheepish expression etched more deeply into his face. "Never does," he said wryly.

"What happened?"

"I was out patrolling. I caught a glint of light on metal and came over to investigate. It was a booby trap." He looked at his upper arm in disgust.

"A booby trap?" Rook repeated. "How in hell—"

"Hold still," Fiona snapped at Brock. She'd unwrapped the roll of gauze and was positioning it over the bandages.

She spoke to Rook without taking her eyes off her handiwork. "The bullet went through the meaty part of his biceps. I've sterilized the wound and I'm wrapping it. It missed the humerus, or it would have shattered. He's lucky he's still got his arm."

"I'll tell you who's lucky," Brock growled. "Whoever rigged that rifle. But his luck's going to run out once I catch up with him."

"Stop fidgeting," Fiona snapped, as she wound the gauze around one last time and taped it. "Let's get you to the emergency room."

"No. We don't have time for that nonsense," Brock growled. "Rook, I want to examine the area before those guys stomp all over it."

Rook looked at Fiona, who raised a perfectly shaped brow. She wanted Brock's arm looked at by a physician. "We'll try to keep it clean for you."

As he rose, he caught the victorious glare Fiona threw at Brock.

"Taylor, can you spare a man to take Captain O'Neill to the ER? Fiona, go with them."

Taylor nodded and gestured to one of his men.

"Now, where's the booby trap?"

"Over here, sir," one of Taylor's agents called. "It's a pretty simple setup. The brilliant part is the placement."

Rook saw what he meant. The trip wire was placed so that anyone getting close enough to trip it would be dead in line with the barrel. The weapon used was simple—a .22 with a silencer, very reliable and very deadly at close range. It was a miracle that Brock wasn't dead.

Actually, he amended to himself, it was a testament to Brock's uncanny awareness of everything around him and his lightning-fast reflexes.

Rook looked around. From where he was standing he could see the front of the ranch house and the roofs of the guesthouses. A high-powered sniper rifle in the right hands could pick off anyone.

"And take a look at this," the agent said. "The rifle's

trigger mechanism is hooked up to a cell phone, probably prepaid."

"A cell phone?"

"Yes, sir. It was rigged to call a number, almost certainly another prepaid cell. Someone was notified that the trap had been tripped."

"Can you trace that phone? Find out where it was bought? Or trace the numbers by area code?"

Taylor walked over. "We'll do what we can, but it's pretty unlikely. If they have any sense at all, they wouldn't have bought them anywhere near here. Besides, you can get all the anonymous phones you want over the Internet."

He glanced over his shoulder at the ranch house. "What's the point of a booby trap? It just calls attention to itself."

"Hang on a minute, Fee." Brock's voice came from behind them. He walked over to stand by Dan. "We were taking shifts patrolling the perimeter. My guess is—" he swept his uninjured arm through the air "—they were planning to set up a sniper's nest up here. Think about it. They already tried to pick off Rafe and Aaron in the hospital parking lot. I'm guessing the trap was set up to kill anyone who found it, and the cell phone notified them to come remove the rifle and the triggers before anyone found the body."

"So the plan was that whoever got too close would die, and they could swoop in, grab the evidence, maybe even the body, and get out. Sounds like they didn't expect you to outrun the bullet," Rook commented.

Brock's lip curled up. "I lost an eye, but I've still got two good ears. I heard the wire sing just before it tripped."

Rook clapped his friend on the back. "Glad your hearing works. Now get to the hospital and get patched up."

Dan stepped over to Rook's side and held out his hand to Fiona, who was putting away her first-aid kit. "Major Hathaway? I'm Special Agent Dan Taylor, with the Secret Service."

She took his hand. "Special Agent Taylor. Glad to meet you."

"My agents told me you'd arrived. I understand you have a newborn baby."

Rook met Brock's gaze and both of them winced.

"Is my child a part of your investigation, Special Agent Taylor?"

Dan's cheeks brightened. "No, ma'am. Of course not. I—"

"Then I fail to see the pertinence of your statement."

"Fee," Rook broke in. "Make sure that Brock rests for a while when he gets back. Now you two need to get going."

Fiona's golden brown eyes shot daggers at the Secret Service agent, but she nodded. "Come on, Brock. Get in the car like a good boy."

Then she turned back to Rook. "I don't think I've ever been more glad to see anyone, but I hope for Irina's sake that you had amnesia or something. She's been shattered without you."

He nodded, not meeting her gaze.

As the SUV pulled away, Rook studied the view of the ranch buildings below and then assessed the ridge. He walked back and forth, measuring with his eyes.

"Sir?"

He held up a hand, still concentrating, then he saw it.

"Here." He stood back, squinting, then stepped over to the suspicious-looking area. Leaves had been scattered artlessly over the flat ground.

"Take a look."

Dan followed his gaze. "What am I looking at?"

"That blanket of leaves. That tree limb. Take a closer look. I'll bet the smallest branches have been cut or broken off."

"You think it's—"

"The sniper's nest. He hides behind the limb and uses it as a brace for his rifle. Another two minutes and Brock would have seen it." Rook crouched and looked downhill. "I don't want to disturb any evidence, but I'm betting that if you sight just above the level of that fallen branch, you'll see the front door of the ranch house."

Rook bent down and sighted along the trajectory. "This is very well done. Well thought out. Hidden in plain sight. I agree with you about the booby trap. Why did they bother? Why not just leave this as is? Very few people would figure out at a glance what it is."

"Hey, Dan," one of the agents called out. "Come take a look at this." He was standing a few feet behind the booby trap.

Dan walked over. Rook followed him. The agent hadn't moved. He pointed.

Rook saw another blanket of leaves, thicker than the sniper's nest.

"What is it, Ferrell?" Dan asked.

"See that? Under the edge of that bush?"

Then Rook spotted it. "Something metallic. Right there."

"I didn't want to disturb anything until you'd seen it," Ferrell said.

"Check it out, but be careful. If that's what I think it is, this area could be booby-trapped, too."

Ferrell worked carefully and smoothly. After a minute, Rook could see that the hidden piece of metal was a sniper rifle. After Ferrell uncovered the rifle, he dug out a pair of high-powered binoculars from underneath.

"Okay, so this is the reason for the booby trap, I take it," Rook commented. "But still, the hiding place was good enough to fool anyone who wasn't combing the area." He propped his fists on his hips. "Now I have two questions. Why booby-trap a hiding place this good? And for that matter, why leave the equipment here at all? Seems as if these guys were begging to be caught."

Another agent came hiking up the ridge from behind them. "Dan, we've found the breach in the fence where they got in. It's a tiny break, back that way."

"That's an old farm road back in there," Rook said. "Hardly used anymore."

Dan nodded. "Probably exactly why they chose it. I'm guessing they didn't want to haul the equipment in each time they came, in case they were spotted."

Rook nodded. "Carrying a super-long-range rifle and state-of-the-art binoculars wouldn't be easy to explain. Without them, they could say they were lost and looking for someone to help them." He straightened.

"Get Deke over here to take a look at this. I'm not familiar with that model, but he knows all of them. He might even be able to give you a short list of shooters. There aren't many who are good enough to make a shot this long."

Dan nodded. "Ferrell, get the kits. See if you can lift any fingerprints or shoe prints."

Rook walked back over to the sniper's nest with Dan beside him. "Get Deke and Brock to look at this, too. Brock can give you a good estimate of the height and weight of the sniper, and Deke just might know him. And listen. I'd like for you to hold off disturbing the scene until Brock has a chance to go over the area. If there's any trace here, he'll find it."

"Sir, I have a crime scene expert on my team."

"A good one, I'm sure. How much experience?"

Dan took a long breath. "Five years."

"Impressive. Brock O'Neill has been tracking and hunting in these mountains since he was old enough to walk. So he has thirty years' experience."

"All due respect, sir, O'Neill is still a suspect—"

Rook leveled a gaze at the young Secret Service agent that had silenced four-star generals. "Fiona will have Brock back here within a half hour. Use him. You and your expert will learn a lot."

The sound of boots crunching unevenly on grass and twigs caught Rook's ears.

He whirled, pulling his gun. At the same time, Dan and three of his agents did the same.

"Whoa. It's just me." It was Rafe Jackson. He spread his hands. He couldn't exactly hold them up because of his crutches.

Dan lowered his weapon and sent his men a quick nod. "Mr. Jackson, what are you doing here?" he asked. "Everyone was ordered to stay in their quarters."

Jackson smiled. "I didn't get that message. Sorry. I saw the activity up here and thought I'd investigate." He gestured with his head. "If I'd realized how steep that grade is—" He stopped, craning his neck. "Is that a rifle over there? Was someone hurt?"

Dan shifted slightly, just enough that Jackson would have to move to see beyond him.

Rook holstered his weapon and crossed his arms. "Special Agent Taylor asked you a question. What are you doing up here?"

Jackson's eyes narrowed and his jaw muscle flexed.

"I saw the activity and was curious about what was going on."

"Saw the activity from where?"

"Down there. The guest quarters."

Rook looked down. From his vantage point so close to the booby trap, all he could see was the roof of the guest quarters.

"Mr. Jackson," Dan said. "An agent will escort you back to the guesthouse. I hope it won't be a problem if we search your rooms. We'll be searching the entire guest quarters."

Jackson's gaze wavered then. "Search? If you'll tell me what you're looking for—" He stopped and laughed wryly. "Strike that. Of course, Agent Taylor. No problem whatsoever."

He planted his crutches and turned. A slight grimace marred his face, but he recovered immediately. "G'day, Colonel Castle."

Rook nodded.

Dan stood beside Rook, not speaking, until the agent and Jackson had started back down the hill.

"His leg is hurting. You could have had the agent drive him," Rook commented.

"I know," Taylor replied. "What do you think about him?"

"Hard to say."

"Nice for them, if they have someone on the inside that could check on their booby trap."

"What will be nice is if we can prove it."

Chapter Nine

After informing the agents that Brock and Deke would be handling the preliminary examination of the sniper's nest and booby trap, Dan and Rook headed into town. They left the ranch via the driveway from the underground garage to avoid any reporters who might be hovering around the front gate.

On the way, Rook called Deke, finding him at the hospital, visiting Mindy and his baby, and told him about Brock, the booby trap and Rafiq Jackson.

"Sure," Deke said. "They got spotlights out there? I'll head out right now. You really think Jackson could be Novus's mole?"

"Right now he's looking pretty good for it," Rook replied. "See if you can see the site from the house. At the time he got up there, we hadn't turned on the spotlights yet. And see if anyone else noticed the 'activity' that Jackson noticed. I want to know what you think about the booby trap, too. Is it rigged to kill, or to just look like it could kill?"

"What does that mean? Are you thinking Brock could have set it up and then shot himself?"

"We can't afford to rule out anyone at this point.

Three of our four agents have been wounded. I'm making the assumption that we can eliminate Fiona, since she was having a baby when Irina called off her search and alerted Novus Ordo. That means if it's any of the other three, then they had to have taken a bullet on purpose. And I'm here to tell you, nobody does that without a lot of soul-searching." He swallowed. "I mean, would you rather be grazed at the temple by a long-range sniper shot, take a chance on bleeding out from your femoral artery or have confidence that you're fast enough to dodge a rifle shot at close range?"

Deke didn't say anything for a couple of seconds. "Or," he said slowly, "trust your best friend to shoot you in the chest without killing you?"

Rook was stunned by the emotion in Deke's voice. He knew he'd asked a lot of his friend, but it hadn't really hit him until now just how much. He'd essentially asked Deke to kill him.

And let him think he had. What kind of arrogant bastard was he, to do that to his best friend?

And his own wife.

"Deke, I—"

"I'll get back with you," Deke said quickly, and hung up.

Taylor pulled up in front of a nondescript government building in Sundance. A weathered sign out front identified it as a U.S. Treasury building. A smaller, dimly lit sign beside the front door read Census Bureau.

Rook nodded. "Good cover," he said.

Taylor nodded. "The Treasury guys moved to the downtown federal building several years ago. Secret Service took over this building when they arrived." He smiled. "Nobody bothers the Census Bureau. The first floor is mostly empty. A receptionist desk that's never manned. We've got locks on the elevators, so no one wandering in can get upstairs. Third floor has been converted into sleeping quarters for the agents."

He led Rook through the lobby and into an elevator. "We're holding the prisoners on the second floor. No one-way glass, but I do have monitors."

"What have you gotten out of them?"

"Nothing yet. They're acting like they don't understand English. I'm trying to locate a translator, but—"

Rook blew out a frustrated breath and shook his head.

Dan raised his brows. "Are you thinking about—"

"Jackson? He speaks the language," Rook replied. "We'd need to record and verify what he says, though."

"We can send the recording to Homeland Security's language lab, but I don't know what kind of lag time they're experiencing right now."

"Can't we claim executive order as a top priority? We're listening to people who are directly linked to the most murderous, most elusive terrorist on the planet."

"Colonel, I wish it were that easy." Taylor shook his head. "But at any one time Homeland Security is listening in on dozens of conversations from different sources, not to mention other agencies. Any one of those conversations could be a discussion of a plan to attack the U.S."

Rook knew Taylor was right, but it still chafed. "Let's do it. Let's bring him in to translate. You call your boss, and I'll put a call in to the Pentagon."

As they stepped out of the elevator on the second floor, Taylor pointed to a door several feet to the right. When he unlocked and opened the door, a man in a white T-shirt and blue jeans with a shoulder holster got up from a table where three monitors and three keyboards sat.

He picked up a half-eaten burger and tossed it in the trash. Then he picked up a cup of coffee.

"This is Special Agent Shawn Cutler. Shawn, this is Colonel Rook Castle."

"Pleasure, sir," Cutler said. They shook hands.

Rook sat down in front of the monitors. Two were trained on the two prisoners. One a wide-angle shot of the entire room, the other at a much closer angle. The third was a high, exterior view of the door.

"What's been going on, Shawn?"

"Not much. They're not talking. Not even to each other." He looked at the paper cup in his hand and shook his head. "This stuff is cold. I'm going to make some fresh. Can I bring you a cup?"

Rook shook his head. "Thanks, Shawn. I'm fine. Why don't you take a break while we're here."

Shawn nodded and left.

"I have two men posted outside that door," Taylor said. "As you see, the prisoners are stripped down to their underwear. They're handcuffed and hobbled. They've been thoroughly searched."

Rook grimaced at the tactics necessary for dealing with individuals who represented threats to national security. He understood that the safety of the nation and the free world was more important than the comfort and even dignity of a single criminal, but he didn't like it.

"Can you get me a closer look at their faces?"

"Sure." Taylor typed a few commands, and the monitor zoomed in.

Rook studied the men, who sat unmoving. One had his eyes closed. The other was staring at a spot on the table.

Rook shook his head. "It was a long shot. I hoped that in the flesh I might recognize one of them. But I'm sure I've never seen either of them before."

He sat back. "Where's the casualty? I want to see him, too."

"He's in the morgue at Crook County Medical Center. I don't advise going there, after all the business Black Hills Search and Rescue has given to the hospital in the past two weeks. There are already reporters waiting outside the gates at the ranch every day. If they find out you're alive, we won't be able to control them. In fact, we're lucky the networks haven't picked up on this yet."

"Good point," Rook said. "Okay. Let's get Jackson in here to question them. Are these monitors recording?"

"Not now. I can make them, though."

"Do it. Make sure you record Jackson's face, as well as the prisoners'. I'll get Matt to put together a word-for-word script for him to follow. We can send that in with the recording." Rook stood. "What about prints or DNA? Anything?"

"No ID on any of them. One had a push-to-talk, but we haven't found any others to connect it with. We're trying to trace it through the carrier. We've sent prints and DNA swabs, but I don't hold out much hope there. These guys are almost certainly here illegally."

"Okay then, what next?"

"I haven't had a chance to talk to you about Jackson, Gold and O'Neill. I questioned them individually after our meeting. Their stories seem to hold up, as far as they go. Not a one blinked. If one of them is the traitor, he has nerves of steel. If it's Jackson, I'd say more than just his *nerves* are made of steel, to come walking up to the booby trap like that."

"Right. It shocked him to see me, but he recovered quickly."

"For that matter, what about Brock? I agree with Deke. I think Brock is least likely to be the traitor. I've known him a long time, and I trust him almost as much as I trust Deke and Matt. But if it is him, then he walked right into the trap he set himself."

"Speaking of recordings, what about the meeting this morning. Do you have those disks ready?"

"Yeah. Haven't had a chance to go over them yet, though."

"I want to do that first thing in the morning. I want to study each specialist—see their reaction to the pictures of Ordo and Frank James. And then I want to call a meeting with everyone, talk about Brock's near miss and see what happens when I announce that they're all suspects."

"What about meeting here at 8:00 a.m.?"

"Okay, but let's get Deke and Brock over here by seven. I want to hear what they think about the sniper's nest before I face the other two. Get one of your agents to get them in here by 8:00 a.m. No, make it eight-thirty." He covered a yawn and continued. "Can we meet in your observation room?"

Dan nodded.

"When Aaron and Rafe come in, have those monitors running. Record them watching the prisoners. Unless I'm badly mistaken, one of them betrayed me."

Dan jotted some notes on his dog-eared notepad and then stood, looking at his watch. "I'll take care of all of that. It's after seven. This has been a long damn day. Even longer for you, I imagine."

Rook was taken aback. "Are you saying it's still Thursday?"

"I am. Why don't we got you away from here. Maybe take you to D.C., where we can protect you properly."

"No. I'm going back to the ranch. That's where my staff is—my family. Do what you have to do to keep us all safe there."

"Yes, sir. I suggest we get going then. I'm guessing you haven't slept since you got back to the States."

Rook thought about it. He actually couldn't remember the last time he'd really slept. The short nap earlier hardly counted, considering that he'd been dreaming he was in Mahjidastan when Irina had startled him awake.

ROOK WAS PREPARED to spend the night in the guest suite. But when he got back to the ranch, he realized all his stuff was with Irina, in the suite that used to be theirs.

He unlocked the door as quietly as he could and slipped inside, easing it shut behind him. A pale night-light kept the room from being totally dark.

When had she started sleeping with a night-light? His heart squeezed in his chest. He knew the answer to that question.

When he'd died.

He glanced around the shadowed room. There near the door to the dressing room was the battered fake-leather bag that he'd lived out of for the past two years. He picked it up and headed for the suite across the hall.

Just as his hand closed around the door handle, he heard her stir.

"Rook?" Her voice was soft and blurry with sleep. He closed his eyes, pushing away memories of her words, her touch, her taste, in the middle of the night.

"Just getting my bag," he said tightly.

"You should stay here."

"I need a shower, and I need to stretch out, get some rest. The sofa doesn't quite fit me."

"You don't have to sleep on the sofa. I mean, there's plenty of room here on the bed."

Her sleepy words awakened his body. He felt himself respond. Felt himself grow.

He clamped his jaw. His hand tightened on the door handle. He should refuse. If he stayed, he wouldn't get a wink of sleep.

With a sigh, he dropped his hand and turned around. "If you're sure," he said.

Her eyes glittered in the glow of the night-light. "Like I said earlier, it will avoid unnecessary awkwardness."

The sleepy sexiness was gone from her voice. Her tone was even. Her words crisp and clear. Their intent unmistakable.

I'm willing to do you this favor. Don't make any assumptions.

"Fine. I'll try not to disturb you."

She didn't say anything more. Rook heard the rustle of silk against satin as she lay back down.

For a few seconds he stood there, unmoving. Whether his senses were unnaturally heightened or whether his eyes had dark-adapted, he didn't know, but he could see her pale shoulders and arms against the paler sheets. He saw the undulating curves as her breasts rose and fell with her breaths. And he remembered, for the first time since the bullet slammed into his chest, how they felt—warm and firm and supple under his fingers.

Her body had always turned him on. It was perfect. The long, delicate bones, the generous breasts and buttocks, the tiny waist. And those legs that went on forever. She was so perfectly proportioned that she was almost a caricature of herself. A mockery of the perfect woman.

He ached with want, with need. His erection rubbed against the material of his briefs, ultra-sensitive. He didn't know what to do about it.

If he hadn't been dead in body for the past two years, he'd certainly been dead in soul. The long months stretched out behind him—an emotional black hole. He remembered nothing. No feelings of any kind, except a vague sense of emptiness, and an obsessive need to find Novus Ordo.

Now his body was reawakening, and lying beside her was going to be torture.

So he picked up his bag, went into the dressing room and turned on the water in the shower. After a second, he sighed and, with a small shudder, twisted the knob to cold.

IRINA TOOK A long breath and relaxed more deeply. She was deliciously warm, and she couldn't remember the last time she'd slept better. The familiar scent of soap and clean hair filled her nostrils. Smooth flesh, like silk over steel, was vibrant and warm under her fingertips.

How she loved waking up like this. Warm and safe and relaxed. She couldn't remember what day it was, and she had no sense of the time, but it didn't matter. It was night, and Rook was beside her.

She slid her fingers down from his chest to his flat stomach, and back up, feeling the ridge of breastbone under his warm skin. She turned her nose into the hollow of his shoulder and breathed deeply of the clean scent she could never get enough of.

Then she slid her fingers across his right nipple,

pausing to tease it until it hardened under the slight pressure she brought to bear on it.

He stirred, and she laughed softly. He'd never been quite comfortable when she played with his nipples. He wasn't sure if he was supposed to like it.

But she knew he did. She knew how sensitive— how erotically charged—they were. It turned him on when she touched them. She knew. Just like she knew that nibbling on his earlobe turned him on.

She knew because she knew his body.

With her eyes closed, she trailed her fingers across his pecs and up the side of his neck to his cheek, where she laid her open palm and pressed gently, turning his head toward her.

He turned slightly toward her, enough that she knew he was aroused, and splayed his hand over her tummy, then slid his palm upward and caressed the underside of her breasts.

He pressed his lips against her forehead and drew in a ragged breath. "Irina—"

A quiet whimper escaped from her throat. He'd said her name in his warning, longing voice. The voice that too often reminded her that he needed to get up and race to a meeting, or that she was late for an important charity event, or even just that he was too tired after some long, drawn-out mission.

"No," she whispered. "No protests. You do not protest. Not right now."

Something niggled at the edge of her brain, trying to interrupt her slow, lazy seduction of her husband. But she pushed it away. She'd woken up with a fiery need blazing deep within her, and *life,* with all its drudgery and problems and monkey wrenches, was not going to intrude, at least not until morning.

"Irina, it's—"

"I don't care what time it is, or what day. Right now you are under my spell." She lifted her head and sought his mouth, kissing him with languid, relaxed lips, darting her tongue in and out, teasing him the way she loved to do.

Rook Castle spent most of his life in a type A personality jet stream. She herself was focused, deliberate and slightly obsessive, but Rook was the poster child for type A.

Just about the only time he relaxed was when they were making love. And for some reason that she was too drowsy and too lazy to explore right now, it seemed particularly important to hold him with her in this erotic netherworld between sleeping and waking for as long as she could.

She nipped at his mouth with her teeth, then ran the tip of her tongue across his lips and down his chin to its soft underside. Just as she knew it would, his head lifted and his breath caught. Another erogenous zone she'd discovered.

Maybe today was the day to find a new one. She started on her quest. She trailed her fingers down his neck, following them with her mouth and tongue.

He cradled her head in one hand and groaned low in his throat as she slid farther down, getting into position to lave and suck on his nipple.

Good, she thought. She had him. She slid her leg up his and nearly moaned herself when she felt his erection pulse.

Flattening her hand against his rib cage, which rose and fell rapidly with his breaths, she tasted his skin, inch by inch, as she crept toward his left nipple.

Then her lips hit a rough spot.

She froze.

Rook's fingers curled inward, fisting in her hair. "Irina, I tried—"

She sucked in a long breath. It cleared her head. Her sleepy, erotic haze vanished.

She looked at his chest and saw the round, rough-edged scar where the bullet had hit him.

"No," she whispered as the swirling special world dissolved and the nightmare trapped her again. The nightmare that had haunted her for two years.

Rook, rising above her, moving within her, then sinking into the dark bloody waters of the Mediterranean.

She raised her gaze to meet his eyes. They burned into hers and she knew that this was no nightmare. It was her life.

"Please," she begged. "Stop haunting me."

A strong arm tightened around her bare shoulder. Panic built inside her. Why couldn't she wake up?

"Irina, shh. It's okay. I'm here."

His voice slid through her like the reverberation of a kettle drum—low, ringing, real. His breath whispered across her cheek.

She was in his arms, her head resting in the hollow of his shoulder. He was here.

No. She shook off the fantasy. He wasn't here. Not really. He was dead. Her loving, gentle husband was dead. She'd been dreaming again.

Beneath her cheek, his chest expanded and he sighed. Her fingers tingled with the life, the vibrancy that pulsed beneath them.

He was here.

She stiffened. He'd come back from the dead, and brought danger with him. Danger to her, to himself, to the people who depended on them and cared about them.

She pushed away and sat up.

"Did you have a bad dream?"

She laughed. "A bad dream?" She pushed her fingers through her hair. "No. Not a bad dream. I am having a bad reality."

She scooted across the bed, away from him, alarmed at how easily and instinctively she'd gone to him and slept in his arms, as if he'd never been gone.

Desperately, she struggled to grasp onto reality. To think about anything other than her pathetic reaction to his presence.

"Oh— Brock." Something had happened to Brock. She rubbed her eyes and pushed her hair back. "Brock was shot? How is he?"

"He's fine. The bullet went through his biceps." Rook threw back the covers and got up with his back to her. He was dressed in nothing but briefs. He reached for his pants.

Irina's eyes went straight to the scar on his upper back. It was nothing like the neat circular scar on his chest. This one was jagged and ugly.

"What happened?" she asked.

He half turned as he finished zipping and buttoning the pants. "What?"

"There. Your back."

He grimaced. "The old farmer who saved me took the bullet out. He said it would poison me if it stayed in. Said he'd dug bullets out of his cows before, and a dog or two." He arched his shoulder, as if it hurt him. "He had trouble finding it."

The words hung in the air.

He had trouble finding it. A simple sentence, spoken calmly, no bitterness, no resentment. Certainly no whining. Just a fact.

It made her want to cry. Made her realize that she could never imagine the pain he'd gone through, or the loneliness.

"Did you—" She stopped. She couldn't even ask that question. He'd been out there alone for two years. If he'd found someone to share the lonely nights, could she blame him?

Something burned deep inside her. The hurt was so deep, so ingrained, that she thought nothing could make it worse, but the idea of him making love with someone else, of sharing even one night with another woman while she lay alone, thinking he was dead, hurt her through to her soul.

"Did I what?" He turned and glared at her. "Go ahead and ask. You've earned the right not to trust me."

She shook her head, swallowing hard against the lump that was growing in her throat and blinking away the stinging behind her eyes.

"I'll answer your questions, Rina. I told you I would. But could you hurry? I'm meeting Deke and Dan at seven."

"Did you have anyone to talk to?"

"That's what you wanted to ask?" He stared at her in disbelief. "The farmer was nice. But, no. I stayed away from people as much as possible. As I worked my way closer to Ordo's hideout, I became more visible because of my differentness, and the danger increased."

He headed for the dressing room. "Now, if there's nothing else," he said on a sigh, "I've got to shave." His gaze held hers for another instant, then faltered.

She didn't speak.

He stepped into the dressing room and closed the door.

When she heard the latch catch, the sob that she'd

been trying to swallow escaped, followed by another and another and another.

Her first thought upon coming face-to-face with him less than forty-eight hours ago was right.

She didn't know him at all.

Chapter Ten

By the time Rook showered, shaved and dressed, it was six-thirty. He needed to get a move on if he was going to meet Deke and Dan at seven.

The light from the dressing room illuminated Irina's face. Her eyes were closed but he knew she wasn't asleep. The line of her body was stiff. Her eyelids quivered.

Because of him.

He clenched his teeth and gave his head a short shake. He had a lot to make up for, but it was going to have to wait. He looked at his watch. Quarter to seven.

Keys. He had no idea where keys to the cars might be. Hell, he didn't even know what cars they had. He started toward his dresser, but its surface was polished and empty.

If everything was the same as it had been when he left, there were extra keys to each vehicle hanging on hooks down in the garage. His mouth curled up at the irony. Everything the same? Hardly. Nothing was the same as it had been.

Just as he reached for the door handle, the phone rang. The sound slashed through him. Something else he was going to have to get used to again—all the sounds of America. Phones. Cars. Televisions. Buzzing and ringing and humming and blaring. The sounds of technology.

He grabbed the handset before it could ring a second time.

"Castle," he said.

Irina lifted her head, met his gaze briefly, then turned over.

"This is Taylor. We've got an explosion at the Treasury Building."

Rook instinctively snapped into emergency mode. "Casualties?"

"Unknown. I'm on my way there. I'm calling Cunningham on his cell now."

"I'll be there in ten." He hung up with a curse.

"Rook?" She sat up and pushed her hair out of her face. "What happened?"

"There's been an explosion in town, at the building where the prisoners are being held." He pointed a finger at her. "Lock the door behind me. Don't use the phone. Don't open the door. Not for anybody."

"Who do you think—"

"Do you understand?"

She frowned and lifted her chin. "Yes, sir. But how will I know—"

For a fraction of a second, Rook paused. But time to reassure her was time that could be used to catch the person responsible for the blast.

"I'll call you," he snapped, then turned on his heel and left, locking the door behind him.

EVERYTHING WAS ready. He was just waiting to hear that the diversion went as planned. He looked at his watch. It should have happened twenty minutes ago.

His room phone rang. Taking a deep breath, he picked up the phone.

"We have an incident." It was Brock with his typical terseness.

"An incident?" he said drowsily.

"Explosion at the Treasury Building. Rook's on his way."

"I'll get dressed."

"Stay there in case this is a diversion."

"Yes, sir." He fumbled as he hung up the phone. His hands were shaking that badly. He already had the prepaid cell phone in his pocket, along with his passport, all the money he'd managed to save and one photo. He looked around the room. Nothing else mattered. He was on his way to his new life.

He looked at his watch. He had forty minutes to kill, then he'd walk down the hall to his fellow specialist's room and inform him of the phone call he'd just received from Rook, outlining a change of plans.

In slightly over twenty-four hours, the finders fee would be his, his personal mission would be accomplished.

IRINA PACED BACK and forth. It had been over an hour since Rook left. She'd showered and dressed. She should have heard something by now. Rook had had plenty of time to get into town and check out the damage.

She understood why he'd told her to keep the door locked until he got back. What she didn't understand was why she couldn't make a phone call. Of course he could call her any minute, but one brief call to find out what had happened wasn't going to hurt anything. In fact, she could use her cell and not even tie up the house phone.

She could call Aimee out in the guesthouse and ask if she'd heard anything from Matt.

But her cell wasn't on the charger, and it wasn't in her purse. She must have left it in her office after she'd called her accountant yesterday—no, the day before. Wednesday.

She picked up the phone on her bedside table. She didn't know which room Aimee and Matt were in, but she could call the main guesthouse number.

Then she spotted the phone book on the lower shelf of the bedside table. The hospital. *Mindy*—she'd know what was going on, if anyone did.

Just as she pressed the first number, a knock came at the door.

Thank heavens. He was finally back. She hung up and rushed over to the door, but stopped with her hand on the deadbolt.

"Rook?" she called through the door. "Is that you?"

"Irina? It's Rafe. Aaron's here. Colonel Castle sent us to get you."

"Rafe? Aaron? Why? What has happened? What about Rook? Is he okay?"

"He's fine, ma'am. We're to bring you into town, to the Vick Hotel."

"What? He told me to stay here. Why didn't he call me?"

After a minuscule pause, Aaron spoke up. "He did. On your cell. You didn't answer."

Irina unlocked the door and looked at the two earnest young men. "What happened? Where is he?"

"Still at the explosion site," Aaron said. "There were several casualties. They're digging them out."

"Oh, no. Not anyone we know?"

Aaron glanced at Rafe.

"Oh, no. Who?" Irina picked up a jacket that matched her outfit.

Aaron led her out, with Rafe following. "Two of the Secret Service agents were injured, and one of the suspects."

They went down to the basement, where Aaron grabbed the keys to the Yukon. "Get in the back, Irina. You'll be safer back there."

Aaron climbed into the driver's seat and Rafe got in on the passenger side. When Aaron started the engine, an annoying beeping began.

"Seat belts," he said.

Irina pushed the belt's clasp into the lock. It seated easily.

Aaron glanced in the rearview mirror.

"What about Aimee?" Irina asked. "And her baby? She's in the guesthouse."

"One of the Secret Service agents is going to drive them to the Vick, too. But Rook gave us specific instructions to bring you through the delivery entrance in back of the hotel." Aaron started the engine and reached up to dial in the code that opened the garage door.

"Ah, hell," he said under his breath.

"What?" Rafe asked.

"We're supposed to reset the password on the garage door." He sighed and reached to unfasten his seat belt. "We should have been out of here five minutes ago."

"I'll set it," Rafe said.

"Let me watch. I can't remember the sequence."

Aaron jumped out, then bent and leaned back in. "We'll be right back, Irina. You sit tight."

"That's what I'm doing," she responded with a tiny smile.

Aaron and Rafe disappeared through the metal door into the safe room.

Several seconds later, Aaron came out alone. He sent Irina a small smile as he got in and started the engine. He opened the garage door.

A twinge of apprehension hit Irina just beneath her breastbone. "What about Rafe?"

"He decided to stay here and guard the house."

"But you said Rook sent you both."

"I did."

Aaron glanced in the rearview mirror at her, his expression stony, his eyes glittering.

Her apprehension grew. "I don't understand."

Aaron turned the car around and drove up the driveway to the road.

"You will." His voice took on a hard quality. His fingers whitened around the steering wheel.

Alarm arrowed through her. "Please let me use your phone. I want to call Rook."

"I'm afraid I can't do that right now."

"Aaron, what is going on?"

He didn't answer as he pulled out of the driveway onto the road.

"What has happened to Rafe? Where are you taking me?"

"You need to calm down, Irina. Everything's going to be all right."

It wasn't all right. She knew it wasn't. Aaron was driving too fast. He was acting too odd.

"What happened to Rafe?"

He glanced at her in the rearview mirror. "Rafe didn't have your best interests at heart."

Rafe? "What do you mean? Is Rafe the traitor?" She'd hired him. If he was in league with Novus Ordo, then she'd caused all the injuries, the deaths. The awful things that had happened were her fault.

"That's what *I'd* call him."

"What did you do to him?"

"Nothing permanent. He was trying to put you in harm's way, so I had to incapacitate him, and I had to make it bad enough to put him out of commission for a while. I kicked him in the thigh and locked him in the conference room."

Shock flashed through her like lightning. "I don't understand. What did he do?"

"Let's just say he has his own agenda."

"His own—?" Irina had never gotten to know Aaron very well. He was always polite, but he'd rarely spoken to her unless she deliberately engaged him in conversation. She'd decided that he was painfully shy around women.

But he was acting odd, even for him. And something didn't feel right about this whole thing.

Rook's warning echoed in her brain. *Lock the door and don't open it to anyone but me.*

"Please let me use your phone, Aaron. I want to talk to my husband."

"Not now," he snapped. "I'm sorry. I don't mean to yell at you. But things are a little tense and I'm on a very tight schedule. You'll get to talk to him just as soon as we're safe."

Aaron slowed down to pull into the left lane at the intersection of Midway Road and Highway 43.

"Aaron wait. You turn right to get to the Vick Hotel."

He didn't respond, but when the left arrow lit, he pulled forward and turned left.

"Aaron, stop this car immediately!"

He shook his head without turning around.

"Aaron!" Irina reached for her seat belt. She punched the release button, but nothing happened. She punched it again. And again.

Twisting, she tried to examine it. She didn't see anything physically wrong with it. But no matter how she tugged and struggled, she couldn't get it to unlock.

"Aaron, I can't get the seat belt off."

"Don't worry about it. We'll be there in a few minutes."

"Be where? Aaron, talk to me. What are you doing?"

But he didn't speak.

Panic burned her temples and scalp. Her fingers shook with dread knowledge. She was being kidnapped.

Aaron was the traitor.

They were approaching another intersection.

Please turn red, she begged the light. *Please. Come on.*

The light turned yellow. For a split second, Aaron held on to his speed, but a big truck approached from their right, so he had to slow down.

The light turned red.

Send a car, she prayed. *Please. Give me a chance to attract someone's attention.*

But they sat there alone. Irina kept her eyes on the back of Aaron's head as she tried to slide excess seat belt through, to give her enough room to slide out of the constraining straps. But there was something wrong with the automatic locking mechanism. She couldn't pull but an inch or so of strap through before the lock engaged. She kept working.

Just then a car drove up beside them—on the driver's side—opposite of where she sat behind the passenger seat.

Forgetting caution or threats, she leaned as far to her left as she could and waved her arms and shouted.

"Help! Help me!" She stretched as far as she could, but the wide seats of the huge SUV made it impossible for her to bang or even tap on the window.

"Help!" she screamed.

"Irina, you're wasting your time and your breath. Nobody's going to take you seriously. Besides, the glass is tinted so dark that they can barely see you anyway. You're wasting your strength, too, and I promise you you're going to need it."

The light turned green and the other car sped away, oblivious of Irina and her plight.

As Aaron pulled away, she leaned forward as far as she could and tried to beat on Aaron's head and neck with her fists. She was barely able to touch him, much less hurt him. The best she could do was distract him.

"If you don't stop," he threatened, "I'll stop the car. Believe me, you'll regret it if I do."

She thought about it. If he stopped the car, at least she'd have a chance she didn't have now. But the tone of his voice told her that she was at best a noisy annoyance. He was in too much of a hurry. He wasn't about to waste time stopping the car.

So she looked around the seat and the floorboard. Usually, there was an umbrella lying behind the driver's seat. But, no. He must have inspected the SUV and cleaned it out.

The center armrest was closed. Maybe someone had left a pen or a mini-umbrella in there. But it was empty, too.

"Settle down, Irina. We're almost there."

"You go to hell!" she shouted, and kept punching at him. "Almost where?"

She looked at her shoes. She was wearing loafers. Not even a high heel for a weapon.

The car careened to the right. She looked up and knew where they were heading. The only thing on this road for miles was a small airfield.

Oh, no. "No," she gasped. "Aaron, what are you doing?"

He ignored her, pulling a cell phone from his pocket. He dialed a number and paused, then spoke. "We're here."

The voice on the other end of the phone was barely audible. Irina couldn't make out anything that was said.

By the time the conversation was over, Aaron had pulled up beside a dilapidated hangar.

"Aaron—please. Do not do this. You will be in so much trouble. Kidnapping is a federal crime."

He stopped the car and turned around, amusement lighting his dark features. "A *federal* crime?" He shook his head. "Really, Irina, surely by now you know that a U.S. federal kidnapping charge is the least of my worries."

Then the reality hit. The truth she'd managed to deny until this moment.

Aaron wasn't just kidnapping her. He was taking her out of the country.

He was taking her to Novus Ordo. She was going to be bait to lure Rook to his death.

A deep, visceral fear shrouded her, taking the place of the panic. Aaron had fooled everyone, including Deke and Rook.

"You don't want to do this, Aaron. When they catch you, they will execute you."

"They'll have to find me first. I'll be safe with Ordo."

"Why, Aaron? You're an American citizen. Why are you betraying your own country?"

He turned in his seat to look at her.

"My country? My country isn't America. My country is Israel. My relatives were killed in the Holocaust." His eyes burned with obsessive zeal. "And your famous husband—do you know where his family came from? They came from Germany."

"You can't believe that Rook—"

"I can and I do. Do you know that he killed my father? He let him *die*. Norman Gold was a hero. And Castle let him die like an ordinary grunt. Then he had the gall to hire me, as if it made up for what he'd done. For what his ancestors did."

"Oh, Aaron. Rook was devastated about your dad. He felt responsible for you—"

Aaron cut her off with a string of curses, then got out of the car. When he did, Irina saw the two men dressed in black with black ski masks over their faces approaching.

Aaron spoke to them and nodded. The three had a brief conversation. Then Aaron gestured back toward the car.

Irina tugged at the door handle, but nothing happened. She pressed the UNLOCK button, then tried it again, pulling on the handle and pushing her shoulder against the door.

It wouldn't budge. She couldn't tell if it was locked or somehow jammed. "Come on. Open," she whispered desperately.

How had Aaron managed to sabotage the SUV without anyone noticing?

She answered her own question. Aaron was their computer expert. He'd have no problem disabling or avoiding the security cameras. With everything that had been going on, and the fact that the specialists had always had unrestricted access to the ranch house, it was no wonder that Aaron had found time to break the auto-release on the seat belt and activate the child-proof locks. She even understood why he'd chosen the Yukon. It was huge, with ultra-dark tinted windows. He could sneak her out past the guards with no trouble.

She should have anticipated this. Should have planned for any contingency. After all, Rook had warned her.

But seeing Aaron and Rafe at her door, looking so solemn and earnest, had fed right into her fear that something had happened to Rook. She'd been so worried that she hadn't even grabbed her purse. She didn't have any money or any ID. Maybe that was a good thing. Maybe it would make it difficult for Ordo to get her out of the country.

As the two masked men stalked toward the car, she braced herself. As soon as they opened the door, she'd start screaming. Surely there was someone around the airfield who would hear and come to the aid of a woman in distress.

One of the men reached for the door handle. The other took something out of his pocket.

She took a deep breath.

When the first man opened the door she screamed at the top of her lungs—for about half a second.

Then the second man clapped a wet cloth over her face, muffling her voice. She grabbed his wrist, doing her best to push him away, gasping and coughing at the sweet, acidic smell of whatever was on the cloth.

She held her breath and struggled as long as she could. It felt like a long time, but she figured it was only seconds. The man holding her was strong. Very strong.

Finally she had to breathe. The caustic vapor burned all the way through her throat to her lungs. She coughed again, weakly, and gagged. Despite her best efforts, her hands fell away from the man's thick wrists.

Her last coherent thought was that they would need a knife to get the seat belt undone.

Chapter Eleven

The Sundance fire chief pointed toward the smoking pile of rubble that had been the east end of the ground floor of the Treasury Building. "You see how the blast took out all of the first floor on this side, but only a small portion of the second floor? That's the danger. Now there's nothing supporting the second and third floors."

Rook nodded and turned to Taylor. "Is it confirmed that there were no casualties?"

"A couple of agents have bruises and minor burns, but this end of the building was empty. Makes you wonder if whoever set the explosive knew that, or if he just couldn't get inside the building."

"Yeah," Rook responded. "This is the least visible spot, back here next to the parking lot. Could be why they chose it."

The fire chief shifted from one foot to the other. "That's what we'll be able to determine, once it cools off enough to get inside. Meanwhile, I need to check and be sure everyone's been evacuated."

"The prisoners have been taken to Casper," Taylor said. "And my men will relocate to Castle Ranch."

"I'll tell you right now," the chief continued. "I'm sure we're going to have to blow the building. This area's too unsafe to leave it as is. The safest thing will be to bring the building down. So as soon as I can let you in to pull out all your papers and equipment, I'll let you know."

Taylor nodded. "Thanks."

Rook checked his watch. "I need to call Irina, let her know everything's all right."

Dan handed him his phone. "Go ahead."

Rook dialed the private line that only rang in their suite, but there was no answer.

A sick dread settled under his breastbone.

"Dammit, Rina," he mouthed. "I told you—" He stopped. She wouldn't have left. He knew it. Something had happened.

"I've got to get back to the ranch, now!"

There must have been something in his voice, because both the fire chief and Dan turned and stared at him.

"Let's go," Dan said. "I'm going with you."

On the way, Dan made several rapid phone calls. "No one entered or left through the main gate. Your housekeeper is checking your suite and Lieutenant Parker is trying to locate Gold and Jackson."

Rook turned into the driveway that led to the underground garage. He hit the high-security garage-door opener and pulled inside.

"There's a car missing...I think," he said as he screeched to a halt at the entrance of the garage and jumped out. "The Yukon."

He pointed to the empty space as he jogged past, heading for the conference room. The elevator there was the most efficient way to get upstairs.

As he got close enough to see, he noticed that the

safety door separating the garage from the conference room was ajar.

"Dammit." He stopped in his tracks and held up his fisted hand, signaling Dan to stop and nodding toward the door. The Secret Service agent drew his handgun.

Rook was forced to hang back while Dan went into the conference room first.

"Clear," Dan called. Then in the next breath, "Jackson!"

As Rook rounded the corner, he saw Dan bending over a crumpled figure lying in a pool of blood.

"It's Rafe Jackson," Dan said. He tossed his cell phone to Rook. "Call 911. Looks like somebody smashed his thigh. Damn."

Rook dialed and reported to the 911 operator what they needed, then called the gate to let them know an ambulance was on its way.

"Can you handle this?" he asked Dan. "I've got to check on Irina."

Dan nodded. "Go."

Rook rode the elevator to the executive office. Then he raced through the house to the east wing.

Just as he feared, the suite was empty. Irina's purse sat on her dresser. But there were no signs of a struggle, and no blood. Thank God for that.

His cell phone rang. "Yeah?"

"Colonel Castle? This is Special Agent Shawn Cutler. I just received word back from the FBI. They've got a match for Frank James."

Rook started to interrupt him, but he needed this information. It would help him find whoever had abducted Rina.

"His name is Franklin Hill, age forty-three. No criminal record."

"How'd they get his prints?"

"Seems he worked one summer for the Forest Service."

"Get the full report to Taylor. Right now I've got a situation."

"Yes, sir."

"And, Cutler, see what you can dig up about his relatives. Specifically if he has a brother." Rook hung up.

So Novus Ordo's real name was Hill.

"You did this," he said aloud. "Didn't you, *Novus Ordo?* But how?" Irina wouldn't have gone without a fight—unless she knew and trusted the person.

Rafe was downstairs, fighting for his life. Matt and Deke were accounted for. It had to be Aaron Gold or Brock O'Neill.

He slammed his palm against the door facing, putting his weight behind it. "Damn you, Novus. You win, for now. I'm coming to get my wife. But don't think for a minute that you've won the war." He flexed his throbbing hand.

"In a little while I'm going to know exactly who you are. And I'm coming after you."

IRINA'S HEAD WAS pounding and her stomach felt queasy. She opened her eyes, but it didn't help. Wherever she was, it was dark as hell. And cold.

The last thing she recalled was a wet cloth over her face and a sweetish odor that burned her throat, turned her stomach and knocked her out. Something not quite remembered made her think the liquid was ether.

She sat up, groaning. She tried to stretch her legs, but something was in the way.

She recoiled when she heard metal scrape against

metal, and a sliver of light appeared in front of her. Someone was opening a door.

Blinding light hurt her eyes, before a shadow blocked it. A man loomed over her.

"Who are you?" she rasped. Her throat burned. "Where am I?"

He didn't say anything. He grabbed her upper arm.

She wanted to fight, but she was too drowsy, and her limbs felt like they were made of lead. She felt a sharp prick and then a burning pain.

"Ouch!" She tried to jerk her arm away, tried to kick him, but she didn't have enough room to put any strength behind it.

He grunted. She'd like to think with pain, but she had a sinking feeling he was laughing at her. He withdrew, and for the few seconds the light shone in, she tried to make sense of what she saw. Dark metal with bumps on it. Wooden crates and canvas bags stacked all around her. Then the light disappeared.

A bitter taste suffused her mouth. Her eyelids wouldn't stay open. She tried to push herself up into a sitting position. Tried to sing, stretch, anything to stay awake, but she couldn't fight the drug.

THE NEXT TIME she woke up, the bitter taste was still with her, and the inside of her mouth felt like cotton. Her limbs were stiff and sore. A dull ache drummed in her temples—like a hangover headache.

She opened her eyes—a chore, because she was so drowsy—and found herself in a tiny, dismal room, lying on a narrow bed with threadbare sheets and a thin blanket. On the other side of the room, the midday sun shone blindingly hot through a small window with broken glass.

The room smelled of sweat and sand and heat. The air was still, oppressively still. She felt claustrophobic, smothered, like she couldn't breathe. She sucked in a lungful of warm air. It didn't help.

She closed her eyes, but that made her stomach flip over, so she sat up, groaning at her stiff, achy muscles, and rubbed her face and eyes. A fine grit under her fingertips scraped her skin, like sand or salt. She tasted it. Salt. The hot, dry air was drawing all the moisture out of her skin.

She licked her dry lips and grimaced when she tasted more salt. Squinting against the sun's glare, she checked out her surroundings. The room was barely big enough for the bed and a small scarred table. She saw a glass jar of water sitting on it.

She whimpered aloud as she reached for the jar, ready to turn it up and pour the liquid down her throat.

But the memory of the foul, nauseatingly sweet-smelling cloth and the prick of the needle stopped her.

What if the water was drugged?

Her throat spasmed and her jaw ached. She craved the liquid so badly that she didn't care.

In this awful place that looked and smelled like hell, maybe she'd be better off asleep.

Without pausing to taste it first, she turned the jar up and drank. The water was flat and lukewarm and slightly brackish, but it was wet.

When she'd drunk all she could, she poured some in her cupped hand and splashed it on her face and eyes. It washed away a little of the salt and drowsiness that clung to her.

Pushing herself to her feet, she walked weakly over to the window. She'd expected to find herself on the second or third floor to prevent an escape. But the room looked right out onto the street. The cracked window was coated with dust and sand. Still, she could see through it.

The latch was rusted. She tried it. It squeaked and she let go as if it were hot. Apparently it still worked.

All she would have to do was turn the latch, push the window open and slip through it. Then she could run. Find someone to help her. Maybe to take her to the American embassy.

But as she studied the scene before her, she realized that there would be no one to help her in this town. The United States didn't put embassies in small towns like this.

How impossibly naive she was. It was obvious why her captors hadn't bothered to secure the window.

The dull gray scene before her gave her the answer. So what if she did escape? What would she be escaping to? A dusty barren alien land, where women were draped from head to toe in dark, hot burkas. Where men stalked the streets dressed in military garb with menacing weapons cradled in their arms and ammunition belts draped across their torsos. Or slunk from doorway to doorway, wall to wall, dressed in rags, with fear and defeat in their eyes.

Her choices for shelter were buildings riddled with bullet holes and draped with barbed wire strung like Christmas lights, or mud huts less sturdy than where she was now.

She was in a Muslim town—a Muslim country. A place halfway around the world from Wyoming.

Out of habit, she glanced at her left wrist. Her watch! She'd been unconscious for over twenty-four hours.

She touched the watch's crystal, remembering when

Rook had given it to her on their first anniversary. She still had her rings, too. The beautiful diamond solitaire and wedding band.

It terrified her that the people who had kidnapped her had no interest in jewelry that could buy them enough food for a year.

She began to feel eyes on her. Some of the people slinking along the street spotted her. A child in rags with bare feet and a grimy face pointed in her direction. A burka-wrapped woman walked past her window. Her eyes widened when she met Irina's gaze through the smeared glass.

Irina backed away and sat down on the bed. It took some thought, but she finally forced her blurry brain to piece together what had happened to her.

Aaron Gold had kidnapped her. Aaron, whom Rook had hired after his father had died under Rook's command.

She knew Rook felt responsible for him, because of his father's death. And Aaron admired Rook. He'd never given any indication that he resented him. He'd always seemed fascinated by Rook's stories about his dad. He'd always acted grateful.

Had his quiet shyness been a mask to cover his true self? The expression he'd worn as he drove off with her in the Yukon had been hard and sinister.

He hadn't blinked an eye as the two men drugged her. She didn't know what had happened next, but she could imagine.

After they'd knocked her out, they'd put her on a plane, probably a small one, judging by the cramped space.

After that she remembered almost nothing. How had they taken her from that small plane to one big enough to cross the Atlantic? How had they smuggled her out of the country? Where was the security that America was so proud of, if a few men could steal a person and get them out of the country unnoticed?

Of course, she had no way of knowing whether alarms had been triggered. Homeland Security, the Secret Service and the USCIS could all be looking for her at this very moment.

Rook could be looking for her.

She waited for the sense of relief to flood her at that thought, but it didn't come.

She looked down at herself. She was still dressed in the slacks and shirt she'd had on when Aaron and Rafe had knocked on her door. Her shirt was sweat stained and wrinkled, and the black slacks were gray with dust. Her jacket was gone, as were her loafers. At least they hadn't undressed her.

A noise outside the door made her jump. Then the rusty sound of a key turning in a lock.

Irina moved to the far side of the room in front of the window. She wasn't sure what she thought that would accomplish. Maybe if someone saw her being attacked, they'd come to her aid?

Judging by the eyes of the people she'd seen, they were too afraid to risk helping her.

Two men in military garb entered the room with weapons in arms. One carried a length of dark cloth. The first man, the one in charge, yelled gibberish at her. Then he looked at the other man and jerked his head.

The soldier tossed the dark cloth at her feet. Then the one in charge pointed at it and yelled some more.

Irina looked down at the cloth. Was this a burka? She had no idea, but she wasn't about to put on that heavy, hot cloak over her clothes, and she wasn't about to take off her clothes.

So she looked up at the man in charge and spat a few choice phrases at him in Russian.

His heavy, dark brows went up in surprise. He muttered something and then gestured at the other soldier with his head.

The soldier said something back to him. He half turned and cocked his weapon, and the soldier held up a hand. He slung his rifle over his shoulder by its strap and started toward Irina.

She crossed her arms. "I am not taking my clothes off," she said in English.

The soldier didn't react. He merely picked up the length of cloth and held it out.

She shrugged.

The one in charge said something that Irina was sure would translate to "Hurry up. We don't have all day."

The soldier shook out the cloth and snapped at her.

All she could think of to do was shrug again.

He held his hand up, forefinger down, and made a twirling motion.

With a glance at the other soldier, she obeyed. She'd shown them she was no pushover—she hoped—but she didn't want to make them angry enough to hurt her.

When her back was to him, he draped the cloth over her head and shoulders. Then he spoke again.

After an instant's hesitation, she turned back around. He wrapped the burka around her until she felt like a mummy.

At least they didn't take her clothes off.

The man in charge gave her an order, and the second man nudged her with his rifle.

Irina stood her ground and pointed to her bare feet. "Where are my shoes?" That earned her another nudge.

They forced her out the door, where the soldier pointed at the floor.

Her shoes. Thank heavens. She slipped her feet into them gratefully. From what she'd seen of the streets outside, she did *not* want to walk out there barefooted.

She was hustled out of the building and into a dusty, battered Jeep. She kept her eyes closed for the entire trip. She even dozed off a few times—thanks to all the sedatives she was sure were still in her body.

When the Jeep came to a halt, she opened her eyes, and wanted to cry. They were parked in front of a tent, set against the side of a mountain and surrounded with armed guards.

She was ordered out of the Jeep and manhandled through the flap. Inside was dark and heavily scented with incense.

All Irina could see were flickering candle flames, and even those were pale and dim. A rifle barrel nudged her in the back again, causing her to stumble forward. She put her hands out, afraid of the dark, afraid she was going to walk into something. Around her she heard the rustle of clothes, the creak of leather, metal scraping against metal, people breathing. The same sounds she'd listened to while traveling in the Jeep with the two soldiers.

The gunman behind her kept nudging her forward. She moved slowly, shuffling, still afraid she would trip and fall. Then the toe of one loafer slammed into something. It felt like rock.

As her eyes adapted to the darkness, she saw the difference in the color of the ground beneath her feet. The road outside, and the floor of the tent, was dirt, but now she was stepping onto rock. Big rocks, smooth rocks.

Then, from in front of her, a voice barked orders in

the same language the soldiers had used, and the two soldiers backed away, leaving her standing alone.

She was becoming more accustomed to the dim candlelight. It helped her to see, but the smell of tallow was making her queasy.

The farther she went into what she could only guess was a cave, judging by the stone floor, the more candles lit her way and the hotter the air grew.

Slowly, the outline of a man in light-colored robes came into focus. He was sitting above and in front of her, on some kind of raised platform. His face looked unnaturally pale in the candlelight.

She blinked and looked around her. She could make out several soldiers standing or sitting in the darkness. She could see the candlelight glinting off their weapons and the belts of bullets.

Turning back to the pale man, she spotted a woman in a glittering dress sitting on the floor at his feet. She looked from the woman's sepia-toned face to the man's.

There was something strange about his face—she couldn't see his features. Just his eyes and that pale… mask.

Mask.

The heat, the smell of many bodies in a hot close place and the weight of the burka on her head and shoulders made her head spin.

The man barked another order. Someone grabbed the burka and yanked it off of her, almost knocking her off her feet. Then a blow to the backs of her calves sent her sprawling backward onto a cushioned surface. She'd landed on some kind of upholstered stool.

"Take a load off, Mrs. Castle."

Alarm ripped through her like lightning. English?

She cast about. Who was speaking in English—and American English at that?

As quickly as her gaze snapped to his featureless face, her brain told her the answer.

Novus Ordo. It had to be. The CGI image Rook had described popped into her head, followed by the photo of the dead Frank James.

A pale mask. An American accent. A hidden cave in the farthest regions of the world. Of course it was Novus Ordo.

And with the help of a once-trusted employee, he'd captured her to lure Rook here.

And he would come. Not necessarily for her sake—although she had to believe that he cared enough to want to save her—but because finding her would mean finding Ordo. And she knew that would happen. Because Ordo had brought her here as bait to force Rook to come to him.

"No, it's not some man behind the curtain. It's me."

"Am I supposed to know who you are?" she asked, doing her best to affect an attitude of disinterest.

He laughed. "Supposed to? No. You *do* know who I am. Just as well as I know who you are. Can I get you some water?"

"No."

"Okay, but you're going to get awful thirsty. I might forget to ask you again."

"What do you want with me?"

"Now, come on, Mrs. Castle, you know that, too. You are here so you'd bring your nosy, arrogant husband to me."

Irina folded her hands in her lap and tried not to look as terrified as she felt. She knew the terrorist was ruthless. She'd seen what he'd already done and tried to do.

She'd listened along with Rook to the news stories recounting Ordo's terrorist attacks. The power plants, oil tankers and who knew what else?"

The man she knew only as Novus Ordo looked at his watch. "It's getting late," he said. "Let's go ahead and make that call. I've waited a long time to get my hands on him."

He snapped an order in that language she couldn't understand, and a soldier stepped out of the darkness to hand him a satellite phone.

Irina squeezed her hands together tightly. Maybe in the shadow of her lap, Ordo wouldn't see her white knuckles and know how scared she was.

He stood up. Immediately, all the people in the room stood. It was a sign of respect. Irina didn't stand.

One of the guards grabbed her arm and yanked her to her feet.

"Nyet," she exclaimed, pulling her sleeve away from his grasp. Then she glared at Ordo. "What will you do if I refuse? Exile me to a worse place than this? To a life lonelier than mine has been for the past two years? *Kill* me?" She stood and crossed her arms.

"I'll do all of that, and more, if it helps me reach my goal. How do you think your husband would feel if I sent him one of your fingers? Or an ovary?"

Irina felt the blood drain from her face. She shivered at the icy chill that ran down her spine. She looked into Novus Ordo's eyes and remembered Jung's words. *If you stare into the abyss long enough, the abyss stares back at you.*

"Why are you doing this?" she cried. "What has Rook, what has the United States, done to you?"

Ordo smiled benignly. "Your husband saw my face. That's enough to condemn him. But the U.S. What has the U.S. done? The U.S. continues to ignore the dangers to the environment that they are perpetrating, not just on home soil but all over the world."

Irina stared, astonished. She wasn't sure what Ordo was talking about.

"Do you know who I am? I graduated magna cum laude from MIT in environmental engineering. My IQ is over 180. If they would just listen to me, I could save the planet. Did you know that within the next decade we could see the demise of every species of insect?"

"Insect?"

Novus snorted. "You have no idea what I'm talking about. Let's get back to what I'm going to do to your husband. You heard what I planned for you. Take that to the next level, and you'll understand what I'll do to Colonel Castle if you don't cooperate. Because you know he'll come. You know that. If you help me, I promise to execute Colonel Castle with dignity—by firing squad."

For a moment, Irina couldn't tear her gaze away from his. He didn't have to say the specific words for her to know what torture he implied. Her knees collapsed and she fell back onto the stool, gagging. She'd vomit if she had any food in her stomach.

Distantly she heard Novus say something. A white cloth was thrust under her nose. She used it to wipe her mouth and eyes, then she looked up at Novus.

"*Ya sdyelayoo eto,*" she rasped. "*Vi gryaznaya svin'ya.*"

"You're talking in Russian again."

Irina lifted her head and swallowed against the nausea. "I will do it," she said as strongly as she could. "Whatever you say." She left off the last bit of her Russian comment. *You filthy pig.*

Chapter Twelve

Rook drove the dusty, beat-up Jeep through the narrow streets of Mahjidastan, his stomach churning at the remembered smells of heat, sweat, dung and dust.

He'd been through a lot in his career as a combat rescue officer. He'd seen and heard some awful things, but nothing he'd ever been through in his life had prepared him for the abject horror in Rina's voice on the staticky satellite phone twenty-four hours before.

Please, Rook, do what he says. You can't imagine what he'll do if you don't follow his instructions to the letter.

Sadly, he *could* imagine.

But the next thing she'd said had baffled him. She'd spoken in Russian, and he hadn't understood a syllable. Thank God he'd insisted that every call that came in from the moment Irina went missing be recorded.

When he'd played the recording for Tanya, a friend of hers in Casper, Tanya had been baffled, as well.

"The last bit says 'I love you,' of course. And the middle part essentially translates as "ecological technical degree." But *provyer'tye em ay'tye?*" She sighed. "Check something. Check mit? Does that make sense?"

He'd written it all down. He spoke it out loud, over and over and over.

Check em ay'tye. Ecological technical degree. I love you.

Check em ay'tye. Ecological technical degree. I love you.

Finally, the answer had coalesced in his brain.

They weren't words, they were letters. MIT. Massachusetts Institute of Technology!

A call to Dan to check MIT for graduates with the last name of Hill who'd majored in ecology hit pay dirt.

Frank James's fingerprints had traced him back to Laramie, Wyoming. His name was Franklin Hill, and he had a brother who'd attended Wyoming University and then graduated summa cum laude in environmental engineering from MIT.

Frederick Hill had graduated with a brilliant future ahead of him. But as of eight years ago, he'd disappeared off the face of the earth—no tax returns, no driver's license. Nothing.

Novus Ordo. Frederick Hill.

As soon as Rook hung up from talking to Dan, he went to see Deke and had a long, somber discussion with him. Then he caught a plane for Kabul—alone. He couldn't take the chance that anyone would stop him.

So now he was here, where Ordo wanted him. All he had to do was wait. Ordo would find him.

At the door to the rooming house, he paused and looked around. Not to familiarize himself with the town—it was burned into his memory forever—but to ensure that everyone in town knew he was here.

Ordo had ordered him here. He was here.

The number of curious stares he attracted didn't scare him. Rather, he scrutinized each one. Trouble was, all of the dark eyes had shadows in their depths. Any one of them could be Ordo's spy.

He sure as hell hoped so. It had been well over forty-eight hours since Aaron had abducted Irina. He had no time to waste.

Turning on his heel, he headed inside. Ironically, the old woman who ran the inn had put him in the same room he'd been in before. A frisson of disgust spread through him. He'd hoped never to see these dingy walls again.

Just like the last time he'd left his home with little hope of returning, he'd brought nothing of value with him, except his watch, his wedding ring and his Sig Sauer.

He fingered the ring. This time was different. This time, the thing he valued most was here, in this desolate corner of the world.

And nothing—not his inherited millions, not his accomplishments, not even his connections with people like the president of the United States—could save her. He had nothing but his wits. That and faith.

He lay down on the narrow bed and closed his eyes. He had nothing to do now but wait. He thumbed the smooth surface of his wedding ring, and his thoughts turned backward, to his childhood.

It seemed to him that everything he'd ever done had led him to this time and place.

How would his life have been different if he and Matt and Deke, his oath brothers, had never gotten caught in that storm? If a good and honorable man hadn't lost his own life that day to save four boys?

He'd have probably taken over his father's diverse and lucrative media conglomerates, instead of joining the Air Force. He'd likely have married a hometown girl and had a nice, safe, normal life.

He'd have never rescued Leonid Tankien. Never met and fallen in love with Tankien's daughter, Irina. He'd have never sat in the Oval Office and chatted with the president about covert missions to rescue innocent Americans. He'd certainly have never had to ask his friends to lay their lives on the line for him.

He didn't regret any of his choices except one. If he could live his life over again, he'd never lie to Rina. She deserved better. She always had.

The banging on the door startled him out of his daydream. He rolled off the bed, gun in hand. "Who is it?" he yelled.

The snarling answer was in Arabic.

His breath whooshed out in cautious relief. Soon he'd be in front of Ordo. He'd be able to see for himself that Irina was all right.

He called out one of the few phrases he'd learned in the local language. From what he'd been told, it translated loosely as "Hang on a minute."

Gripping his weapon, Rook unlocked the door. When he saw the soldiers in their desert camo with ammunition belts criss-crossing their chests and heavy guns cradled in their arms, he raised his hands, letting his gun dangle from his fingertips.

The guy in charge stepped close and knocked the gun away.

Interpreting what was expected of him, Rook spread his hands in surrender. One of the armed soldiers turned around and put his back to the door facing, obviously guarding the door. The other stepped inside and trained his rifle on Rook's midsection.

The leader gestured to Rook. His meaning was unmistakable. He wanted him to undress. Probably for a strip search.

Rook stood without moving.

The leader gestured a second time and snapped an order.

Rook shrugged, affecting a puzzled expression. The skin on the back of his neck prickled. He hoped like hell that the man would give up if he played dumb.

No such luck. The rifle barrel pushed painfully into Rook's side.

Fine. He gave in, praying that the men weren't sadistic. They weren't. The search was almost cursory and was over inside of two minutes.

As soon as he got his shirt buttoned, the leader pulled a square of cloth from a pocket and gestured for Rook to turn around.

He decided further delays would only hurt his own agenda, which was getting himself in front of Ordo as quickly as possible, so he obeyed.

Within seconds, he was blindfolded and his hands were tethered behind his back. He had to quell his instinct to fight. This was not about him. Certainly not about being a hero, or getting revenge.

He was a player in a much bigger undertaking. Sure, he was here to get Rina to safety. But as much as he wished he could just somehow grab her and go, she wasn't his primary mission.

He didn't resist as the soldiers led him outside and pushed him into the backseat of an open vehicle—probably a Jeep.

They were taking him to Novus Ordo. And everything—*everything*—depended on how he handled himself.

If he were a desperate international terrorist whose true identity was in danger of being uncovered, and the one man in the world who could destroy him were brought before him, he'd execute him on sight. But he wasn't Novus Ordo.

And the plan depended on his expatriated American's need to gloat.

Because Rook was offering him exactly what he wanted—with one caveat.

Let Irina live.

The ride was a long one, and bumpy. Blindfolded, and with his hands behind his back, he was at the mercy of the dysfunctional shocks in the Jeep. His exhausted body took a battering by the time the vehicle finally stopped. Judging by how long it took, and the condition of the roads they'd ridden, he figured they'd driven up several hundred feet in elevation into the mountains.

He was manhandled out of the Jeep and shoved forward. He shuffled and stumbled as he tried to stay upright. Every time he paused, feeling his way for his next step, a rifle barrel prodded him in the kidneys.

Through the blindfold and his closed lids, he could tell when they entered a dark shelter, probably a tent. The odors of too many bodies in too close a space, combined with sweetish incense and cigarette smoke, made his nose burn. The heat was oppressive, and it wasn't helped by all the candles that flickered redly in front of his closed lids.

The toes of his boots hit something solid. He fell forward. His knees landed on some sort of wooden riser, or step.

The soldier growled in the language Rook had heard a lot here in Mahjidastan.

From in front of him, he heard another voice. Same language, but sounding very different. Then the same voice greeted him, and he understood what the difference was.

"Colonel Castle. Nice of you to drop by."

The voice belonged to an American.

He was standing in front of Novus Ordo.

Ordo barked a command. Someone yanked off Rook's blindfold, although they left his hands tied. He raised his head, blinking, waiting for his eyes to finish adapting to the dark.

Then he saw Ordo, his pale face illuminated by the wan light of the flickering candles. His face with no mask.

It was the face from the sketch. Almost identical to the face from the autopsy photo of Frank James.

"Ordo," he breathed. He pushed himself backward, trying to get his feet under him so he could stand. He'd just about straightened when a staggering blow struck the back of his knees. He fell forward, banging his cheek on the hard wooden platform.

Ordo snapped an order, and a hand in his hair jerked him upright.

"Sorry, Colonel. My soldiers don't like to see me disrespected."

The man who named himself Novus Ordo, or "New Order," sat in a crudely built wooden chair draped with lengths of cloth in various tones. The candlelight rendered everything nearly monochromatic. Novus wore a plain white shirt and tan pants that had seen better days.

His head was bare. His matted light brown hair completed his resemblance to Frank James—Franklin Hill, his younger brother.

"Where's Irina?"

"I figured that would be your first question. Let's just say she's safe, for the moment. So what's your second question?"

"Where's Aaron Gold?"

"Okay, good one—and easy. Aaron was a big help. A *big* help, but he's outlived his usefulness."

The relief he'd felt at hearing that Irina was safe faded and was replaced with dread. He closed his eyes briefly. "You killed Aaron?"

"Not yet. I thought you'd enjoy watching. Just like I'm certain that Mrs. Castle will get a kick out of watching you die."

Rook clenched his jaw. Let the man get his jollies. He knew Ordo was trying to get a rise out of him, but Rook was not going to give him the satisfaction.

He tried to relax. If Novus could see something as subtle as a muscle tensing, then let him enjoy it.

"Let's hear your third question," Novus said.

"How many questions do I get?"

Novus's brows drew down and his jaw tightened in irritation. "As many as I want to give you. Until I get bored. And by the way, that question—*very* boring."

"What happens when you get bored?"

That amused him. "I have a question for you."

Rook nodded. "Okay," he said. Inside, he felt the swell of triumph in his chest. He'd figured it wouldn't take long for Novus to get around to talking about himself. To do what he'd done took the mind of a megalomaniac, the soul of a sociopath, the distorted assurance of a messianic delusion.

"Have you figured out why you haven't been able to identify me?"

"What makes you think we haven't?"

Novus rolled his eyes. "Oh, please. Give me some credit. If the United States had confirmed my identity, my face would be plastered all over the Internet and the TV, searching for people who knew me, who might still be in touch with me. And I have spies everywhere."

"Maybe we're smarter than that. How did you feel about your brother's death?"

Even in the dim light, Rook saw Novus's face darken. "That was unnecessary," he said. "And your mistake. You probably could have bullied him into talking. So I guess I should be happy he's dead."

Rook looked at him questioningly. "Can I ask another question?"

Novus sat back on his makeshift throne and crossed his legs. "Sure. I've got nowhere to be."

"What are you doing here? You don't seem like the type to embrace Islam, or enjoy these primitive conditions. What made you leave your cushy life to come and live like this?"

"Cushy life?" Novus's head snapped up and his eyes narrowed suspiciously.

Rook winced inwardly. He hadn't meant to go there—at least not yet.

"What are you talking about? What do you know about—" Ordo stopped, studying Rook.

Finally he smiled and shook his head. "Oh, no. You're just trying to get me riled, You don't know anything about me."

Rook thought fast. "I know that when you were a kid, you didn't dream of becoming a terrorist. I know you're fairly intelligent, and extremely clever. What's the attraction? The fame? The money?"

"Haven't you been paying any attention to my radio messages? My blogs on the demise of this planet? Why do you think I bombed that nuclear plant in India? And that supposedly *secret* chemical munitions warehouse in Mexico. Why do you think I took three American oil tankers hostage?"

"That was you?" Rook goaded.

That angered Novus. His face turned bright red. "Of course that was me. What the hell's wrong with you?"

Rook shrugged. "I guess I forgot. From what I understand, a lot of people think you're dead. It's been two years since you've carried out a major attack. So what was your problem with those places? The oil tankers carry fuel to move food and necessary supplies around the world. The nuclear plant brings electricity to hundreds of thousands of people who couldn't otherwise afford it. And that munitions plant? It produced one-third of the chemical munitions used by the U.S. and NATO nations to protect their people."

"Do you know what happens to the waste from those places—not to mention the waste from people's everyday lives? We're destroying our planet. At the rate we're going, we'll be lucky if any species of insect survive the next decade."

"And that's not a good thing?" Rook asked innocently.

Novus pressed his palms against his temples. "You're baiting me. You can't be that dumb. Without insects, the entire ecology of the planet will fall apart. Mankind—hell, *everything*—will be extinct."

"If I'm understanding you correctly, you're committing acts of terrorism to save the planet? I'm not quite sure I can make that leap. You're murdering hundreds—thousands—of people in order to what, save some insects?" It was all Rook could do to keep from smiling. Ordo was right. He *was* baiting him.

"You don't understand. How could you, with your narrow point of view and your privileged life? Don't think I don't know who your father is. Be thankful I haven't bombed his National News Network yet. Although I do have plans to see what I can do to get my hands on some of those millions, after I've sent your body and your wife's back to the U.S." He smiled benignly. "I wonder who inherits all that money when you and your wife are dead?"

Jennie. His baby sister. Rook used every ounce of strength in his body not to react. "You'll never have the chance, Novus."

Ordo laughed. "Tall words. You act brave. It's going to be interesting to see how brave you really are."

"Bring it on, Novus. Without your rag-tag bunch of soldiers, I doubt you can hold your own."

"These hyenas? They don't understand my real purpose. I don't expect them to. They're useful just like they are. They think they're fighting a holy war. Makes it easy to send them on suicide missions." He stood and walked around the wooden chair and leaned on the back of it.

"Everyone is so hot on their religious icons," he continued. "They think Allah is their savior. Christians think Jesus is." He shook his head.

Rook frowned. "What do you think?" he asked, pretty sure he knew the answer.

Ordo thumped his chest. "I am the savior. I'm the only one who can really solve the world's problems. I tried to explain to your wife. No one would listen to a new PhD graduating in environmental engineering. Not even at MIT. I advocated for change. I wrote papers. I testified before Congress. I did everything I could to convince people that the destruction of the planet is almost out of hand."

Novus doubled his fists and pounded on the back of the chair. "I had no choice. They'll see. By the time I've taken out all the nuclear plants in the U.S., the world will know me and will see that I'm right. That I have saved the planet."

He was going to destroy over a hundred nuclear plants?

"You don't have the manpower to blow up a hundred plants at once."

"You have no idea."

With a start, Rook realized that the terrorist was right. There was no intel on how many followers Novus had.

"If you blow up all the nuclear plants in the U.S., you could potentially kill every person in North America."

"America is the biggest offender."

"When are you planning this attack?"

Ordo held up a finger. "Oh, no. Nobody knows the answer to that question. I trust my people, but not that much."

"I'm impressed, but I don't see you gathering enough people to carry out a plan like that."

Ordo yawned. "I'm bored. I thought you came here to rescue your wife."

Rook assessed the terrorist. What was he up to? "Of course, that's my top priority. But stopping you is a close second."

"Would you like to see her?"

Rook's throat seized. "Yes." He didn't trust himself to say anything more. He'd been so afraid that Ordo had hurt her, so afraid that he'd killed her already. He knew that all Ordo had wanted was to provide Rook with proof that he had her. It's why he'd forced her to call him. After that, Ordo had no reason to keep her alive.

"Good." Ordo came around the chair. "One thing I've never been accused of is being a bad host. Although you, Colonel Castle, are too big a liability to my cause and my anonymity, you obviously deserve some respect for your rank and your perseverance."

Rook waited, maintaining a neutral expression. At least so far, Novus had no idea his anonymity had been compromised.

"I've prepared my bedroom for you for tonight. Tomorrow morning I'm afraid I've got to execute you. But for now, I'm offering you a gesture of respect. Enjoy my hospitality, and enjoy your wife, on the last night of your life."

Rook laughed. "You've got to be kidding."

"No, sir. I am serious. It's a tradition amongst warriors. The night before the final battle should be spent in love. I'm offering you a warrior's final night."

There had to be a trick. Hidden cameras? Hidden microphones, in hope that he might whisper some secret plan to Irina?

"However," Ordo added.

And here it was. The trick.

"You'd do well to remember, Colonel Castle, that my bed is better guarded than any place in this entire province. If you try to escape, you'll be shot down like the mangy coyote you are. I'll put your head on a pike. And then I'll do what you failed to do. I'll enjoy your wife, right on top of your bloody corpse, before I leave her to my soldiers, who have few enough chances to see a beautiful woman such as her."

He took a deep breath and smiled. "Do I make myself clear?"

Rook looked Ordo full in the face and nodded. "I accept your offer."

Chapter Thirteen

Rook walked through a narrow passage into another candlelit room—an anteroom to the main cave, cut or worn into the mountain. It actually was set up as a bedroom.

Most of the candles were on wooden boxes that served as bedside tables for the surprisingly contemporary king-size bed. The mattress was draped with colorful quilts, spreads and pillows in jewel tones.

A carafe of water and one of wine sat on a low table beside the bed, along with bowls of figs and almonds.

On a low stool beside the bed was a porcelain chamber pot. The rest of the cave was bathed in darkness. Two candles flickered on a side table. In the glow, he made out a bowl and pitcher and a small stack of folded cloths.

Was this how Ordo lived, or had this ersatz honeymoon suite been put together for Rook's benefit?

More importantly—was Irina really here? Just as he asked himself that question, a shadow moved across the surface of the bowl and pitcher.

"Irina?" Her name was wrung from his throat unwillingly, in case Ordo was watching or listening. A testament to his fear and hope.

The shadow froze, then through the dimness a small figure moved toward him. The candlelight's glow picked up the person's silhouette, then began to chase the shadows away from the curves and planes of her body. *Her* body.

"Rina?" His voice broke.

"Rook?"

She stepped out of the shadows. She was dressed in a simple white *abaya* with embroidery across the front and down the sleeves. Her hair had been washed but not styled, so it floated like golden fog around her drawn face. Her blue eyes were huge and frightened.

He tore his eyes away from her and looked around the room, wishing he could somehow sense where microphones or cameras might be.

She touched his arm and gasped quietly. "You're really here."

His gaze snapped back to hers. He took a step forward and held out his hand.

For an instant she stared at his fingers as if she didn't quite know what to do, but then she laid her hand in his.

When she raised her frightened blue eyes to meet his, he tugged lightly, pulling her to him and wrapped his arm around her. For a few seconds, she just stood there, unmoving in his arms. Then he felt it, the giving in, the yielding. He knew she couldn't stay detached if he touched her. Just as he couldn't with her body pressed against his.

He embraced her fully, pressing her sweet familiar body to his, branding himself with her. How had he lived without her? Burying his nose in the sweet curve between her shoulder and neck, he knew the answer. He hadn't lived—he merely existed.

"Oh, Rook," she whispered. "Why did you come? Did you not figure my message?"

"Shh," he breathed in her ear, so low he couldn't hear himself. Then he nodded, twice.

Irina's breath blew out in a ragged sigh and her arms came up around his neck. "Then why—"

He tightened his arms. "Shh," he breathed again. "He could be listening."

She shook her head. "Nothing on me. I checked."

He was relieved. But what about him? Had the soldiers placed a bug on him during the strip search, or on the ride here? "Wait," he whispered.

He pulled away from her and shed his shirt, then brought his hand up around her neck and bent until his mouth was against her ear. "Check me."

She did, running her hands through his hair and down his neck. Over his shoulders, his upper arms, forearms and hands.

He stood stiffly, knowing the touching was necessary, knowing that losing himself in the soft caress of her fingers could be deadly, and yet unable to keep from reacting.

When she moved to his throat, his collarbone, his pecs, his heart rate went up and his breathing grew ragged. She wouldn't touch his nipples, would she? Not in this dangerous place as she performed such a dangerous job.

Her hands slid across his pecs and down his breastbone.

Then she did it. She ran her fingertips across his already distended nubs. He gasped. He lifted his hands to stop her before the intense shock of lust spread through his whole body, but he was already too late.

He groaned as his erection pulsed and grew.

She ran her fingers across his rib cage, his waist and his abdomen. When they touched the waistband of his pants, he caught her wrists.

"Back," he grated, and turned around. "If it's down there they won't be able to hear much."

She quickly checked his shoulders and back. When she was done, she pressed a kiss to his shoulder blade.

He turned around and pulled her close again. Her chest rose and fell rapidly, and she didn't try to pull away from his obvious arousal. In fact, she slid her arms around his waist and pulled him close.

"We need to find a way out of here," he whispered.

Her breath caught. "No." She shook her head.

"Yes. We might be able to make it. He can't have enough men to guard every inch of this mountain."

"You don't know what he'll do to you if you try to escape."

He cradled the back of her head in his palm. "He's going to kill us if we stay here."

She stiffened and shook her head again. Her fists doubled against the small of his back. "Rook, he'll torture you and leave you to bleed to death on the ground."

"So I should just give up without a fight? Without trying?"

She brought her fists around and up to pound on his chest. "You—man!" she hissed. "Your reasoning makes no sense. It will be better, because he promised me. He will give us this night together. He will give you—" her breath caught in a sob "—a dignified execution by firing squad."

"And for you?"

She didn't answer.

"That's what I thought. What would you have me do?"

"Preferably? Rain the punishment of God down on his head. Kill him, no matter if we die with him. Rid the planet of his insane power."

Rook nodded. "That's the plan," he breathed in her ear. Then he tugged on her earlobe with his teeth and followed them with his tongue, tracing its delicate curves all the way around and back to the lobe, which he nibbled again.

Irina's entire body tingled with arousal as Rook teased her ear. He knew what he was doing. He could always get his way by nibbling on her earlobe.

Right now, his teasing added to her already turned-on state. Her body soared to the brink of climax.

The dire task of making sure Rook's torso hadn't been bugged had turned into an erotic interlude unlike anything she'd ever experienced. She had no way of measuring how long it had taken to search every inch of his upper body, but for her, time had stood still, as if she'd been trapped forever in an erotic time warp of foreplay. Every place she'd touched, every millimeter of his skin had hummed with warmth, with life, with sexual stimulation.

"Rina." His voice buzzed in her ear, like a bee.

He took her fist in his hand and uncurled it gently, then guided it to the ball of his shoulder. "Feel," he whispered.

She ran her palm and then her fingers over his smooth skin, his shoulder bone, his strong, tense tendons.

Then she felt it. The tiny hard circle, right behind the ball and socket of his right shoulder.

"What is that?" she whispered, her heart pounding at the possibility that formed in her mind.

"A GPS locator chip. Brand-new technology. But I need to get outside."

A tracking device. He'd done what Ordo had ordered him not to do, on pain of death—his *and* hers. He'd brought reinforcements.

She lifted her face until her lips were almost touching his.

"Blow out the candles."

"What?"

"I slept here last night. Trust me."

His brows rose, but he did what she'd said. As he extinguished the last candle, he realized there was still light coming from somewhere. He glanced around but didn't see any other flames.

While he'd been busy with the candles, she'd lain on the bed. He could see her skin, pale against the dark, rich colors of the spread and drapes.

"Come here," she said softly.

After an instant's hesitation, he climbed onto the bed and lay beside her.

"Look up," she whispered in his ear.

He did. Directly over the bed was an opening in the cave roof. Not a large one. Just enough to let moonlight in and to see a few stars.

Just enough to—

Rook's astonished gaze met hers. She nodded.

Then she saw something she'd only seen a few times since she'd known him, and not once since he'd come back from the dead.

His smile.

No diamond could match it for beauty, or rarity. It transformed his stern, angular face into dimpled, boyish, heartbreaking sweetness.

With a little luck, the skies would stay clear tonight, and Deke and whoever else Rook had brought with him could zero in on the chip embedded in his shoulder.

"You should stay on top," she said, her voice breaking with hope and happiness and fear.

"I suppose I should." He touched the hem of her *abaya,* and she raised up so he could slip it off.

Then he reached for a length of gauzy cloth and draped it over them from head to toe.

She slid her hand between the cloth and his shoulder and touched the chip. He lay his hand over hers. "Thin cloth—not a problem."

Then in one smooth motion, he raised himself above her, and the hairs on his chest tickled her breasts' distended tips. His hips met hers, and his erection pushed against her with exquisite pressure. He leaned on his elbows and caressed her face, her cheeks, her lips, with his fingers.

All she wanted to do was surround herself with him. To have him in her and around her for this one last time.

Maybe his plan would work. Maybe they'd be rescued in the morning. But she knew that all she could count on was right now. All anyone ever had was now.

As much as she'd ever wanted anything, she wanted to hold on to it, to experience every single nanosecond of it. For this one brief instant of time, she had her heart's desire.

But more than that, she longed to hear him say the words he'd never said.

She hated herself right now. She knew this moment was fleeting, and she knew she was going to ruin it. But her insecurities were stronger than her will.

"Rook?"

"Hmm?" He kissed her deeply, thoroughly, a kiss to transcend time and space. A kiss between lovers. Then he pushed into her waiting body with exquisite slowness.

The sensation of him filling her made her cry. She'd been alone for so long. She'd given up hope, and yet hope had never given up on her.

He made a noise deep in his throat and sank deeper. He pressed his forehead against hers. She felt his chest rise and fall rapidly.

"This feels so good," he whispered. "I missed you so much."

"Why, Rook?" she murmured brokenly. "Why did you leave me?"

"Rina," he muttered, his tone hovering between a warning and an endearment. Dipping his head, he sought her mouth.

She longed to kiss him, to surround herself with his powerful body, to feel him at once in her and around her as she had so many times before.

But inevitably, her hands pushed at his chest, resisting. She struggled to maintain eye contact.

"Why?" she repeated, like lines in a play she was being forced to perform. She wished she could stop, but she was too caught up in her nightmare.

"You know why," he whispered, and his breath fanned her eyelashes. He kissed her eyelids, her cheek, the sweet spot beneath her earlobe.

She tasted sweat on his neck—salty, delicious. "Rook, I need to know."

"I had to," he said. "It was the only way to keep you safe." His erection pulsed inside her.

"But you left me alone."

"Don't," he whispered, moving within her, rocking her with the slow rhythm she knew so well. His chest rumbled with languid laughter when she gasped.

But then she pushed him away again, helpless against the current of her insecurity and need.

He stopped again. "Rina, I know you don't trust me. I know I destroyed that when I did what I did. But you have to try. You have to believe me. I did it because I love you. So much that I believed that nothing, not even death, could tear us apart. I loved you then. I love you now. I will love you forever, wherever we are."

He held her gaze and pushed into her, once, twice, again and again, stealing the doubt from her mind and replacing it with uncontrollable desire.

"Now shut up and come with me." He pushed her over the threshold, and all the stars in the heavens burst in front of her eyes.

THE NEXT THING Irina knew, a man was poking a rifle into her neck. Her eyes flew open and her hand clutched at the thin cloth that covered her.

Rook was already awake and sitting up, his hands spread in a gesture of surrender. He spoke sharply, in the language of the area, and jerked his head toward the cloth-draped doorway that divided the bedroom from the main cave.

The rifle at her throat jabbed, choking her. She coughed.

The other soldier barked a command, and her guard took a step away. Then the two of them backed out of the room.

Rook's gaze met hers. "Are you okay?"

"What did you say to them?"

"Told them you were a lady and needed your privacy to dress."

She looked around and then up, at the opening in the roof. "It is barely dawn." Her heart leapt into her throat. "Is it time?"

He nodded grimly. "Apparently."

Rising, he walked naked around the bed and picked up the carafe of water. He poured a cup, handed it to her and turned the carafe up to his lips.

She drank some of the flat-tasting water, but it was hard to force it past the lump in her throat.

This was it. They were going to die today. A flood of regret washed over her. She wasn't old. Not even thirty-one.

There had been times in her life when she'd almost wanted to die. *Almost*. But today wasn't one of them.

Rook bent and picked up her *abaya* and tossed it to her. He looked her way but didn't meet her eyes. That could only mean one of two things—he was hiding something from her, or he'd lied to her.

She longed to ask him if they were really going to die here. To ask him why Deke wasn't on his way to rescue them. And why he wasn't fighting to live. But she was afraid of his answer. She'd thought she knew him, sometimes better than she knew herself. But he'd planned to fake his death, and she'd never suspected.

She pulled the *abaya* on over her head and stood so the hem fell to her ankles.

Rook buttoned his wrinkled, dirt-stained shirt and pulled on his pants, then shot his cuffs as if he were wearing a tux.

"Rook?"

In the dimness, his eyes, which were usually the color of peridot, looked much darker. A ghost of a smile played around his lips. "Don't be afraid, Rina," he murmured.

Her heart leapt and her breath caught. Was that assurance she heard in his voice? Maybe Deke was on his way.

He put an arm around her shoulders and pressed a kiss to the top of her head. "It's not so bad."

Death.

He was talking about death. Her throat closed and her eyes stung. Because he knew. She slid her arms around his waist and pressed her face into the hollow of his shoulder.

It was too late.

"I cannot help it," she whispered brokenly. "I wanted more. More time, more life. More *you*."

"Shh. Don't cry."

She *was* crying and she hated that she was that weak. He'd been so strong through everything. He'd been her rock. Her savior. Her lover.

She heard heavy footsteps. The guards.

Rook gently pushed her away but kept his hand on the small of her back. The guards entered and stood on either side of the cave opening, their rifles cradled menacingly in their arms.

Pressing firmly on her back, Rook urged her forward. She lifted her head, doubled her fists at her sides and walked through the opening with as much dignity as she could gather.

In the large main cave, Novus Ordo sat with a cup in his hand. "Coffee?" he said conversationally. "It's strong."

Rook pulled her a few millimeters closer. He didn't answer the terrorist.

"No?" Ordo drained the cup and held it out. The old woman standing behind him took it. "See that?" he asked with a grin. "There's nothing like it. Think I could ever have all this in the U.S.?"

"And I thought you were crazy and misguided, but at least you had a worthy cause." Rook's voice dripped with revulsion. "Looks like your thing isn't saving the planet—it's power and money."

Ordo's face turned dark. "Don't even presume to judge me," he shouted, his hands white-knuckled on the arms of his chair. But immediately, he let go and held up his hands, palms out.

"No," he said, shaking his head. "I'm not going to let you bait me this morning. I intend to enjoy this."

He turned to Irina. "Mrs. Castle, you kept your word. I'm going to keep mine. Your husband will be executed by a firing squad this morning."

Irina couldn't speak. She could hardly breathe. To hear those words, spoken in that calm, slightly amused voice chilled her to her soul.

"What about my wife?" Rook asked. "You'll let her go?"

Ordo laughed. "Sure. Sure thing. I'll let her go." He said something else, in that language Irina couldn't understand, and all the soldiers in the room laughed, too.

Rook's whole body went rigid against her, and she felt his hand double into a fist at her back.

What had Ordo said? She looked fearfully at the terrorist and the two guards standing on either side of him. They were leering at her. Her knees gave way, and she'd have fallen if Rook hadn't caught her.

"Kill me," she whispered to him as he held her close against him.

He didn't answer her, but his arms tightened and his heartbeat against her ear tripled.

"Mrs. Castle. I'm guessing you figured out what I said." Ordo grinned at her. "And, no, your husband won't be able to kill you. He doesn't have the means or the guts, do you, Colonel—?"

The last of his sentence was drowned out by the sound of an airplane overhead.

Ordo's head jerked up sharply, then he eyed Rook with suspicion. He gestured to one of his guards and whispered in his ear. The guard nodded. He stepped away from Ordo's chair and headed for the main entrance to the cave, taking another soldier with him.

Novus Ordo slammed his fist on the chair arm. "I *knew* it. You couldn't keep your word, could you?" he thundered. "You coward! You cheat! Well, I hope that's your best buddy up there in that plane, because it's coming *down!*"

He pointed to one of his guards and spat an order, then pointed to a second one. The two men slung their rifles over their shoulders. One grabbed Rook, the other grabbed her.

He was separating them. Irina struggled helplessly against the guard holding her, as she tried to maintain eye contact with Rook.

He hadn't reacted to the guard who'd dragged him across the room. He stood tall and straight, and when his gaze met hers, he gave her a tiny shake of his head.

Don't struggle. It was as clear as if he'd said it aloud.

From outside, she heard several small explosions, one right after another. She sent a questioning glance toward Rook but he was looking at Novus, who held his hand up.

He waited. The whole room waited.

Another short burst of explosive, then a deafening blast that went on for a couple of seconds.

No one in the room moved.

Finally, the unmistakable sound of metal crashing to the ground.

Irina gasped. Rook closed his eyes. Novus Ordo

sent up a shout of triumph, and the roomful of guards cheered with him.

There could be only one explanation for what she'd heard.

Novus had shot down their rescue plane.

Chapter Fourteen

Rook looked Novus Ordo in the eye and watched him light up like a child on Christmas as the sickening sound of metal crashing to the ground filled the air.

Novus smirked at him in triumph. "Did you think I wouldn't have anti-aircraft missiles? Did you think I couldn't shoot your little planes right out of the air?"

Rook let the words roll off him like beads of water. He didn't change expression, didn't move a muscle. The hardest thing was not to look at Rina, but he managed. He held Ordo's gaze.

After a beat, Novus snapped an order and all the guards stood at attention. Best Rook could translate was something on the order of "It's time. Make ready."

He figured Novus was ordering his men to set up the firing squad. A shard of fear ripped through Rook. He hoped his courage held out. He wasn't sure how much he had left. It had been draining away ever since the moment he found out Novus had gotten his hands on Irina. And now, if he died, or maybe even if he managed to get out of this alive, his sister was a target.

As he expected, a second guard stepped up beside

him. From the corner of his eye he saw one move to Irina's right.

With a rifle barrel pressed into his kidney, he was marched through the tent and outside. The bright sunlight was obscured by black smoke. To his left, a coil of fire and smoke rose several hundred feet into the air.

The planes. He turned his attention to the guard in front of him, who gestured toward the south corner of the small open area. The guard behind him prodded him until he reached the edge of a stand of scrubby trees.

The guard drew a line with the toe of one boot, then pointed his rifle barrel at it. Rook stepped to the line and turned around.

The first thing he saw was Irina's pale face as she was prodded through the tent opening behind Novus Ordo. Her blue eyes were wide and dark with fear. When she spotted him, she swayed and caught at Ordo's shirt. He slung her off with a growl.

Immediately two guards grabbed her and pulled her away from their leader. One jerked her backward and shoved her toward an older woman, who grabbed her arm.

At least she was no longer beside Ordo.

Rook caught her gaze, wishing he could send her a telepathic message to reassure her. But if she could read his mind, she'd know how little reassurance he had to offer.

Then a small commotion to his left caught his attention. A man with a cloth over his head, hobbles on his feet and his hands tied behind his back was thrust into the clearing. He fell without even trying to right himself.

Ordo smiled at Rook. "That's right, Colonel." He

walked over to where the man was lying on the ground, pulled the cloth off the tethered man's head and lifted it by his hair.

It was Aaron Gold.

Rook frowned. Irina uttered a little cry.

Aaron's face was a mask of terror. A cut above his eye and a dark bruise on his cheek told Rook that Ordo hadn't welcomed him like a hero for betraying his boss and his country.

"So," Ordo said, turning to look at Rook. "Say hi to your employee of the month. I think he expected me to hand over the keys to the kingdom, or at least to a sizable reward." Ordo grinned at Rook. "Tell him why he's here."

Rook didn't speak.

"Tell him!"

Rook gritted his teeth. He didn't know how far he could push Ordo, so he answered, never taking his eyes off him. "Not even a traitor can trust a traitor."

Ordo laughed out loud. "That's right." He gestured to the guard, who yanked Aaron up and half dragged him over beside Rook.

"Tell him how lucky he is to be executed nobly, along with you."

Rook kept his mouth shut. Beside him, Aaron whimpered.

"Never mind." Novus Ordo waved a hand. "He knows. Since he's been here he's seen an example or two." He looked up at the morning sky. "Okay, let's get this show on the road. I've got a shipment of weapons coming into port in forty-eight hours. So I've got a long drive and a long flight ahead of me."

He gave an order, and ten soldiers stepped forward from various places in the clearing. They took their positions in an invisible line about twenty feet in front of Rook.

Rook lifted his head and tensed his muscles. He couldn't resist one last glimpse of Rina. When their gazes met, his heart leapt into his throat and tears burned at the backs of his eyes.

"Ready..." Ordo shouted.

Rook nodded at Rina. "Close your eyes," he whispered, but she didn't react. Of course she didn't. She couldn't hear him.

"Aim..."

Irina couldn't tear her gaze away from Rook's. He'd mouthed *Close your eyes,* but she couldn't. Wouldn't. She tried to jerk away from the old woman, to run to him and die beside him, but the woman's grip was too strong.

She waited, cringing, determined to stand strong for Rook, as Novus Ordo uttered the final word—

"Fire."

Something popped.

Rook's head jerked. Aaron screamed.

Ordo made a strangled noise, then collapsed, not two feet in front of her.

Then everyone was shouting. Gunfire burst all around her. Irina felt as if every single bullet hit her heart. Suddenly the black smoke from the downed planes swirled with white smoke from the guns and she couldn't see anything.

The old woman pulled on her sleeve, trying to force her to the ground out of the line of fire, but she had to find Rook.

The woman let go, and Irina fell to her knees, just as something hit her and knocked her backward.

"Stay down!" The command was growled and

constant gunfire obscured the words, but she knew who it was.

"Rook! Thank God!"

He slid his arm underneath hers and dragged her through the tent into the cave. "Stay!" He thrust a long rifle into her hands. "Shoot to kill. It'll keep firing as long as you hold the trigger down."

"Wait!" she shrieked, but he was already gone.

Back out there.

The guns still spat unrelenting staccato bursts. She knew the sound. From her childhood in Russia. Back then, she'd believed that her mother and father would keep her safe.

Now she knew better.

She scooted backward until the rocky cave wall stopped her. She quickly examined the heavy rifle. She'd never seen one like it, but it seemed to have all the necessary parts.

Did it matter that she'd never shot a gun like this in her life?

Hold the trigger down—it keeps shooting.

She planned to do exactly that.

ROOK CROUCHED behind the dead body of an enemy soldier and swung the barrel of his weapon around, squinting to see through the smoke. The ground was littered with bodies. He prayed none of them were his men.

He knew going in that his rescue squad would be grossly outnumbered, but it looked as if he'd been right in his assessment of the situation.

Most of Novus Ordo's rag-tag band of soldiers had scattered at the sight of Ordo with a bullet hole in the middle of his forehead. They'd probably fled to higher and more remote caves. Obviously, they were braver carrying a suicide bomb than fighting hand-to-hand.

Ordo's fatal mistake was that he hadn't recruited soldiers—he'd recruited zealots.

Rook scooted backward awkwardly, still eyeing the carnage, alert in case one of the sprawled bodies moved or another soldier came into sight.

Finally he reached the opening. With difficulty, he pushed himself up to a crouched position and cautiously stepped inside. Empty.

He ran his hand down his right pant leg, feeling the blood that soaked it. Gingerly touching the painful wound, he decided it had stopped bleeding, which was a relief.

He limped across the stone floor, planted his back against the wall and angled around, leading with the automatic rifle he'd taken off one of the casualties.

The cave was dark, the air inside it still. It felt and sounded empty. Without breathing, he turned toward the corner where he'd left Irina.

"Stop!" she cried.

He froze. "Rina? It's me."

For an instant he heard nothing. Then a small sound, like a sob. "Is it over?"

"I think so." He braced himself on his good leg and waited for her to throw herself into his arms. Once he felt her body, vibrant and warm against him, then he'd know for sure it was over. That they had survived. *Then,* he could reassure her.

But she didn't run to him. He could see her, pale skin lighter than the shadows. She stood slowly and walked carefully toward him, cradling the rifle like an expert.

"Rina, are you all right?"

Without speaking, she stepped into the thin blade of

light that shone from the cave opening. Her wide, blue eyes assessed him from head to toe. When they reached his legs, she gasped audibly, then raised her gaze to his.

"Who died in the planes?"

He gave her a small smile. "No one. They were drones. Piloted by remote control. I didn't see any Americans on the ground, either, so I'm hoping we haven't lost anyone. Most of Ordo's men have scattered. We'll never see them again. Brock and Deke should be here any time."

"You lied to me," she stated calmly.

"No, Rina—" He held out a hand, but she ignored it.

"Yes, you did." She lifted the heavy rifle to her shoulder, aimed the barrel at his eye and lay her cheek along the stock.

He didn't move. If she shot him, he couldn't blame her. But it wasn't her style. She wasn't vengeful.

After a few seconds she lowered it again. "How many times do you expect me to watch you die?"

"Rina, you have to understand—"

"I do not *have* to do anything except endure until I can get home."

He heard footsteps outside the cave. He turned, raising the rifle.

"Rook? Irina?" The voice was unmistakable.

"Deke," he said on a relieved sigh. "In here," he called.

Deke strode into the cave, dressed in desert camo with matching paint on his face. His dark eyes took in the tense scene immediately. "Everything okay?"

Rook nodded. "Anybody hurt?"

Deke shook his head. "A couple of guys got winged, but this new body armor is amazing." He nodded at

Rook's leg with a frown. "I see you weren't quite so lucky. We need to get that looked at."

He glanced at Irina. "Irina? You're all right?" he asked gently.

"I'm fine." Her voice cut the air like a bayonet.

Deke's head shot up a fraction. "O-kay. Good. Let's get you two out of here and into one of the choppers."

As if conjured by Deke's words, the slap of helicopter blades hit Rook's ears.

Irina heard them, too. She carefully set the rifle down on the floor of the cave and then addressed Deke.

"Is it safe to go out there now?"

"Yes, ma'am," Deke replied. "Brock's waiting right outside the tent."

She turned and stalked out.

Rook waited, his mouth compressed into a thin line. Sure enough, as soon as she disappeared, Deke turned on him.

"I told you to tell her."

"You're out of line," Rook said evenly. "You do *not* know my wife better than I do."

"Oh, yeah? You still think she's the innocent young daughter of Leonid Tankien that you brought out of the former Soviet Union. You still think she needs to be sheltered. But you're wrong. That's not who she is."

Rook eyed his best friend and oath brother. Something scary filled his insides. Something he'd felt only a couple of times in his life.

Self-doubt.

Deke stuck his finger in front of Rook's face. "See. You *know* I'm right. Hah. You've dug a deep hole for yourself this time, Castle. I told you not to hurt her. I hope you can dig yourself out. Now, let's get that leg bandaged—" Deke paused, enjoying himself way too much "—unless you're going to heal it with stubbornness."

Rook pushed past his best friend and strode out of the cave, mustering as much dignity as he could. He'd have done a better job of it if his damn leg hadn't been hurting so much.

Chapter Fifteen

Rook looked around the conference room at his two oath brothers. They were a little worse for wear, but they were alive.

"There was a time there when I wasn't sure we were going to make it"

Matt nodded.

Deke leaned back in his chair.

"As soon as we get back from Washington, I want each of you to take your families on a long honeymoon. You've earned it. You deserve it."

"Yeah?" Deke responded. "What about you?"

Rook looked over Deke's shoulder at the big picture window. He rubbed his chin. "I've got a couple of things I need to take care of."

"You need to take care of? What about Irina? If you want my opinion—"

He glared at his best friend. "I don't."

"Maybe not. But you need it," Deke continued. "Matt, help me out here."

Rook turned toward Matt, daring him to speak.

Matt didn't look away, but he didn't speak, either.

"Tell him, Matt. Tell him what an idiot he is, hanging on to his pride. How being too damn stubborn to admit he's wrong could lose him the best thing that ever happened to him."

Rook and Matt both turned toward their friend, whose face turned red. "Hey. It's just my opinion."

Rook shook his head. "I can't fix this. I hurt her too much. Betrayed her too many times. She'll never trust me."

Deke growled. "You don't give her enough credit. You never have."

Matt pushed back from the table. "We've only got about twenty minutes before the limos get here to take us to the airport.

"I've got to make sure Aimee and William are ready."

"Yeah," Deke responded. "I need to say goodbye to Mindy. She's not happy that the doctor won't let her fly."

"Why don't you stay with her?"

"I would if she let me. But she's threatened me with bodily harm if I don't go to D.C. to meet the president."

Rook nodded. "Thanks, guys. See you on the plane."

SHE DIDN'T LOOK ANY DIFFERENT.

Irina stared at her reflection in the mirror, disbelieving. She turned sideways. The simple teal-blue jersey dress hugged her curves exactly the same way it always had. Her silhouette wasn't any leaner—or curvier.

She leaned in closer, inspecting her face. No new wrinkles or gray hairs.

Of course it had only been three weeks since she'd

found out her dead husband wasn't dead. Twenty days. She shook her head. It felt like twenty years.

The tears started again. She hadn't been able to control them since she'd started the seemingly endless journey from Mahjidastan back to Wyoming.

She'd never cried so much in her life. Crying never helped anything, and it could be dangerous. She'd learned that during her childhood in Russia. Her mother, and later her father, had warned her countless times that if she cried, the soldiers would find them.

She yanked another tissue from the box and dabbed at her eyes, lecturing herself silently.

She heard a knock on the door to her suite.

"Come in," she called, working to keep her voice steady. "My bags are ready to go."

She quickly gathered up all the wadded tissue, cardboard packaging and other rubbish from the countertop and tossed it into the trash, looked at herself one more time and stepped out of the dressing room.

And stopped dead still.

It wasn't the limo driver come to pick up her bags.

It was Rook. He was as handsome as ever in crisply pressed khakis and a green crewneck sweater that matched his eyes. The slight bulge of the bandage on his thigh was hardly noticeable.

She pressed her lips together and braced herself to meet his gaze. He was watching her warily, unsure of what she was going to do or say.

Good. He deserved to experience the fear and uncertainty she'd lived with for the past two years.

"You look beautiful—"

"Don't," she snapped.

His jaw tensed. "The limo will be here in a half hour."

Smoothing her dress over her ribs and tummy with her palms, she took a deep breath and nodded. "I'm ready. Thank you."

He didn't move.

"There is no need for you to wait. I will be out in a few minutes. I just want to—"

"Rina, you've been crying."

"No, I haven't."

Did he have to be so observant? So gentle? She hated the way he was acting—had acted ever since they got back—as if she were fine porcelain and he was terrified she might break.

Where was the arrogant commander who took charge and damn the consequences?

"We need to talk. You haven't said two words to me since we got back. It's been eight days."

Her stupid tears were clogging her throat again. She swallowed hard. "Please go. I'll be right out there—"

"No," he barked.

Great. *Now* he pulled out his commander ammo.

She turned her back on him. "Go," she choked. "I will get my purse."

"I'm not leaving."

He'd come closer. Too close. He put his hand on her arm. Any second now she was going to break down in front of him. And he'd be proven right. She was weak. She did need his protection.

She really couldn't live without him.

She had only one line of defense left. She hadn't wanted to tell him this so soon. She'd wanted to keep it a secret as long as she could, because it was the one weapon she knew would find its mark.

The one thing guaranteed to send him hightailing it away from her like a jackrabbit from a fox.

She whirled, her face only inches from his.

"I'm pregnant," she spat. For the moment, abject terror and heavy dread dried up her tears.

He'd never wanted children. She'd always known that.

Early on, he'd listened when she brought it up. He'd never commented, but he had listened. In the months leading up to his death—his disappearance, rather—he'd refused to even talk about the possibility.

Now, standing so close to him she could feel his heat, she watched in fearful fascination as her words sank in.

His head moved almost imperceptibly, as if he were dodging a glancing blow. Then his brow wrinkled and his eyes glittered with something she couldn't identify.

"You're pregnant? How?" he shook his head.

She swallowed a giggle that could have just as easily been a sob. "How do you think?"

He shook his head slowly, dazedly. "I don't know," he muttered. "I never thought—"

He dropped his gaze to his boots and rubbed his palm across his mouth, then shook his head again. "I never—"

Rook Castle, speechless? She wasn't sure what she'd expected. Anger? Indifference? But not this uncertainty.

The adrenaline rush of fear and dread was fading and the tears were pushing their way to the surface again. She felt one slip over her lower lid and tickle its way down her cheek.

Dammit. She swiped at it.

Rook pressed his knuckles against his lips, then looked up at her from under his lashes. After a second, his gaze drifted downward to her tummy and back up.

"You're really—?"

She nodded, dislodging another tear. "I'm sorry. I

know you never did want children. I understand why. I do. It was wonderful of you to marry me. You felt responsible, and I will always appreciate that."

While she was babbling, Rook's head shot up and his brows drew down in a frown.

"Rina, what the hell are you talking about?"

His eyes were glittering strangely, and his dark, thick lashes were matted, almost as if—as if they were wet.

"I—don't know," she answered.

"I've lived my life on the edge. I never thought it would be fair to a child. Especially after I saw every day what living that way had done—was doing—to you."

"Why did you marry me?"

A knock on the door interrupted his answer.

Annoyance briefly marred his features. "In a minute," he called.

"Rina—" His tone was something between a warning and an endearment, and there she was, back in the nightmare.

Her heart stood still.

"Colonel Castle?" a deferential voice called. "The limo is here."

"Tell them to wait!"

He put his hands on either side of her head and wiped her tears away with a gentle brush of his thumbs. Then he pressed his forehead to hers.

"You know why I married you," he whispered, his breath tickling her eyelashes.

"I don't," she said, caught in her recurring dream, dreading the words she knew she was destined to say. Dreading the answer she already knew he would give.

"Tell me," she begged. It was happening just like in her dream. Oh, she was pathetic.

He sighed, then lifted his head. A jagged shadow defined the clean line of his jaw.

"I had to marry you," he said. "I thought it was the only way I could protect you."

"But what about love?" *Stop! Don't say it.* But it was too late.

"Love? Rina—" His voice rasped. "Don't you remember what I said that night in the cave?"

Her broken heart ached. Of course she did. Every word was tucked away in the farthest corner of her heart. She would remember and cherish those words forever. That didn't mean she believed them.

"You didn't believe me." An echo of her thought.

He kissed her forehead and then straightened. "I don't know how to fix this. I made a cocky, arrogant assumption, that just because I loved you, I could keep you safe."

He sighed. "I'll do whatever you want. I'll let you go. I'll stay away from my—" his voice broke harshly "—my child. But whatever you decide to do, please try to believe me. I do love you. I loved you the first moment I laid eyes on you. And I'll love you forever."

Irina could barely breathe around the squeezing of her heart. She'd wanted desperately to believe those words he'd said that night in Novus Ordo's cave. And she desperately wanted to believe him now.

But he wasn't meeting her gaze. And she knew from long experience that it meant he was holding something back. She touched his chin.

"Look at me," she said as evenly as she could. His olive-green eyes met hers. In their depths, she saw why he'd avoided her gaze. Not because he was hiding a secret.

Not this time.

What she saw was doubt—self-doubt. That was

what he was trying to hide. The fact that he was doubting himself pierced her heart like an arrow.

"No," she murmured.

Pain flickered across his features.

"No. My husband will not stay away from his child. Not for one moment—until at least she is twenty-one."

She'd read in books about people's faces lighting up, but she'd never witnessed it in real life—until this moment. Rook's face glowed with an angelic light.

"Rina?" he whispered, twirling her around and pulling her back against him. "I'm sorry—"

She put her fingers to his lips. "Shh. I accept your apology."

He kissed her shoulder, the side of her neck and her ear. Then he whispered, "You didn't let me finish."

His hands slid over her belly, where their tiny new baby lay, protected by her womb.

She laughed through tears. "Please then," she murmured, laying her head back against his shoulder and closing her eyes. "Finish."

"I'm sorry, but this—" he patted her tummy "—is not a girl. He's all boy."

Laughter bubbled up from her throat. Laughter, joy, love. She turned in his arms and lifted her face to his. "We'll see."

In one motion, Rook picked her up and headed toward the bed. But before he'd gotten two feet, a sharp pounding stopped him.

"Colonel Castle. Is everything all right? Because if we don't leave now, you're going to miss your plane to Washington. And that means you'll miss the ceremony with the president tomorrow morning."

With a growl, he set her back down.

"We're coming, right now," Irina called breathlessly.

Rook held on to her for one more second, long enough to whisper in her ear.

She laughed and shook her head. "You will do no such thing in the limo. And not on the plane, either. We have plenty of time."

Saying the words, she realized that, for the first time, she believed them.

"We have a lifetime," she whispered to herself, as her husband opened the door for her.

* * * * *

CAVANAUGH PRIDE

BY
MARIE FERRARELLA

Marie Ferrarella has written more than one hundred and fifty books, some under the name Marie Nicole. Her romances are beloved by fans worldwide. Visit her website at www.marieferrarella.com.

To Jacinta, who lights up Nik's life
and made him smile again.

Chapter 1

Detective Julianne White Bear didn't want to be here. And she was sure the four detectives looking her way in the homicide squad room didn't want her here. They weren't openly hostile, but she knew resistance when she saw it.

She couldn't blame them. She knew all about being territorial and, if the tables were turned, she would have felt exactly the same way.

But Captain Randolph had sent her here and she wasn't about to argue with the man. Years before she joined the force, she had learned to pick her battles judiciously. When she did decide to dig in and fight, the very act carried an impact.

Besides, who knew? Maybe it was fate that brought her here. Maybe this was the place where she would finally find Mary. This was where her leads had brought her.

For a moment, Julianne silently scanned the small, crammed room, assessing its inhabitants. The lone woman looked to be about her age, maybe a couple of years older. She'd been talking to two men, both of whom had a number of years on her. The man off to the other side was younger.

He was also studying her.

She wondered which one of the detectives was in charge of the newly assembled task force and how long it would be before she butted heads with him—or her.

"Can I help you?" Detective Francis McIntyre, Frank to anyone who wanted to live to see another sunrise, asked the slender, dark-haired woman standing just inside the doorway.

His first thought was that a relative of one of the dead girls had finally shown up, but something about her had him dismissing the thought in the next moment. He couldn't deny that he'd be relieved if she wasn't. Though he'd been working homicide for a while now, breaking the dreaded news to people that their child, spouse, loved one was forever lost was something Frank knew he would never get used to.

Mentally taking a breath, Julianne crossed to the good-looking detective. A pretty boy, she thought. Probably used to making women weak in the knees. She didn't get weak in the knees. Ever. She knew better.

"Actually, I'm here to help you." Saying that, Julianne held out the folder she'd brought with her from Mission Ridge's small, single-story precinct. She was acutely aware she was being weighed and measured by the tall, muscular dark-haired man with the intensely blue eyes. A glance toward the bulletin board indicated the others were following suit.

"You have some information about the killer?" Frank asked, looking at her curiously as he took the folder from her.

Was the woman a witness who'd finally decided to come forward? God knew they needed a break. Something didn't quite gel for him. Most people who came forward, whether over the phone or in person, usually sounded a little uncomfortable and always agitated. This witness—if she *was* a witness—seemed very cool, very calm. And she'd obviously organized her thoughts enough to place them into a folder.

"No, those are my temporary transfer papers—plus all the information we have about our homicide."

"'Our'?" Frank repeated, flipping open the manila folder. He merely skimmed the pages without really reading anything. Three were official-looking papers from the human resources department from Mission Ridge, the rest had to do with a dead woman, complete with photographs. As if they didn't have enough of their own.

"I'm from Mission Ridge," she told him, pointing to the heading on the page he'd opened to. "Detective White Bear, Julianne."

He frowned.

"I don't know if we have any openings in the department," he began. "And besides, I'm not the person to see about that—"

Julianne's belief in the economy of words extended

to the people who took up her time, talking. She cut him off. "It's already been arranged. My captain talked to your chief of detectives," she told him. "A Brian—"

"Cavanaugh, yes, I'm familiar with the name."

Frank was more than familiar with the name and the man, seeing as how Brian Cavanaugh had been part of his life for a very long time, starting out as his mother's squad car partner. Just recently the man had married Frank's mother and made no secret of the fact that he was absorbing Frank, his brother, Zack, and two sisters, Taylor and Riley, detectives all, into what was by now the legendary Cavanaugh clan.

He would have expected a heads-up from Brian about this turn of events, not because he was his stepfather, but because Brian was his boss.

"And just why are you being transferred here?" he asked.

"*Temporarily* transferred." Julianne emphasized the keyword, then pointed to the folder. "It's all in there."

Frank deliberately closed the folder and fixed this unusually reticent woman with a thoughtful look. "Give me the audio version."

She smiled ever so slightly. "Don't like to read?" she guessed.

"Don't like curves being thrown at me." And this one, he couldn't help notice despite the fact that she was wearing a pantsuit, had some wicked curves as well as the straightest, blackest hair he'd ever seen and probably the most exotic face he'd come across in a long time. "Why don't you tell me why you're here?" he suggested.

"I'm here because my captain and your chief of detectives seem to think that the body we found in Mission Ridge the other night is the work of your serial killer."

Frank didn't particularly like the woman's inference that the killer was Aurora's exclusive property. That placed the responsibility for the killing spree squarely on their shoulders—the squad's and his.

Damn it, they should have been able to find the sick S.O.B. by now.

He was just being edgy, Frank upbraided himself. Edgy and overly tired. Ever since he had put two and two together and realized they had a full-fledged serial killer and had gotten his new stepfather to give him the go-ahead to put a task force together, he'd been working almost around the clock. As far as he was concerned, this was *his* task force and *his* killer to bring to justice. The fact that they were getting nowhere fast tended to rob him of his customary good humor.

"And why would they think that, White Bear, Julianne?" Frank asked, echoing the introduction she'd given.

Julianne didn't even blink as she recited, "Because the woman was found strangled and left in a Dumpster. There was no evidence of any sexual activity." To underscore what she was saying, she opened the folder he still held and turned toward the crime-scene photos. "That's where your killer puts them, isn't it? In a Dumpster?"

Both questions were rhetorical. Ever since Randolph had told her he was loaning her out to Aurora, she'd read everything she could get her hands on about the serial killer's M.O. Lamentably, there hadn't been much.

"He's not my killer," Frank corrected tersely.

"Sorry," she apologized quietly. There was no emotion in her voice. "No disrespect intended."

The blonde she'd first noticed standing by the bulletin board came forward, an easy smile on her lips. The first she'd seen since entering the room, Julianne noted.

"Don't mind Frank. He gets a little testy if he can't solve a crime in under forty-eight hours. To him life is one great big Rubik's Cube, meant to be aligned in record time. I'm Riley McIntyre," the woman told her, extending her hand. "This is my brother, Frank." Riley nodded toward the two men she'd been talking with. They were still standing by the large bulletin board. Across the top of the bulletin board were photographs. Each one belonged to a different woman who had fallen victim to the Dumpster killer. There were five photographs, each heading its own column. "That's Detective John Sanchez and Detective Lou Hill." Each nodded in turn as Riley introduced them.

Julianne saw the flicker of interest in their eyes. Assessing the new kid.

How many times had that happened in her lifetime? she thought. Enough to make her immune to the process, or so she wanted to believe.

Julianne nodded politely toward the two detectives, then looked back at the smiling, petite blonde. Despite her manner, Julianne had a feeling the woman could handle herself quite well if it came down to that. "And which of you is in charge?" she wanted to know.

"That would be me," Frank told her.

Of course it would, Julianne thought. She glanced at the folder he held. "Then maybe you'd like me to read that file to you?" she offered.

This one was going to be a handful, Frank thought. Just what he *didn't* need right now. "Riley, get your new little playmate up to speed," he instructed, heading for the door.

"Where are you going?" Riley asked, raising her voice.

Frank paused only to glance at her over his shoulder, giving his sister a look that said she should be bright enough to figure that out.

It was Julianne who was first to pick up on the meaning behind the expression. He was going to the chief of detectives, she would have bet a year's pay on it—and she wasn't one who gambled lightly.

"Before you go," she called out to him, "you should know that I don't want to be here as much as you don't want me here."

"Not possible," was all he said as he exited the squad room.

"Don't mind Frank," Riley told her again. "He hasn't learned how not to take each case he handles personally." She led Julianne over to the bulletin board to bring her up to speed. "Don't tell him I said so, but he's really not a bad guy once you get to know him. Authority has made him a lot more serious than he usually is," she explained. "He's still working things out."

Julianne had always believed that, up to a point, everyone was responsible for his or her life and the way things turned out. "If he's not comfortable with it, why did he agree to be in charge?"

"Because Frank was the first one who made the connection between the latest victim and the other bodies." She gestured toward the bulletin board. "Until then, they were on their way to becoming cold cases," Riley told her. "C'mon, I'll get you settled in first. This is a pretty nice place to work," Riley assured her with feeling, a smile backing up her words.

Julianne glanced over her shoulder toward the doorway where Frank had disappeared. She supposed she couldn't blame the man for being abrupt. She wasn't exactly thrilled about all this, either. "I'm willing to be convinced."

"An open mind," Riley commented with a wide grin. "Can't ask for more than that."

Julianne thought of Mary and all the months she'd spent trying to find her seventeen-year-old cousin—afraid that when she did find her, it might be too late—if it wasn't already.

"Yeah," Julianne answered quietly, "actually, you can."

The blonde spared her a curious look, but made no comment.

Frank knocked on Brian Cavanaugh's door. "Got a minute?"

He'd waited outside the glass office, curbing his impatience, while his new stepfather had been on the phone. But the moment the chief of detectives had hung up, Frank popped his head in, attempted to snare an island of the man's time before the phone rang again or someone walked in to interrupt them.

Brian smiled. This was an interruption he welcomed, even though he had a feeling he knew what it was about. He'd known Frank, boy and man, for almost as long as he'd known Lila and was proud of the way Frank and his siblings had turned out. They were all a credit to the department—as well as to their mother.

"For you? Always." Brian beckoned his stepson in and gestured toward one of the two chairs in front of his desk. "Take a seat."

About to demure, Frank changed his mind and sat down. He looked less confrontational sitting then standing, even if he preferred the latter.

"What's up?" Brian asked.

Frank didn't beat around the bush. "Did you assign a detective from Mission Ridge to my task force?"

Brian nodded. He'd guessed right, but he hadn't expected to see Frank in his office for at least a day or so. Had he and White Bear locked horns already? Had to be some kind of a record.

"I meant to tell you, but then the mayor called with another one of his mini-emergencies. With the police chief out on medical leave, I get to wear more than one hat." With the current mayor, however, it was more a case of constant placating and hand-holding. The mayor was highly agitated about the serial killer, afraid that if the man wasn't captured soon, it would bring down his administration when elections came around in the fall. "Don't know how Andrew took it for all those years," he added, referring to his older brother, who before taking early retirement to raise his five children had been Aurora's chief of police.

And then Brian took a closer look at Frank. If the young detective clenched his jaw any harder, his teeth would pop out.

"Why? Is something wrong? You did say you could use more of a staff."

"Yes, but I meant someone from *our* homicide

division." He'd never thought someone from the outside would be brought in. He didn't have time to integrate this woman. "Maybe Taylor, or—"

"Granted, we have the superior police department," Brian agreed, tongue in cheek. Mission Ridge's police department numbered twelve in all, but he'd been given White Bear's record and found it exemplary. "But I thought, since the captain called from Mission Ridge and the killer's M.O. was exactly the same as the serial killer we're dealing with, that it wouldn't hurt to bring in a fresh set of eyes." That said, Brian leaned back in his chair to study his stepson. "Is there a problem?"

Other than feeling as if he was being invaded, no, Frank thought, there wasn't a problem. At least, not yet. And then he replayed his own words in his head before speaking. He was coming across like some kind of grumpy malcontent.

Leaning back, Frank blew out a breath and then shook his head. "No, I guess I just would have liked a heads-up."

"Sorry I couldn't give you one," Brian apologized, then added, "I'm sure that the dead women would have liked to have been given a heads-up that they were about to become the serial killer's next victims."

"Point taken," Frank murmured. Brian was right. Nothing really mattered except clearing this case and getting that damn serial killer off the streets before he killed again. If bringing in some detective from a nearby town accomplished that, so be it. And then, because it was Brian, the man who used to bring him and his siblings toys when they were little, the man who he'd secretly wished was his father when he was growing up, Frank let down his guard and told him what was really bothering him. "I just thought that maybe you thought—"

"If I didn't think you were up to the job, Frank, I wouldn't have let you head up the task force," Brian informed him. "My marrying your mother has nothing to do with what I think of you as a law-enforcement officer. And if I have something to say about your performance, I won't resort to charades—or to undermining your authority. You know me better than that," he emphasized.

"Yeah, I do," Frank agreed, feeling just a little foolish for this flash of insecurity. This, too, was new to him. Self-confidence was normally something he took for granted.

"I hear that White Bear's good," Brian continued. "Maybe what she has to contribute might help you to wind up this case."

If only, Frank thought. Out loud, he said, "Maybe," and stood up, turning toward the door. He'd wasted enough of the chief's time.

"Frank?" Brian called after him.

Frank stopped and looked at the man over his shoulder. "Yes, sir?"

"Go home at a reasonable hour tonight," Brian instructed. "Get some sleep. You're no good to me—or anyone else—dead on your feet."

Frank turned to face him again. "I'm not dead on my feet," he protested.

They both knew he was, but Brian inclined his head, allowing the younger man the benefit of the charade. "Almost dead on your feet."

The last thing he wanted was preferential treatment.

There'd already been some talk making the rounds about that. Since his mother had married Brian, there'd been rumors sparked by jealousy. He was beginning to have new respect for what the younger Cavanaughs had to put up with, working on the force.

"Just one thing." He saw Brian raise a quizzical brow. "Are you speaking as the chief of detectives, or as my new stepfather?"

Brian was not quick to answer. "Now that you mention it, both," he finally said, then leaned forward, lowering his voice. "And if you don't comply, I'll tell your mother." He punctuated his threat with a grin.

"Message received, loud and clear." For the first time in two days, Frank McIntyre grinned.

"And if you get a chance," Brian added just before his stepson went out the door, "Andrew would like to see you at breakfast tomorrow."

Everyone knew about Andrew Cavanaugh's breakfasts. More food moved from the former chief of police's stove to the table he'd had specially built than the ordinary high-traffic restaurant. The family patriarch welcomed not just his immediate family, but his nieces and nephews and their significant others as well. There was no such thing as too many people at his table and, like the miracle of the loaves and fishes, Andrew never seemed to run out of food no matter how many people turned up at his door.

"If I get the time," Frank answered.

"Make the time," Brian replied. There was no arguing with his tone.

"Is that an order, sir?"

At which point, Brian smiled. "That's just a friendly suggestion. You really wouldn't want to get on the wrong side of Andrew."

It was an empty threat. Even though everyone knew that in his day, Andrew Cavanaugh was a formidable policeman, when it came to matters concerning his family, Andrew always led with his heart. "I'll keep that in mind, sir," Frank promised.

"You do that, Frank. You do that. And don't forget to tell me what you think of this White Bear—once you give her a chance," he added knowingly.

Frank nodded. "Will do."

He still wasn't all that happy as he went back to the cubbyhole that served as the task force's work area. Becoming integrated into the Cavanaugh family was enough of an adjustment without having some outsider suddenly thrust upon him. It was the *last* thing he needed.

At any other time, he thought, pausing in the doorway and quietly observing the newest addition to his task force, he would have welcomed someone who looked like Julianne. The woman was a head-turner, no doubt about that. But he was in charge of the task force and that changed the rules.

He'd never much liked rules, Frank thought with an inward sigh, but there was no arguing the fact that he was bound by them.

Squaring his shoulders, he walked into the room.

Chapter 2

"So, did Riley get you all caught up?" Frank asked as he came up behind Julianne.

Five victims were on the board, five women from essentially two different walks of life who, at first glance, didn't appear to have anything in common. If there was a prayer of solving this case and bringing down the serial killer, each victim would require more than just a glance. More like an examination under a microscope. No way could she have even scratched the surface in the amount of time that he'd been gone.

Was he testing her?

"She gave me a thumbnail sketch of each victim," Julianne answered guardedly, watching his face for an indication of his thoughts. "It's going to take me a while to actually get caught up." She pulled a folder out from the bottom of the pile of files she'd been given and placed it on top. "While I'm at it, you might want to go over Millie Klein."

The name was unfamiliar to him. "Millie Klein?" he repeated.

"The woman found in the Dumpster in Mission Ridge," Julianne elaborated.

She leaned back in her chair as last Tuesday came rushing back at her. The woman, an estate planning lawyer, had been her first dead body. When she closed her eyes, Julianne could still see the grayish, lifeless body half buried in garbage, her bloodshot eyes open wide and reflecting surprise and horror.

"It looks like your guy was off on a field trip when he had a sudden, uncontrollable urge to kill another woman," she speculated.

"That the way you see it?" Frank asked. Crossing his arms before him, he leaned back and perched on a corner of the desk that Riley had cleared off for the Mission Ridge detective.

McIntyre studied her more intently than was warranted, Julianne thought.

Stare all you want, I'm not leaving.

"Right now, yes," she said flatly. "There's no other reason for him to have strayed from his home ground. Plenty of 'game' for him right here." She'd already gotten a list of clients that Millie had seen that week she was murdered, but so far, everyone had checked out. And every one of them lived in Mission Ridge.

"Maybe it's not the serial killer." He studied her face to see if she was open to the idea—and caught himself thinking she had the most magnificent cheekbones he'd ever seen. "People have been found in Dumpsters before this serial killer started his spree."

"Not in Mission Ridge," she informed him. "We don't have a homicide division in Mission Ridge. Stealing more than one lawn gnome is considered a major crime spree. It's a very peaceful place," she concluded.

Frank's eyes narrowed. He'd been laboring under a basic misunderstanding. "Then you're not a homicide detective?"

"I'm an all-around detective," she answered succinctly. Then, in case he had his doubts and was already labeling her a hick on top of what he probably perceived as her other shortcomings, she was quick to assure him, "Don't worry, I won't get in your way."

It didn't make any sense. Why would they send over someone with no experience? And why had Brian agreed to this? "If you don't mind my asking, why were you sent here?"

That, at least, was an easy enough question to answer. "Because Captain Randolph isn't the kind of man who sweeps things under the rug, or just lets other people do his work for him. This is kind of personal."

Riley walked by just then and without breaking her stride, or saying a word to her brother, dropped off one of the two cans of soda she'd just gotten from the vending machine, placing it on Julianne's desk. Julianne smiled her thanks as she continued.

"Millie Klein was the granddaughter of a friend of his, and he wants justice for his friend. That means seeing her killer pay for her murder. You have the superior department," she informed him without any fanfare. "It just made sense for him to send the case file over here as well as someone with it."

Okay, he'd buy that. But he had another question. "Why you?" She'd just admitted to not having experience and from the looks of her, she couldn't have been a detective *that* long. They had to have someone over at Mission Ridge with more seniority than this lagoon-blue-eyed woman.

Julianne studied him for a long moment before she said anything. "Is your problem with me personal or professional?"

"I don't know you personally."

And he knew better than to think that just because the woman was beautiful she'd gotten ahead on her looks. If he would have so much as hinted at something like that, his sisters—along with all the female members of the Cavanaugh family—would have vivisected him.

So he was saying that his beef with her was professional? She took just as much offense at that as she would have had he said it was personal.

"Professionally, I worked my tail off to get to where I am." Her eyes darkened, turning almost a cobalt blue. "And you don't need to know me personally not to like me 'personally.'" She set her jaw hard. "I've run into that all my life."

Prejudice was something he'd been raised to fight against and despise. "Because you're Native American," he assumed.

"You don't have to be politically correct," she told him. "*Indian* will do fine." The term had never bothered

her, or any of the other people she'd grown up with. She
didn't see it as an insult. "Or *Navajo* if you want to be
more specific."

"Navajo," Frank repeated with a nod. He'd bet his
badge that there was more than just Navajo to her. Those
blue eyes of hers didn't just come by special delivery.
"And you won't find that here," he informed her.

"Other Navajos?"

"No, prejudice because you happen to be something someone else isn't. I don't care if you're a
Native American—"

"Indian," she corrected.

"Indian," he repeated. "What I don't like is not
having a say in who works for me." But even that could
be remedied. "But you prove to me that you can pull
your weight, and we'll get along fine."

That sounded fair enough. "Consider it pulled,"
Julianne told him.

With that out of the way, he nodded at her desk. "I'll
look at that folder you brought now."

Julianne held the folder out to him. It was thin
compared to the ones that Riley had given her. There
was a folder complied with random notes and information on each victim posted on the board.

"You know, all that information was input on the
computer," he told her. He indicated the small notebook
computer Riley had managed to mysteriously produce
for the new detective. It had to have come from one of
the other squad rooms, but he wasn't about to ask which
one. This was a case where "Don't ask, don't tell" applied
particularly nicely. "You can access it easily enough."

Rather than draw the notebook to her, she moved the folders closer. "I like the feel of paper," Julianne told him. "If the electricity goes down, the paper is still here."

Frank laughed shortly. He didn't hear that very often, and never from anyone under thirty. "Old-fashioned?" he guessed.

She'd never thought of herself in those terms, going out of her way not to have anything to do with the old ways to which grandmother had clung.

"I prefer to say that I like the tried and true." With that, she lowered her eyes and got back to her reading.

Frank knew when to leave well enough alone.

Julianne was still going through the files and rereading pertinent parts at the end of the day, making notes to herself as she went along.

She did her best to remain divorced from the victims, from feeling anything as she reviewed descriptions of the crime scenes. She deliberately glossed over the photographs included in each file.

The photographs posted on the board showed off each victim at what could be described as her best, before the world—or the killer—had gotten to her. The photographs in the files were postmortem shots of the women. Julianne made a point of flipping the photographs over rather than attempting to study them.

"Pretty gruesome, aren't they?" Riley commented.

Julianne looked up, surprised to find Riley standing in front of her desk. She'd gotten absorbed in the last folder, Polly Barker, a single mother who made ends meet by turning tricks. Her three-year-old daughter,

Donna, had been taken by social services the day after
the woman's body was discovered. Despite her best
efforts, Julianne's heart ached, not for the mother, but
for the child the woman had left behind.

She closed the folder now. "Yes."

"I don't blame you for not wanting to look at them,
but I really think you should."

Julianne glanced at Riley, somewhat surprised
though she made sure not to show it. She'd sensed that
the other woman was watching her, but more out of curiosity than a of desire to assess the way she worked.

"Why? I've got all the details right there in the files."
She nodded at the stack.

"You're supposed to be the fresh pair of eyes," Riley
reminded her. "Maybe you'll see something we didn't."

Taking a deep breath, Julianne flipped over the set of
photographs she'd just set aside. It wasn't that she was
squeamish, just that there was something so hopeless about
the dead women's faces. She'd fought against hopelessness all of her life and if given the choice, she would have
rather avoided the photographs taken at the crime scene.

But Riley was right. She *was* supposed to be the fresh
set of eyes and although she doubted she would see something the others had missed, stranger things had happened.

The first thing she saw was a tiny cross carved into
the victim's shoulder.

Just as there had been on Millie's.

In his own twisted mind, was the killer sending his
victims off to their maker marked for redemption? Was
he some kind of religious zealot, or just messing with
the collective mind of the people trying to capture him?

After a beat, she raised her eyes to Riley's. "How long?"

Riley looked at her, confused. "How long what?"

Julianne moved the photographs away without looking down. "How long before you stopped seeing their lifeless faces in your sleep?"

Riley nodded. She knew exactly what the woman meant. "I'll let you know when it happens," Riley told her. And then she smiled. "The trick is to fill your life up so that there's no time to think about them that way. And to find the killer," she added with feeling, "so that they—and you—can rest in peace." Riley glanced at her watch. It was after five. "Shift's over. Would you like to go and get a drink?"

While she appreciated the offer, getting a drink held no allure for her. Her father had been an alcoholic, dead before his time. Her uncle, Mary's father, while not an alcoholic, was a mean drunk when he did imbibe.

Julianne shook her head. "I don't drink."

"Doesn't have to be alcohol," Riley told her. "They serve ginger ale there. And coffee." It was obvious that she wasn't going to take no for an answer easily. "I just think you need to unwind a little. And it wouldn't hurt to mingle," she added. "Might make the rest of this experience tolerable for you."

What would make the experience tolerable would be finally finding Mary, but, having kept everything to herself for most of her life, she wasn't ready to share that just yet. For a moment, Julianne debated her answer. Turning Riley down would make her seem standoffish and she didn't want to generate any hard feelings beyond the ones Frank seemed to be harboring.

"All right." She rose, closing her desk drawer. "I'll follow you."

"Great." Riley grinned, moving over to her desk to grab her purse. "I'll drive slow."

"No need. I can keep up," Julianne told her.

Riley nodded. "I bet you can."

Rafferty's was more a tavern than an actual bar. While it was true that on most nights, members of the Aurora police force went there to unwind and shed some of their more haunting demons before going home to their families, the establishment just as readily welcomed spouses and their children. In many cases it was a home away from home for detectives and patrol officers alike.

And Rafferty's was also where, on any given evening, at least several members of the Cavanaugh family could be found.

This particular evening there were more than a few Cavanaughs in the bar and Riley made a point of introducing Julianne to all of them, as well as her older brother, Zack.

"Taylor's probably out on a date," Riley told her matter-of-factly, carrying a mug of beer and an individual bottle of ginger ale over to the small table she'd staked out for the two of them as soon as they'd walked in.

Julianne took a seat, accepting the ginger ale. Riley had refused to let her pay. "Taylor?"

"My sister." Riley sat down opposite her. "She's the social butterfly of the family. Like Frank," she tagged on as an afterthought. "Or he was until he got assigned to this case."

After having met the man, it was hard for Julianne to picture Frank McIntyre as anything but solemn. Except for that one instance, he hadn't smiled during the course of the day, not even when the smaller of the two detectives, Sanchez, had made a joke.

Keeping her observation to herself, Julianne scanned the crowded room. As she recognized faces, it struck her that she'd been introduced to more people than she'd realized.

"And you're related to these people?" she asked Riley, slightly in awe as the fact sank in.

Riley nodded, taking a sip of her beer before answering. "Through marriage," she qualified, although she'd gotten to know a great many of them from day-to-day interaction ever since she joined the police force. "My mother is married to the chief of detectives, Brian Cavanaugh. Real good guy," she said with a wide, approving smile. Brian was the man her mother was meant to have married. He treated her far better than the man who had fathered all four of her children. Brian Cavanaugh was the man she herself had always pretended was her father, when times became rocky. "They used to be partners back when they were on patrol."

Julianne looked at her in surprise. "Your mother was on the job, too?" This police department really *was* a family affair, she thought. It made her feel even more of an outsider than usual.

"Yes. Almost everyone I know is on the job," Riley told her.

It was on the tip of Riley's tongue to mention her late

father, but since his career ended in disgrace, she decided not to go into something she didn't really want to talk about. Besides, if Julianne remained on the task force long enough, she was pretty sure the woman would hear about it from one source or another. Facts had come to light not all that long ago about how her father had faked his own death and bided his time to come back for the money he'd stolen from drug runners. That wasn't something to discuss with a stranger.

"My father made her quit the force after she was shot—"

"Shot?" Julianne echoed.

Riley nodded. The story was so much a part of her life, sometimes she forgot that not everyone knew about it. "While on the job. Brian saved her. Stopped the blood with his own hands and all but willed the life back into her as he waited for the paramedics."

"I can see why your father wanted her to quit."

He had pressured her mother to leave the force because he was jealous of Brian, not because he feared for her life, but Riley kept that to herself as well.

"Being off the force didn't suit her. Being a law-enforcement officer was in her blood so, once Frank was in high school, she got back into it. To keep peace in the family, she took a desk job, but she figured that was better than nothing." She took another sip, then added, "I guess you just can't keep a good cop down."

Julianne heard the pride in Riley McIntyre's voice and a trace of envy surfaced.

What was that like, she wondered, being proud of your parents? Of what they'd done and were doing, and the effect all that had on the lives of other people? She would have given *anything* to experience that.

But there was no sense in wishing. Those weren't the cards that fate had dealt her and she'd already made her peace with that years back.

There'd been no other choice, really, except maybe to wind up the way her father had. But she absolutely refused to go down that road and let that happen. Pride wouldn't allow her to.

"How's it going?"

The deep, baritone voice asking the question came from behind her. Rather certain the question wasn't directed at her, Julianne still turned around in her chair to see who was doing the asking. She found herself looking up at yet another law-enforcement officer. He wasn't in uniform, but there was just an air about that man that fairly shouted: authority. He was older and had a kind, intelligent face, not to mention a handsome one. He also had the ability to take over a room the moment he entered.

She guessed his identity a second before he told her.

Smiling, Brian extended his hand to her. "Brian Cavanaugh," he said easily, as if he was just another cop on the force rather than the chief of detectives. Julianne started to get up out of respect for the man and his rank, but he waved her back into her seat. "No need for that," he told her. "I stopped by the task force and Sanchez told me that Riley was bringing you here for a quick orientation session," he laughed.

His deep blue eyes scanned the room quickly. "They're a bit overwhelming at first," he agreed. "But they grow on you." He turned his eyes on her again. "Glad to have you aboard for the ride."

Something about the man made her feel comfortable. As much as she was able to be.

"Glad someone is." The words came out before she could tamp them down. Living off the reservation had made her lax, she upbraided herself.

"Don't let Frank get to you," Riley said. "He's channeled all his usual enthusiasm into solving the case and I know he can come on strong sometimes, but there's the heart of a puppy underneath," she guaranteed. Turning around, she saw the door opening. "Speak of the devil."

"Riley," Brian laughed, "that's no way to talk about your brother."

"No offense, Brian, but you don't know him like I do." And then she winked at Julianne, as if they shared a secret.

Julianne wondered what it meant. Before she could make a comment or frame a question, she saw that Frank was crossing the room.

And coming straight toward them.

All her natural defenses instantly rose.

Chapter 3

Riley dramatically placed her hand to her chest, like a heroine in a 1950s melodrama, feigning shock.

"I didn't think I'd see you here, mingling with the masses," she said to her brother as Frank approached their table.

Frank spared her a slight, reproving frown. He was bone tired and desperately in need of unwinding. "Give it a rest, Riley. This is after hours."

Stealing an empty chair from the next table, he pulled it over to the one occupied by his sister and Julianne. He straddled the chair and folded his arms over the back.

Raising his hand, he made eye contact with the bartender and nodded. The barkeep took a mug and filled it with beer on tap and handed it to the lone waitress working the floor. Only then did Frank look at the detective from Mission Ridge and ask, "Mind if I join you?"

"No, I don't mind," she answered crisply. "I was on my way out, anyway." Rising from her chair, she nodded at Riley. "Thanks for the ginger ale and the introductions."

"Don't mention it," Riley replied, doing her best to hide her amusement.

"I'll walk you out," Brian volunteered, then told his stepchildren, "I promised your mother I'd be home early tonight. I just wanted to stop by and see how the new detective was doing." And then he smiled at Julianne. "From the looks of it, I'd say she's doing just fine."

Not accustomed to compliments, Julianne murmured a barely audible, "Thanks," before turning on her heel and heading for the front door.

Brian was right beside her.

"Well, that's a first," Riley said the moment she judged that Julianne was out of earshot. She looked at her brother with no small amazement. "I don't think I ever saw a woman go out of her way to get away from you before."

Frank handed the waitress a five and then picked up the mug she'd placed on the table in front of him. He shrugged, dismissing the incident. "She said she was leaving anyway."

"She only said that *after* you sat down," Riley pointed out. The waitress cleared away Julianne's ginger ale and made her way back to the bar. "Face it, Frank, you're losing your charm."

Frank eyed his sister over the rim of his mug. "I'm also losing my patience with smart-alecky sisters." He took a long sip, then added, "If you weren't so damn good at your job, Riley, I'd have you taken off the task force."

To which Riley merely shook her head, as if at a loss whether to pity him or hand his head to him. "Careful, Frank, this job is turning you sour." And then she leaned in, her expression becoming more serious. "Really, Frank, lighten up a little. You're trying too damn hard."

They had a difference of opinion there. He'd had the case for over a month and in that time, they'd compiled nothing but data. Data and no viable suspects. And he had an uneasy feeling they were running out of time.

"Way I see it, I'm not trying hard enough." His expression turned grim. "The killer's still out there somewhere, daring us to catch him. Every second he's out there is a second less the next victim has."

"We'll get him," Riley said confidently. "*You'll* get him," she emphasized. It wasn't often that she told him she thought he was good. But he was. "Just don't alienate everyone else while you're doing it."

Rising, he turned his chair around so that he could sit in it properly. He sighed and picked up the mug again. Another long sip didn't change anything. "Sometimes I think I'm in over my head."

"We all are." Riley laughed shortly. "This is where the dog paddle comes in *really* handy. We're all just treading water until the killer makes a mistake. When he does, we've got him."

The shrug was careless. He didn't know if he bought into that philosophy. So far, the killer had been anything but careless. It was as if he was a ghost, depositing lifeless bodies into Dumpsters. Six in all, counting the one in Mission Ridge, and *nobody* had seen him.

To get his mind off the case, Frank changed the subject. "So, did you learn anything about the detective from Mission Ridge?" he asked, doing his best to sound offhanded.

Riley slanted a glance at her brother's face. There was interest there, she'd bet a month's pay on it. Personal probably although he'd try to keep it professional.

"Not a thing, except that she's thorough." The woman had studied the files without getting up from her desk all afternoon. "But she's not exactly chatty."

"Yeah, well, that might be a nice change," he speculated, looking at her deliberately.

Riley swatted him.

"Hey," he warned, pulling his head back. "You're not supposed to hit your superior."

"We're off duty, remember?" Riley countered. "You've got to learn how to turn it off, little brother, or it'll take you apart."

Frank said nothing to confirm or deny the wisdom of her words. Instead, he just took another sip of his beer and thought about the woman fate—and his stepfather—had brought into his life.

Julianne could have driven back home. "Home" was only about forty-two miles away. But in the interest of time, Julianne had decided to rent a room in a hotel close to the police headquarters.

Taking the suitcase she'd thrown together last night out of the trunk of her car, she walked into the Aurora

Hotel, a wide, three-story building that, from the outside, resembled one of those 24/7 gyms that had become the rage.

The decor inside could have used a little modernizing and upgrading. But in comparison to what she'd lived with when she was growing up, it was on par with the Taj Mahal.

The lobby was empty. No one sat in the five chairs scattered about, their gray color all but fading into the equally gray rug. The bored, sleepy-eyed desk clerk came to life as she approached the front desk, obviously grateful for any diversion that would make this long, drawn-out evening move a little faster to its conclusion.

Ten minutes later, with her keycard in her hand, Julianne got out on the third floor and walked to her room. As uninspired as the lobby, it at least gave the semblance of cleanliness, which was all she required. Setting her suitcase down by the pressboard writing desk, she didn't bother unpacking. There was time enough for that later.

Right now, she had a job to do, which was the real reason she hadn't balked at being loaned out to an adjacent police department. She had streets to drive up and down, people to question and show the picture she carried with her at all times.

Throwing some water into her face, Julianne was ready. Dinner would be fast food. She didn't care what; it was just fuel anyway.

She wasn't one to believe in miracles, but, as she'd said to Riley, she liked to think that she had an open mind about things. Silently, she challenged God to prove her wrong about miracles. Someone had told her that finding Mary would come under the heading of a miracle.

Mary.

Her cousin was out there somewhere because living on the street was preferable to living at home, subjected to nightly abuse at the hands of a father who didn't deserve the name. "Monster" would have been a far more fitting title.

But he would never bother anyone again. Events had arranged themselves so that she could make that claim to Mary—when she found her—with certainty.

She hadn't gone over to her uncle's house to kill him even though she'd wished the man dead more than once. But when he'd come at her the way she knew in her heart that he had come at Mary time and again, she'd had no choice but to defend herself any way she could.

Julianne wasn't even sure just how the knife had come into her hand. She only knew that when she'd told him she'd use it if he didn't back off, her uncle had laughed at her. He'd mocked her, saying that she was just as cowardly as her father had been.

And then he'd told her what he'd do to her for daring to point the knife at him. She remembered her blood running cold. Remembered feeling almost paralyzing guilt for not having taken Mary with her before her cousin had been forced to run away.

Her uncle had lunged at her, knocking the knife from her hand and screaming obscenities at her. There'd been a struggle for possession of the weapon. They'd wrestled and though to this day she wasn't certain how it happened, somehow the blade had wound up in his chest—up to the hilt.

Her first inclination had been to run. But she knew she could never outrun her own conscience, so she'd gone in to the captain without bothering to change her torn clothing. Numb, in shock, she'd told him the whole story.

People who lived in the vicinity knew the kind of man her uncle had been. In short order, Harry White Bear's death was ruled self-defense, and she was free to go on with her life.

Her search for Mary began that day.

She wanted to bring her cousin home with her, the way she should have done right from the beginning instead of fleeing herself and leaving Mary behind. She'd left because her uncle had made advances, but she'd never, in her wildest dreams, thought that he would force himself on his own daughter.

That was when she still believed that there was some good in everyone.

She didn't believe that anymore.

Julianne wanted to find Mary to let her know that she didn't have to look over her shoulder anymore, that her father wasn't going to hurt her again, that she could become something other than a woman who lived on the streets.

"I'm going to make it up to you, Mary. Somehow, someway, I'm going to make it up to you," she murmured to the photograph she'd placed face up on the passenger seat. "But first, I've got to find you."

Julianne knew she had a long night ahead of her. It didn't matter. All that mattered was finding Mary.

* * *

The next morning, after only about four hours of sleep, Julianne was at her desk by seven-thirty. She wanted to go over the last of the files she hadn't gotten to the previous day.

When she heard someone entering the squad room shortly after she arrived, Julianne was surprised. From what she'd been told, the detectives came in at eight-thirty. She'd assumed that she'd have some time to herself before the room filled up with noise.

Her surprise doubled when she looked up and found Frank standing over her desk. Something instantly tightened inside of her. Every nerve ending had inexplicably gone on high alert and she wasn't completely sure why.

"Can I help you?" she asked, successfully stripping her voice of all emotion and the tension.

He studied her for a moment before asking, "Whose picture were you showing around on McFadden last night, White Bear?"

The question caught her utterly off guard. Stunned, Julianne couldn't answer him immediately. How had he known where she was last night? Was he following her? That had to be it, but why?

A sudden thrust of anger surged through her. This wasn't going to work. She wanted out. Her eyes narrowed. "You were spying on me?"

He heard the accusation in her voice, but managed not to rise to the bait. While she was part of his task force, he was accountable for her. He needed to know exactly what he was getting himself into. "I was driving down McFadden when I saw you."

Julianne pressed her lips together, trying to choose her words carefully. She had a temper, but most of the time managed to bury it. Now it was closer to the surface than usual. She wasn't sure she believed him, and yet, what sense did it make for him to be spying on her?

For now, she gave him the benefit of the doubt—as long as he could answer her question to her satisfaction. "What were you doing there?"

How had this gotten turned around to be about him? Still, he'd learned that in order to get something, you had to give something. So rather than pull rank, which he was obviously entitled to do, he answered her question.

"I was retracing what I thought might have been the last victim's steps. What were *you* doing there?"

He waited to see what kind of an answer she'd give him. It didn't seem plausible that she would be out, her first night on the case—her first night in Aurora—showing around one of the victim's photographs to the ladies of the evening on that particular corner of the world.

She hated being accountable to anyone. It had taken her a while before she could trust Captain Randolph and follow instructions. This was not going to be easy. But she owed it to Randolph to try. The man had put his reputation on the line and taken her side during the investigation into her uncle's death.

"Asking questions," she replied tersely.

His eyes never left hers. It impressed him that she didn't flinch or look away. "Isn't that a little in the over-achiever range?"

She shrugged carelessly. "The sooner this case gets

solved, the sooner I can go back to Mission Ridge—and get out of your hair."

"Very noble of you," he commented. She wasn't sure she detected a note of sarcasm in his voice. And then he pressed, "So that's all you were doing? Showing one of the victim's photographs around?"

She raised her chin, silently daring him to disprove her. "Yes."

His eyes pinned her. "Which one?"

Julianne blinked, her mind scrambling for a name. She stalled for time. "Excuse me?"

"Which victim?" he asked. "Which victim's picture were you showing around? Seems like a simple enough question." The longer she didn't give him an answer, the less he believed her.

Damn him. She didn't like being cornered. It took Julianne only half a beat to make a selection. He wouldn't know the difference. Not unless he'd gotten out of the car and questioned the hookers she'd talked to after she was gone. And even then, he wouldn't get an answer. Some of them seemed pretty out of it.

"That one." Julianne pointed to the photograph of a somewhat bedraggled woman whose picture was heading up the third column.

He turned to look, then approached the bulletin board. "That's Andrea Katz. She was a computer programmer for Dulles and Edwards." He looked back at Julianne. "Why would you be asking around about her there? Andrea Katz wasn't found anywhere near that part of town."

Why was he pushing this? "Okay, so it was the one next to her."

Again, he turned just to verify what he already knew. He'd gone over and over this board time and again, searching for the one connection he needed. The women's likenesses were all embossed in his brain.

"Ramona Hernandez. Hooker. Found in a Dumpster behind a diner in the older part of the city," he recited. "Want to try again?" he asked cheerfully.

It was getting harder and harder to hang on to her temper. "What do you want from me, McIntyre?"

"The truth, White Bear. I'd like the truth. Is that too much to ask?"

He was crowding her space. She was a very, very private person, one who had trouble filling out anything beyond her name on a form, feeling that it was her business, not anyone else's. But what harm would telling him do, Julianne silently argued with herself. And if it would get him off her back, maybe telling him would be worth it.

"Okay," she bit off the word. "In my off hours, I thought I'd try to find my cousin, Mary. Mary White Bear. She's a runaway. Just before I left Mission Ridge, someone told me that they thought they saw her in Aurora." Again Julianne lifted her chin pugnaciously. He'd agitated her and part of her was almost spoiling for a fight. "Satisfied?"

Questions about the woman before him began materializing in Frank's head at a prodigious rate. "No."

Her eyes narrowed into annoyed slits. "Well, there's nothing I can do about that, is there?"

Now there they had a difference of opinion. He allowed a smile to curve his mouth. "You could tell me why you thought you had to lie about that and keep it to yourself."

She hadn't told Randolph about Mary and she got along with the Captain fairly well. Julianne couldn't see herself voluntarily sharing something so personal with a stranger. She shrugged carelessly, combing her fingers through her hair and sending it back over her shoulder. She said the first thing that came to mind. "I figured you wouldn't want me distracted."

"I don't," he agreed firmly. "But what you do in your time away from the job is none of my business." And then, because there was an aura of danger about this woman he needed to find out more about, he qualified his statement. "Unless you wind up killing someone."

Julianne looked at him sharply, adrenaline rushing through her veins. Had he looked into her background? Did he know about her uncle?

Frank saw the heightened awareness, saw the wary look that entered her eyes. White Bear, he realized, just might be capable of anything. If she turned out to be a loose cannon, he wanted her off his task force. "*Did* you wind up killing someone last night?"

"No."

Well, that was a relief. But he was still going to keep an eye on her. Ordinarily, that wouldn't have been a hardship. But her looks were distracting and he couldn't afford to be distracted, not until the killer was caught and this case was closed.

"Okay then, I've got no problem with you looking for your cousin during your downtime." Turning away from her, he began to walk toward the cubicle that served as his office. "Can I see it?"

"See what?" she asked warily.

This woman trusted no one, he thought, as more questions about her came to mind—the first being why was she so distrustful? "The photograph you were showing around. Maybe I've seen her," he added when she made no effort to retrieve the photograph from her purse.

Maybe he had, Julianne thought.

No stone unturned, remember?

She was going to have to do something about her defensiveness, Julianne silently upbraided herself, taking her purse out of the desk's bottom drawer. Opening it, she pulled out the photograph of her cousin and held it up to him.

The girl in the photograph looked like a younger version of Julianne. She had incredibly sad eyes. "Pretty girl," he commented.

"She would have been better off if she wasn't," Julianne answered grimly, looking at the photograph herself.

"Meaning?"

Julianne raised her eyes to his. "Meaning that she looked a lot like my dead aunt. And the first one who noticed was my uncle."

Her tone of voice had Frank quickly reading between the lines. Incest was a crime he could never quite wrap his head around. It was just too heinous. "So she ran away from home before he—"

"No," Julianne contradicted angrily, "she ran away from home *after* he…"

She deliberately let her voice trail off without finishing the sentence, but there was no mistaking her meaning.

Frank took a breath. Maybe that was why this woman was so angry. It would have certainly made him angry to have a cousin of his violated by the very person who was supposed to protect her.

"Sorry to hear that," he said, his voice as full of feeling as hers was monotone.

She thought he honestly meant that and it made her regret the tone she'd taken with him. When she reached for the photograph he was still holding, he didn't surrender it immediately.

"Why don't I have copies made of this?" Frank suggested. "Pass it around to the beat cops. Maybe one of them will see her and get back to us."

Us. It was on the tip of her tongue to say that she hadn't asked for his help, but she swallowed the words. She had to start trusting someone somewhere along the line or she was just going to wind up self-destructing. That wasn't going to help Mary at all.

Julianne pressed her lips together. Time to take the hand that was reaching out to her, she silently ordered. Taking it didn't automatically make her weak.

"That would be good, yes," she agreed.

But just as he began to head for the copy machine, the phone on Riley's desk rang. Since he was closer to it than Julianne was, Frank picked it up.

"McIntyre."

Julianne saw his face darken as he listened. His eyes went flat.

"We'll be right there," he said grimly before hanging up. "C'mon," he told her, putting the photograph down on her desk. For now, it was going to have to wait. "They just found another body."

Chapter 4

The Dumpster was clear across town behind a popular restaurant that served Chinese cuisine, buffet style.

Gin-Ling's was a popular food source for the homeless. Confronted with the all-you-can-eat philosophy, more than half the patrons who came to Gin-Ling's had a tendency to overload their plates. Discovering that their stomachs weren't really as large as they'd surmised usually followed shortly thereafter. Since the restaurant didn't provide doggie bags, most people left the uneaten portions on their plates.

Most evenings, the twin Dumpsters behind Gin-Ling's were filled to overflowing.

This time, one of them was more "overflowing" than the other.

Parking his Crown Victoria sedan at the end of the

alley bordering the crime scene, Frank got out. As he began to make his way to the Dumpster where the newest gruesome discovery had been made by a homeless man with, it turned out, a very weak stomach, he pulled a pair of rubber gloves out of his pocket and started to put them on.

Mentally, Frank wished he had coveralls on instead of the suit he was wearing. But when he'd dressed this morning, he hadn't been planning on undertaking a safari through a Dumpster.

Just before he reached the Dumpster under scrutiny, Frank glanced toward Julianne and saw that she was putting on her own pair of plastic gloves. He noted that her mouth was set grimly and recalled what Riley had told him last night. The detective from Mission Ridge wasn't used to homicides.

"You up to this?" he asked her suddenly.

Busy taking in everything around her, significant or otherwise, it took Julianne a second to realize that McIntyre was talking to her.

"Excuse me?"

He stopped walking. "Riley said that you mentioned that the woman who was killed in Mission Ridge was your first dead body." These things could be pretty unsettling and he didn't want to be sidetracked by a detective throwing up her breakfast.

Julianne wasn't sure where the detective was going with this, only that she probably wasn't going to like it. "So?"

"So," he continued patiently, "if you'd rather sit this

out—until at least the rest of the team gets here—I understand."

Right. He understood. And then he'd use that against her to send her back. She didn't need those kinds of favors. She was here and she planned to remain here until she found Mary and, oh yes, helped to find the serial killer as well.

"Thank you but there's no need to worry about me," she told him coolly. "And Millie Klein wasn't my first dead body," she informed him. "Just my first homicide."

Her uncle had been the first dead person she'd seen. And that scene had been made that much more brutal because he was dead by her hand. Blood had been everywhere. She could still see him staring down at the knife, anger and shock on his face as the life force fled from his veins.

But there was no way she was about to go into that now.

Frank could sense she was holding something back. He had a feeling that if she were drowning, White Bear'd throw the life preserver back at his head, determined to save herself on her own. Pride was a good thing, but there was such a thing as too much of it. For the time being, he let it go.

"Okay."

As he approached the Dumpster, he saw that the crime scene investigators had already been called in. A slight, younger man was busy snapping photographs of the area directly surrounding the one Dumpster, while another man, older and heavyset, was inside the Dumpster. Wrinkling his nose involuntarily against the pungent smell, he was taking close-ups of a woman who could no longer protest.

Overturning a wooden crate that, if the image painted on the side was correct, had once contained bean sprouts, Frank pushed the box next to the Dumpster and used it as a step to facilitate his getting into the Dumpster. The thought of just diving in seemed somehow repugnant.

The smell of death and rotting food assaulted him. Still, a job was a job. The first thing he noticed, before he climbed in, was the wig. A blond wig, obviously belonging to the victim, had slipped halfway off her head.

The second thing he noticed was the woman's face.

He'd seen that face before. Less than an hour ago.

Stunned at the way fate sometimes toyed with them, he turned to see that Julianne was gamely about to follow suit, waiting her turn to use the wooden crate as a stepstool.

"Stay back," he ordered.

The barked commanded caught her off guard. "Why? I said I can handle it."

Not this. "I don't think so," he told her tersely. There was no arguing with his tone.

Except that she refused to be browbeaten. Nor would she accept any special treatment that he could later hold over her head.

"Why don't you let me decide that?" It was a rhetorical question and she didn't wait for an answer. Bracing her hands on the front of the Dumpster, she was about to vault in.

"Might get crowded in here," the investigator speculated.

"White Bear, I said get back," Frank ordered angrily.

He shifted, trying to block her view, but it was too late. Because that was when Julianne saw her. Saw the face of the serial killer's latest victim.

She could almost feel the blood draining out of her face. "Mary."

Frank jumped down from his perch in time to catch her as her knees gave out.

Julianne vaguely felt arms closing around her even as fire and ice passed over her body. For a split second, the world threatened to disappear into the black abyss that mushroomed out all around her.

Only the steeliest of resolves enabled her to fight back against the darkness, against the overwhelming nausea that almost succeeded in bringing up her hastily consumed dinner from last night.

Sucking in air, Julianne struggled against the strong arms that held her prisoner.

"I'm all right," she insisted, hot anger mingling with hot tears she damned herself for shedding. "I'm all right," she repeated, almost shouting the words at Frank.

The sound of an approaching car had Frank looking down the alley. He recognized Riley's vehicle. "Look, why don't I have Riley take you back?" he suggested kindly.

She bristled at what she thought was pity. "No." The word tore from her throat like a war cry. Shrugging out of Frank's hold, willing her legs to stiffen, Julianne moved back to the Dumpster. "I'm not going anywhere," she cried defiantly.

"You're off the case, White Bear," he told her tersely.

Her head snapped around and she glared at him. "No, I'm not," she insisted. "You can't do that."

Oh, but he could. And he had to. "You're related to the victim."

Her eyes blazed and she took out all the pain she was feeling on him. "You wouldn't have known that if you hadn't invaded my privacy."

He wasn't going to get sucked into nitpicking. "Doesn't change anything. You can't—"

Suddenly grabbing his arm, Julianne dragged him over to the side, away from the investigator who had made no secret of listening to the exchange. It killed her to beg, but if she had to, she would.

"Please, I'm asking you not to take me off the case. That girl in the Dumpster is the only family I have. I had," she corrected. Even as she said it, she could feel her heart twisting in her chest. *I'm sorry, Mary. I'm so sorry.* "She's in there because of me."

"How do you figure that?"

"You're not going to be satisfied until I rip myself open in front of you, are you?"

This woman could raise his temper faster than anyone he'd ever encountered, but his aim wasn't to irritate her. He had only one focus. "My only interest is in solving the case. Now if you have anything to contribute that might be helpful—"

The words, propelled by her guilt, rushed out. "If I'd taken her with me instead of leaving her with her father, she wouldn't have run away, wouldn't have tried to support herself by resorting to the world's oldest profession."

He didn't buy that. There was *always* another choice.

"Lots of other ways for a woman to earn a living besides that," he told her.

Julianne knew she would have never resorted to that, but she wasn't Mary. Mary's demons had branded her. "Not if she thinks she's worthless. Her father didn't just steal her innocence, he stole her soul. And I let him." She pointed toward the Dumpster. "That's on me."

His eyes held hers. Frank could all but feel her misery. "You knew what was going on?"

"No, but I should have." If she hadn't been so involved in making a life for herself, she would have realized what was going on, would have understood the desperate look in Mary's eyes.

If there was the slightest case for her staying, he thought, White Bear wasn't going to do either of them any good by blaming herself for something she had no control over.

"Listen, I'm not up on my Navajo culture, but I don't recall hearing that the tribe had a lock on clairvoyance. If you didn't know, you didn't know. What happened to your cousin isn't your fault." But he could see that his words made no impression on her. It was as if they bounced off her head.

He had to let her work the case. He *had* to. "Please don't take me off the case. I've got to find her killer. I owe it to Mary."

"Hey, anything wrong?" Riley called out as she came up to join them. Sanchez and Hill stood directly behind her. Both veered over to the Dumpster that had become Mary's final resting place. Their expressions grim, each detective pulled on a pair of plastic gloves.

Frank saw the unspoken plea in Julianne's eyes as she looked up at him. This was, for the time being, still between the two of them. Being leader sucked, he thought. But there was no way he was about to relinquish the position.

"Turns out White Bear's got a delicate stomach," he told his sister after a pause. "I'm trying to tell her she doesn't have to look at the victim. Plenty to do around here besides staring at a dead woman."

"No shame in that," Riley assured her. "First murder victim I saw, I emptied out my stomach and didn't eat for a week. Frank's right," she continued, placing herself between Julianne and the Dumpster. "There're enough people to document the vic's position and whatnot." She looked at her brother. "Want us to canvas the area?"

The question was a mere formality. She knew procedure as well as Frank. Better probably. But since he was the lead on this, in front of others she'd played along.

"Good a start as any," Frank commented.

He turned back to the Dumpster, intent on doing his own examination of the immediate area as well as getting as concise an overview of the victim as possible.

As he crossed back to the Dumpster, he saw Sanchez stand up and look at him over the side. It was obvious by his grimace that this was *not* the other detective's favorite place to be.

"There's no ID on the vic from what I can see, Frank," Sanchez called out.

"We've got an ID," Frank informed him. "Her name was Mary."

"Mary?" Hill echoed. The older detective clambered

out of the Dumpster. He was less than graceful. "Mary what?" he asked, trying to brush some of the debris off his clothing.

"For now, just Mary," Frank said.

Tagging the victim White Bear would bring immediate focus on the Mission Ridge detective in exactly the fashion she didn't want. He hadn't made up his mind about her. And, he had to admit to himself, in all honesty, he sympathized with what she had to be feeling.

Behind them, the coroner's vehicle pulled up at the mouth of the alley, ready to take victim number seven to the morgue.

Frank turned to glance in Julianne's direction. He saw her looking at him. Very deliberately, she mouthed, "Thank you," before turning away and following Riley to the front of the restaurant.

Don't thank me yet, White Bear, he thought.

Julianne caught a ride back to the precinct with Riley rather than Frank even though she'd initially arrived with him. She was grateful that Riley didn't press her to talk, respecting the fact that she needed some time to process what had happened. She was sure Riley just believed she was traumatized about seeing a murder victim.

Eventually, she had to tell the woman that the serial killer's latest victim was her cousin. Right now, she couldn't bring herself to talk about it. Or Mary. She needed to pull herself together and focus. One thing she knew: She wasn't going home until Mary's killer was caught.

By the time she walked into the room the task force had taken over and made their own, there were two bulletin boards in the room instead of one. Mary's photograph was pinned to the new board. Rather than the unsettling crime-scene photographs, Frank had used the one that she'd brought with her. The one she'd used to show the prostitutes last night.

If only one of them had remembered seeing Mary, maybe she could have gotten to her before …

She was going to drive herself crazy, Julianne silently reprimanded. She had to deal with what *was,* not with what might have been.

It almost hurt her to look at Mary's photograph. Despite the sad eyes, Mary was smiling in the photograph. She had been so young, so pretty. The whole world could have been at her feet had she been allowed to grow up like any normal girl.

It wasn't fair, Julianne thought angrily. It just wasn't fair.

Like someone in a trance, she walked up to the second bulletin board because the one they had had grown too crowded to handle any more victims. Right now, Mary's photograph was the only one on it.

How long would that last?

In the middle of saying something to Hill, Frank abruptly stopped and crossed over to her. "I need you to fill me in on things."

She was grateful that McIntyre was letting her stay, but a wariness crept over her nonetheless. "What things?" she asked.

Because her connection was going to be kept private for the time being, he lowered his voice. "You said she was your only family."

"Yes?" The single word inferred that he had heard correctly.

Same confounding pattern, he thought. "Then she had no brothers or sisters, nobody to ask after her, except for you?"

Where was he going with this? She didn't like moving blindly into something. "Right."

"Just like the others," Frank murmured under his breath, looking at the first bulletin board.

"The others?" She'd read through all the files, but didn't recall seeing that each woman was an only child. Was he referring to something else?

"The other victims," Frank clarified. "That's the only thing they had in common." He looked from one photograph to another, thinking what a terrible waste it all was. "None of the women had anyone in their lives to ask after them if they suddenly went missing."

Julianne took offense at his statement. "She had me," she protested.

He pointed out the obvious. "But you didn't know where she was. So you weren't a presence," he said matter-of-factly. "Or a factor. All these other women, they were all single, or divorced."

"Our second victim was a widow," Riley reminded him, walking into the room from the opposite end. She tossed down her purse on her desk, weary beyond reason. She hated coming up against dead ends and that was all their canvassing had yielded: dead ends.

Frank shrugged. "Same difference. For all intents and purposes, they were all alone. No immediate family in the area to ask about them if they suddenly vanished.

Employers assumed they were taking a sick day. And who misses a hooker?" He deliberately avoided looking at Julianne as he posed the question. "A cold trail is harder to follow than a hot one," he concluded.

His eyes swept over the photographs thoughtfully. There *had* to be something else. Something that tied them together. Something they were all missing. But what?

"Maybe he just picks them at random," Hill suggested. That had been his theory all along.

But Frank shook his head. "One or two, maybe. But the chances of all seven of them being loners is astronomical," he insisted. "No, the killer hand selected them."

"Okay, assuming you're right," Julianne said, crossing her arms before her, waiting to be convinced. "Why? Why these particular women and not another group?"

"If we knew that, we could narrow our search, couldn't we?" Frank countered, banking down a wave of sarcasm before it entered his voice.

He looked at her for a long moment, still not certain he was doing the right thing by letting her remain on the task force. Rules dictated that he take her off if she had a personal stake in it and this was really personal.

"I need to talk to you in private," he said abruptly, walking into the hall.

Those were the exact words the principal had used the day he'd called her into his office. He called her in to tell her that her father was found dead. She was eighteen and four days away from graduating high school.

Julianne struggled against the chill that slipped down her spine now as she walked out of the room and followed Frank into the hall.

The moment they were out of earshot of the others, he turned to look at her. "I'm not sure that letting you stay is the right thing to do," he told her honestly. "The rules—"

She didn't let him finish. "You're not someone who goes by the rules."

She said it with such certainty, he was sure Riley had to have tipped her off. "Who told you that?"

"Nobody," she replied quietly. "I can see it in your eyes."

"That Navajo clairvoyance again?" This time he allowed a touch of sarcasm to come through.

"No, that's gut instincts. Cops are supposed to have them," she reminded him. He wasn't coming around, she thought. She needed something more. There was only one card she had left to play. She hoped it would do the trick. "You come from a big family, McIntyre. How would you feel if that was *your* cousin's picture posted on the bulletin board and you thought you let her down? Would you just back away, pack up and go home and let someone else take over finding her killer?" she challenged. "I don't think so."

Frank didn't answer immediately. But he knew how he'd react. He'd track down the bastard and make him pay for what he'd done.

But this wasn't his cousin, it was hers and that made all the difference in the world.

Being leader was a no-win situation, he thought darkly. But, for what it was worth, it did allow him to call the shots—until he wound up shooting himself in the foot, he thought cryptically.

"Okay, you can stay. For now," he qualified. "But that means that you don't go Lone Ranger on me, understand?"

"Wrong character," she corrected with a glimmer of a smile on her lips. "Tonto was the Indian."

"Yeah, but Tonto followed the rules."

She laughed shortly. It was all in how you viewed things, she thought. "Tonto teamed up with a white guy in a mask." That was back in the day when stereotypes were the rule, not the exception. And pairing the two together had gone against type. "There *were* no rules."

"There are here." She couldn't mistake his meaning. There were rules and she was to abide by them.

Julianne took a deep breath. "Duly noted," she said. Mentally holding her breath, she asked, "So, do I get to stay?"

"You get to stay."

"Thank you. Anything else?"

"Not at the moment," he told her.

With a nod of her head, Julianne turned around and walked back to the squad room.

Unconsciously noting the almost infinitesimal sway of her hips as she moved, Frank had an uneasy feeling he was going to live to regret his decision as he followed Julianne back into the squad room.

Chapter 5

"We're going to start from scratch," Frank announced once he walked back into the squad room.

Hill set down the coffee—his twelfth cup of the day—and frowned. "Come again?"

"We're going to question anybody who had any interaction with our victims. The career women," he specified. "Talk to their coworkers, their neighbors, find out what supermarkets they went to and talk to the checkers. Sometimes people share things with strangers they wouldn't tell their friends."

"These people didn't have friends," Sanchez reminded him. "They had stepping-stones. They climbed up on the backs of others," he elaborated, when Julianne gave him a puzzled look.

"Maybe somebody had it in for one of them," Frank theorized.

"And did what, killed all these other women to hide it?" Riley asked, incredulously.

"Maybe he killed the first one for a reason—and discovered that he liked the feeling. Liked being God in that tiny universe," Julianne said, thinking out loud.

Frank nodded, the movement becoming more enthusiastic as he thought over what Julianne was saying. "Good. Go with that. Talk to Andrea Katz's employer, her neighbors, her coworkers, anyone you can find. Get her credit history and see where she shopped, what restaurants she went to, what movie theaters she frequented. Who her boyfriends were," he added.

"You heard the man," Riley said to Julianne. "Let's go."

Julianne rose, but her attention was focused on the lone photograph on the second bulletin board. "I thought that—"

He didn't let her finish. "You thought wrong. We're going to do this in order."

"The first forty-eight hours after a crime are the most crucial."

He didn't want her investigating her cousin's death for a number of reasons, not the least of which was that she was too involved and could very possibly make an emotional call. "Thank you, I'll try to remember that. Now get going. Sanchez, Hill, you take the next two."

"How come we get two and they get one?" Hill protested.

"What is this, kindergarten?" Frank challenged. "The next two are prostitutes. There are less people to talk to."

Hill grunted as he went out with Sanchez, clutching his wilted coffee container.

Frank was right.

The prostitutes proved to be harder to get a handle on. Although some of the working girls staked out particular corners and guarded them zealously, for the most part, the faces along the "Boulevard of Easy Virtue," the label that McFadden had come to be known by, changed. Hookers moved around, they dropped out of sight and no one seemed to notice their absence. If they did, they weren't talking.

Despite having two sets of steps to retrace, Sanchez and Hill were back in the office before Julianne and Riley.

Julianne had expected Frank to allow her to question the various strolling hostesses of the evening about Mary and was disappointed when he'd told her to check out Andrea Katz. The killer's first victim had been a software programmer supposedly away on a business trip when she was killed. She never made it to the meeting that her firm had sent her to.

Andrea, blond, shapely and in her late twenties, had been missing for almost a week before the connection was made between her and the body found in a Dumpster within a trendy apartment complex.

Up until that point, the detectives handling the case assumed that the woman lived within the complex. The fact that no one recognized her only testified to the transient nature of the residents who lived there. People came and went without taking note of one another.

Andrea had been strangled from behind. Like all the victims who came after her.

The people at Andrea's firm had nothing new to add to the testimony they had given before. Andrea was a hard worker, a go-getter who kept to herself for the most part. The people who worked closest to her desk said that there'd been no photographs on it, no treasured mementos. She was very orderly, very neat, almost pathologically so, according to one woman. She made it evident that there was no love lost between them.

"Andrea didn't go out for drinks after work, didn't share lunch with anyone—Lord knows we asked and tried to get her to come, but she always said no. So we stopped asking. She was too interested in getting ahead to make friends," the woman concluded dismissively.

Her testimony echoed that of the other coworkers.

"Makes you think of Thoreau, doesn't it," Riley commented as they left the building and walked up to the car she'd driven to the firm. Julianne looked at her silently, waiting for enlightenment. "You know, the guy who said that most people live lives of quiet desperation."

Julianne shrugged. Other than being an overachiever, there was nothing to set the woman's life apart, nothing that made her a prime target.

"Maybe she liked a quiet life," Julianne speculated. "It wasn't as if someone was holding a gun to her head, saying she had to be a top-notch programmer. It was what she wanted. This day and age, women have a lot more options opened to them than they used to."

Getting into the vehicle, Riley strapped in, waiting

for Julianne to do the same before she started the car. "And yet," she commented, "some of them still choose to go the easy route and sell their bodies for money."

Julianne felt her throat tightening. "What makes you think it's easy?" she challenged.

Riley spared her a glance. "I meant that they didn't have to spend time studying, or sacrificing anything."

Riley couldn't have been more wrong, Julianne thought. She'd come away from questioning the hookers last night with a very distinct impression. It killed her that Mary had numbered among those lost souls. "They sacrificed their pride, their self-respect. They sacrificed everything just to survive. And sometimes, they *do* have guns held to their heads."

"Did I just offend you somehow?" Riley asked. "If I did, I didn't mean it. I was just talking. Thinking out loud."

Julianne blew out a breath. She had no right biting Riley's head off. Riley was right, she hadn't meant anything by it. "Sorry, I'm just edgy."

Riley made a right turn at the next light. "Yeah, I kind of noticed."

It wasn't often she apologized. Wasn't often she felt she was in the wrong. But she had and she was. She supposed some kind of an explanation was in order. "I'm not used to having a partner. The police department over at Mission Ridge isn't very big. I usually go off on my own."

She'd had her suspicions about that, Riley thought. "That kind of thing is frowned upon around here," Riley warned her. And then she winked. "Although it does happen. I'll try not to get on your nerves," she went on to promise amiably.

Julianne looked straight ahead. "It's not you, it's me."

Stopping at a red light, Riley turned toward her, humor curving her mouth at hearing the classic line. "Are you breaking up with me, Julianne?"

Julianne laughed. God, it felt good to laugh. She couldn't remember when she last had. "No, just trying not to be so on edge." Even her hands were clenched in her lap, she realized. She deliberately spread her fingers out in a effort to shed the tension she felt.

Riley inclined her head. "Homicide'll do that to you."

Riley sounded completely laidback and relaxed, Julianne noted. "Doesn't do that to you."

Grinning, Riley lifted one shoulder in a careless little shrug. "I'm one of the lucky ones. I've got a great support system."

"Your family." It wasn't a guess on Julianne's part, not after watching Riley at Rafferty's last night.

Riley nodded. "Nothing beats it."

A sliver of envy momentarily wove its way through her. Had to be nice, Julianne thought, knowing people cared about you. Her father had, in his own way, when he wasn't floating in the bottom of a bottle. "I wouldn't know."

"No family?" Riley asked, surprised.

Julianne thought of Mary, thought of the way her cousin had looked in the Dumpster, her face forever frozen in fear. Had Mary called out to her? With her last breath, had she called to her to come save her the way she used to do when they were both growing up on the reservation? Mary always managed to get into some kind of scrape and then she'd come running for help.

She hadn't been there for Mary when it counted. There was no getting around that.

"No," Julianne finally said flatly.

Riley looked at her, puzzled. "But you're a Navajo, right?"

"Yes."

Riley searched for the right words, not wanting to give any offense. Afraid of treading on feelings that already seemed rather raw. "But isn't the tribe supposed to—"

"Be my family?" Julianne guessed where her partner was going with this. "Ideally. But it doesn't always turn out that way."

Riley was quiet for a long moment, taking advantage of another red light to look at the woman seated next to her. The light changed and she shifted her foot back to the gas pedal.

"Uncle Andrew's going to want to see you," she finally said to Julianne.

"Uncle Andrew?" Julianne echoed. She'd heard several of the Cavanaughs referring to the man last night with more than a little respect. "Is that anything like Marlon Brando in *The Godfather?*"

Riley laughed. "Not hardly. And for the record, he's not really my uncle, although it feels nice to call him that. I did sort of inherited him when my mother married Brian." She slowed down to merge into the next lane, allowing an SUV to pass first. "I'm talking about Andrew Cavanaugh. He used to be the chief of police in Aurora until he retired early to raise his kids." Glancing at Julianne, she noticed that she had the detective's full attention. "His wife disappeared, leaving him with five kids."

Julianne immediately thought of her mother. "She walked out on the family?"

"No, she left for the store and just didn't come back. Actually they thought she was dead. They found her car in the lake. Everything pointed to her accidentally driving off the road."

"But it was murder?" Julianne guessed, picking up on Riley's phrasing.

"No, turns out she actually survived the accident. Rose dragged herself out of the lake, but she'd hit her head and couldn't remember who she was." Even talking about it brought a chill down her back. She didn't know what she'd do if that had been her mother. "A Good Samaritan traveling north took her to a hospital. For the next eleven years, she was someone else, a waitress who worked in a diner up north. Andrew was the only one who didn't think she was dead. He used every spare minute he had to go over and over the evidence."

"Did he ever find her?" Stupid question, Julianne admonished herself. Of course he had, otherwise how would Riley have known the woman had amnesia or where she was all that time.

Riley grinned. "You can meet her at breakfast tomorrow."

Riley was taking an awful lot for granted here. "I can't just barge in—"

Riley stopped her before she could get any further with her protest. "That's just it, you wouldn't be. Uncle Andrew likes to have family over for breakfasts. His family refers to it as 'command performances.' He has this industrial-type stove and is able to make breakfast for veritable legions of people. There're always people at his table and he likes it that way," she concluded as if that was the end of the discussion.

"I'm not family," Julianne pointed out.

"You're a cop, that's family enough for him." She slanted another glance in her direction. "It might make you feel better."

"Thanks, I'll think about it." She had no intention of either thinking about it, or showing up, but it seemed like a polite way to end the conversation.

She'd underestimated her partner.

"I can swing by in the morning, pick you up," Riley volunteered, convinced that the woman would do well to interact with Andrew. "Or Frank can…"

"I'll give you a call if I decide to go," Julianne told her, keeping her tone friendly but firm. She had no desire to mingle with anyone. She wanted to mourn her cousin's passing, find her killer and go back to where she came from. Where people knew not to intrude into other people's lives unless invited.

Frank pushed himself away from his desk. Squaring his shoulders, he pulled them back, stretching muscles that had gotten cramped as he'd hunched over his keyboard. No doubt he would find the serial killer way before he learned how to type quickly.

There was definitely too much paperwork that went with this position. It had been bad enough when he was one of the regular detectives. Now he was drowning in it.

This leader of the pack had more cons than pros, he thought.

He was the last one left again, he noted, looking out at the squad room through the glass partition. And then he stopped.

Someone else was in the squad room.

The lights had dimmed and he'd almost missed her. White Bear. Typing something on the keyboard.

He put his computer to bed and got up. Leaving the tiny cubicle that served as his office, he crossed over to her desk. She was so intent on what she was doing, she didn't seem to hear him.

"So you do know how to use the computer."

Julianne's head jerked up. Frank stood over her desk. Again. Didn't the man have anything better to do? She'd heard that he was quite the ladies' man. Didn't he have any ladies to impress?

"Didn't say I didn't know how to use it," she answered, lowering her eyes back to the keyboard. "I just don't like using it."

So why was she still here? "The shift's over," he told her. "You can go home."

Julianne didn't bother looking up. She went on typing. Faster than he could, he noted. "It's a hotel room."

So, it was like that, was it? He could play along. "Okay, you can go to your hotel room. Or better yet, Rafferty's if you don't want to think. There's enough noise there to freeze your brain."

Julianne raised her eyes to his and he caught himself thinking how beautiful she was.

Her voice was low and devoid of emotion. "What makes you think I don't want to think?"

It amazed him that the woman wasn't stoop-shouldered from the weight of the chip she carried around with her. They both knew the answer to that question. If he had lost a cousin—his only family—he wouldn't want any free time to think, either. Not until he could handle the grief.

Frank debated saying as much, then decided that it wouldn't do any good. The only thing that possibly would could be summarized in two words.

"I'm sorry."

Julianne shrugged, trying to seem nonchalant. "You didn't say anything that—"

"I'm sorry about your cousin."

Julianne lapsed into silence as myriad sensations and emotions warred within her. Her first inclination was just to snap at him, to tell him that she didn't need his pity or whatever it was he was offering, and neither did Mary.

But that would have been wrong. McIntyre was just trying to be nice. Julianne sighed. She supposed she should give him points for that. She was just too thin-skinned lately and would have to adjust.

"Yeah, me, too," she answered quietly. Pressing her lips together, she tried to keep the words back. But maybe, just this once, it wouldn't hurt to share things. For Mary's sake. She didn't want him thinking of her as just some ignorant little runaway who turned tricks to get by. "I wish you could have seen her when she was little. She was always so happy. Always tagging after me." A sad smile played on her lips. She could feel the tears gathering in her eyes. Talking was a mistake. "She thought of me as her big sister, I guess."

It didn't take a rocket scientist to see she was beating

herself up about her cousin's death. "You're not responsible for what happened to her."

"Yes I am," she shouted back, her temper cracking. "All I thought about was me. About making some kind of life for myself. About not winding up like my father. I didn't think about her and what she was going through, didn't even consider the possibility that she might have been living in some kind of hell." Julianne stopped then, covering her mouth with her hands before more words came spilling out. "I'm sorry," she said hoarsely. "I didn't mean to yell."

He waved his hand at the apology, as if the fact that it was unnecessary was a given.

"Beating yourself up isn't going to change anything," he told her. "It's not going to bring her back." He looked at her meaningfully. "And it's not going to help you catch the killer."

She looked away. Seeing Mary in her mind's eye. "No," she agreed in a hoarse whisper, "it's not."

"Shut down your computer, White Bear," he ordered abruptly, making a decision. After all, he was responsible for the welfare of his task force, and this newest member was in serious need of an intervention. "I'm taking you out for a drink."

"I don't drink," she told him flatly. There was no need for the man to do anything. She was responsible for herself.

Rather than come up with alternatives the way his sister had done, Frank looked at the woman before him incredulously. Everyone he knew drank. Not to the point where they were a danger to themselves and others, but everyone liked to unwind by imbibing something with a kick, however minor.

"But I saw you at Rafferty's last night," he protested.

"And I was drinking a ginger ale," Julianne informed him.

He'd seen the color of her drink and had assumed it was a beer, his sister's beverage of choice at Rafferty's. Apparently he was wrong. "Okay, your secret's safe with me. You can have another ginger ale."

Julianne remained where she was. "What is it about your family that makes you all want to pull people out of their nice, dark corners and drag them into loud, noisy places?"

"We're all terminally social," he said matter-of-factly without missing a beat. Deliberately reaching over her desk, he closed the folder that lay open. "Serial killers, though, tend to be loners."

So now he was equating her to a serial killer in waiting? "Not all loners are serial killers."

"No," he agreed amiably, "but all loners run a greater risk of becoming serial killers. They lack the skills for successful interaction with people."

She glanced at the bulletin board as she finally rose from her desk. "I don't know about that. I think our killer has skills. Skills that help him get his victims to lower their guard. Either that, or they all knew the killer."

He turned around and scrutinized the bulletin board, trying to see what made her think so. "What makes you say that?"

She recalled the medical examiner's reports she'd read. "None of the victims had any skin under their nails. There were no defensive wounds. No one fought for their life. The most we have is a frozen look of surprise on a couple of the victims' faces."

He put his hand on her back, gently guiding her out the door. She felt small and delicate under his hand. And she'd probably carve his heart out with some kind of an ancient Navajo ceremonial knife if he said that out loud.

"You're going to have to come up with something more than that to wiggle out of going to Rafferty's," he told her.

"What if I tell you I just don't want to go?" she challenged.

"Overruled, White Bear," he said glibly. "I'm team leader and I say you need to." He eyed her sternly. "Remember, I have the power to have you removed."

She blew out a breath as she crossed the threshold. "Blackmail. Nice."

Frank grinned as he shut off the lights and closed the door. "I thought so."

Chapter 6

"You weren't at your hotel room when I swung by this morning."

Completely lost in the files on her desk, it was all Julianne could do to keep from jumping at the unexpected sound of Frank's voice.

He was just walking into the room.

Julianne stifled a sigh. Miscalculated again. She'd hoped to buy herself a little time alone before anyone showed up in the office. It was a lot easier for her to think when there were no distractions. And although she hated to admit it, McIntyre was proving to be a major distraction. Sanchez and Hill usually strolled in on time, if not late. And this morning, because he'd talked about it yesterday, she'd assumed that both McIntyre and his sister would be busy attending a command breakfast with Andrew Cavanaugh and their wildly extended family.

So much for the best laid plans of mice, men and one struggling police detective trying to catch a break. Or find one, she added silently.

"No, I wasn't. I was here," she answered, pointing out the obvious. Then, because her comment sounded a little sarcastic, even to her own ear, she added, "I thought I'd get an early start." And then, just like that, his words replayed themselves in her head. "Wait, you know where I'm staying?" She didn't remember telling him the name of the hotel. She eyed Frank suspiciously, hating her privacy invaded. The city was littered with hotels and motels. Knowing which one was hers hadn't been just a case of pure luck. "How?"

"I'm team leader. I know everything," he cracked.

She raised her chin. Okay, she'd let the fact that he snooped into her life pass. This was only a minor infraction.

"If you know *everything,* then you have to know that I prefer taking my breakfast alone."

He gave her a tolerant smile. "Just because I know doesn't mean I agree."

Which meant that he still thought it was a good idea to socialize her and he fully intended to. In their off hours. For now, he nodded at the folders spread out all over her desk. It didn't take a genius to guess that she was searching for the common thread. They all were.

"Find anything?" he asked.

"Not yet," she admitted grudgingly. "Re-creating these women's last day doesn't point us in any common direction." Her expression was grim. She hated being stumped. Granted, she'd never been involved in anything of this magnitude before, but that didn't change the ground rules. She *needed* to resolve this. "They didn't all pass by the same place, didn't do anything alike from what I can see. Not to mention that the career professionals had absolutely nothing in common with the street vendors."

Frank's dark brows drew together. "Street vendors?" he echoed, puzzled.

"I'm having a little difficulty calling them what they were, considering that Mary was one of them. I can't picture her letting anyone touch her, not after..." Her voice trailed off and she looked away. Her shoulders lifted and lowered in a defensive, careless shrug.

It didn't take much for Frank to understand what she was going through. If a member of his family had been reduced to Mary's tragic circumstances, he would have handled the situation with a great deal less calm than White Bear appeared to be doing.

"Say the word and you can be off this case."

She began to understand him a little. It was an offer tendered in kindness, not because of some rules and regulations written down in a book. She knew that, heard that, and yet, she couldn't control the way her answer came out.

"No!" Julianne snapped.

He really hadn't expected her to say anything else, he just wanted her to know there was no shame in bowing out.

"Then if you want to do Mary and all these other

dead women any good—" he waved a hand in the general direction of the bulletin boards "—you're going to have to handle it and her murder like anything else you've come across."

He saw Julianne square her shoulders. The thought that she looked like a warrior princess about to go out into the field crossed his mind. So did the word *magnificent*.

"Won't happen again," she promised stoically.

"What? You being human?" Because that was what her reaction was like, pure and simple. "I'm not asking you to be a robot, White Bear, just to keep your personal feelings out of it." Without intending to, he moved in a little closer. So close that there was less than space enough for a deep breath between them. "Save them for something else," he told her, his eyes holding hers. Frank lowered his voice. "Something important."

Damn, but the woman was just *too* attractive. It hit him sometimes, as if it was a new perception on his part instead of something he'd already noted more than once and, basically, right from the start. If he'd run into her anywhere else but on his own task force, there was more than a strong possibility that by now, he would have worn down her barriers and gotten to know the real Julianne White Bear. The one hidden behind all that barbed wire and harsh rhetoric.

It was something that he was looking forward to. Later.

Julianne let out a long, slow breath. Working in this office would be a great deal smoother if McIntyre was old and balding. Or at the very least, married with six kids and battling a bad case of terminal halitosis.

Didn't matter what he looked like, or that, at this

distance, the very breath he exhaled drew her in. She was entirely focused on finding Mary's killer....

And yet, if she were being honest with herself—and she had to be—there was something that was going on here, a strong undercurrent of—what?—she wasn't sure.

With steely resolve, she replied, "I'll keep that in mind."

"Keep what in mind?" Riley asked, walking into the squad room.

Surprised, Frank turned to her. "I thought you'd be here later." She couldn't have already eaten. Even toast at Andrew's table took time. Conversations engulfed people like quicksand. No one got out in under half an hour. "Didn't you stop by Andrew's?"

"Got up late," Riley explained. "If I went by Andrew's, there's no telling how late I would be." She draped her jacket over the back of her chair and dropped her purse into her drawer. "Besides, there are always so many people there, I don't think he'd notice if I didn't show up."

Frank gave her a dubious look. "From what I hear, Andrew notices everything, including who *isn't* there. Story has it that the man's got one of these minds that records everything and plays it back at will."

Unfazed, Riley countered, "He was also a cop. He understands being consumed by a case that just won't open up." She looked from her brother to Julianne. "Did I interrupt something?"

"Saved me from something, actually," Julianne answered quickly. "The 'team leader' was in the middle of giving me a lecture."

"He's good at that," Riley commented. "Years of

being the youngest and having to take everything the rest of us dished out undoubtedly had him storing up a lot of lectures." She smiled at her brother, giving his face an affectionate pat before he pulled back. "Don't get carried away. We need every single body we can get. Live bodies," she qualified, looking at Julianne. They'd started going over the women's apartments yesterday but were by no means finished. "Want to hit the streets, or sit here and listen to Frank pontificate?"

She hardly finished her question before Julianne was reaching for her jacket. "Did you really have to ask?"

Riley laughed. "No, I guess not. Streets it is," she declared, pulling out her car keys. "I'll drive."

Since she didn't know her way around yet, that only made sense, Julianne thought. "No problem."

Her answer drifted back to him as she and his sister left the room.

No problem.

But there was a big problem, Frank, thought as he watched as Julianne make her way down the hall next to Riley. The detective loaned out from Mission Ridge was getting to him. Through no fault of her own, or his.

Tamping down any further thoughts, he went to get a cup of coffee. His stomach rumbled, making him acutely aware that there were consequences to skipping out on one of Andrew's breakfasts.

The smell of despair was everywhere within the four-story pre-1950s walk-up. In the dark hallways with its peeling paint and its scribbled obscenities, echoing in the cries of neglected babies and rising up in the acrid odor of human waste. She was accustomed to poverty. She wasn't accustomed to this.

"Even a dog knows not to go where he sleeps," she murmured under her breath.

"Dogs are smarter than some people," Riley answered.

Julianne did her best not to shiver as she followed Riley into the run-down one-room apartment. The place had once belonged to Rachel Reed, the first prostitute to have made the serial killer's list.

The building was located in the poorer section of Aurora. Here the sun never shone, she thought. Here were housed the hopeless and the just barely not homeless, trying to hang on for just another day until they either died or somehow wandered into the path of a stray miracle. Either way, their misery would be over.

Had Mary lived in such a place? Or was this horrid place actually something she would have aspired to? Mary might have huddled somewhere out on the street, fighting for a space that had no vermin, no bugs that would crawl along her body while she slept.

Oh God, Mary, why didn't I take you with me? I'm sorry, so sorry.

Riley glanced in her direction, interpreting her reaction. "Pretty grim, isn't it? Hard to picture someone actually living like this."

"Yeah," was all Julianne permitted herself to say. And then she looked at Riley. "How can you sound so upbeat?" she asked. The woman sounded as if none of this, the squalor, the wasted lives affected her on any significant level.

"Because if I let it get to me," Riley answered simply,

"I don't function. And these women need me to function so that I can get the bastard who cut them down in the prime of their lives." That said, she started to go through the prostitute's meager belongings. "Well, let's see if there's something that might have been missed the first time," Riley murmured. Sanchez and Hill had gone over the one-room apartment initially. There was always hope something had been overlooked. "Not much to see," she speculated. "Shouldn't take us too long."

"Hard to believe that this is the sum total of someone's life," Julianne murmured, opening up the single, narrow closet. Only a few items of clothing were hanging inside.

Riley and Julianne methodically went through everything, including the miniature refrigerator. They were finished almost before they started. There wasn't much in the apartment. No books, no signs that this was anything but a place for the victim to put her head down, except for the television set.

Julianne paused in front of it the old-fashioned analog type TV with rabbit ears. Possibly left behind by a previous tenant, she judged. She turned it on. Nothing but snow appeared on the screen even when she flipped to a few different channels. It seemed to emphasize that there was nothing in the victim's life. She shut the set again.

A couple of fliers the woman might have picked up along the way were on top of the set. One from a homeless shelter somewhere in the vicinity, the other from a fast-food place she noted was around the corner.

"Nothing," Riley sighed, shaking her head as she finished going through a rickety bureau that contained several pairs of undergarments, some sweaters and a graduation yearbook that was several years old. The victim's, or was it something she'd stolen? She decided it might bear a look. Turning, she glanced over at the dark-haired woman across the room. "Anything stand out for you?"

Julianne looked around at the dust and dirt. "Only that she wasn't a very good housekeeper."

Riley grinned. "Well, if that was a crime, the jails would be *really* overcrowded." Picking up the yearbook, she gave the place one last scan. "Might as well get back."

"Drop me off at McFadden," Julianne told her as Riley closed up the apartment. The boulevard was only a few blocks away from where they were right now.

"Why?" Riley asked as they started back down the stairs. "What's there?"

Maybe she'd gotten her information wrong. "Isn't that the place where most of the prostitutes gather?"

"Not so much before dusk."

"Still, there might be some out, getting an early start and who knows, someone might have seen something suspicious."

"We've already canvassed the area," Riley pointed out. "Right after each hooker was found."

"Can't hurt to show some of the photographs around again." She was thinking of the copy she had with her of Mary's photo. "Maybe you missed talking to one of them, someone who could remember a detail." She was grasping at straws, but stranger things had happened. "And it's not like we have any leads to chase down," Julianne told her.

Riley thought it over. "Okay, we'll both go. It'll go faster that way," she theorized. About to get into her car, she heard her cell phone going off. Half a beat later, so did Julianne's.

"McIntyre."

"White Bear."

Riley looked over the roof of her vehicle at Julianne. It was obvious that they were getting the same call from two difference sources. She saw the other woman's eyes widen. And then she heard why.

"Two?" Riley echoed in disbelief. She struggled to keep the horror out of her voice.

But Julianne heard her and she nodded as she closed her cell phone and slipped it into the pocket of her jacket. "That's what the man said. I think our killer is looking for a greater high," Julianne said grimly. The deaths were happening closer together. According to the files, the first had been almost a year ago. Now only days separated one from another.

The killer's bloodlust was growing.

Riley started the car. McFadden was going to have to wait. They had a date with two Dumpsters. "Either that, or he's enjoying rubbing our noses in it."

Julianne shook her head. Something in her gut told her that it wasn't that. "It's not about us, I don't think. It's about them. His victims."

Riley looked at her sharply. "You found something you want to share?"

Something had occurred to her, but she wasn't ready to elaborate just yet. "I'll let you know after we see the latest victims." Even as she said it, she started to brace herself for the ordeal that lay ahead. She glanced at Riley's profile and saw her own feelings reflected in the set of the woman's jaw. She remembered what Riley'd said to her. "It doesn't get easier, does it?"

"Nope," Riley replied as she turned on the siren. "It really doesn't."

Victims number eight and nine were both very successful in their chosen fields. Zoe Martin was a criminal lawyer from one of the more renowned law firms in the country and Christina Wayne was an interior decorator with her own business and a client list that extended to the rich and famous—the very rich and famous.

Their bodies were discovered buried beneath a thin layer of debris in two different Dumpsters arranged side by side behind one of the fancier hotels located in the heart of the city. The debris was not meant to hide them so much as to highlight the fact that, like the rotting food and refuse, the dead women were trash, too.

The crime-scene investigators, three of them, were already on the scene when she and Riley arrived. As was Frank. Sanchez and Hill were just pulling up.

Julianne got out and strode over to the first Dumpster. Steeling herself off, she climbed up and looked in, virtually over the shoulder of one of the crime-scene investigators. Without a word, she climbed down and then went to the second Dumpster. The second C.S.I. had just finished taking pictures.

The second woman had been tossed in just like the first, as if she was nothing more than just trash, not even worthy of an afterthought. God, but this was one cold S.O.B. they were dealing with, she thought grimly.

"Well?" Riley asked as Julianne moved away from the second Dumpster.

"Well what?" Frank asked. He'd crossed over to them and caught the expectant note in his sister's voice.

Riley turned toward him, more than willing to share. "Julianne thinks she might have a theory about our serial killer."

"Okay, let's hear it," Frank said. "At this point, I'm ready to go with anything if it makes the slightest bit of sense."

"He's killing the same woman," Julianne told him, trying in vain to distance herself from what she'd just seen. Like Mary, these women were going to haunt her for a very long time.

Frank looked at her. "What do you mean, the same woman?"

What had set her thinking along this path was Mary's wig. "They all have the same coloring, are approximately the same age—give or take. Somewhere along the line, our killer was rejected by a blond-haired, blue-eyed woman with high cheekbones and undoubtedly higher standards. Standards that he didn't measure up to. Mary had black hair, but you found a blond wig in the Dumpster with her. Maybe she was trying to disguise herself, to pretend to herself that it wasn't her. The point is, this guy's got it in for blondes. Rejection seems to be the likely conclusion."

"So if he's taking revenge, why didn't he rape them?" Riley asked.

It was a good question, and she only had a partial answer. "Maybe he thought that was withholding the ultimate intimacy, something he's not capable of or didn't want to share."

There was merit in the thought, Frank decided. "You think it all started with the first victim? That she was his real target and he just got carried away?" he asked her.

She hadn't worked that out yet. "Maybe. Maybe not. Maybe he didn't have enough courage to kill the woman who actually rejected him. Could have been a girlfriend, could have been his mother, but somewhere along the line, she rejected him and he's been nursing his wounds until now." She moved out of the way as another C.S.I. set down a plastic marker to denote where a piece of jewelry was found on the ground. "Once started, he kept taking his frustrations out on the surrogates he's been picking out."

"Why now?" Frank posed. "Why not earlier? What makes now different?"

Again, she had no answers except this feeling in her gut. She shook her head. "Some kind of trigger. A meltdown, a personal tragedy, I don't know, but something set him off and he's not going to stop until we stop him. Which means there'll probably be more dead women."

Even as she said the words, Julianne had to struggle not to shiver.

Chapter 7

Frank looked at the woman before him thoughtfully. Obviously, there was more to her than just an undercurrent of sensuality and quiet beauty.

"That's pretty good," he finally acknowledged. "Ever consider working as a profiler?"

"For the FBI?" Even as she asked, Julianne shook her head. The bureau was the last place she'd want to work. "Too many rules and regulations."

That was an odd thing to say, Frank thought, considering her present position. "And being a police detective has less?"

It all depended on whether you worked in the big city, or a small township. She'd chosen accordingly. "In Mission Ridge it does. Captain Randolph gives me pretty much free rein. But then, there's hardly any crime in Mission Ridge." Which could account for the lax regulations. It wasn't a matter of "them" versus "us." To a greater extent, they were all just neighbors with jobs to do. "Kids joyriding once in a while. Lawn sculptures placed in suggestive poses, things like that."

He'd thought places like that only existed in idyllic novels. "I can see why you wouldn't have wanted to have a dead body on your hands. Spoils paradise."

Paradise. She'd never thought of Mission Ridge in those terms. "Wouldn't exactly call it that," she told him. "In my experience, paradise doesn't exist. There're too many people around out for only themselves for that to happen." Even in Mission Ridge. After all, her uncle had lived on the outskirts of the town.

One rotten apple …

Definitely in need of Cavanaugh exposure, Frank judged, looking at Julianne. And as soon as possible. The woman with the incredible blue eyes was in pain, whether she realized it or not. And he hated seeing anyone in pain. The fact that he was attracted to her would have to be put on hold. Helping her, however, was necessary, what he needed to do.

He still had a crazed serial killer on his hands, not to mention a new, double homicide to contend with. He had a gut feeling that the new victims weren't taken and killed at the same time. One victim had to precede the other, the medical examiner would sort out.

And it was up to them to do everything else.

"Okay, people, you know the drill," Frank announced, raising his voice so that Hill and Sanchez could hear him as well. "Canvas the area. Talk to everyone with a pulse. Somebody *has* to have seen something," he insisted. "This bastard can't continue being the luckiest S.O.B. on the face of the earth. His luck has to run out some time." When he saw Riley begin to leave with Julianne, he called out, "Wait up." Both women turned around, waiting for him to give them further instructions. "White Bear, you're with me. Riley, get the names of the hotel guests on the second and third floors facing the alley. I want them all giving statements."

With that, Frank quickly walked out of the alley. Julianne hurried after him. The man had freakishly long legs, she thought, having almost to run in order to catch up.

"Don't trust me?" she asked when she was finally abreast of him. Was that why he suddenly had her pairing up with him?

He gave her a look that told her she was off base. "I like to rotate positions when I work," was all he said to her.

She knew there had to be more and, because she was the outsider, she was pretty certain that her first assessment was accurate. He wanted to keep an eye on her. Something she'd done or said had gotten under his skin.

For the moment, she played along with his answer. "Too bad, your sister and I were beginning to hit a routine."

"Now you can hit a routine with me." He stood back and let her go through the hotel's revolving door first. Except that she didn't. Stepping to the side, she pulled open the door that was on the side.

Everything she did made him wonder about her. This was no exception. But for now, a desk clerk needed questioning and an initial report compiling. His own, personal questions were just going to have to wait.

When the task force finally made it back to the squad room several hours later, Brian Cavanaugh was waiting for them. With him was a solemn-faced, dark-haired man who looked as if he'd emerged from a standard government agency cookie press. He had on a black suit, a white shirt and appeared to Julianne as if his face had never entertained even a glimmer of a smile in his forty-something years on the planet.

Brian made the introductions quickly. "This is Special Agent Elliot Solis," he said, then pointed out each of his detectives by name, refraining from mentioning that his stepson and daughter were in the group. Julianne was introduced separately, with an addendum that she was on loan from a neighboring town. "I was just showing him the task force area."

Frank was instantly on guard. There was only one reason the FBI would send one of their agents. "Are you here to take over?"

Julianne glanced at him. He was being territorial. She could understand that. It gave them something in common.

The man's expression remained unchanged. "No, just to give you the benefit of my expertise."

"You're a profiler," Julianne guessed, her voice just as expressionless as his face.

"Yes, I am. And Chief Cavanaugh has been filling me in on the case." Julianne thought she detected a touch of elitism in his tone. She wondered if Frank took offense at it. He must.

The special agent looked at the bulletin boards. Sanchez was just tacking up the two latest photographs beside the lone photograph that bore silent testimony to Mary's murder. Until they located better photographs, the ones taken at the dump site of the last two would have to do.

"He's escalating," Solis commented.

Frank folded his arms before him. He reminded her of a portrait of a warrior she'd once seen. "Certainly looks that way," he agreed stoically.

Moving toward the bulletin boards, Solis glanced from one photograph to another in silence, then turned around. He wasted no time in rendering his profile.

"Most likely, you're searching for a loner, someone who's always been on the outside, looking in. He's white, between the ages of late twenties to early forties and he has trouble holding down a job. He might even be homeless, which just feeds his rage." As he spoke, he looked from one detective to another, as if to watch his words sink in. "Women won't give him the time of day and he's sexually frustrated." The FBI profiler stopped. "You're frowning, detective." His observation was addressed to Julianne. "Something I said?"

She didn't like being singled out, especially since she really wasn't part of the group. It made her feel as if she was on a tightrope. But Solis was expecting an answer, so she gave him one—in the form of a question. "Are you aware that none of the women were raped, Special Agent?"

Unfazed, Solis shrugged his shoulders. His black jacket barely moved. "Just means he's impotent, that's all. More to be angry about."

She didn't think so. "No, if he were impotent and this was about sexual rage, he'd used anything he could get his hands on to penetrate them. Rebar, a stick, a bottle, whatever did the trick if that was his ultimate goal. Plenty of things like that in the Dumpsters—and most likely wherever the murder happened." Because, like Frank, she subscribed to the theory that all the women were killed somewhere other than where they were found.

It was obvious that Solis wasn't pleased with her take on it. "So what are you saying, he's 'respectfully' murdering them?"

She wished she hadn't started this. But if the special agent intended on making her squirm, he was going to be disappointed, she thought. "No, I'm saying that maybe he's just trying to get rid of them, to rid the world of them," she elaborated, and then added, "And I don't think he's homeless."

The man's eyebrows rose as he pinned her with a skeptical look. It was all Frank could do to keep from laughing.

"Oh?"

Julianne forged ahead, even though she fought back an urge to tell the profiler what he could so with his high-handed, disapproving tone.

"More than half the women are professional career women. They'd never let a homeless man near them. Neither would the prostitutes." She saw Riley look at her in surprise. "Homeless men don't have the kind of money the hookers are looking to make."

Solis snorted, dismissing her theory. "And how long have you been profiling?"

"About an hour," she answered evenly. "But I've been

observing people for a lot longer than that," she added just as a smug expression began to come over the man's angular face.

Sensing that they were on the verge of having the situation become *really* uncomfortable, Brian quickly intervened.

"Special Agent Solis, are you going to be sticking around to help us with this case?" Forewarned was forearmed, he'd always believed. The man had said nothing about this possibility when he'd arrived, so Brian was hoping the answer to his question was no.

And it was. "Sorry, but I've got to be getting back," Solis told him. "I was just asked to come out and form a profile of the man you're looking for." He looked pointedly at Julianne. "Now that I have—"

"You need to be getting back to the field office, I completely understand." Without wasting any time and afraid that the man might change his mind, Brian looked over toward Hill. "Detective Hill, would you mind driving Special Agent Solis to the airport?"

Hill looked a little surprised at being chosen, then inclined his head. One outsider was enough to get used to. This one was going to make too many waves in the way they worked.

"No problem." He offered Solis a large, toothy smile. "Come with me, Special Agent."

Once the profiler had left, Brian looked at Julianne. "Well, I was going to ask if you'd found a niche for yourself, but I guess I've got my answer."

Julianne pressed her lips together.. At least he wasn't reprimanding her. "I didn't mean to step on any toes, it's just that I don't think that Solis's right. I think whoever this serial killer is, the women trust him. Trust him enough to let them come within five feet of them. That's not someone who's been living on the streets, or gives off vibes that he's sexually frustrated."

Riley picked up on the word Julianne used. "Trust him how? Like a priest?"

Julianne thought about it. "No. Only two of these women were Catholics." The rest were a scattering of different religions and at least one was an avowed atheist. "Why would the others seek out a priest?"

Offhand, there was no answer for that. "So we're back to square one?" Brian asked.

"Not exactly square one," she said. They had learned a few things, she thought. "More like version one point one."

Like software, Brian thought. He supposed it was something. "Keep at it," he said to Frank. "The city's getting very jumpy about having a serial killer in their midst."

Frank knew his stepfather would have rather kept the whole thing under wraps without involving the news media, but the papers broke the story several weeks ago. Since then, they'd set up a tip line. It was almost never silent. And nothing had come of it.

"Maybe that's a good thing," Frank theorized. "It'll make women be more careful."

"Or paranoid," Brian countered. He'd been around long enough to have seen these kinds of things go bad. "That's all I need, a city full of women with concealed weapons, ready to Taser—or worse—the next poor slob who make the mistake of tapping them on the shoulder."

"At least they'll both be alive," Riley pointed out. "And that's a good thing."

"Just get this loony for me," Brian requested with weary feeling. Before leaving, he turned toward Julianne. "And, White Bear?"

She'd been waiting for the chief to get around to her. She had embarrassed a special agent with the FBI and now it was time to pay the piper. Was he going to send her away? "Yes, sir?"

Brian smiled at her warmly. "Nice job just now."

She blinked, confused. Praise was something she was essentially unacquainted with. "Excuse me, sir?"

"Coming up with your own profile," the chief explained, amused by her disoriented expression. "I think yours works better than the one that special agent gave us."

She wasn't sure how to react. Something warm opened up in her chest. "Thank you, sir."

"*Chief* will do," Brian told her. *Sir* made him feel as if he was ready to be put out to pasture. With a new bride at home, out to pasture was definitely one place he wasn't ready to occupy.

"Chief," Julianne echoed with a nod of her head. The corners of her mouth curved ever so slightly.

"Anything else strike you about this man?" Frank asked as soon as his stepfather had left the room.

Julianne shook her head. "Nothing I can think of, offhand." She paused, then added, "Except that maybe he has a nice face."

"A nice face," Frank echoed. "What is that supposed to mean?"

"A nice face," she repeated. "Again, like someone you'd trust. Like someone who looks like he'd never even think of hurting anyone, much less a perfect stranger."

Sanchez joined their circle. "You mean like Ted Bundy?"

The infamous serial killer had been able to conduct his bloodthirsty spree because he was so good-looking and so nonthreatening in appearance. No one suspected him of being capable of the gruesome crimes he actually committed.

Julianne nodded. "Something like that."

"You think this serial killer stalked them?" Frank asked, wondering just how much thought White Bear had put into this and if it all was just speculation on her part, or if she was working with some sort of insider information they didn't know about.

Confronted with the question, Julianne thought for a moment. "I think he comes across them in his daily life and then, yes I think he starts watching them until he feels the time is right."

"And when is the time right?" Riley pressed eagerly, caught up in the theory.

Julianne shook her head, frustrated. "That I don't know."

Frank said nothing as he went back to his office. There was a great deal to think about, though.

He put her on phone duty, explaining that everyone had a turn listening and taking down what eventually turned out to be false pieces of information, usually rendered with the best of intentions.

Several hours of that had all but flattened her ear and made her feel as if she was close to being brain dead. She had a hard time not commenting on obvious stupidity, but somehow, Julianne managed to make it through the shift.

Returning to the squad room for her things, she passed Frank's office. Everyone else had already gone home for the day. Mercifully, there'd been no other sightings, no other bodies discovered in Dumpsters.

In his office, his back was to the entrance and he was on the phone. She was about to knock on his door to give him the courtesy of saying she was leaving.

But since she had no idea how long he was going to be, she turned on her heel, about to leave, when she heard him say, "I appreciate you taking the time to talk to me, Captain Randolph. I'd also appreciate it if you keep this conversation just between the two of us. Right," he said, answering something the man on the other end of the phone said. "I agree. She wouldn't understand. Glad you do, sir. Good night."

All sorts of thoughts ricocheted through her head. The second McIntyre hung up, she charged into his office, ready for a confrontation. Her initial thought had been just to get away. But that never solved anything. Besides, she was mad. Who the hell did he think he was, checking up on her?

"You called Captain Randolph about me?" she demanded hotly.

Startled, Frank swung around in his chair. He

hadn't even heard her walk up. "Julianne, I thought you were gone."

It was the first time she'd heard him say her first name. Somehow, that made everything that had just happened that much more personal. And it made her angrier.

"Well, I'm not!" she snapped. Her hands were on her hips as her eyes flashed blue lightning. "Were you just pumping Captain Randolph for information about me?"

"Just trying to get a few things straight," he answered vaguely, then added, "And I'd tone my voice down a few notches if I were you." He didn't appreciate her tone of voice, no matter how magnificent she looked when angry.

"Well, you're not me," she fired back. "Nobody just delved into your life history—"

He held up a hand to stop her. "Not exactly your life history—"

She charged right over it. "Then *what* 'exactly'?" she demanded, her temper flaring higher. Digging her knuckles into his desk top, she leaned over it, her face inches from his. "What could you have possibly asked the captain that you couldn't ask me firsthand?"

He rose from his desk, his eyes darkening to match his expression. "And if I asked you questions, you would have answered them?"

"Yes!" she snapped at him.

He had his doubts. Everything about the woman was secretive. She played her cards close to the vest. "Truthfully?"

Her eyes widened. The question all but took her breath away. This was her integrity he was bandying about. "So now you suspect I'm a liar as well as whatever else is going on in your mind?"

He backtracked. "I just wanted to be sure about you."

"Sure about what?" she demanded. What was he accusing her of?

"That you were here because he sent you, that you didn't falsify your papers—"

She let him get no further. "Falsify my—" She was too stunned to finish the sentence. "Why the *hell* would I do that?" she cried.

"Because you seemed to know a lot about the killer," he told her honestly. "I thought maybe there was some kind of connection."

"There is." Her voice was dangerously low. "He killed my cousin."

Frank shook his head, dismissing her answer. "I mean more than that."

"Did you also accuse the FBI profiler?" she asked. "He claimed to know what made the serial killer tick. Why didn't you check him out? Why just me?"

"Because you seem to be dead-on." He looked at her for a long moment. Had she seen the killer? When that one woman was murdered in Mission Ridge, had White Bear stumbled across him and let him go for some reason? Had guilt brought her here, and now she wanted to make amends?

"So I'm better at putting some of the pieces together than he is. Is that a crime?" Angry, insulted, Julianne drew herself up. "Look, if you don't want my help, just say the word."

They'd gone around about this thing just the other

day. And she'd asked to stay. Was she changing her mind now? "You'd go back to Mission Ridge?" he asked incredulously.

"No, I'd take some time off and try to find this sicko on my own." And then she allowed sarcasm to enter her voice. "But don't worry, I wouldn't want to interfere with your work."

He didn't respond immediately. Instead, he studied her for a long, unnerving moment.

"Under the heading of 'Works and plays well with others,' did you get straight 'unsatisfactories' when you were in elementary school?" he finally asked her. A hint of a smile played on his lips as he asked.

Julianne tossed her head. "I was a happy kid," she informed him defiantly.

"So what happened?"

He was standing much too close to her. Invading her space. She would have taken a step back if it wouldn't have given him the impression that he intimidated her— because he didn't.

"I grew up."

He watched her mouth as she fired back at him and felt something stir inside. He was more than familiar with the reaction.

Too bad, he lamented silently.

"Takes more than that," he told her. He wanted to know what pressed this woman's buttons. Why she looked as if she was a firecracker about to go off without warning. Maybe if he knew, it would curb his desire to find out what her mouth tasted like. "Tell you what, why don't we grab a drink and we can talk about it?"

What was it with these people and their attention spans? "I told you, I don't—"

"Drink, right, I know. Water, then," he suggested easily. "What we're doing as we talk isn't important. Talking is."

"Frustrated shrink?" she guessed sarcastically at his reasons.

"Frustrated detective." He looked at her pointedly. "Won't cost you to talk to me."

She supposed he wanted to go to his usual place. She didn't. She didn't want to be on display for all the other members of the police department to gap at. "Rafferty's?"

He shrugged. "Or someplace else. The drink and the place don't matter," he emphasized.

Okay, so what would it hurt? If he was determined to spend some time with her after hours, she might as well get something out of it. "All right. You can buy me dinner."

Frank grinned. "Consider it done."

He was grinning. She wished he wouldn't grin. It got to her.

The word *mistake* whispered across her brain as she left the squad room with him.

Chapter 8

Frank brought her to a well-lit family-style restaurant with checkered tablecloths and friendly ambience. The food, although not fancy, was appetizing, and the service was fast.

Ordering a Black Russian for himself, he was surprised when Julianne agreed to the waiter's suggestion of sparkling cider. He watched with interest as Julianne drained her glass while waiting for their dinners to arrive. The waiter came by to refill the glass after setting their meals down in front of them.

For a woman who didn't imbibe, Frank mused, she certainly did do justice to her drink.

He waited until he was fairly certain that Julianne had taken the edge off her hunger before he asked the question that had been on his mind since she first walked into the squad room.

"All right, Detective White Bear, tell me what makes you so angry."

She raised her eyes to his, wondering, at the same time, why the room was just the slightest bit out of focus. "I'm not angry."

He said nothing in response. Instead, he put down his fork and he took out his cell phone. Aiming it at her, he snapped a picture. Then, switching the camera's function to the still mode, he placed his phone on the table and turned it upside down so that she could see it.

"Then I'd say that you're doing a good imitation."

Snapping the phone shut, she pushed it back to him. "Okay," she allowed grudgingly. "Point taken. Maybe, if I look angry," she qualified, not giving in completely, "it's because I don't have any control over where I'm being sent. One day, I'm at Mission Ridge dealing with the city's first homicide in ten years, the next, I'm here, being shoved in with a group of people who all know each other and most likely resent having someone forced on them, but are too polite to say it." She paused, taking another sip to wash down her words before continuing, "Maybe I'm angry because this serial killer found Mary before I could—and took her away forever." She drew in a breath, her head swimming just a little. "And maybe I'm angry because despite the fact that the group leader is invading my space and thinks someone appointed him my social director, I'm so attracted to him, I'm having trouble concentrating."

The moment the words were out of her mouth, she

appeared more surprised than he did to hear them. Eyes widening at what she viewed to be a very basic tactical error, Julianne looked down at the empty glass beside her in awakening horror. "That's not just apple cider, is it?"

Well, that explained that, he thought. Playing along, Frank reached over for her glass and sniffed it.

"Nope," he confirmed. "I'm no expert, but I'd say that was some form of white wine. It does have a hint of apples to it," he allowed, setting the glass back down on the table. He couldn't resist asking, "Couldn't you tell the difference?"

She drew herself up, trying to appear formidable. At five-four and with a slight build, she usually relied on her expression to do the trick. Right now, lightning was all but shooting from her eyes.

It wasn't his fault, she reminded herself, trying to be fair. McIntyre hadn't ordered the drink for her, she had, going with the waiter's suggestion.

"Obviously not." Sighing, she pushed the glass away from her. Locking the barn door after the horses had run away, she thought, upbraiding herself. "I should have told him to bring me a ginger ale." And then, because there was a need to blame someone, she eyed him accusingly. "Did you tell him to switch drinks?"

He didn't take offense. "You were sitting here the entire time. Unless you think I have some kind of secret powers and can communicate with people through telepathy, I think you know the answer to that." And then, because he couldn't help himself, he smiled warmly at her. Regulations dictated that he ignore her confession and pretend that nothing had said about the electricity humming between them. But he was too intrigued, too taken with her to just let her words pass without some sort of acknowledgement. "You're attracted to me?"

She could feel herself reddening and gave him a look that bordered on murderous, deliberately daring him to make a comment about her changing complexion. "It's the wine talking."

His gut told him that this wasn't the case here. "Sometimes alcohol loosens tongues."

Her eyes narrowed. "And sometimes it turns people into useless drunks."

She said it with such feeling, Frank was certain that someone close to her had to be the focus of that statement. A lover? An ex-husband? He'd seen her file and there was next to nothing personal in it. Other than her having grown up on a reservation and the fact that both her parents were deceased, nothing in it gave him a clue about her childhood. He was filling in the blanks as he went.

He leaned forward, lowering his voice. Sounding kind. "Who did it turn into a useless drunk, Julianne?"

There he went again, using her name and making it personal. She wished he'd stop that. She raised her chin defiantly.

"That has no bearing on anything."

"Doesn't it?" he challenged. "We're all made up of a million different little pieces that are fit together. Some of which go back to our childhood," he added tactfully. He saw resistance enter her eyes.

Maybe, if he was lucky, it would be a matter of "I'll

show you mine if you show me yours." It was worth a try. But that meant that he had to go first.

More than most, Frank understood her reluctance about talking about her personal life. He didn't exactly like talking about parts of his past, either. But if his talking about his past would free her up to talk about hers, then it was worth it.

Besides, it wasn't as if no one knew. That was the problem. Too many people knew. It was something he and his brother and sisters, not to mention his mother, had had to live down.

So, when she said nothing, he took the plunge. "I've spent the last few years fighting the specter of my father. Rumor had it that he was a dirty cop, that he was trying to rip off the very people he was supposed to be busting." Talking about it brought back the anger. It surged through him. He wondered if he was ever going to be able to revisit this time without feeling betrayed and defensive. "The worst of it was when they started whispering things about my mother, saying that she was in on his plan, or that she knew where the money that had disappeared was buried. It got me pretty crazy for a while," he admitted.

"How did you handle it?" she asked.

"Instead of getting into fights, defending her, defending his name, I learned how to just ignore what was being said." His expression turned grim as he remembered the events of the previous year. Of how his mother had tried in vain to protect them all from the fall out. "But then my father came back from the dead and everything that had been said about him turned out to be true."

"Wait, wait." Julianne grabbed his hand, as if that would stop him from going any further. Suddenly realizing what she was doing, that her hand was covering his, she pulled it back. "What do you mean, he 'came back from the dead'?"

He was so used to the people around him being aware of the details, he forgot that she wouldn't be. "We all thought he was dead. There'd been a gun battle and my father's mutilated body wound up washing up on the shore. At least, we *thought* it was his body. We held a closed-casket funeral service for him and buried him in the family plot." The ironic smile on his lips had no humor in it. "Turns out it wasn't him. It was his drug contact who was killed in the shoot-out. My father was probably the one who pulled the trigger," he added grimly. "He dressed the other man in his clothes, then bashed his face in. We made a natural mistake."

She knew what it felt like wanting to be proud of your father and knowing that you couldn't be. That he was nothing more than a huge disappointment, a weak man who thought only of himself.

Her sympathy aroused, she looked at him for a long moment. "How did you stand it?"

Frank shrugged. He hadn't intended for his "confession" to go this far. He'd brought her here to find out more about her, not talk about his own past. "You get through it. And it helps to have someone like Brian Cavanaugh on your side," he told her. "Not to mention siblings to turn to."

She thought of the people Riley had introduced her to the other night. She vaguely recalled that a couple of them, a man and a woman, had been named McIntyre. That made him far better off than her.

"Yeah, well, things are different when there's nobody to turn to."

Nobody. That had to be one of the loneliest words he'd ever heard. "Nobody?"

She shook her head. From what she'd heard, her mother, already convinced that she'd made a huge mistake marrying her father, hadn't wanted any children. After she was born, her parents stopped sleeping in the same bed.

"I'm—I was," she amended with a great deal of difficulty, "five years older than Mary. When the bottle finally did my father in, I was a couple of weeks shy of turning eighteen. My uncle volunteered to take me in." Her mouth hardened. "According to him, it was my father's dying wish that I move in with him and my cousin. It didn't sound like my father, but I just wanted to be part of something so much, I believed him. Turned out that it was my uncle's wish, not my father's."

It wasn't hard to pick up on her tone. "What did your uncle do to you?"

"Nothing," she answered firmly, and then she relented, adding, "Not for lack of trying. Every time I walked by, he tried to pull me onto his lap, grab me…" Julianne shrugged, letting the momentary silence take the place of any further explanations. "I lasted exactly eight days, then packed up and left in the middle of the night." If she'd tried in the daytime, she knew her uncle would have tried to physically stop her, and he was twice as big as she was. "I got a job and put myself through school," she continued without any fanfare, then sighed heavily. "It never occurred to me that he would try to do the same thing to his own daughter." Just saying it made her feel ill all over again.

He'd seen it time and again. People who blamed themselves for things they had absolutely no control over. "That's because you don't think like a sick child predator."

"I should have. I should have known," she murmured more to herself than to him. "Now, because of me, Mary's dead." And she was never going to forgive herself for that.

"What happened to your cousin is *not* your fault," Frank insisted firmly. What was it going to take for her to believe him?

"Yes, it is," she answered quietly. There was no way that she couldn't take responsibility for this. "I failed her when she needed me."

Stopping abruptly, Julianne looked at him. Most likely it was the wine talking. But maybe McIntyre was right. Maybe it just loosened tongues instead of fabricated stories.

Julianne leaned in closer and said, "I don't want to be alone tonight."

Her breath was warm on his face and he could feel his pulse accelerating. But even though he felt himself responding to her and to what she was saying in myriad ways, he knew nothing would come of it. Because he wouldn't allow it. He didn't believe in taking advantage of vulnerable women no matter how attracted to them he was. There were rules, rules of his own making, that he followed.

"I'll take you to your hotel room," he told her. "Tomorrow, Riley will come by and bring you to your car," he continued, answering Julianne's question before she could ask.

Signaling for the check, Frank paid the amount in cash, leaving a healthy tip. He slipped his wallet back into his pocket and placed his hand under her arm. "Let's go, Julianne."

"White Bear," she corrected, rising to her feet. "Call me White Bear."

It seemed like an odd request. Usually, a woman who wanted to sleep with you wanted things to be more intimate, not less. "Why?"

Julianne took a breath, trying to keep things from slipping into a haze. "Because when you say my name, it feels too personal." They walked outside and the cool evening air made her feel a little better. "This isn't going to be personal," she informed him.

This was absurd, she thought, annoyed with herself. Why was her head buzzing like this? It was just one stupid glass of wine. Okay, maybe two, she amended, remembering that the waiter had come by to refill her glass. The problem was, she suddenly remembered, that she'd consumed the wine on essentially an empty stomach. And because she blamed it for her parents' breakup, she had never built up any sort of tolerance for alcohol.

A little tolerance would have been wonderful right about now.

They'd reached his vehicle and she realized that he was looking at her. "It's not going to be personal, huh?" It was a rhetorical question.

She began to shake her head, then thought better of it. Her head was throbbing as it was. "Nope."

"Then I take it we're going to be using puppets?" he asked mildly, unlocking her door.

"We're going to be having sex," she retorted, getting into his car. Sinking into the seat, she took a moment undertaking the ordeal of buckling up. "That doesn't have to be personal."

Getting in on the driver's side, Frank laughed shortly. There was a lot that had to be straightened out about this woman.

"Sorry, whenever I make love with a woman, it's *always* personal." He spared her a look before backing out of the parking space. "Otherwise, why bother?"

Confusion wove in and out of her brain as Julianne tried to think. "To release energy, tension," she finally answered.

Wow. He shook his head in disbelief. "You've just reduced a beautiful thing to a science theorem. Bet you have to beat men off with a stick."

She took his last sentence literally. And remembered. "A knife," she corrected.

They were on the road. Rather than pass through the amber light, he slowed down and watched the traffic signal turn red. This wasn't the kind of conversation to be had while staring through the front windshield. "You used a knife?"

She shut her eyes and found that wasn't such a good idea. Things began to swim. She opened her eyes again. "Just once."

To defend herself? To exact revenge? With her, it could have gone either way. He didn't know her well enough to make the actual call, but his gut told him it was probably self-defense. "Want to talk about it?"

The light turned green. He wasn't moving. "No."

The driver behind him tapped his horn. Frank put his foot on the accelerator. His hands tightened ever so slightly on the steering wheel. "He deserve it?"

The laugh gave him his answer before she did. "In spades."

There was silence for the rest of the trip, which wasn't long. Within ten minutes, he was guiding his vehicle into the parking lot. Frank found a spot close to the entrance.

Pulling up the hand brake, he turned the engine off and then looked in her direction. Ordinarily, he would have just waited for her to get out but his gut told him that, despite her pride, Julianne might need a little help navigating. Without saying as much, he got out on his side and rounded the trunk of his car, getting to her door before she had a chance to pull the handle.

Opening the door for her, he extended his hand and then helped her out. Her left heel got caught in the gravel and she sank slightly when her shoe refused to move with her.

Frank's hold on her tightened automatically and he pulled her to him.

Big mistake.

His brain instantly telegraphed the observation to him as electricity shot through his body.

Before he knew exactly what was happening, he found himself kissing her.

Under penalty of death, he wouldn't have been able

to say if he was the one who made the first move, kissing her or if she had set the ball in motion, kissing him. Either way, the next moment, their lips were pressed against each other and someone had set off an entire giant string of Fourth of July fireworks approximately three months too early.

Her mouth tasted exactly the way he'd thought it would.

Impossibly sweet, impossibly enticing.

Without meaning to, Frank deepened the kiss, wanting to savor her lips before he did the right thing and stepped back, away from her and what was clearly the line of fire. However, since his intentions were good and his plan laid neatly out before him, he thought that he could be forgiven, just this once, if he extended the time limit by a few precious seconds. He needed to absorb the sensations that were—even now—shooting wildly through him, setting off sparks and, inadvertently, a hunger that he hadn't been aware of harboring.

While it was true that he couldn't remember a time when he hadn't been attracted to women and acted on that attraction, for some unknown reason, this felt different.

Was different.

To begin with, it was going against rules, both his own and, to a lesser degree, the department's. Julianne was someone from his own department—at least she was for the time being—and that meant that there was supposed to be a hands-off policy in force.

A policy he couldn't seem to make stick.

But he would. In a minute. Maybe just a tad bit longer.

She'd never been drunk before, had sworn to herself, at a very young age as she tended to her father, that she never would be.

Because being drunk made you stupid.

Except that she didn't feel stupid. She felt, in a word, glorious. Superhuman. Right at this moment, she felt as if she could leap a tall building in a single bound and do all sorts of wonderful, incredible things.

All because he was kissing her.

No, it wasn't a kiss. The man was setting fire to her. And she didn't have enough brains to try to get away. To run for cover.

Julianne could swear that she could actually *feel* her blood rushing through her veins. Could feel her head begin to spin wildly as an unprecedented hunger began to consume her.

Was that the alcohol at work?

Or him?

Wrapping her arms around Frank's neck, leaning her body into his, she stood up on her toes and deepened the kiss.

As she did, her tongue briefly flirted with his, sending shockwaves through her body to the point that she couldn't understand how she was keeping from trembling all over.

She was a responsible woman. This *had* to stop.

In a minute.

In just another minute.

A sigh escaped her lips as, rather than stop, she kissed him harder. Kissed him with all the feeling that was running rampant through her.

This was just sex, nothing more than sex, Julianne silently insisted, even as something inside of her really craved for it to be more.

But even in her unfocused state, she knew that wasn't possible.

More was for people who won more than they lost. For people who hadn't found themselves abandoned at every turn by people they loved.

By people who were supposed to have loved her.

For her, just sex and nothing more, would have to do.

But even as she resigned herself to that, the ache inside of her grew.

Chapter 9

The heat continued to build up within her. Julianne could sense it all but consuming her. Burning the edges of her fingers and toes.

And then, suddenly, she felt hands closing down on her shoulders. Firm hands that exerted just enough force to gently push her back.

Julianne blinked, disoriented. There was space between them where, only a moment earlier, there'd been none.

Frank looked down into her face, a squadron of emotions flooding him. "Good night, Julianne."

Those were probably the hardest words he'd said in a long time. Somewhere, a medal of honor waited for him.

"You're not coming in?"

For two cents… Struggling, he shook his head. "No."

Julianne stared at him, dazed. "But I just threw myself at you."

And he would have liked nothing more than to catch her. But he knew he couldn't. Not if he wanted a clear conscience.

"Yes, you did."

And then it suddenly all became clear. "Oh." Julianne felt naked and vulnerable and every inch an idiot. This had never happened to her before. The opposite had always been true. She'd have to fight men off. "You don't want me."

Frank laughed then and shook his head. God, was she ever off base.

"Lady, you are definitely not as good at reading people as you think you are." Because they were standing outside her hotel and not inside her room, he allowed himself a second more to drink her presence— and all that could have been—in. "I don't think the word *want* even *begins* to cover what I'm feeling right now."

He wasn't making any sense. "Then why…?" Her voice trailed off as she regarded him, mystified. Was he afraid that she was trying to trap him? "I'm not expecting anything."

He laughed shortly. "Always flattering to be told that."

She waved an impatient hand at him. "You know what I mean. I'm not expecting our spending the night together to mean anything to you—to us," she corrected herself quickly, not wanting him to think that her attraction was reaching critical mass. "Isn't that what every man wants, sex with no strings?"

He would have thought so, yes. But somehow, when

she was the other party involved, it wasn't as pleasing as it should have been.

"In theory."

Her brain was in a fog. Was he trying to tell her something? Right now, subtlety was wasted on her. "And in practice?"

The smile on his lips was a fond one. She didn't want fond, she wanted passion. Fireworks. A release from all the tension she'd been experiencing.

"You're tipsy, Julianne," he told her gently. "Go in and sleep it off." Rather than kiss her again and run the risk of giving in to his baser feelings, Frank paused to brush his lips along her forehead. "I'll see you in the morning."

Frank turned on his heel and walked away. Quickly before he had a chance to change his mind—or act on a mind that was already calling him a fool.

He left her standing before the hotel, open mouthed and deeply puzzled. And torn between deep disappointment and a budding ray of admiration.

Morning crept into her system, dragging with it a really annoying headache that was not about to be ignored and an even more annoying sense of embarrassment. For a moment, she pulled the covers over her head and tried to will herself back to sleep.

Nothing happened. Because her mind launched into high gear. Throwing herself at McIntyre, what was she thinking? What the hell had gotten into her last night? she demanded silently.

And McIntyre—he'd turned her down. Was he displaying superior morals, or was it just that she wasn't to his liking?

Didn't matter. Either way, she really didn't want to have to see him today. But there was no way around it. She couldn't just not come in. After all, this wasn't her normal stomping grounds. She was a loan-out.

Okay, might as well face the music, she thought grimly, sitting up. Putting it off wasn't going to solve anything. It would only fester and grow if she hid out for the day—and the next.

Julianne dragged her hand through her long, straight black hair, wishing with all her heart that she could just as easily drag the cobwebs out of her brain and the sour taste out of her mouth.

What in God's name did people see in drinking anyway? Why would they want to deliberately wake up the next morning, feeling like sewage? A momentary surge of exhilaration the night before just wasn't worth the price.

Julianne stumbled into the shower and turned up the cold water in a desperate attempt to wake up and come to. She supposed she would have felt twice as bad this morning if they'd actually *had* sex. Grudgingly, she had to give him his due. McIntyre had saved her from that.

She supposed she should feel grateful to him. But she didn't. It was all she could do to bank down the hostility.

Frank was already in the office when she came in a little less than an hour later.

Restless, frustrated, unable to sleep more than a few minutes at a time, he'd decided he might as well come in and try to do something useful instead of tossing and turning all night, thinking of the warm mouth and warmer body he'd walked away from.

Something else to hold against this job. But even as he thought it, he knew that wasn't it. It wasn't the job that had him walking away from her last night; her judgment had been seriously impaired by the alcohol. As little as she drank, it had hit her hard. He couldn't just satisfy his own needs at her expense.

If they did wind up coming together, she would have to be clearheaded, not have her judgment clouded by either alcohol or emotions that had run rampant.

Until then, Frank mused, watching the woman walk in as if on cue, he was just going to think of her as the one who got away.

"'Morning," he called out as she passed by his opened door.

Julianne barely glanced in his direction. "Yes, it is."

And then, because there was no one else in the squad room yet, she decided to say something before the matter took on the proportions of an elephant standing in the living room, something to be acutely aware of but not mentioned.

She stopped and turned around, walking into his office. "About last night—"

He smiled at her. "You really don't drink, do you, White Bear?"

Good, she was White Bear again, not Julianne. That made talking easier. "No. But I just wanted to say—" Julianne paused. What was it, exactly, that she wanted to say?

Why didn't you want me? Why didn't you take me

when I literally threw myself at you? Is the idea of making love with me that repugnant to you?

But even as the questions formed in her mind, she knew that wasn't it. He hadn't turned her down for any of those reasons. She hadn't imagined the electricity, the chemistry that crackled between them. Hell, she could feel it now, just standing in the same room with him.

She pressed her lips together, then said, "I just wanted to say thank you."

The surprise in his eyes melt into a smile. Something inside of her said that this was far from over, which meant that she was far from out of danger. Because she could care about him. And she didn't want to care. Not about anyone. Caring only led to pain—and she'd had enough of that to last her a lifetime.

"Don't mention it," he told her, his voice low. "Just know this. The next time you do it—"

Her head snapped up as her eyes met his. "There won't be a next time," she cut in.

Frank continued as if she hadn't said anything. "—I might not be able to walk away. Consider yourself warned."

"Right." He was warning her? Did he think she couldn't take care of herself? Julianne blew out a breath, then forced herself to focus on the only thing that actually mattered, she silently insisted. "What's on tap for today?"

He glanced down at the notes he'd made to himself early this morning. "More apartments to search, more people to question. Nothing else matters until we get this creep off the streets."

Well, at least they were in agreement on that. She looked at him for a long moment, not sure how she wanted him to answer the next question. "We still partnered?"

"Yes."

Then she was going to have to dig up her A game and be on her toes at all times. "I'd better get some coffee."

He pretended that they were talking about being alert, and nothing more. "Sounds like a good idea," he told her, already turning his attention to the screen he'd pulled up on his monitor.

But as Julianne walked away, he couldn't help looking in her direction, observing the soft sway of her hips as she put distance between them.

Frank held back a sigh.

Sometimes he wondered if he was just too noble for his own good.

The tiny third-floor walk-up held the dust and grime of several tenants who had come before the victim they were investigating.

Julianne looked around with an impartial eye, deliberately leaving her emotions out of it. This was no more a home than a public restroom at a bus station. But it was the last known residence of Candy Cane, whose real name was still unknown and very possibly always would be.

Julianne couldn't help thinking of her own place, a small one-bedroom apartment she'd moved into right after joining the force. She thought of it as her haven, some place to take shelter. Periodically, she scrubbed it until it shone, determined to keep her tiny space immaculate.

No such wish here, she thought, running her hand along the bureau. The plastic gloves instantly turned grimy. Suppressing a sigh, she got down on her knees to look under the bed.

"Find anything except dust bunnies?" Frank asked a moment later, walking over to her. A search of the cupboards had yielded nothing of interest, other than telling him that the victim had a weakness for marmalade, something he himself actively disliked.

"Dust bunnies?" Julianne echoed, amused despite herself as she lowered her stomach to the floor and snaked her way under the double bed with its sagging springs. "Strange term for a head detective to use."

"Thanks to two sisters and a mother, I'm in touch with my feminine side," he cracked. He came around to her side of the bed. Only her legs were visible. "What are you doing down there?" he asked, crouching beside her. Instead of answering him, she sneezed. "Besides sneezing and getting dirty?"

He tried not to notice how firm her butt looked as the slender Mission Ridge detective undulated her way out from underneath the bed.

"Getting this," she announced, holding up a piece of crumpled paper. She sneezed again.

"Bless you." Taking the balled up paper from her, he smoothed it out. It was from a homeless shelter in the vicinity, asking for volunteers and donations. "Just a flyer," he told her.

Sitting on her heels, Julianne took the paper back from him and scanned it. Something rang a bell. "I've seen this before."

She'd gotten some dust in her hair. Leaning forward, Frank gently removed it. He heard her draw in her breath, as if the contact surprised her. Glancing at the paper again, he raised his eyes to hers.

"Where?"

"Yesterday. At the first prostitute's studio apartment. She had it on top of her TV set along with another flyer. Something from a local fast-food place." Was this finally something to connect the women? "You think it's a coincidence?"

Frank rose to his feet, offering her his hand. For a moment, she debated not accepting it, or his help, then decided that maybe, at this point, they were past playing games. Wrapping her fingers around his, she got up. And found herself standing a little too close to him for either of their own good, she thought.

Damn chemistry, anyway.

Frank regarded the flyer in her hand. "Maybe, maybe not. Both women probably lived on the street at one point or other. According to the address, this is just the closest homeless shelter. St. Vincent de Paul's Homeless Shelter," he read. "Stands to reason that they'd stay there to get a warm meal and a place to sleep."

Something about his voice didn't sound as if he was completely convinced about what he was saying. "Are you thinking what I'm thinking?"

He was thinking he wanted another chance at last night. This time around, he would have suggested she have ginger ale. And if something happened afterward when he brought her to her hotel, there'd be no reason for recriminations or acts of conscience.

What he was thinking made him grateful that the woman before him wasn't clairvoyant.

Pushing his thoughts before they took him in a whole different direction, Frank nodded. "I am if you're thinking that we should go back and get copies of the victims' pictures to show around to the staff at St. Vincent de Paul's Homeless Shelter."

A glimmer of a smile curved her mouth. "I guess then we're on the same page," she told him with approval.

"Mostly," was all he allowed himself to say before he turned around and led the way out.

The present director of St. Vincent de Paul's Homeless Shelter, Colin Wilcox, had been on the job a little less than a year. Of average height and slight build, he had a round head made that much more apparent by his swiftly receding hairline. His eyes moved like small brown marbles as he looked at the array of photographs spread out on the rickety card table before him.

If the man concentrated any harder, Julianne thought, she was certain smoke would come out of his ears. Finally, he looked up at her.

"Some of them, yes, they look familiar. But after a while—" he moved his shoulders in a vague way "—they all start to look alike. At least the ones without kids," he added hurriedly. "Kids make a difference. They tend to stick in your mind."

"Do you have some kind of sign-in list, records you keep of the people who've passed through here?" Frank prodded.

"We used to," the homeless shelter director answered.

And then he shrugged haplessly again. "But then, after a while, there didn't seem to be much point to keeping it going."

"Why not?" Frank wanted to know.

"Because all we wound up collecting were a bunch of aliases. Most of the people who stayed here were too ashamed to use their own names and some of the others, well, they hadn't heard someone say their name for so long, they just forgot it."

"These are all young women," Julianne pressed. "They wouldn't have forgotten their names." She pushed Mary's photograph in front of him. "How about this one? Do you remember ever seeing her come by? Did she ever stay here?"

Colin shook his head. "No." And then he paused, wispy eyebrows drawing together. Just as she began to pick up the photograph, Wilcox pulled it back over and studied it. "No, wait. She did," he amended. "A few months ago, I think. But she didn't have black hair. She was a blonde. Yeah, I'm almost sure of it. A blonde." Frowning, he began to look at the other photographs again, as if seeing them for the first time. "They're all blondes, aren't they?"

"One way or another," Frank commented. It was very obvious that the prostitutes were all dyed blondes, getting color out of the cheapest product they could find. The career women were another story. If they weren't natural blondes, they would have gone to salons to have their hair dyed.

"Guess California is the place for blondes," Colin murmured. His small, dark eyes darted toward the woman next to him, taking in her midnight black hair. "No offense."

"None taken," she replied, dismissing his comment. All she cared about was piecing together Mary's last few weeks. Maybe if she did, they could get that much closer to who had killed her. "So she was here? This one?" she emphasized, taping Mary's photograph when Wilcox looked as if his mind was wandering.

"Yeah, she was here. I'm certain of it now. Didn't talk much."

"What was her name?" Frank asked. Julianne looked at him, puzzled. "She might have used an alias," he explained, then looked at Wilcox, waiting. "Apparently everyone else did."

The man frowned again, trying to remember. "She had such an innocent face, I thought she was still a kid. I tried to ask her about her family, but she said they were all dead."

The comment was like a knife to her heart. Stoically, Julianne pressed, "Did she tell you her name?"

He thought for a moment. "Karen, Krystle, something like that." He shrugged helplessly. "I'm not good with names. I can't remember—no, wait," he said, his eyes widening with excitement. "I do." He looked at Julianne. "It was the same as yours."

Julianne stared at him. "What?"

Wilcox's head bobbed up and down. "Julie, that was it, she called herself Julie."

Mary couldn't stand what she'd become, so she'd fantasized about being someone else. About being her, Julianne thought.

Why did that hurt so much?

"Do you have any idea where she went when she left here?" Frank asked.

Wilcox looked at him as if he thought the detective had lost his mind. "They never tell me. Least-wise, most of them don't. The kids, though, they talk. It's like they need someone to listen to them.

"The others, the older ones, they just stop coming around. Sometimes they get a place of their own, some-times they go to another shelter and sometimes, well, they just go," he said tactfully, but they both knew he meant that they died. He tapped Mary's photograph. "This one, though, she hardly said two words in all the time she was here. Just kept to herself. Didn't talk to the other homeless people, either."

Julianne had heard only one thing. She exchanged looks with Frank. "She was here for more than a few days?"

"Yeah, at least a couple of months." And then his eyes widened again, as if remembering caused his pupils to dilate. "Christmas," he said suddenly. "She was here during Christmas. I even caught her helping decorate the tree. Mayfair Department Store always donates one every year," he explained. "When I said something to her about what a good job she was doing, she smiled. First smile I ever saw on her. Only smile I ever saw on her," he qualified.

Yes, that sounded very much like Mary, Julianne thought. "She didn't have anything to smile about," she told the homeless shelter director quietly.

Chapter 10

At the detectives' urging, Colin Wilcox slowly reperused the photographs of the serial killer's victims who had been prostitutes. He wasn't able to answer whether they had been there or not with any more certainty.

"Is there anyone else who works with you who might have a better memory for faces?" Frank asked, doing his best to bank down his impatience.

"We're badly underfunded," Wilcox lamented. "Most of the people who do work here are strictly volunteers—and they don't always show up when they say they will. Some of them come once or twice and then just never come back."

"I understand that—but is there any one else who's *paid* to be here?" Frank asked.

"Well, there's Jon and Suzy."

"Great. Are Jon and Suzy here?" Frank asked through gritted teeth.

"Yes."

"Could you ask them to come here?" Julianne suggested. As Wilcox ambled off, she leaned into McIntyre and whispered, "I think you have steam coming out of your ears."

Frank took a breath, letting it out slowly. "I have trouble dealing with stupid. It's a failing of mine."

For once, she understood exactly what he meant because she had the same problem. She'd grown up believing that everyone was blessed with a reasonable amount of intelligence. With age, she realized that axiom was erroneous.

She allowed herself a fragment of a smile. "Not such a failing." Wilcox returned to the room, bringing two people with him. Julianne lowered her voice. "Let's hope these two have more than half a brain between them."

As it turned out, Jon and Suzy each seemed to possess far more intelligence than their boss. After looking through the photographs, both agreed that each of the deceased prostitutes had passed through the shelter's doors at least a few times in the last nine months, although neither could be more specific than that. At least, it was a start, Frank thought as he gathered up the photographs.

None of the career women who'd been slain were familiar to either of the two shelter employees. Half was better than none.

"You're not going to say anything to the media, are you? About them being here, I mean. The dead women,"

Wilcox elaborated haltingly as he walked them to the entrance of shelter. He paused to pick up a mop that had fallen on the floor, leaning it back against the wall. He muttered something about no one knowing how to do a decent job these days, then looked at Frank for an answer to his question. "You're not, right?"

Frank had little use for the media. They tended to sensationalize everything. He believed the dead women should be allowed to rest in peace—as soon as their killer was caught.

He fixed Wilcox with a penetrating look that made the man squirm. "Why don't you want the media to know?" he asked.

Wilcox looked genuinely horrified. "That kind of publicity will keep them from coming here, the ones who need this place the most. If they think someone's watching, picking them off…" He fumbled for a conclusion to his statement and his voice just trailed off.

Frank didn't know whether to feel sorry for Wilcox or disgusted by him. The man was obviously worried about keeping his job, not the people he was supposed to be helping.

"I doubt the people who come here have the time or the opportunity to watch TV," Frank replied sarcastically.

"We do a lot of good here," Wilcox called after them. "We do."

"Jerk," Frank muttered under his breath.

"He's just afraid for his job," Julianne said, getting into the car on the passenger side. And then she looked at Frank as he got in on his side. "You think there might be two serial killers at work?"

Turning on the ignition, he pulled out of the space before glancing at her. "What?"

"Do you think there might be two serial killers?" she repeated. "One killing prostitutes, one targeting career women."

Now there was a horrific thought. "Two killers with the same M.O.? Highly unlikely." He noted the flashing red light in the middle of his dashboard. It meant a seat belt wasn't secured. "Buckle up," he instructed.

Julianne glanced down and realized her oversight. She pulled the belt over and slid the metal tongue into the slot. "Maybe they're playing tag team, like wrestlers."

Frank shook his head. There were no documented cases to support that theory—and he hoped to God there never would be. "Any time there's been a team, they've worked together. One dominant, one subservient, but always both together." Again, he glanced quickly at her to bring his point home. "And, before you say it, I don't think it's a copycat killer, either. Not all the details have been released to the press, so someone reading about the murders and deciding to go off on their own killing spree wouldn't be able to follow the M.O. to the letter."

She knew he was referring to the fact that no mention had been made that there had always been a tiny cross carved on the victim's right shoulder. That part had been deliberately left out.

Thinking, she sank deeper into her seat. "Okay, so what have we got? A rather loose connection between the prostitutes," she said, answering her own question. "How does this relate to the career women?"

"Oh, my turn?" he asked, tongue in cheek, then grew serious. "It doesn't. Yet."

The last word surprised her. "You know, when I first met you, McIntyre, you didn't strike me as the optimistic type."

He sped up in order to pass a car in the next lane, then changed lanes to get in front of it. "Just for the record, that's not optimistic, White Bear, that's tenacious."

She nodded. "So, then you're not optimistic."

"Didn't say that," he pointed out. "Just trying to clear up a point."

Okay, if it wasn't A, then it was B. "Then you *are* optimistic."

He spared her a fleeting glance even though he was driving. "Yes."

She studied his profile for a moment. It had noble lines. And, if she were to draw conclusions from last night, so did he. "About solving this case?"

She thought she saw the corner of his mouth curving. "Among other things."

Was this about last night? she wondered. Had he just pretended to be noble, in effect laying groundwork for later? To what end? He could have had her last night if he wanted. And this morning, there would have been no recriminations.

The man was complicated, she decided. "They all involve you being tenacious?"

"Yup."

Definitely complicated. She knew she was better off for not having anything happen last night, and yet…more than a little curiosity had been aroused.

And that wasn't the only thing to have been aroused.

"I see," she murmured.

"By the way, there's a party being thrown for my mother and stepfather this Saturday," he said without any preamble. "You're invited."

She ignored the invitation for the time being. "What's the occasion?"

"Their six-month anniversary." In some ways, it felt as if his mother had been married to Brian forever. Maybe because that was the way it should have been, from the beginning, he mused.

Her frame of reference when growing up had been life on the reservation. Even though it had been eight years since she'd left, she still wasn't fully acclimated to the outside world. "Do people usually throw parties for that around here?"

He thought that was an odd way to phrase it, but didn't comment. "They're not throwing it, Andrew Cavanaugh is."

She connected the name to what she'd been told previously. "The former chief of police to whose house both you and Riley have tried to get me to go."

He was unaware of Riley's efforts, but nodded. "That's the one," he replied with a grin. It was obvious that he was fond of the other man. "His parties are usually loud and noisy, but the food is incredible and you can't beat the atmosphere. Wall-to-wall cops and family," he elaborated when Julianne said nothing.

Wall to wall *Aurora* cops and family. And she was neither. "And I'm invited."

He nodded. "You're invited."

It wasn't the former police chief who was inviting her, it was McIntyre. Even if she liked parties, she wasn't about to crash one. "Andrew Cavanaugh doesn't know me from Adam."

They were at a light, and Frank gave her a very thorough once-over. One that made her feel as if her clothes had evaporated.

"Oh, he could tell you from Adam, trust me. Besides, *I* know you—and you're a cop. That's more than reason enough for an invitation."

She was about to point out that she was on loan, that she didn't belong here and that she didn't believe in crashing parties, but only got as far as the first two words.

"I don't—"

He didn't give her a chance to refuse. "What have you got to lose?" he challenged. "I'll give you the address and you can come over on your own. You don't like it, you're free to leave. Nobody's going to handcuff you to the banister."

The way he said it suggested to her that he'd considered that an option. "So that's already crossed your mind?"

"No, but I'm guessing it probably crossed yours," he countered.

Of course it did, since she said it, she thought. "Good call. Okay. Maybe," she qualified, knowing that when tomorrow came, more than likely, she wouldn't show up at the gathering.

"All I heard was *okay,*" he told her, putting her on notice.

She laughed shortly, amused. "Is this where you being tenacious comes in?"

McIntyre merely grinned at her. She had her answer.

* * *

For the rest of the day, they went over the list of St. Vincent de Paul's employees, past and present, and the handful of volunteers that Wilcox had ultimately given them. While Sanchez, Hill and Riley reexamined the late prostitutes' living quarters, she and Frank remained at the precinct, checking into backgrounds and any prior histories that the employees and volunteers might have had for any arrests or run-ins with the law.

By day's end, Julianne's frustration had grown to huge proportions.

"Other than one of the volunteers being arrested for lewd behavior on the beach almost a decade ago, the worst thing I could come up with are several unpaid traffic tickets—all belonging to Wilcox," she told Frank when he came by her desk to check on her progress—or lack thereof. "Maybe that was why he looked so nervous when we came in," she speculated.

"That," Frank allowed, "or maybe he just had a natural aversion to having the police come by to question him."

Frank leaned in to look at her screen. What he accomplished was simultaneously invading her space and clouding her thinking. In an effort to get him to move, she repositioned her monitor so that he had a better view. He remained where he was. Crowding her.

"Looking for something?" she finally asked.

He hit a key, then another. The screen changed, but enlightenment didn't come. "Yeah."

She looked from the screen to Frank. "What?"

This time, Frank did straighten up. A sigh escaped

his lips as he did so. "I don't know. Just that magical something that'll put us on the right track. I was really hoping that we had a former mental patient or someone with a history of violence in that pack. But from the looks of it, we've got nothing but average people and solid citizens." He tapped two of the names on the list on her desk. They corresponded to the two screens he'd just perused. "One's a lawyer who also volunteers his time at a free legal aid clinic in Oakland and the other's a C.P.A. who's a scout master and he used to volunteer at a soup kitchen in Santa Cruz when he lived there. Even sings in the church choir."

Perching on a corner of her desk, Frank scrubbed his hand over his face, as if that could somehow sharpen his focus, or bring something to light.

"Nothing," he repeated more to himself than to her. "Nothing."

"I think we need to get away from this for a while," Riley suggested, getting up from her desk. The day she and the other two detectives had spent had bore no more fruit than Frank and Julianne's day. "Take a break and come back fresh. Maybe something will come to us then."

The look Frank gave his sister was both skeptical and weary. "Let's hope the serial killer takes a break, too."

"After upping the kill to two? Not damn likely," Sanchez scoffed. Julianne saw Riley shoot him a dirty look. Sanchez shrugged his stocky shoulders, backpedaling as swiftly as he could. "But hey, what do I know? Anything's possible."

Frank looked at the string of dead women neatly

tacked up on the bulletin boards. His gut told him this wasn't the end of it. "That's what I'm afraid of."

She had no intention of attending the six-month an-niversary party, just as she'd had no intention of showing up at Andrew Cavanaugh's breakfast table when both Riley and Frank had suggested it. It wasn't even on her mind when her cell phone rang a little before noon on Saturday. She was on her way back to McFadden Boule-vard with Mary's photograph in her purse.

When she saw Frank's name on her caller ID, the first thing she thought of was that there'd been another murder.

"Where and when?" she snapped out as she got on the line.

"18931 Riverview."

She began to program the address into the car's navi-gational system, then stopped. She'd heard that address before. "Isn't that Andrew Cavanaugh's house?"

"Yes." She heard the smile in his voice.

Julianne sighed. For a second, she was sorely tempted just to terminate the call and keep driving to McFadden. But, technically, McIntyre was her boss. For now. She couldn't just blow him off no matter how much she wanted to.

"I thought there'd been another murder," she said impatiently. "Look, I'm in the middle of something—"

"Still trying to find out where your cousin was staying." It wasn't exactly a guess. And the silence that met his statement told him what he needed to know. "I might have some information for you along those lines."

She was instantly alert. *"Might?"* she echoed expectantly.

"Actually," Frank amended, "I do."

She wanted to demand the information, but knew that wasn't the way the game was being played. "And, let me guess, if I want it, I'm going to have to meet you at Chief Cavanaugh's house."

"Captain Randolph did send us the sharpest knife in the drawer, didn't he?"

She knew he was smirking, she would have given anything to wipe the expression off his chiseled face. She had absolutely no patience with games, or people who played them. "If this turns out to be a ploy just to get me over there—" And why it should even matter to him that she should be there left her completely baffled.

Frank stopped her before she could—he instinctively felt—begin to elaborate about the slow torture she could devise for him. "It's not. I do have some information you'd be interested in."

"About?" It was going to turn out to be something trivial—if he actually had something, which she still doubted.

"Where your cousin lived."

Four words. Just four words. And they went straight to her chest, rendering her immobile. He was probably bluffing, but she couldn't afford to just discount it. Because McIntyre was just perverse enough to actually *have* exactly what he said he had.

"And if I show up, you'll tell me?"

"Yes."

She didn't believe him. There was more of a catch to it. "Immediately?"

Julianne heard him laugh. Though she tried to block it, the sound encompassed her, warming her like a fire on a cold night. She wished it wouldn't, but there was no getting away from the fact.

It had been her hope that having sex with Frank McIntyre would have permanently laid to rest her attraction to him, but that hadn't happened. Yet.

"No, not immediately," he told her. "I want you to stay at the party for a little while."

She knew better than to agree outright. He had her over a barrel, but she still wanted to be clear on as much as she could be. "How little a while?"

She heard him pause, considering her question. "Give it two hours."

Two hours. An eternity. "And after that?"

"I'll tell you," he said cheerfully. "So, do we have a deal?"

She was already turning her car around and heading back to the hotel. "Do I have a choice?"

"Sure. You don't have to come."

Right. He knew that wasn't going to happen. For only one reason. "And you won't tell me."

"You catch on quick."

Stopped at a light, she looked down at what she was wearing: worn jeans and a T-shirt that had seen better days. She'd put them on so she'd appear nonthreatening to the prostitutes. Ordinarily, she didn't care what people thought, but she didn't want to look like a raga-muffin, either.

"I'll be there as soon as I can," she told him.

"Don't bother changing," he told her, guessing for the reason for the delay. "It's strictly casual. Come as you are."

"And if I'm naked?" she posed.

"You wouldn't be driving around in your car if you were."

"Good hearing," she commented.

"I like to keep all my parts in top running order," he quipped.

She refused to let her imagination run off with that. "Yeah, that's what they all say. I'll be there soon," she promised, ending the call with a snap of the lid on her cell phone.

When had it gotten so warm in her car?

Forty minutes later, after stopping at the hotel to put on a shirt, a long-sleeved white one that buttoned in the front and had been freshly ironed, and black, thin pinstriped slacks, then picking up a bottle of wine as a last-minute gift, Julianne showed up at Andrew Cavanaugh's residence.

The noise—music, laughter and overlapping conversations—was not fully contained by the closed door. The people inside sounded as if they were having fun. She didn't know if she was up to facing that.

For a moment, she debated just turning around and getting back into her car. McIntyre was probably putting her on about the information, using it to get her over here.

But she couldn't leave any stone unturned, Julianne silently insisted.

She forced herself to knock on the door before she

could leave. She knocked hard, instinctively knowing that the doorbell would go unheard. The moment she knocked, the door sprang open, giving her the impression that someone had been waiting and watching for her.

She expected to see Frank standing there. Instead, she found herself looking up at a tall, distinguished-looking man in his early fifties with possibly the warmest smile she'd ever seen.

He looked enough like Brian Cavanaugh to convince her that she was in the presence of the family patriarch and former chief of police, Andrew Cavanaugh. But before Julianne could say a word or introduce herself, the man was enveloping her hand warmly between both of his.

She felt both power and tranquility radiating from the contact.

"You must be Julianne."

Chapter 11

"I guess I must be," Julianne heard herself murmuring, a faint smile rising to her lips almost of its own accord. Had Frank said something to him about her attending? "How did you…?"

His eyes crinkled as his smile deepened. "I'm the former chief of police, Julianne. It was my job to know everything. I still like to keep my hand in, exercise the old brain cells every now and then." His eyes skimmed over her, taking full measure, no doubt. He made her think of an eagle, majestic and in control of all he surveyed. A nice eagle, she amended. "According to my brother, Brian, Frank and Riley speak very highly of you."

Julianne was at a complete loss as to how to respond to that. She wasn't accustomed to being confronted with compliments. Criticism, yes, she knew how to react then. But this was unfamiliar ground for her.

She cleared her throat. "Yes, well, I think they're pretty good cops, too."

Andrew smiled at her, as if to indicate that her being a good police detective hadn't been the focus of the conversations he'd been privy to. But he said nothing further along those lines.

Because she made no effort to come in, he took the lead. "Would you like to come in?" he coaxed.

She flushed. "I guess I'd better, if I want my hand back."

Andrew chuckled. "Good call." But she noticed that the former police chief didn't release her hand until she was across the threshold. Just long enough for Frank to reach them.

To reach her.

"I was beginning to give up hope," he told her cheerfully.

"Hope is something you *never* give up," Andrew told him. "Not while there's a breath left in your body." And then he winked. "Remember that." And then he turned to her again. "I'd better go see to the food. A pleasure finally meeting you, Julianne."

"Likewise," she said, still a bit dazed. Suddenly realizing that she was still holding on to the beribboned bottle of wine she'd brought, she held it out to him. "Oh, this is for the Chief and Mrs. Cavanaugh."

Andrew accepted the bottle. "Thank you. I'll be sure to let them know you brought it."

As the former chief melted into the crowd, Julianne turned around to face Frank. "*Finally* meeting me?"

She echoed the word Andrew had used. "I haven't been in town that long."

"It's all relative," Frank assured her. He subtly maneuvered his body so that she was no longer facing the door—and could escape.

Julianne looked around the large living room—and whatever she could see beyond. More than half the people there were Cavanaughs, the people she'd been introduced to at Rafferty's the first night.

"Yeah, so I noticed," she commented. There were more people in this room than on the reservation, when she'd finally left it. "You people could go off and form your own city."

Frank grinned. Figuratively, they already had. Andrew had five children, all married with families of their own. Brian had four in the same state, not to mention that when the man had married his mother, he'd inherited four more "unofficial" Cavanaughs. And his stepfather's late brother, Mike, had two offspring that he'd owned up to and three that he hadn't. That made for quite a full house.

"What makes you think we haven't?" he teased. Changing the subject as he eased Julianne farther into the room, he asked, "Would you like a drink?"

She didn't want to stay any longer than she absolutely had to. "What I'd like is that information you promised me."

She wasn't thrilled with the enigmatic smile that curved his mouth. "All in good time, Julianne. All in good time. First, let's go see about that drink."

Before she could argue with him, or accuse Frank

of luring her out on false pretenses, he floored her by taking her hand and leading her over to one of the side tables against the wall. This particular one had a bar set up on it.

His brother Zack was manning the bar, aided and abetted by a pretty dark-haired woman she heard him refer to as Krystle. By the look on both their faces, she gathered that they were more than just casually friendly. The next moment, she noticed the winking diamond on Krystle's left hand. The ring silently confirmed her suspicions.

"I see he got you to come," Zack said, offering her the same warm smile she'd seen on Frank's lips. The family resemblance was hard to miss. The same bone structure, the same black hair and intense blue eyes. "Some shindig, isn't it?" Zack raised a glass in a silent toast to his step-uncle. "Andrew Cavanaugh really knows how to throw a party."

"What's really amazing," Riley chimed in, coming up behind her and Frank, "is that Uncle Andrew can do this kind of thing at the drop of a hat—and often." She placed herself between the two couples. "You should have seen our mother's wedding reception." And then Riley rethought her words. "Come to think of it, you probably will." She grinned at her older brother and his fiancée. "I heard that he's already busy putting together Zack and Krystle's reception." There was laughter in her eyes. "Should be some blowout," Riley predicted.

"Congratulations," Julianne murmured, addressing her words to the couple behind the makeshift bar.

Frank took the bottle of beer his brother handed him without a word. He saluted his future sister-in-law with it. "My money's still on Krystle coming to her senses and making a mad dash out of town."

"No," Krystle said softly, her eyes shining as she looked at Zack the way a woman might look at her hero, Julian though. "My dashing-out-of-town days are all behind me, thanks to Zack."

Lost, Julianne looked at Frank for an explanation. "Long story," he confided, lowering his mouth to her ear. "I promise to tell it to you if you stick around long enough."

That was just it, she really wasn't planning to stick around at all. These were very nice people, but she had no real business being here. She didn't fit in. But she let Frank's words slide without bothering to correct him. She'd discovered long ago that the less she said, the less she had to be accountable for.

Making a noncommittal noise, she accepted the glass of ginger ale that Zack poured for her and subtly glanced at her watch.

Eight hours later, Frank said to her, "Okay, it's getting late and I guess it's time to go."

Seated on a sofa in the living room, Julianne looked at him in surprise. She had no idea how it had gotten to be so late. The hours seemed to have melted away and she'd been having too much of a good time to notice. That in itself, she realized, was a rarity. If she attended a party at all, she was accustomed to standing on the perimeter, observing.

That sort of thing wasn't allowed at one of Andrew Cavanaugh's gatherings. Everyone was drawn in, from the youngest to the oldest. No excuses were accepted. By anyone. Cavanaughs-by-marriage were just as apt to reel people in as the core family members—and quite possibly were even more intense about it. In the last eight hours, she'd gotten completely absorbed by the Cavanaughs, there was no other word for it.

During the course of the evening, it seemed to Julianne that every single person at the party came by at least once to talk to her. Frank's mother, Lila Cavanaugh, had spent nearly an hour with her, talking to her the way she might have talked to a daughter. There were no barriers, no awkward pauses. Everything was straightforward and friendly.

They looked very good together, Julianne observed. Lila and Brian seemed perfectly matched, as if they'd been created as a set. Julianne could easily see why they—and their children—were so happy about the union.

Happy, that was the word for them. They were all happy.

Another foreign concept, Julianne thought, trying to remember when she'd last been in that state. Nothing came to mind.

That was when Frank told her that *they* were leaving.

She glanced at him, wondering if she'd misheard. There was no *they.* She and Frank had come in separate cars. And she was quick to point out that fact right after they'd said their goodbyes and Frank mentioned something about dropping her off at her hotel.

"In case you've forgotten," she told him patiently, "I came in my own car, McIntyre."

Frank seemed utterly unfazed. "Okay, then you can

drop me off at my place," he countered without missing a beat.

"What about your car?"

His attention fully focused on her, he dismissed the question with a careless shrug. "I can always have Riley pick me up in the morning and bring me back here to pick it up."

"Why go through all that trouble?" she asked.

That was when the look in his eyes almost undid her. "Because a little extra time with you would be well worth it."

Something tightened in her stomach. She was reacting to him again. With effort, she held it in. "Are you supposed to be talking to me like that? I'm mean, you are technically my temporary boss."

"Not here I'm not." As far as he was concerned, they were equals away from the precinct. "Here I'm just Frank McIntyre, hoping to snag a few minutes alone with a beautiful woman."

Smooth, very smooth, she thought. How many women had this man sweet-talked? "That just glides off your tongue, doesn't it?"

The expression on his face was innocence personified. "Never had trouble with the truth."

Julianne rolled her eyes. He was good, very good. He sounded as if he meant what he said. But she was very aware of his reputation.

"Okay, I'll take you home," she told him, then gave him her conditions. "But only if you promise to tell me whether or not you actually have that information about where Mary lived."

Shouting a general goodbye to the room as he headed out the front door, Frank took her hand as easily as if he'd always been doing it. She did her best to ignore the warm feeling that came over her.

"I do," Frank said, answering her question.

Julianne stopped walking. Hunk or no hunk, she wasn't going to let him yank her around anymore. "I'm not taking another step until you tell me where her apartment is—or was," she corrected. God, but it was hard thinking of Mary in the past tense. She didn't think she'd ever get used to it.

He looked at her for a long moment, as if debating whether or not she meant it. He obviously decided that she did because the next words out of his mouth were, "All right, you lived up to your part of the bargain I'll live up to mine. I'll tell you where she was staying when she was murdered."

The mere mention of the word wounded her. She forced herself to focus on what he was saying.

"I want to go there," Julianne insisted as a surge of adrenaline appeared out of nowhere and found her. She felt her blood rushing in her veins, excitement skipping through her.

The look on his face was incredulous. He checked his watch. It was past eleven. "Now?"

"Now," Julianne declared firmly. There was no room for argument.

Frank sincerely had his doubts about the wisdom of going to that part of Aurora at this hour. "Why don't we wait until morning?" he suggested. "It's a really seedy part of the city." And it would only look more so with the absence of light.

But she refused to be talked out of it. This was where Mary lived. Possibly where she died. She *had* to see it.

"I'm not afraid," she told him crisply, then tried her best to smile as she added, "I have the chief of detectives' stepson with me."

Frank set his mouth grimly. "Okay."

He agreed, but it was against his better judgment. Not because the area wasn't safe, but because viewing the squalid living quarters at night would make them appear even more depressing than they already were. She didn't need that, he thought.

When they reached her car, she got in on the driver's side. "Why don't you let me drive?" he suggested. "I know where it is."

But she shook her head. She was too wired to sit quietly in the passenger seat. "You can guide me," she told him.

Resigned, Frank got in on the passenger side. Like a live version of a global positioning satellite, he doled out the directions in a modular voice as they came to each turn.

As she drove, she became increasingly aware of the changes that came over the scenery. For the most part, Aurora was upper middle class with all that entailed. But here, in the older part of the city, the moon didn't cast as bright a light. It somehow seemed darker along the more narrow streets with their aged buildings. Darker and sullenly hopeless.

Parking in the street before a graffiti-laden building that had, for the last ten months, been condemned by the city—Mary's building—Julianne tried to brace herself.

"You sure you want to do this?" Frank asked,

opening the heavy iron door that marked the entrance to the building and holding it ajar.

Julianne squared her shoulders and looked straight ahead. "I'm sure."

She wasn't prepared for this.

Coming from a reservation where poverty was the general a way of life, Julianne discovered that she was still unprepared for the levels of poverty, of hopelessness that she found within the condemned building.

The smell was appalling and she came close to gagging. The acrid odor that pervaded the dank, dark hallway, was made up of many components: urine, dead rats, garbage left out to rot and other things that were better left unidentified.

Because there was no electricity, they used the flashlight that she kept in her glove compartment to illuminate their way inside the building. The lone beam intensified the poverty.

"It's right here," Frank said, pointing to the apartment to the left of the stairwell.

Walking ahead of her, he pushed open the door that no longer had a lock on it. Frank crossed the threshold and waited for her. He shouldn't have told her. But then, she would have found out anyway. The discovery had to be made part of the report and she would have held it against him once she found out that he knew and hadn't told her.

"And she *lived* here?" Julianne whispered in disbelieving horror. In comparison, the home Mary had run away from had been a palace.

Complete with its own monster, Julianne thought cynically.

She could hardly bring herself to move out of the doorway. The single barren space, once advertised as a studio apartment, almost screamed of despair. It was completely devoid of furniture. Beyond the dirt, there was only one thing in the apartment.

An old, worn-out blanket spread out on the cracked wooden floor.

Mary's bed.

Finally moving forward, Julianne crossed to the blanket and crouched down to examine it. But even as she did so, her heart felt as if it was constricting in her chest.

"I gave this to her," Julianne said hoarsely, only vaguely addressing her words to Frank. "Years ago. It was our grandmother's. Oh, God." Her voice nearly cracked. She felt hands on her shoulders, felt Frank raising her to her feet. She turned to him. Angry, confused. Hurting. "How could she have lived like this? How could *anyone* have lived like this?" she demanded, struggling not to cry.

"There were people she could have gone to," Frank told her. "Missions. Homeless shelters. Organizations." All the places they were presently checking out for any spare information about the victims. "She chose not to. Pride?" he guessed.

Julianne shook her head. She had a better answer. "Fear. Mary was afraid of everyone," she told him. Her uncle had done that to Mary. Made her afraid to trust anyone. If you couldn't trust your own father, who could you trust?

A sob racking her lungs, she squeezed her eyes tight, trying to push back the tears. They managed to seep through her dark lashes anyway.

Seeing her this way got to him. He *knew* it was a bad idea, telling her. "C'mon," he coaxed. "You don't belong here."

"Neither did Mary," she insisted, raising her voice angrily.

"No," Frank agreed gently, guiding her out the door and down the hall to the front entrance. "Neither did Mary."

The air outside the building smelled almost sweet in comparison. She took in several deep gulps, trying to regain control over herself. He waited, then brought her over to the car.

"I'll drive," he told her.

She would have taken it as a challenge, had she any energy left to her. But she suddenly felt too wiped out, too numb to argue with him. Very quietly she surrendered her keys.

He drove her vehicle to his apartment.

Becoming aware of her location, Julianne eyed him quizzically. After what she'd just been through, she'd assumed that he'd bring her to her hotel.

"I thought you might want to talk for a while," he explained.

"No," she whispered, shaking her head. "What's there to talk about?"

"We'll find something," he promised, getting out. Rounding the hood, he came over to her side and opened the door for her. He took it as a bad sign that she made no cryptic remark about her capabilities regarding opening her own door. "At any rate, you shouldn't be alone right now."

She wanted to argue with him. To lash out at

McIntyre. At *anyone*. But instead, she merely nodded and allowed him to help her out of the car.

Unlocking the door to his ground-floor apartment, Frank brought her inside. "I can put on some coffee," he volunteered.

She was finally beginning to understand why her father crawled away from life and into the bottom of a bottle. The pain ripping her heart apart was almost too much to bear. She ignored his offer for coffee. "Do you have any whiskey?"

He thought of the bottle left over from celebrating his mother's marriage. It was on the kitchen counter, next to the canister of sugar. "Yes."

She took a deep breath, nodding. "Whiskey, then."

"No."

Julianne looked at him in surprise, wondering if she'd heard right. "What?"

"No," he repeated. He could guess at what was on her mind and he wasn't about to let her make that kind of a mistake. "That won't help you. It'll just give you a headache. Tomorrow the same feelings will be there and you'll have one hell of a killer hangover."

What kind of a man was he anyway? She stared at him, stunned. "I thought men liked getting women drunk. Hoping to get lucky."

"I don't want to 'get lucky,'" he deliberately enunciated the phrase. "I want you to be okay."

She bit her lower lip to keep it from trembling. "Well, that's not going to happen. I don't think I'm ever going to be okay again." Her voice broke in the middle of her words and she covered her mouth with her hands, trying to pull herself together and still the sobs that threatened to break out. "Oh God, Frank. Oh God," she repeated, unable to finish.

Because she was crying, he took her into his arms, trying to quiet her, trying to offer her what comfort he could.

"I know," he said softly against her hair. "I know. And I'm sorry. I'm so very sorry."

It was the worst thing in the world he could have done or said. The show of sympathy made the dam inside of her break apart into a million pieces.

Chapter 12

He made her feel safe. As if having his arms around her created some sort of a haven, was some kind of a barrier against all the hurt that the world had to offer. Knowing she shouldn't, Julianne clung to that. Clung to him.

Later, looking back, she wasn't really sure how it all happened.

One minute, she was holding on to Frank, on to the tiny fragment of peace he magically created for her. And then the next, she'd raised her mouth, salty with her fallen tears, to his.

In less than a heartbeat, the kiss sealed her to him, evolving from a quest for comfort to sheer exploding passion. Her arms went around his neck as she poured her entire soul into the kiss. Her fragile world was rocked because Frank McIntyre kissed her back the way she had never been kissed before—except, perhaps, that one time. By him.

Damn it, Frank silently cursed. Instead of easier, Julianne White Bear was getting harder and harder to resist.

This absolutely *had* to go under the heading of being close to superhuman, he thought, as he struggled to put distance between himself and her. Struggled to just separate himself from her.

It wasn't easy.

But he had to. For her sake if not for his. She wasn't thinking clearly and he couldn't allow himself to get carried away when she was like that.

Drawing his head back, he attempted to remove her arms from around his neck. "Julianne, you're upset—"

"Don't say no to me, Frank," she pleaded quietly. "Don't say no."

He had expected her to take offense and pull away. She didn't.

Frank bit back a frustrated groan, convinced he was going to hate himself in the morning for what he was valiantly trying to do tonight.

He had to keep talking until she came to her senses. "I didn't bring you here for this, Julianne."

She believed him. God help her, she believed him. With eyes and a mouth like sin, the man still had his own honorable code of ethics.

But she didn't want honorable, not tonight. If she couldn't lose herself in a bottle, then she was going to lose herself in him. She *needed* to.

"New plan, then," Julianne told him less than a half a beat before she sealed her mouth to his again.

He felt intoxicated. His head was swimming. And when he tried to draw her away a second time, the look in her eyes stopped him cold. It was a mixture of pleading and sadness. Sadness of a kind that he'd never seen before. Sadness that went clear down to the bone. Clear *into* the bone.

All he could think of was wiping that sadness away. He brought his mouth down to hers.

The next moment, he found himself engulfed in sensations running rampant through him. He felt as if he was about to burst into flame. A completely new experience for him. Considering the fact he was far from a novice with women, that was saying a great deal. He'd honestly thought there were no new experiences left for him.

To find out he was wrong was both humbling and earthshaking at the same time. The revelation didn't even involve any sort of new, exotic technique on her part. She wasn't doing anything different, anything extraordinary. She was just kissing him.

There was no "just" about it.

The mere sensation of her velvet lips against his awoke something inside of him, something that made him want to comfort her at the same time that it urged him to take solace within her.

In the eye of the storm, there was peace.

Rather than lyrical, the lovemaking that erupted between them sizzled and was close to frantic. Clothes went flying in all directions. Mouths, teeth, tongues went exploring, tasting, sampling. Glorying. And with each pass bringing a giant wave of extreme pleasure, the magnitude of which, heretofore, had not been felt or even suspected.

Frank came to realize it was his soul quaking, as close to an out-of-body experience as he would ever hope to have.

The more he kissed Julianne, the more he wanted to kiss her. Every single tempting inch of her.

His hands skimmed over her body, caressing, touching, possessing and questing until he was fairly certain he could re create her shape blindfolded. And all the while, as he was trying to deal with an expanding host of emotions, something inside of him was building up a huge head of steam, threatening an even greater eruption than he'd already experienced.

He'd never felt out of control before, not even marginally. Here he was barely holding on with his fingertips.

The very scent of her was driving him wild.

More than anything else, Julianne wanted to get lost in him, to literally disintegrate and maybe, just maybe, reinvent herself and come back as something new. Someone else. Someone who had no bad memories coloring each and every fiber of her life, casting shadows so engulfing that there was no space for happiness.

She *needed* happiness.

That's what this emotion was, Julianne suddenly realized with a start. *Happiness.* Frank had the ability to make things glow inside of her. The ability to bring happiness into her life, however briefly.

Close to breathless, Julianne felt herself scrambling

to embrace the warmth, to embrace the completely foreign sensation of well-being radiating all through her.

And then, out of nowhere, she felt herself in the midst of fireworks exploding throughout her body, beginning with her very core.

Startled, Julianne's deep blue eyes widened as she struggled to both absorb the experience and, at the same time, prolong it.

Was this what she thought it was?

Arching against him, pressing her lips together to keep a sob from escaping, she felt the heat of Frank's breath on her belly.

The explosion left her wanting more.

She grabbed his shoulders, barely getting her fingers around them as she urgently tried to pull Frank up toward her, desperately wanting to seal her mouth to his. To give back a little of what she'd received. It was only fair.

As Frank slowly snaked his body over hers, rising to her level, she saw his smile through the haze swirling around her brain. It wasn't a superior smirk, which would have all but killed her, but a smile, as if he could read her thoughts. As if he was enjoying her enjoying what he was doing to her.

Her heart slammed against her rib cage, tired of its prison.

Her breath all but gone, coming in ragged snatches, Julianne spread her legs for him, silently inviting Frank to become one with her.

Not to have sex with her, she suddenly realized, but to become one with her.

What had he done to her?

And then, there was no time for silent questions, no time to think, only to react. Frank was driving himself into her. The rhythm of life took hold as he infused her with the same melody that he was moving with. The same melody that he heard in his head.

Their rhythm of life.

The tempo increased, going faster and faster. Together, they raced toward the promise of stardust and dreams, however fleeting it might be. And then, just as the singular golden moment arrived, Frank, his hands joined with hers, kissed her.

Hard.

As if they belonged together forever.

The glow began to recede seconds after it had arrived and she struggled to hang on to it for just a little longer. If she could have, she would have pressed the feeling between the pages of a book.

A sense of sorrow moved to take its place. Sorrow because she'd never experienced anything even close to this level of excitement and passion before and was more than convinced she never would again.

When Frank shifted his weight off her, she expected him to get up and hurry into his clothes. Expected him to say something not too subtle about the fact that she should be leaving soon.

The one thing she didn't expect was for Frank to thread his arm around her and draw her closer to him. And she certainly didn't expect him just to hold her.

Moreover, she didn't expect to have the feel of his heart beating hard against hers generate such a sensation of comfort within her.

What was going on here? She had no answer.

The sound of their combined breathing was the only sound that drifted through the apartment. Confused by her feelings, by his actions, by everything that had transpired this last hour, Julianne turned toward the man who'd set her world on fire and demanded, "Aren't you going to say anything?"

Smiling, Frank brushed his lips over the top of her head and murmured, "How about those Dodgers?" The next moment he was laughing because she'd hit his shoulder with the heel of her hand. Hard. She packed quite a wallop, in more ways than one.

"Wrong thing to say?" he guessed.

She sat up then, pulling her knees up to her chest and huddling her body into almost a tight ball. She said nothing, her midnight-black hair raining down along her arm.

His amusement faded to concern. Frank sat up beside her. But when he tried to put his arm around her, she shrugged it off, making an unintelligible sound. "Julianne, are you all right?"

No, I'm not all right. I'm confused. Up is down, down is up and all I want to do is make love with you again. And again.

"What did you just do?" she demanded hotly. The question sounded as if it was a trick one, meant to trip him up. Frank didn't answer her immediately. "What did you just do?" she demanded again, more angrily this time, turning her face toward him.

Like a man trying to survive his way crossing a minefield, Frank picked his path slowly. "If you have to ask, I guess I must have done it wrong."

"Yes, you did it wrong," she accused. She felt like crying and laughing at the same time. Was she going crazy? "I *felt* something," she fairly shouted the words at him. "I'm not supposed to feel anything."

He stared at her. She couldn't be serious—could she? "Who told you that?"

"Me, I told me that," she snapped. "If you don't feel, then you're safe."

He had his answer. It was starting to make sense now. Julianne was angry at him because she'd just lost her defense mechanism.

"No," he corrected her quietly, skimming his fingertips along her face ever so lightly. "Then you're isolated—and you might as well be dead. Life is about reaching out, Julianne. About feeling. And you, lady, whether you like it or not, made the earth move for me."

She wished she could believe him. But she knew better. "Is that your usual speech?" she asked, trying her best to sound haughty and disdainful. Anything but naively trusting.

"No," he told her honestly. And then he smiled at her. It was a small, intimate smile and, like a rose-tipped arrow, it went straight to her heart. "It's okay to be afraid, Julianne."

He was reading her mind and that scared the hell out of her. Her chin shot up. "I'm not afraid," she retorted.

He saw right through her. Right through the lie, but

he allowed her to have it. "Good," he answered, "because I am."

What kind of a game was this? Men like Frank didn't admit to fear. They didn't *have* fear, not when it came to women. "You?"

In his own way, he'd played it safe all his life when it came to the fairer sex. It was time to risk something in order to win something.

Still, it took him a moment before he could. "Something just happened here that never happened before— and you scared the hell out of me."

She made no effort to bank down the smirk. "You're not going to tell me that you've never made love before, are you?"

"Oh, I've made love before," he assured her. "But I've never felt as if I wasn't in control of the situation before." His eyes skimmed over her, creating swirls of warmth throughout her body. And then he grinned. "Must have been a fluke."

If that was the way he wanted to play it, fine. "Must have."

But his eyes wouldn't release hers. And she could feel her heart accelerating again, just as it had the last time.

"Only one way to find out if it was or not," he told her.

It took her a second to realize that her breath was just sitting in her throat, stuck. She could barely squeeze the words out.

"And that is?"

Frank kissed her shoulder, sending all sorts of delicious sensations scrambling through her—again. And they all felt stronger than they had the first time. "Guess."

Julianne turned her face toward his and within a moment, there was no need to guess. Because he was showing her.

Exhausted, spent, Julianne fell back, snuggling against the space that Frank had created for her with the crook of his arm.

Incredibly, it had happened again. He'd had her climaxing, one overwhelming, breath-stealing sensation flowering into another until she thought she was going to die from the myriad sensations assaulting her body. Die willingly and happily.

Granted, she was as confused as she'd been the first time around, but this time she caught herself smiling more. Willing to accept the pleasure at its face value. The proof was that she found herself curling into him rather than into herself.

She knew it was all just temporary, all just an illusion. But for now, she wanted nothing more than to hang on to it for however short a time period she had left to her.

Was this what it was like, she wondered. To be normal? Not to be the prisoner of dark memories and a childhood that had had the blush of innocence stolen away all too soon?

If she could just pretend….

And then, the ribbon of a melody sliced through the sound of their joint, uneven breathing. The song was vaguely familiar to her, although she couldn't place it immediately.

The next moment, she heard Frank groaning. With a resigned sigh, he sat up. "That's my phone," he told her, looking around.

It was evident that he hadn't the slightest idea where his cell phone was. Frank began sorting through their clothes, trying to locate the evil instrument that had called a halt to their euphoric state.

Just as he found his pants, and, by association, his cell phone, a high-pitched ringing noise chimed in.

That was her phone.

They exchanged looks, both knowing what that meant. Neither one wanted to say it out loud, hoping that they were wrong, that their night of lovemaking wasn't being capped off by the discovery of yet another body cast off into a Dumpster.

"McIntyre," Frank announced crisply as he snapped open his phone.

"White Bear," Julianne said, following suit with her own silver phone. She fell silent, listening to the voice on the other end.

The world had found her again, she thought, pulling her out of paradise and back down to earth. She'd expected nothing less, but she'd hoped for just a little more time.

The man on the other end, Sanchez, stopped talking. He and Hill had been the first called on the scene and now they were calling in the rest of the team.

"Right," Julianne said, apropos to nothing in particular. "I'll be right there."

Frank had already ended his call. Putting the cell

phone down, he started getting dressed. When he spoke, his voice was vibrating from suppressed emotion.

"This guy isn't going to give it a rest until we get him," he speculated grimly.

Julianne merely nodded, hurrying into her clothes. She tried to assess what had just happened, but her efforts were futile. Finally, dressed, she looked at Frank.

"What do we tell people?" she asked.

He slipped his phone into his pocket, his mind charging in a dozen different directions at once. "About?"

She slanted a look at him, but he wasn't playing games, he was actually asking her. "About why we're driving in together."

That was when he looked at her. She couldn't read his expression. "The truth."

He had to be kidding. But just to be safe, she put the question to him. "That we were going at it like rabbits when they called?"

"That we went to investigate where one of the serial killer's victims lived and then stopped to get some coffee. We don't have to tell them where we stopped," he added, seeing the reluctance in her eyes. "Or what happened after we did."

She felt relieved and yet, at the same time, oddly put off. "Embarrassed?" she finally asked.

"Just trying to protect your privacy," Frank countered. He strapped his gun on, then checked to see if it was secure. "And to answer your question, no, I'm not. Why should I be?"

Julianne shrugged, trying her best to seem careless. She was about to stride past him to the door when he caught her by the shoulders and spun her around to face him. The look in her eyes was both defiant and confused.

"This isn't over, Julianne," he told her. "Not by a long shot."

"We've got a crime scene waiting for us," she countered, deliberately ignoring what he was saying.

She didn't know if what he said made her uncomfortable—or the exact opposite. All she knew was that she'd never been as confused, as conflicted as she was at this very moment. Making love with him had undone everything that she had believed to be true up to this evening. Not the least of which was the fact that she could take or leave sex—and it certainly never made her take leave of her senses before.

She couldn't claim that anymore. At least, not truthfully.

Once they were outside, he dug into his pocket. "Here—" he handed her the keys to her vehicle. "You drive."

She took the keys gladly. At least this was one thing she could be in control of. Her car.

As if that made a difference, something inside of her scoffed. Her world was jumbled up. And, she slanted a grudging look in Frank's direction, it was all his fault.

Chapter 13

According to the information found in her purse, victim number ten was Anastasia Aliprantis. She was a pharmaceutical representative for Geneva Labs who'd been with her company more than five years and had done very well for herself. Up until now.

The M.E. had determined that she'd been dead approximately thirty-six hours and that her murder had occurred at a location somewhere other than the site of the Dumpster.

Like the others, she'd been strangled but not sexually violated. Also like the others, she was blond, slender, under the age of forty and with no known family in the state.

And that was where the connection appeared to end. Again.

"Now we've got an equal number of women from

both walks of life," Frank observed with a mounting feeling of disgust. "Five of each."

He'd long since discarded the notion that the women were picked at random solely for their looks. The fact that the victims had no families in the immediate area was too much of a coincidence.

"Somehow, some way, the killer knew his victims." Frank repeated the obvious out loud for what seemed like the umpteenth time. "He studied them before he moved in for the final kill."

Hill frowned, moving out of a C.S.I.'s way as the latter searched the scene for anything out of the ordinary that could be tied to the murder. "Hey, it sounds plausible, but—"

"I know. How?" Angry at the way the killer seemed to be thumbing his nose at them, Frank looked at the assembled team. "I don't have an answer. Yet," he emphasized. But he was going to find one, he silently vowed, and soon. "So we start at the beginning. Sanchez, canvas the area. Maybe someone saw something. A car that shouldn't have been there, someone lugging a rolled up rug. *Something,* anything that stood out or struck them as off or odd. Riley," he turned to his sister, "you and Hill go to Geneva Labs and see if anyone there can shed any light on Anastasia's lifestyle after hours. Get a list of the doctors she gave out samples to on a regular basis."

Julianne looked at him. "You think this could be the work of a doctor?"

"Right now, I don't know what to think," he said honestly. "But I'm open to anything." He got back to assignments. "I'm going to check out the victim's apartment." The address he had was for a trendy part of the city, a newly built apartment complex directly across from a popular, recently expanded shopping center. "Julianne, you're with me."

Out of the corner of his eye, Frank caught his sister's badly hidden smile. Now wasn't the time to take her aside and ask questions as to what she thought she knew. Everything else, including his personal life, was going to have to be placed on hold until they got this maniac off the streets. At this present pace, it wouldn't be long before he was killing a woman a day.

"Okay, people. We'll compare notes when we get back to the precinct," he told them. "Now let's go get this bastard."

The apartment complex where Anastasia had lived boasted several pools and Jacuzzis, two fully equipped exercise rooms and a "common" area that was anything but. It was the last word in single living and Julianne sincerely doubted any space went for under three grand a month.

It struck her as a sinful waste of money.

Their latest victim's apartment was located in one of the complex's corners. It came with a view of the shopping center's imported Ferris wheel.

"My God, I didn't think anyone short of a celebrity lived like this," Julianne murmured more to herself than to Frank as the landlord unlocked the door to Anastasia's apartment.

She took a moment to look around and get her bearings. Spacious with cathedral ceilings, the split-level living quarters were completely done in white, from the rugs to the walls to the furniture.

The landlord backed away, taking his leave as he said something about needing to rent the apartment out as soon as possible.

"I feel like I'm lost in a blizzard," Frank commented with a shake of his head. Then he looked down at the floor again. "At least anything out of place will be easy to spot. I'll take the bedroom," he told her. "You take that room." He nodded toward what appeared to be a guest room. It was furnished in white as well.

The guest room doubled as an office. Maybe she'd get lucky and find something, Julianne mused. Pulling on her rubber gloves, she sat down at the snow-white desk and opened the deep, single side drawer. The drawer was heavy, filled with folders. All white, all neatly labeled. Julianne went through them one at a time.

For the most part, the folders contained current receipts obviously saved for tax purposes. Behind the folders was an array of expanding manila envelopes. Those housed tax forms from the previous years. They covered the last five. Her time with Geneva Labs, Julianne thought.

She flipped through the collection methodically and noted that four of the 1040 and 540 packets had been handled by a firm called Myers and Sons. The most recent one, however, carried the stamp of another accounting firm, Harlow & Higgins. Beneath the stamp was an all but illegible signature.

Julianne stared at it, trying to make out the person's name. She angled it for better light.

"Anything?" Frank asked, walking in. "All I found out was that our victim had a taste for expensive clothes and even more expensive lingerie—lots of it. I'm hoping you had more luck."

"Probably not," Julianne answered. She was acutely aware of the scent of his cologne as he stood behind her chair, looking over her shoulder. Trying to block it out, she held up the tax forms. "Until last year, Anastasia had her taxes done by the same firm."

Curious, Frank asked, "What happened last year?"

"She switched. I have no idea if that means anything or not." She held up the back side of the 1040 form so that Frank could get a look at the signature of the man who'd prepared it.

Tax accountants. Now there was an angle they hadn't explored. Did that sound as desperate as he thought? Frank felt as if he was clutching at straws, but who knew? Wasn't it about time that someone besides the serial killer got lucky?

He squinted at the signature, then looked at Julianne. "Who did the other women's taxes?"

She didn't remember finding any tax forms, but then, she hadn't looked. "I don't know."

They had nothing else to go on. This was as good as anything. "Let's find out."

Four trips to four different upscale apartments later, they had their answer. And a possible reason for some excitement.

Each of the dead career women had had their taxes done by the same firm as the last victim: Higgins and

Harlow. Not only by the same firm, it turned out, but
also by the same senior accountant: Gideon Gifford.

"Think that's the connection between murders?"
Julianne asked, almost afraid to hope as they left the
last apartment.

"*Any* connection at this point could be something,"
he told her.

"Okay," she agreed, "Let's say it is. But how does
that connect with the five prostitutes?" God, but it killed
her to have to include Mary in that group. "They
wouldn't even file tax forms, much less make use of an
accountant."

Frank started up the car. "That's what we need to
find out," he answered. He set his mouth grimly.
"Maybe Mr. Gideon Gifford can shed some light on
that little detail for us."

Gideon Gifford was an amiable middle-aged, slightly
overweight man who wore rimless reading glasses. His
somewhat faded brown hair was receding daily, leaving
him with an ever expanding forehead. In the middle of
wrestling with a complex computation, he seemed
relieved to take a break.

His smile was wide and welcoming as the firm's ad-
ministrative assistant brought them into the man's office.

Unlike the accountants who did their work while
housed in small, mazelike cubicles scattered throughout the floor, Gifford had a corner office with a pano-
ramic view of the city's skyline.

On his back wall were a number of framed photographs strategically arranged and permanently freezing

Gifford with prized clients and a number of other, famous people, one of whom Frank recognized as the last mayor of Aurora. There were also framed diplomas, one from Stanford and another from Yale's graduate school.

Next to those were plaques commemorating his selfless good works for the Boy Scouts, his local church and a several other organizations to which he'd either donated a good deal of his time or money—or both.

Gifford's desk had several more framed photographs, but these were more personal. They were of his family. A wife, two daughters and a son. There was also a dog. In all, it looked like the perfect American family.

"My wife gets the full credit for the way the kids turned out," Gifford joked. "I put in long hours and don't get to be home as much as I'd like. I'm planning on cutting back," he confided to Frank.

Frank noted that Julianne was oddly quiet and wondered why. "What changed your mind?" he asked the man, pretending to be interested.

Gifford grinned. "Heard that song the other day, the one that goes nobody ever died saying, 'I should have spent more time in the office.' It suddenly hit me that the song could have been about me."

Gifford went on talking, answering Frank's questions, including mentioning his whereabouts the nights of the deaths, and volunteering more information than was called for. And then he lowered his voice and confessed that part of his reason for wanting to cut back was because he'd realized that four of the women who'd been murdered had been his clients.

"I'm not normally superstitious," he quickly explained. "But I'm beginning to think that maybe I'm bad luck. My wife tells me I'm crazy, but…" His voice trailed off as he shrugged.

"Your wife's probably right," Frank told him easily. Because, for now, he had no more questions, just points to ponder, and because Julianne had remained silent through the entire interview, Frank said goodbye and left Gifford's office.

Julianne lengthened her stride to keep up with him as they walked out of the building.

"After a while, I started to get the impression that I was questioning the male version of Mother Teresa," Frank commented.

"Maybe that was what he wanted you to feel," Julianne suggested. She'd spent the whole time studying the man, listening to his answers. Watching his body language as he spoke. Searching for inconsistencies.

"Maybe," Frank allowed. He couldn't help wondering what was going on inside her head. "You were awfully quiet back there."

She had her own agenda to attend to. "You were doing fine without me."

No, there was more to it than that, Frank thought. He was willing to bet on it. "He had a plaque on his wall from St. Vincent de Paul's Homeless Shelter for his hours of selfless work."

Their eyes met just before she got into the car. "I know."

"You're not buying into it?" he asked.

Buckling up, she waited until Frank had gotten in before continuing. She answered his question with a question of her own. "Did you notice his eyes when he was talking?"

Looking in the rearview mirror, Frank backed out of the parking space. "No."

"I did. They were flat. Inscrutable. Eyes are supposed to be the windows to the soul—unless you don't have one."

The way she said it, Frank had the impression that she considered Gifford to belong to that group. Before he could ask what made her think so, she began telling him a story.

"I once knew a boy with eyes like that, back when I lived on the reservation." She stared straight ahead, remembering. "Richard Eagle. He was a few years older than I was at the time." She took a breath before adding, "He took extreme pleasure in torturing and killing animals."

They both knew that those were the classic signs of a budding serial killer. "What happened to him?"

"He disappeared after killing a dog that belonged to one of the tribe's elders."

Frank spared her a glance. Her expression gave nothing away, forcing him to ask, "Did this Richard Eagle run away or—?"

She had her own theories on that. The reservation was a law unto itself, and the outside world couldn't interfere.

"Nobody ever said," she told him, then added, "but if I had to guess, I think it was probably 'or.'" A hint of a satisfied smile played on her lips. It was obvious, though she said nothing more, that she thought that justice had been served.

* * *

"Gideon Gifford?" the director at St. Vincent de Paul's Homeless Shelter repeated the name less than half an hour later. His round face lit up. "Sure I know him. Gideon's one of our best volunteers. Probably *the* best one," Wilcox amended, "Shows up when he says he will. Stays later than he has to." He sighed, looking over his shoulder at the chaotic common room where several of their current homeless people were gathered. "I wish I had a dozen of him."

Not if he turns out to be who we think he is. For now, Julienne kept the comment to herself.

Frank gave voice to her thoughts, though his words were only audible to her. "You might want to change that wish."

The director wrinkled his wide forehead, apparently hearing only Frank's tone but not what he'd actually said. "What?"

Frank shook his head. "Nothing. Thank you. We'll be in touch."

The director stared after them, obviously confused as to why the detectives had come by and then only asked him about his star volunteer. Shrugging, he turned away and walked into the common room.

Frank said nothing until they were outside and sitting inside the car again. They were both thinking the same thing. He could feel the tension and excitement. Their eyes met and he was the first to say it.

"That's our connection between the victims," he declared with a note that was equal parts triumph and relief. "Gideon Gifford."

* * *

The next five hours were spent back in the squad room. Frank put himself and all the task force team members to work gathering every single available shred of information that even hinted about Gideon Gifford. But the more they gathered, the less likely it seemed that Gifford was their suspect. There was no police record, no traffic tickets. Not even a minor moving violation.

From all indications, Gideon Gifford had led an exemplary, pristine life.

Hill leaned back in his chair. It squeaked in protest as he laced his fingers together above his head and sighed in frustration.

"You sure this is the guy?" he asked Frank. "I'm about ready to believe that the man walks on water when he isn't turning it into wine." Frowning, he tapped his monitor. "He was voted Man of the Year at his church three years in a row—beating out the minister." Turning his chair around, he looked over toward Frank. "We bring this guy in for questioning, the whole community's going to be outside the precinct with torches and pitch forks."

"There *has* to be something," Frank insisted. He knew what he saw on his own screen and he knew what his gut was telling him. That the two didn't add up. There had to be *something,* however minor, that gave Gifford away. "A man doesn't just get up one day after leading a supposed model life and say, 'I think I'll become a serial killer today.'"

"Here's a thought," Sanchez volunteered, having come across the same blank wall. "Maybe this Gifford's *not* our killer."

Julianne looked up. For the most part, she'd been silent since they'd returned to the precinct, choosing instead to concentrate on searching for the needle in the haystack.

"No, he's our killer," Julianne underscored with quiet feeling.

Riley sighed. "We're going to need something beyond a gut feeling."

"Yeah, but if we start asking around about him, someone's going to tip him off and he'll go into lockdown mode," Frank pointed out, chewing on the problem that was staring all of them in the face. "If we're right—and I think we are—he's killed ten women—"

"That we know of," Julianne interjected grimly.

"That we know of," Frank echoed. "You just don't escape detection this long without being very, very thorough."

Swinging her chair around to face the man who had caused her to redefine her world last night, Julianne asked, "What do you have in mind?"

The answer was very simple. "We need to catch him in the act."

"What, tail him until he goes to kill somebody?" Riley asked.

"No." That would take too long and if Gifford thought he was being watched, he could just bolt. There was an easier, riskier way. "Now that we know his type we give him someone to focus on."

"You mean to kill," Julianne corrected.

He didn't want it put in those terms. "It's a sting."

It took her less than half a second to raise her hand. "I volunteer," Julianne offered.

Frank shook his head. "Sorry, Gifford already knows you. We can't take a chance on his realizing that we're on to him," he reminded her. "Besides, you're not his type."

He was looking pointedly at her long, black hair.

That wasn't a deterrent. She thought of Mary. "All I need is a blond wig."

"Why go with a wig when you already have a blonde?" Riley injected, flipping her hand beneath her blond hair to make it flare out.

His immediate reaction was to say no. Frank didn't want to use either his sister or Julianne, but he knew he couldn't allow his personal feelings to get in the way. This was police business and the public's welfare was at stake.

He looked at Riley. "You sure you're willing to go through with this?"

"Hell, yes," Riley said with feeling. "I want this killer off the street. Now. And if I can help to get him that way, all the better."

"I'll dye my hair," Julianne said suddenly. The other four people in the room looked at her.

"Julianne—" Frank began.

He was about to point out the reasons against it. She didn't give him a chance. "No offense, Riley, but I'm guessing you've never really been poor a day in your life."

She'd lost him. "What does that have to do with it?" Frank asked.

"Simple." She was talking to Frank now, pleading her case with passion. "She might not be convincing. I know what poverty feels like. What being desperate feels like. And most of all, I know what it means not to have anyone to turn to for support. You've always had your family," she said to Riley and then turned back to Frank. "We've only got one shot at this guy, Frank. He smells anything out of the ordinary, he's gone. Which means that he'll be free to start all over again somewhere else. I didn't say anything when we went to his office. He doesn't even know what my voice sounds like. You did all the talking," she reminded him. "Please, Frank, I wouldn't ask you if it wasn't important. I owe this to Mary. I want to nail this creep to the wall."

The word *no* hovered on his lips. But he knew if he said it, he'd be thinking with his heart, not his head. In his gut, he knew that she'd be the more convincing one. She was the one with that kind of background to draw on. It could make a difference.

His eyes swept over her and he shook his head. "Seems a shame to dye that hair."

He'd given her his answer. Julianne let go of the breath she'd been holding. "It'll grow out," she assured him matter-of-factly.

Frank sighed. It was a done deal. "Okay. We go with you. But we do it my way." He had to be able to exercise some control over the situation. In his gut, he knew it wouldn't be enough, but at least it was something.

"Sure."

Julianne had agreed much too quickly, he thought, fervently hoping he wasn't going to regret this decision.

Too late. The words materialized out of nowhere, whispering across the perimeter of his mind.

Chapter 14

The stiletto heels forced her to slow down as she made her way through the doors of St. Vincent de Paul's Homeless Shelter.

Even mindful of her balancing act, Julianne felt amazingly calm. No nerves stretching themselves to the end of their capacity, no jitters making her stomach turn somersaults. It was almost as if this was what she'd been meant to do all along.

Rid the world of a monster.

Although she was by herself as she walked into the homeless shelter, Julianne knew she wasn't alone. Somewhere out on the street, housed in a repair truck with a local cable company logo slapped on its side, Riley and Frank were listening to her every word, her every breath. She was wearing a wire. Because her clothing was of the tight, abbreviated variety, the computer tech had woven the wire into her bra.

It chafed against her skin as she breathed, but because it represented not only safety, but a way to trap Gifford, she did her best to ignore it. She kept her breathing shallow.

"Gifford, straight ahead," she murmured under her breath, letting Frank know that their target had been sighted. She knew that Frank would be antsy until she said that, despite the fact that the director had shown them a schedule earlier, which clearly specified when the senior accountant, among other volunteers, would be here at the homeless shelter.

Gifford was alone, distributing some sort of literature on vacant tables.

Julianne sauntered over to the man, instinctively imitating the way she'd assumed her cousin had conducted herself in the presence of strangers—afraid, but doing her best not to show it.

There was no hesitation as she confronted him. "Word on the street is that I can get a decent meal here." With hooded eyes, she allowed her glance to go from the top of what was left of his curly hair down to his highly polished dress shoes. "That true, handsome?"

Gifford did her one better. He looked at her for a long moment before he responded and she had the impression that she was being dissected and then put back together. Had she passed? Failed? She couldn't readily tell from his expression.

In any event, she'd been right. His eyes were flat. Flat and mercilessly cold despite the presence of a smile on his lips.

"Absolutely," he told her with no small enthusiasm. "Here, why don't you just come with me? I'll show you where the kitchen is." He began to lead the way to the back of the first floor where the kitchen with its industrial appliances was. "Is this your first time at St. Vincent's?"

"My first time in any place like this," Julianne retorted defensively. Her eyes challenged him to make something of it. When he didn't, she fixed a smile to her lips. "I've always been able to take care of myself until now. But then—" she shrugged carelessly, as if the topic was beneath her "—the economy's been rough on us working girls, too."

They'd reached the kitchen. There was no one there at the moment. Gifford walked in as if he was intimately familiar with the area. Opening the refrigerator, he took out two large pots and began to prepare a small serving of chili with rice. Last night's dinner.

Placing the dish on a silver-topped table where all the meals were usually prepared, he asked, "Where do you work?"

"Here and there." Julianne raised her eyes to his, a smirk curving her mouth. "Why? You planning on looking me up? Hoping to get some kind of a discount because you're feeding me with someone else's food?"

"Just making conversation—" He paused, as if realizing that he was short some crucial information. "What did you say your name was?"

"I didn't." Julianne deliberately waited a beat before telling him. "It's Sally."

He pulled over a stool for her. "Sally what?"

Julianne slid onto the stool. It surprised her that Gifford kept his eyes on her face the entire time. "Just Sally."

"Well, Just Sally, what does your family think about you working here and there?"

"Who knows? Who cares?" Her tone was dismissive as she shrugged carelessly and went on eating. The chili, she thought, was fairly good. "They're back in Oklahoma—if they're still around."

"So that's home?" he asked. "Oklahoma?"

"It was."

He looked at her thoughtfully. "Ever think about going back?"

She put herself in Mary's shoes, reacting to the question the way she imagined her cousin would. Recoiling from the mere suggestion.

"Hell, no. I couldn't wait to get out of there." And then, because her so-called benefactor appeared to be waiting for more, she added, "There's only my mother— and a never-ending parade of men with grabby hands."

"And there's nobody else to go back to?" Gifford prodding, a kindly expression on his face. When she didn't answer immediately, he told her, "I could front you the cost of a bus ride home if you did want to go back."

She allowed contempt to curl her lower lip. "You'd just give it to me?"

"It'd be a loan," he explained. "You pay me back when you can."

Right. Just how naive did he think she was? There was no such thing as a free lunch. But she was curious to see what he would say, so she pushed the envelope a little further.

"And if I stiffed you?"

"Just a chance that I guess I'd have to take," he told her philosophically.

Finishing the serving, she let her spoon clatter in the bowl as she set it down. Her eyes were steely as she looked at him. "I didn't think people like you really existed."

"We do," he assured her with just the right touch of humility. She could see how Mary, hungry to trust *someone* might have been tempted to believe him. "There's more of us than you think, Sally." He dug into his pocket and held out a bill. "Here, take it," he urged.

She looked down and saw that he wasn't holding out a twenty. It was a hundred-dollar bill. Was he trying to lull her into a false sense of security? That had to be it, she decided. Was this the way he'd gotten to Mary? Pretending to be a Good Samaritan?

"Use it to help turn your life around," he was saying to her.

Julianne looked contemptuously at the bill, then laughed harshly at the suggestion. "It's gonna take more than a hundred dollars to do that."

Her answer didn't faze him. "Think of it as a start, then." He urged the money on her. "Please."

She let suspicion enter her eyes. "And you don't want anything from me?"

"No."

Julianne pushed her plate back on the table. Rubbing against the surface, it squeaked. Her eyes on his, she grabbed the bill out of his hand. "Okay, then." Folding the bill into a tiny square, she pushed it into her bra. "Gotta say you're the easiest John I ever had."

"I'm not a John," Gifford answered her with feeling. "I would, though, like to be your friend."

Yeah, right. Was that how he did it? Did he offer to befriend those lost souls before he blindsided them? "Novel approach," she responded sarcastically. "Tell you what, friend, you've got yourself a little credit," she told him.

He didn't look as if he followed her meaning. "Credit?"

"Credit," she repeated. "The merchandise kind. You decide that you want a little something in exchange for that hundred dollars you just surrendered, you come find me." She was certain that her smile left nothing in doubt. "We'll talk."

For the first time, Julianne thought she saw something different in the suspect's eyes. A flare of interest? Or was that something else?

"And let's say if I did want to come find you—to see how you were doing," he qualified quickly, "exactly where would that be?"

Gotcha! "Corner of McFadden and Holloway," she told him. I'll be the pretty one."

With that, she slid off the stool slowly, making sure that Gifford got more than an eyeful of her long limbs. With a seductive smile, she tugged at the bottom of her next-to-nonexistent skirt, the action exposing more than it covered.

He looked surprised when she began to make her way to the front door again. "You're leaving?"

"Didn't come here for the bed," she told him matter-of-factly. "Just a hot meal that wouldn't cost me nothing. Wasn't half bad," she added, then nodded at him. "Thanks."

She walked out slowly, moving her hips in a timeless, hypnotic rhythm because she knew he was watching her. Leaving the storefront shelter behind her, Julianne walked down several more blocks before she turned down into an alley. She listened carefully to the sounds of the city with its passing cars. No footsteps. Gifford wasn't following her.

"Come get me," she whispered to her chest.

"Way ahead of you." She heard Frank's voice in her ear, thanks to the tiny ear bud he'd hidden there. Frank had begun to follow her the moment she'd left the shelter, taking care to keep an eye out for Gifford. The accountant had remained where he was.

Pulling up at the entrance of the alley, Frank waited for her to get in.

"By the way," he told her as she closed the door behind her, "talking to your chest is viewed as very sexy in some circles."

Julianne could feel color rising up to her cheeks. Heat marked its path. "You've got definite voyeuristic tendencies, McIntyre."

He grinned at her. "I've been told that once or twice." *Yeah, I'll bet.*

"That was a hell of a great performance," Riley complimented her. "I even caught Frank checking his pockets, looking for spare bills." And then she grew serious. "You were right. That was a lot better than anything I could have done. Ever think of becoming an actress?" she posed out of the blue.

Settling into a seat, Julianne let out a long breath. She hadn't realized how tense she was until this very moment. So much for thinking she was calm, she silently upbraided herself.

"Too wearing," she commented. Turning away, she snaked her hands underneath the skimpy top and unhooked the wire. She sighed with relief as she turned back around and handed the wire over to Riley. "Got one that doesn't chafe?"

"Sorry." Riley took the tiny device from her. "I don't think they thought about that aspect when they came up with it." She looked at her brother. "Okay, now what?"

Getting up from the console that had helped them monitor Julianne, Frank crossed to the front of the van and got in behind the wheel. For now, they were returning to the precinct. He wasn't going to feel at ease until this charade was over, but he knew there was no point in saying anything to Julianne. The die had been cast.

"We wait until nightfall and then Julianne becomes a strolling hostess of the evening." Frank started up the vehicle. "With luck, Gifford will take the bait."

It turned out not to be that easy. Gifford didn't show that evening. Nor did he show the evening after that. Both nights Julianne strolled back and forth over the restricted terrain, tense and waiting while sending away more than her share of potential customers. Over the course of the two nights, she ignored a series of car horn blasts, whistles and shouted propositions of the baser variety.

All the while, she thought about Mary, about what she had to have felt during what turned out to be the last days of her life. This, and worse, was what her cousin had been faced with night after night. The very thought deadened her soul.

What had it done to Mary's?

And then one enraged would-be John charged out of his car, determined to drag Julianne into it. Watching, Frank had one hand on the door, ready to leap out of the van and come to her aid. But Riley stopped him.

"What?" he demanded.

"She can take care of herself," his sister told him. "Just watch." She indicated the screen that highlighted the corner where their camera was trained.

"What are you, too good for me?" the John demanded, shouting into Julianne's face.

It was the last thing he said in an upright position. The next second, he was flipping through the air, landing flat on his back with a thud. Before he could get up, Julianne had the heel of her stiletto pressed against his throat.

"I'm picky," she told him. "I like to choose whose money I accept." As if to make her point, she pressed the heel a little harder against his throat.

"Okay, okay, I get it." Julianne marginally withdrew her heel and the man scrambled to his feet, coughing. "Crazy bitch!" he shouted at her.

He'd no sooner roared off in his beat-up white coupe than another car drove up. This one was a pristine dark gray sedan. The exact make and model that Gideon Gifford drove.

Adrenaline instantly roared through her veins. Every nerve ending Julianne possessed went on tactical alert.

Gideon Gifford pressed a button on his armrest and

the window on the passenger side rolled down. He leaned toward the opening. There was a hint of admiration in his manner. "You handle yourself pretty well."

"He was an insulting jerk," she said with no attempt to hide her contempt. And then she smiled at Gifford. "Not like you." Leaning into the car, she gave him her most inviting smile. "Here to collect on that hundred dollars you lent me?"

"Just here to talk," he told her. Pressing another button on the armrest released all four door locks simultaneously. "Why don't you get in?"

She pretended to look around and assess the immediate area. "Well, it does look like a slow night," she commented, then shrugged. "Okay." Getting in, she turned toward him. "So, talk."

"Put your seat belt on," he instructed.

"The careful type, huh? Okay." Pulling the belt around her, she slipped the metal tongue into the slot. It clicked into place and she sat back. "So, where are we going?" she asked.

"Just for a drive." He took the car out of park and stepped on the gas. The beverage he had housed in the cup holder sloshed, but didn't spill. "Away from here."

"Okay, but you're just going to have to bring me back."

Gifford slanted a long look at her. "We'll see."

She forced a laugh. "Are you still trying to save my soul?"

"No." His voice was low, dangerous. "Can't save what you don't have."

She felt the hairs on the back of her neck standing up. Something was off. She could feel it. Was he switching persona? Just like that? "What's that supposed to mean?"

In response, Gifford gunned the engine, flying through the yellow light. "It means that you shouldn't be on this earth, taking up space. Women like you are just useless trash, ruining men's lives," he bit off. "Ruining families, just to feed your own needs."

"I don't have to listen to this," Julianne cried. She yanked on the door, as if trying to escape the way she knew Mary would have. The door refused to give. It was locked. She tried to pry up the lock, but it wouldn't budge. He'd done something to it. "Open this damn door," she demanded.

"I will. When I'm ready." Before she could say anything, he grabbed the paper cup from the beverage holder and threw the contents at her chest. The wire short circuited, burning her skin. She bit down hard on her lower lip to keep from screaming.

"That's so your friends in the van don't follow," he said in a mild voice, as if he were commenting on the weather.

He knew.

"Stop the car, Gifford!" she ordered in a voice that rang with confident authority. He only went faster. Julianne reached for the small pistol she had strapped to her inner right thigh.

Just as she did, Gifford accelerated and the car lunged forward. The next second, he threw it into reverse, speeding backward. Julianne was thrown forward, hitting her head on the dashboard, then back just as suddenly. The small revolver flew out of her hands.

She heard Gifford laughing. "Scrappy little thing,

aren't you? Knew you would be the second I laid eyes on you."

Julianne blinked to clear her eyes. Her vision was still blurred, but she tried desperately to focus and see where they were going.

Gifford was taking her out of the city, she realized with a sudden start. The northern portion of Aurora backed up to a game preserve that boasted of several kinds of wild animals, including a couple of mountain lions.

He was going to kill her there.

The terrifying thought throbbed in her head. "Stop the car, Gifford," she ordered, summoning as much bravado as she could. "Now!"

He only went faster. "Not now, *Sally.* Not when we're having so much fun," Gifford taunted, a nasty edge rising in his voice.

They were going at least eighty miles an hour. The vehicle careened through the streets, making twisting turns on what amounted to two wheels. Her fingers felt icy, even as perspiration began to slide down her back. She had to stop him.

Where was Frank?

As if reading her mind, Gifford laughed. "He's not going to come save you, Detective. Right now, Detective McIntyre and the rest of his crew are dealing with four flat tires."

Her eyes widened as she looked at the maniac next to her. He'd called her "detective."

There was nothing but contempt in his eyes as he glanced her way. "Didn't you think I'd see through your little disguise? I've got a 180 I.Q. MENSA comes to me with questions," he crowed vainly. "Which means I'm way too smart for you and those other buffoons, Detective. But it's been nice toying with you."

The nasty laugh that rose to his lips echoed throughout the vehicle.

Gifford stomped down on the gas, whizzing by the sparse traffic as if the other cars were just painted scenery.

A sick feeling seized hold of her stomach. Julianne looked in the rearview mirror. There was no cable van following them.

She was on her own.

Chapter 15

"**P**ick a place," Gifford told her, his voice mild as if they were just passing the time. As if he hadn't just admitted to being the serial killer who had terminated so many young women's lives.

This was surreal. Julianne felt as if she'd just fallen down the rabbit hole. "What?"

"Pick a place," Gifford repeated, his voice growing slightly strained. "Out there." He nodded toward the vast, engulfing darkness beyond the windshield. "Pick where you want to die."

"Paris."

He laughed harshly at her flippant answer. "Sorry, it's going to have to be somewhere closer than that." The smile on his lips when he glanced in her direction made her blood run cold. "You should be honored. I never told the others they only had minutes to live. They went on thinking they had forever." The malicious smile widened. "Until they didn't."

She had to keep him talking until she thought of a way out. "Why did you do it?" she demanded. "Why did you kill all those women?"

"Why not?" he countered, so coldly she almost shivered. The near-maniacal laugh drove fear through her heart and she struggled not to let it overwhelm her. If it did, she knew she was lost. "You have no idea what a rush it is," he told her, still traveling at breakneck speed. Signs of the city began to peel away as they went down a two-lane, tree-lined road. The foothills emerged in the distance. Gifford's voice swelled in volume as he spoke, the vision the words fashioned clearly exciting him. "Feeling the life draining out of someone, passing through my hands. Watching them struggle, then give in to the inevitable. Give in to *me.*"

She could hear the self-importance in his voice as Gifford crowed about his accomplishments, about how the women had struggled and begged him for mercy with their eyes.

"In the last seconds of their lives I was *everything.* I was their God, their deliverer. Their entire *world.*" He took a deep breath, as if awed by himself. "Just talking about it gives me a high."

Feeding his ego wasn't going to work, she thought. In his present state it would just backfire on her. "You're not going to get away with this, you know," she told him, her voice calmer than she actually felt. "They know who you are."

The laugh was contemptuous, belittling. "Won't do them any good," he promised.

Abruptly, he pulled over to the right, all but nosediving into a desolate spot. With a flip of his wrist, he cut the engine. He seemed infused with pride, unable to keep quiet. He talked, as if justifying that his audience would be dead soon.

"I've been preparing for this day ever since the beginning. After tonight, there won't be a Gideon Gifford. I've got a whole new life waiting for me." And with deliberate precision, agitating her all the more, he added, "New unsuspecting lives to cut short."

His eyes seemed to glow as he looked at her. From that moment on, Julianne was certain that she would always remember what the face of Satan looked like.

She had to do something *now,* before it was too late. Because she knew she'd run out of time.

In one swift movement, she hit the release on her seat belt and lunged at Gifford, her fingernails going straight for his eyes. He screamed in pain and outrage. But instead of backing off the way she thought he would, Gifford grabbed her by the throat. His powerful hands closed around the slender column and began to squeeze. Hard.

Julianne clawed at him. But Gifford was a great deal stronger and her own strength, fueled with outrage and anger, began to ebb away, dragging in a darkness in its wake.

Just as she lost consciousness, Julianne felt a jolt from behind and thought, just vaguely, that they'd been hit by another car.

But that wasn't possible. They were alone out here. *She* was alone out here.

The darkness won.

A heavy, dark curtain was still oppressively draped over her, but somewhere beyond that, she thought she felt someone holding her, tugging on her. Calling her name over and over again.

Air and consciousness returned simultaneously.

With a sudden gasp, Julianne bolted upright, her fists swinging. That same someone grabbed them and restrained her despite the frantic fury that propelled her. She was powerless again. He was going to kill her.

"Hold it, Champ. I'm one of the good guys, remember?"

Frank?

Frank!

Her eyes flew open—only then did she realize that they'd been closed.

"Frank!" His name came out in a grateful sob. Her emotions raw, every nerve in her body throbbing and adrenaline racing through her body, Julianne's first reaction was to throw her arms around him and cling for dear life.

Frank did nothing to discourage her. Closing his arms around her, he just held her to him, grateful beyond words that he'd been able to save her.

All around them, the backup that he'd called for were assessing and processing the near crime scene. Sanchez and Riley had taken Gifford away in handcuffs.

Still holding her, Frank breathed in deeply, absorbing Julianne's scent, silently whispering a prayer of thanks.

And then he felt her drawing back. She looked at him in confusion. "Not that I'm not incredibly grateful that you came riding to the rescue just as that sick bastard was trying to choke me to death, but how did you even know where I was?"

Frank laughed, shaking his head. He hadn't thought that she'd underestimated him that much. "You think I'd let you climb into his car without having some sort of way to track you?"

She looked down at the front of her wet peasant blouse. With a single movement, she ripped away the now-defunct wire. "I thought that was what the wire was supposed to be for."

"Some 'backup' way to track you?" he corrected. She raised her eyes to him in a silent question. "I planted a tracking device under Gifford's car while you tottered into the homeless shelter on those stilettos."

"I didn't totter," she sniffed. And then she blew out a breath. She'd been through a lot in her life, but this was the closest she'd ever come to death. When she looked at him again, there was no bravado in her eyes or her voice. "Thanks."

He wanted to tell her that there was no reason to thank him. That when he'd realized that she was no longer transmitting and alone with that maniac, fear had almost rendered him immobile.

But all he said was, "Don't mention it."

She was coming around now. Things were falling

into place. "But wait a minute, Gifford said you had four flat tires."

Frank laughed shortly. "No, but not for his lack of trying. The bastard threw a handful of tacks in the road. The van went over some of them—came close to having a blowout." He shrugged. Sometimes the good guys won. "We were just lucky."

It took all she had to bank down the shiver threatening to undo her. She knew if she gave in, she wouldn't be able to stop shaking. Julianne ran her hand tentatively along her throat. It felt sore, tender. "I was luckier."

The story, with all its gory details, hit the street in the morning edition of the paper. Julianne could have sworn she heard a collective sigh of relief coming from the city when Aurora's citizens learned that the serial killer was under lock and key and apparently would remain that way for the rest of his life. Unrepentant and proud of his deeds, in return for having the death penalty taken off the table, Gideon Gifford cheerfully recounted the history of all his murders.

The first thing he told the D.A. and his assistant, Brian's daughter Janelle Cavanaugh Boone, was that the police took a long time to catch on. With a sly, self-satisfied smile he said that there'd been more than ten victims. Ten more than ten to be precise. The first group, escaping any detection, had long since become one with the city's landfill.

He remembered all their names and surrendered them under the terms of the same bargain.

Mary White Bear's body was released to Julianne that morning. Julianne made arrangements for her cousin to be brought back to Mission Ridge. She wanted to bury her there rather than on the reservation where they'd grown up because she was fairly certain that Mary would have preferred it that way.

On her way back from the funeral parlor, Julianne stopped at a local drugstore and bought another bottle of hair dye. The woman on the box had lustrous blue-black hair. Hers, she knew, would be a flat, cartoonlike black, but at least it would be black until her own hair grew out. She didn't like being a blonde.

She applied the hair dye the minute she got back to the hotel.

Less than an hour later, she was packing. There wasn't much to take with her, she mused. At least, not in a suitcase.

She was almost finished when she heard a knock on the door. She ignored it. After all, she wasn't expecting anyone. All she wanted to do was just get back to Mission Ridge, bury Mary and go on her life.

But whoever was on the other side of the door refused to take a hint and knocked again. And then again. They weren't going away.

With a sigh, Julianne went to the door and yanked it open.

Her mouth dropped.

"It's about time," Frank said, walking in. "I was just about to use my male prowess and break it down." And then he stopped, turning around and doing a double take. "You dyed your hair back. Good. Blonde wasn't your color. I like you better this way."

It took her a second to recover. She certainly hadn't

expected to see Frank here. When she'd left the precinct, Frank had been surrounded by a huge circle of police personnel—friends as well as family. She'd assumed that he'd be there for a good while to come.

It made leaving easier, not having to say goodbye formally. Not easy, but easier.

She could only think of one reason why he'd be here. "Did I forget something?" she asked.

"Yeah. Me." His eyes held hers, saying things he knew he couldn't put into words just yet. Not because he lacked them, but because they would scare her away. "Were you just going to leave?"

She shrugged, turning back to her packing. She struggled to distance herself from him, from her feelings. "The case is closed," she replied simply. "You got the bad guy."

He looked at her incredulously. "You weren't even going to say goodbye?"

She avoided his eyes. "I'm not very good with goodbyes."

Frank deliberately moved her suitcase to the floor and sat down on the bed. "Andrew's throwing a party."

Just a hint of a smile curved her lips. Some things it seemed, Julianne thought, were dependable. "And this is news how?"

"The party's in our honor," Frank went on. "For capturing the serial killer. It's tonight."

This was fast, she couldn't help thinking, even for Andrew. "Then what are you doing here? Shouldn't you be on your way?"

"*Our* honor," Frank repeated, emphasizing the first

word. His eyes held hers. He understood her, he thought. Understood why she was running. Because, in his own way, he'd been running, too. But he wasn't running anymore. And he wasn't going to allow her to, either. "That means you, too."

No, in her mind, she'd already made the break. To go back would mean to go through it all again. She wasn't sure if she could a second time.

"That's very nice, but—"

Frank shifted so that she had to look at him. "You have some pressing place you need to be?"

Why was he making this so hard for her? He knew this couldn't go anywhere, she thought. They had no future together. All they had was the past. One wondrous night. "No, but—"

"You wouldn't want to hurt Andrew's feelings now, would you?" Frank asked, his voice coaxing her to reconsider.

As if that would happen. "I've got a feeling he's a pretty tough guy."

"On the outside," Frank agreed, keeping a straight face. "But he's soft and sensitive on the inside—just like me."

She laughed then. She couldn't help it. The man sitting on her bed wasn't exactly a marshmallow. "Yeah, right."

Not put off, Frank took her hands in his. "Well, I am. C'mon, Julianne. Come with me. Put in a little time at the party." The look in his eyes went straight to her gut. "What have you got to lose?"

Oh, so much, she thought. *I'm already losing it. Losing the ground beneath my feet.*

Giving in but still trying to save face, she offered a

careless shrug. "All right, I suppose. I'll come. But *just for a little while*."

He flashed a smile at her. She realized that he would have accepted no other answer. "Okay, let's go."

She looked down at the jeans and pullover she was wearing. It was fine for traveling, but not for a party that his family would be attending. "Like this?"

"Didn't I tell you? It's a come-as-you-are party."

Julianne sighed, surrendering. He had her out the door before she realized it. "There is no winning with you, is there?"

"Nope," was all he said.

Frank had the good grace not to let her hear him laugh.

The music came from the house before they ever walked in. Rhythmic music that shimmied under the skin and made people want to dance. This time around, as well as incredibly appetizing dishes, Andrew had also provided live entertainment. Riley played a mean guitar and Kyle, one of the triplets fathered by his late brother, Mike, did wicked things on the drum set. Together, they turned out to be greater than the sum of their parts.

People were shouting over the music and dancing, but everything stopped dead when Frank walked in with Julianne. The next moment, the abrupt silence was filled with the sound of applause.

Embarrassed, bemused, Julianne fought back the overwhelming desire to turn around and leave. "Are they always like this?"

"Pretty much, I'm told." It didn't bother Frank. After

years of treading on eggshells because of his father, it was nice belonging to a family where approval and support was the norm, not the unusual. "Why, do they make you uncomfortable?"

Oddly enough, Julianne thought, they didn't. Although she didn't like attention drawn to her, there was something genuine about the spontaneous applause and the quick statements of congratulations that followed.

"No," she told him, her voice barely audible because of the noise, "they don't."

Her answer made him smile. "That's good," he said, his smile widening. "That's good."

"Why?" Why should it matter how she felt about this? She'd be gone soon.

"Want to dance?" Even as he asked, he was already leading her to the small cleared-off space before his sister and Kyle.

He hadn't answered her question, but she shrugged in response to his. She supposed it wouldn't hurt to dance. The music was already moving her feet.

"Why not?"

"You know," he said, lacing his hand through hers and placing the other intimately against the small of her back and, ever so lightly, pressing her to him, "you've got the makings of a really good cop."

She raised her face to his. What was he getting at? "I *am* a really good cop."

"Confidence, I like that." He nodded his approval. "We could always use another good cop on the force. But you'd have to consider another department other than homicide."

Had she missed a step here? What was he talking about? "Why would I want to do that?"

"Because the force doesn't generally approve of a husband and wife working in the same department." He knew because he'd looked it up earlier today. "I guess I could be the one who switches—or, better yet, we might just run off for a secret ceremony." The tempo picked up and he went with it, twirling her around even faster. "That way we could go on working together. Vegas isn't all that far away. Although if Andrew ever finds out—and he will, trust me. The man has incredible powers of deduction—he'll insist on throwing us a wedding reception, which kills the whole secret thing—"

He was bouncing back and forth, and her head was spinning. Julianne held up her hand. "Hold it, hold it, hold it," she cried, overwhelmed. "Back up, McIntyre. Repeat what you just said."

His face was a study in innocence. "What part?"

"The husband-and-wife part."

"The force doesn't like husbands and wives working in the same department," he recited. "That part?"

He'd glossed right over it again. "*What* husband and wife?" she demanded.

He looked at her for a long moment, the rest of the room fading into the background. "Us."

Stunned, she stared at him. Somehow, she just kept on dancing without even being aware of it. "When did you even ask?"

The grin was almost sheepish. "I figured if I talked fast enough, you would have assumed I had and just go along with it."

Julianne abruptly stopped dancing. Shaking off his hand, she spun on her heel and walked away. "We haven't even gone out on a date and now you want to get married? You're crazy, you know that?" she threw over her shoulder.

"Yes I am," he agreed, hurrying after her. She was going for the front door and he was determined to cut her off. She had to hear him out. "Crazy if I let you go."

His hand on the door, he blocked her way out. She glared at him. "What makes you think you have a choice? Or a say in anything I do?"

"Hope," he answered simply. He started again, trying to make her understand. "Look, I've been out with an awful lot of women."

"So now you're bragging?" Was he trying to impress her?

"No, I'm explaining. I've been out with an awful lot of women and I never felt about any of them the way I feel about you. I know it's soon but I know what I want. When I thought that bastard was going to hurt you, I almost lost it." That had been, by far, the worst twenty minutes of his life. "Riley had to pull me off him." He'd bolted out of the car and dragged Gifford out of his vehicle, pummeling him. "If she hadn't been there, I probably would have killed him."

"So I made you want to kill him?"

"The point is—" Frank took her hands in his "—you bring feelings out of me that I didn't even know were there. Protective feelings. I love you, Julianne, and I want to spend the rest of my life proving it to you."

No, she wasn't going to let him talk her into this. She

wasn't going to let him in. She *couldn't.* Julianne shook her head. "Find someone else," she told him. "I can't love anybody."

"Why?" he demanded.

She wanted to leave, to just walk away without a word. Without opening up her wounds again. But he wasn't going to let her, was he? Not until she gave him an answer.

"Because everyone I've ever loved has left me. My mother, my father, Mary. If I don't love," she insisted, "I don't hurt."

But she had missed the most obvious argument against that. "You don't feel."

She raised her chin. "Exactly."

"I don't believe you," he said softly, his fingers skimming along her cheek, tracing a path along her jaw. He saw something flare in her eyes. "You're lying," he told her. "You do feel something. Something for me."

Julianne looked away. "Yeah, well, with any luck, I'll get over it."

Taking her chin in his hand, he made her look at him. "I'm not going to let you."

"What are you going to do about it, Pale Face?" she challenged. Even the nickname she'd used was to emphasize that they came from two different worlds

Frank didn't answer her. Instead, he brought his mouth down to hers.

The kiss was all velvet fire, burning away her barriers, swirling its way to her inner core in lightning speed.

"That's a start," she allowed breathlessly.

"Of the rest of our lives," Frank told her just before

he brought his mouth down on hers again. This time for longer.

In the distance, Andrew watched and smiled his approval. It'd been six months since he'd thrown a wedding reception. Zack and Krystle were up next.

But after that…

* * * * *

Don't miss Marie Ferrarella's next romance
Becoming a Cavanaugh
available April 2010 from Mills & Boon® Intrigue!

*Mills & Boon® Intrigue brings you
a sneak preview of…*

Carla Cassidy's The Rancher Bodyguard

*Grace Covington's stepfather has been murdered, her
teenage sister the only suspect. Convinced of her
sister's innocence, Grace turns to her ex-boyfriend,
lawyer Charlie Black, to help her find the truth.
Although she is determined not to forgive his betrayal,
the sexual tension instantly returns as their
investigation leads them into danger…and back
into each other's arms.*

Don't miss the thrilling final story in the
WILD WEST BODYGUARDS
*mini-series, available next month from
Mills & Boon® Intrigue.*

The Rancher Bodyguard
by
Carla Cassidy

As he approached the barn, Charlie Black saw the sleek, scarlet convertible pulling into his driveway, and wondered when exactly, while he'd slept the night before, hell had frozen over. Because the last time he'd seen Grace Covington, that's what she'd told him would have to happen before she'd ever talk to or even look at him again.

He patted the neck of his stallion and reined in at the corral. As he dismounted and pulled off his dusty black hat, he tried to ignore the faint thrum of electricity that zinged through him as she got out of her car.

Her long blond hair sparkled in the late afternoon sun, but he was still too far away to see the expression on her lovely features.

It had been a year and a half since he'd seen her, even though for the past six months they'd resided in the same small town of Cotter Creek, Oklahoma.

The last time he'd encountered her had been in his upscale apartment in Oklahoma City. He'd been wearing a pair of sports socks and an electric blue condom. Not one of his finer moments, but it had been the culminating incident in a year of not-so-fine moments.

Too much money, too many successes and far too much booze had transformed his life into a nightmare of bad moments, the last resulting in him losing the only thing worth having.

Surely she hadn't waited all this time to come out to the family ranch—his ranch now—to finally put a bullet in what she'd described as his cold, black heart. Grace had never been the type of woman to put off till today what she could have done yesterday.

Besides, she hadn't needed a gun on that terrible Friday night when she'd arrived unannounced at his apartment. As he'd stared at her in a drunken haze, she'd given it to him with both barrels, calling him every vile name under the sun before she slammed out of his door and out of his life.

So, what was she doing here now? He slapped his horse on the rump, then motioned to a nearby ranch hand to take care of the animal. He closed the gate and approached where she hadn't moved away from the driver's side of her car.

Her hair had grown much longer since he'd last seen her. Although most of it was clasped at the back of her neck, several long wisps had escaped the confines. The beige suit she wore complemented her blond coloring and the icy blue of her eyes.

She might look cool and untouchable, like the perfect lady, but he knew what those eyes looked like flared with desire. He knew how she moaned with wild abandon when making love, and he hated the fact that just the unexpected sight of her brought back all the memories he'd worked so long and hard to forget.

"Hello, Grace," he said, as he got close enough to speak without competing with the warm April breeze. "I have to admit I'm surprised to see you. As I remember, the last time we saw each other, you indicated that hell would freeze over before you'd ever speak to me again."

Her blue eyes flashed with more than a touch of annoyance—a flash followed swiftly by a look of desperation.

"Charlie, I need you." Her low voice trembled slightly, and only then did he notice that her eyes were red-rimmed, as if she'd been weeping. In all the time they'd dated—even during the ugly scene that had ended *them*—he'd never seen her shed a single tear. "Have you heard the news?" she asked.

"What news?"

"Early this afternoon my stepfather was found stabbed to death in bed." She paused for a moment and bit her full lower lip as her eyes grew shiny with suppressed tears. "I think Hope is in trouble, Charlie. I think she's really in bad trouble."

"What?" Shock stabbed through him. Hope was

Grace's fifteen-year-old sister. He'd met her a couple of times. She'd seemed like a nice kid, not as pretty as her older sister, but a cutie nevertheless.

"Maybe you should come on inside," he said, and gestured toward the house. She stared at the attractive ranch house as if he'd just invited her into the chambers of hell. "There's nobody inside, Grace. The only woman who ever comes in is Rosa Caltano. She does the cooking and cleaning for me, and she's already left for the day."

Grace gave a curt nod and moved away from the car. She followed him to the house and up the wooden stairs to the wraparound porch.

The entry hall was just as it had been when Charlie's mother and father had been alive, with a gleaming wood floor and a dried flower wreath on the wall.

He led her to the living room. Charlie had removed much of the old furniture that he'd grown up with and replaced it with contemporary pieces in earth tones. He motioned Grace to the sofa, where she sat on the very edge as if ready to bolt at any moment. He took the chair across from her and gazed at her expectantly.

"Why do you think Hope is in trouble?"

She drew in a deep breath, obviously fighting for control. "From what I've been told, Lana, the housekeeper, found William dead in his bed. Today is her day off, but she left a sweater there last night and went back to get it. It was late enough in the day that William should have been up, so she checked on him. She immediately called Zack West, and he and some of his deputies responded. They found Hope passed out on her bed. Apparently she was the only one home at the time of the murder."

Charlie frowned, his mind reeling. Before he'd moved back here to try his hand at ranching, Charlie had been a successful, high-profile defense attorney in Oklahoma City.

It was that terrible moment in time with Grace followed by the unexpected death of his father that had made him take a good, hard look at his life and realize how unhappy he'd been for a very long time.

Still, it was as a defense attorney that he frowned at her thoughtfully. "What do you mean she was passed out? Was she asleep? Drunk?"

Those icy blue eyes of hers darkened. "Apparently she was drugged. She was taken to the hospital and is still there. They pumped her stomach and are keeping her for observation." Grace leaned forward. "Please, Charlie. Please help her. Something isn't right. First of all, Hope would never, ever take drugs, and she certainly isn't capable of something like this. She would *never* have hurt William."

Spoken like a true sister, Charlie thought. How many times had he heard family members and friends proclaim that a defendant couldn't be guilty of the crime they had been charged with, only to discover that they were wrong?

"Grace, I don't know if you've heard, but I'm a rancher now." He wasn't at all sure he wanted to get involved with any of this. It had disaster written all over it. "I've retired as a criminal defense attorney."

"I heard through the grapevine that besides being a rancher, you're working part-time with West Protective Services," she said.

"That's right," he agreed. "They approached me about a month ago and asked if I could use a little side work. It sounded intriguing, so I took them up on it, but so far I haven't done any work for them."

"Then let me hire you as Hope's bodyguard, and if you do a little criminal defense work in the process I'll pay you extra." She leaned forward, her eyes begging for his help.

Bad idea, a little voice whispered in the back of his brain. She already hated his guts, and this portended a very bad ending. He knew how much she loved her sister; he assumed that for the last couple of years she'd been more mother than sibling to the young girl. He'd be a fool to involve himself in the whole mess.

"Has Hope been questioned by anyone?" he heard himself ask. He knew he was going to get involved whether he wanted to or not, because it was Grace, because she needed him.

"I don't think so. When I left the hospital a little while ago, she was still unconscious. Dr. Dell promised me he wouldn't let anyone in to see her until I returned."

"Good." There was nothing worse than a suspect running off at the mouth with a seemingly friendly officer. Often the damage was so great there was nothing a defense attorney could do to mitigate it.

"Does that mean you'll take Hope's case?" she asked.

"Whoa," he said, and held up both his hands. "Before I agree to anything, I need to make a couple of phone calls, find out exactly what's going on and where the official investigation is headed. It's possible you don't need me, that Hope isn't in any real danger of being arrested."

"Then what happens now?"

"Why don't I plan on meeting you at the hospital in about an hour and a half? By then I'll know more of what's going on, and I'd like to be present while anybody questions Hope. If anyone asks before I get there, you tell them you're waiting for legal counsel."

She nodded and rose. She'd been lovely a year and a half ago when he'd last seen her, but she was even lovelier now.

She was five years younger than his thirty-five but had always carried herself with the confidence of an older woman. That was part of what had initially drawn him to her, that cool shell of assurance encased in a slamming hot body with the face of an angel.

"How's business at the dress shop?" he asked, trying to distract her from her troubles as he walked her back to her car. She owned a shop called Sophisticated Lady that sold designer items at discount prices. She often traveled the two-hour drive into Oklahoma City on buying trips. That was where she and Charlie had started their relationship.

They'd met in the coffee shop in the hotel where she'd been staying. Charlie had popped in to drop off some paperwork to a client and had decided to grab a cup of coffee before heading back to his office.

She'd been sitting alone next to a window. The sun had sparked on her hair. Charlie had taken one look and was smitten.

"Business is fine," she said, but it was obvious his distraction wasn't successful.

"I'm sorry about William, but Zack West is a good man, a good sheriff. He'll get to the bottom of things."

Once again she nodded and opened her car door. "Then I'll see you in the hospital in an hour and a half," she said.

"Grace?" He stopped her before she got into the seat. "Given our history, why would you come to me with this?" he asked.

Her gaze met his with a touch of frost. "Because I think Hope is in trouble and she needs a sneaky devil to make sure she isn't charged with a murder I know she didn't commit. And you, Charlie Black, are as close to the devil as I could get."

She didn't wait for his reply. She got into her car, started the engine with a roar and left him standing to eat her dust as she peeled out and back down the driveway.

© Carla Bracale 2009